A woman could fall into his eyes
and travel routes to his soul.

Slowly she stepped back.

His mouth . . . his wide mouth hinted of a heated afternoon spent in exchanging long, slow, shudderingly sweet kisses.

A faint dampness trickled across her palms, and she formed fists to dry them on her gloves.

She already knew he was tall and broad-shouldered. But she hadn't realized how his body defined his clothing, making them superfluous decorations on a perfect form.

This was a stranger to her, but she recognized his breed. He moved, ate and spoke like a normal man.

But he was a walking, breathing heart-ache.

Other Avon Books by
Christina Dodd

THE RUNAWAY PRINCESS
THAT SCANDALOUS EVENING
A WELL FAVORED GENTLEMAN
A WELL PLEASURED LADY

CHRISTINA DODD

Someday My Prince

 AVON BOOKS ⬧ NEW YORK

This is a work of fiction. Names, characters, places, and incidents either are products of the author's imagination or are used fictitiously. Any resemblance to actual events, locales, organizations, or persons, living or dead, is entirely coincidental and beyond the intent of either the author or the publisher.

AVON BOOKS, INC.
1350 Avenue of the Americas
New York, New York 10019

Inside cover author photo by Nesossi Photography
Published by arrangement with the author
Library of Congress Catalog Card Number: 98-94820
ISBN: 0-380-80293-7
www.avonbooks.com/romance

First Avon Books Printing: July 1999

AVON TRADEMARK REG. U.S. PAT. OFF. AND IN OTHER COUNTRIES, MARCA REGISTRADA, HECHO EN U.S.A.

Printed in the U.S.A.

WCD 10 9 8 7 6 5 4 3 2 1

Chapter One

Bertinierre
May 1829

At the ball celebrating her twenty-fifth birthday, Crown Princess Laurentia scrutinized the leering, timid, swaggering, toe-dragging, eloquent, stuttering sea of black and white evening wear and thought she had never seen such a pitiable pool of suitors in her life.

And they were hers. All hers.

"My dear, that smile looks much like the one you don when you suffer the headache, but you are still required to launch a ship."

She didn't look at her father, as was protocol. Each of their gestures, their glances, their words had been choreographed in advance. She stood at King Jerome's right hand while he sat on the gilded, ancient, throne of Bertinierre. Both wore elegant smiles. One by one gentlemen moved forward to the foot of the dais to make their bows to the woman—or more accurately, the *kingdom*—they hoped to win.

Yet King Jerome spoke in a tone that carried no farther than her ears, and he sounded remarkably amused. Moreover she knew *his* smile was sincere.

And why not? She'd made him a promise, and he hoped that promise would lead to the fulfillment of his dearest dream.

Hers, too, she reminded herself. She was the only heir to the tiny Mediterranean kingdom of Bertinierre, and she must produce a child, preferably two, before her fruitful youth vanished.

Too bad the whole thing left her feeling like an unpollinated apple tree.

"And these are the bees." To atone for her uncharitable comment, she rewarded her lady-in-waiting's current presentation, a Mr. Andrew N. Sharparrow, with a slightly warmer smile.

He returned it, and took another bow while Weltrude lifted her smartly-groomed brows in inquiry.

Responding to the prearranged signal, Laurentia blinked twice, and the Englishman was sent on his way, allowing another to take his place.

"Perhaps when you're married you'll stop talking to yourself," said her father.

"Probably not. I enjoy intelligent conversation."

He chuckled, then smothered his mirth behind a regal cough. "You haven't given the poor lads a chance."

She chose to ignore his remark. "Besides, *you* talk to yourself."

Taking her gloved hand, he patted it between his palms. "I used to talk to your mother. I still do, the best way I know how."

Giving in to temptation, she looked down into his warm brown eyes and wished, not for the first time, that she could be more like him—intelligent, yet kind.

Without conceit, she knew she was intelligent, too, but her intelligence contained the sting of acerbity. She had endless patience with children and the feeble of mind, but for those who chose to waste their God-given gifts in idleness and frivolity she felt a vast disdain.

Unfortunately, that included too many of the wealthy, well-born gentlemen milling around the grand cream and gilt ballroom.

A nobleman so ancient he could have been her father's father made his bow before them, and toppled over. Weltrude, large, big-boned, and stern, caught him before his head could make contact with the step.

Jerome indicated that one of his personal guard should assist the aged suitor. "How does he dare to think I would allow my beautiful girl to go to him?"

"Not everyone thinks quite as well of my looks as you do, Papa." Certainly not Beaumont, the English Earl of Burlingame . . . and her first husband. "Have you thought you might be influenced by a parent's prejudice?"

"You look exactly like your mother," King Jerome said with finality.

That, in his mind, settled the matter of her beauty. The portrait of Queen Enid and her four-year-old daughter hung in the royal gallery, Laurentia a miniature of the petite, small-boned, regal Welshwoman who had won his heart thirty years ago. But the wavy black hair, fair skin, and melting green eyes which revealed Queen Enid's true serenity were nothing but camouflage on Laurentia.

Laurentia well remembered the torture of standing

for the portrait, of shouting that she wanted to run outside, not dress in scratchy lace. She remembered the bribes of candy King Jerome offered to keep her still, and the way the artist glared at her when she cried. She knew her protruding lower lip drawn into the portrait aptly represented a sulky princess.

She didn't sulk anymore—much—and she never stomped her foot, but the devil's own temper lurked not far beneath her civilized demeanor, and always she kept a firm rein on it. Always . . . except for those moments when the day had been long, and people had been aggravating, and she sat alone in her chamber. Then an impassive Weltrude shut the door on Laurentia's fury.

Tonight could very well be such a night.

King Jerome spoke. "If none of the rest of them please you, Laurentia . . . I suppose you can have Francis."

Francis? He would allow her to take Francis, Comte de Radcote, her former playmate? Bertinierre's home minister, the man she had concluded she should wed—the man King Jerome himself had refused to consider? Exasperated beyond coherence, she sputtered, "But . . . you said . . . Then what . . . then why are we doing this?"

"You know why."

Her gaze sought Francis toward the end of the line that wound, seemingly for leagues, across the glossy black-and-white checked marble floor. She located him by his height and distinguished bearing, and barely took note of the excessively handsome Sicilian duke making his bow. "Papa, Francis is a good man. He would give his life for me."

"I know. I know." King Jerome lifted his hand when she would have continued to remonstrate him. "But he is proper."

"So he is. That's what I like about him."

"*Like*." King Jerome imbued the word with scorn.

"Yes. *Like*. We have everything in common. He's from one of the oldest families in Bertinierre. He understands my duties as few do. He's knowledgeable and responsible."

"And proper." If anything, King Jerome sounded even more annoyed.

"Papa, I won't ever fall in love again like the first time."

"You won't let yourself."

"Of course not." She would have to be insane herself to fall for a man with the violence and passion she had felt for Beaumont.

"You were a young girl infatuated with a handsome older man. I should have known better."

"How? Who could have ever known Beaumont would be—" She hesitated to put a word to it. Especially here. Especially now. They were saying too much already in too public a venue.

King Jerome, too, must have thought the subject too sensitive to broach, for he said, "You stare out over the crowd, too proud to condemn Beaumont and through him, me and my carelessness. But I know you, Laurentia, and I know you still bear the scars."

"That's quite dramatic." Her gaze flicked impatiently over Prince von Fulda, bowing with a flutter of his white-gloved hand. "Beaumont never laid an unkind hand on me. I'm more resilient than you give me credit for."

"And more armored against love than any woman should be."

"*Love.*" She invested that word with as much scorn as he had given the detested "like." "You brought all these men here. Did you think I would see one across the crowded ballroom, a shaft of lightning would strike us both, the violins would sing, and I'd fly to the arms of my dearest beloved?"

He shifted uncomfortably on the throne.

"Oh, Papa." Confound his fanciful soul! "I don't want a dearest beloved, I just need a husband in my bed."

"A *functioning* husband," King Jerome insisted.

"Francis would be that." And if she suspected lovemaking with Francis would be less than passionate, well, even a little passion would be a new experience for her.

Catching Francis's gaze, she smiled at him, a quirk of the lips. A man like that would be good to have at her side. He would be a tower of strength in the forthcoming years, when her father must inevitably die and she would become queen.

She faced that reality without flinching, as she'd been taught to face all the harsh facts of her life.

The line had dwindled, Francis had been presented, when Weltrude said, "Your Highness?" Her black silk dress was orderly and discreet. Her flawlessly styled brown wig covered the traces of gray in her hair. Although Laurentia suspected Weltrude had been born around the turn of the century, her creamy complexion was almost completely unlined.

She was the perfect lady-in-waiting for an imperfect princess, and Laurentia sometimes wondered if the strain would someday prove too much. Thus far it never had, and now as Weltrude stood on the bottom step of the dais, her smile curved her rouged lips just the proper amount and no more. "Is there a gentleman you would like to have as an escort for the first dance?"

Laurentia thought to take Francis, but King Jerome stood. "I would like the first dance."

"Papa." She smiled, charmed by his old-fashioned gallantry.

"Anyone else you choose will be viewed as your favorite." Her father's gaze swept the ballroom, and in disappointed tones he muttered, "Bloodless worms." Taking her hand, he led her to the center of the empty floor.

As all eyes focused on them, she experienced a chill, like the cold creep of unfamiliar fingers up her spine. How odd to be uneasy in her own ballroom. This disquiet must be the result of so many desperate, hopeful, needy suitors piling their hopes on her slender shoulders.

King Jerome made his bow, and as she curtsied, she determinedly shook off her caprice. "Papa, you are quite the handsomest man in the ballroom."

"I can scarcely deny that." His eyes twinkled at her as the orchestra struck up a waltz—her father was fond of waltzes, having performed them in his youth when they were not respectable—and they whirled around the floor.

A distinguished man of sixty, his face bore the marks of forty years of ruling, of the struggles of war and the constant difficulties of diplomacy. Yet he was handsome, as many eager ladies had noted, with a beak of a nose over gray mustache and trimmed and pointed beard. Bushy gray eyebrows encroached on his receding hairline, and his pristine white uniform was decorated with the insignia of the highest commander of the cavalry.

The scent of his favorite cigars transported Laurentia back to a time when she sat on his knee and he made everything all better. In his arms, she relaxed and enjoyed the impetuous flight around the floor, a petite princess in a rose taffeta gown with her hair upswept in an ethereal creation, dancing with a still-vigorous king who performed his duty with energy and ease.

As the dance neared its end, other couples flooded the floor, allowed on by Weltrude's nod. When the next dance began, Laurentia found herself faced with a suitor chosen at random. Prince Germain of Bavaria was charming and charmed, especially when he realized she remembered him from the Congress of Vienna fourteen years before. He failed to comprehend that she remembered everyone; it was her duty as princess.

The brief dance ended, and another man took his place. He was shy, with little conversation; Laurentia had to draw him out. Another followed, and another, until Laurentia's feet hurt and her cheeks ached from holding her smile in place.

It was Francis who gave her a lull, putting his hand on her waist and pulling her close—but not too close. "You don't have to look pleasant for me," he said easily.

"Thank you." She allowed her face to settle into its at-rest expression. "Although I feel as if I'm scowling at you."

"Not at all. Your dimples appear to have created permanent creases in your cheeks."

She laughed, her smile returning for a natural appearance. "That sounds attractive!"

"It is, perhaps, the sign of things to come. As one grows older, one must face the reality of a less than perfect complexion."

He hadn't been joking about the creases in her cheeks, nor did he see a problem with reminding her of her approaching middle age.

Now only half-laughing, she retorted, "I am not so conceited as to worry about that!"

"Like all women, you have your little vanities."

As he had his. He enjoyed training the little wave of brown hair above his forehead. He rode horses every day because gentlemen exercised their horses. It gave him, he had once told her earnestly, a strong physique.

Yes, he had his vanities, and his drawbacks. He lacked a sense of humor, and stared uncomprehending at her jokes.

But he compensated for his shortcomings with his sincerity. With him, she would never have to portray herself as regal or lofty. They knew each other too well for pretense, which explained why she couldn't imagine him naked, panting, lost in passion. Francis would never give way to any uncontrollable emotion, and just the thought of intercourse with him made her want to giggle.

"You are smiling again." He meticulously kept

their bodies apart at the prescribed distance. "Don't grace me with that gracious, royal smirk, Your Highness. Just say you'll be my wife."

She wanted to, so badly, but she couldn't hurt her father by scorning the celebrations he had planned with such enthusiasm. Even if he agreed to this match, he wanted her to have this night.

Intent on evading Francis's gaze, she stared toward the long row of glass-paned doors that led to the terrace.

"I have waited all through your first marriage, your bereavement, and this inexplicable foot-dragging." He spoke vehemently, but quietly, never forgetting that couples swirled around them and the eyes of the kingdom judged them. "I have waited. Who can say as much?"

"No one," she admitted. "But you make me feel as if I owe you for what you elected to do."

He frowned. "That is not my intent."

It wasn't. Only Francis had decided on the right thing, and he didn't understand why she wouldn't allow him to guide her. She had been taught to think for herself, and Francis had been taught that a man should think for his wife. She foresaw trouble ahead, yet what man believed any differently than Francis?

The music slowed. Francis bowed as formally as if she had never, on the occasion of her ninth birthday, given way to fury and broken a thousand-year-old Ming vase over his head.

She wanted to do it again right now.

If only he would sweep her into an alcove, take her in his arms, and declare his love, or even just his resolve to have her. In one dreadful moment of wavering, she wondered—did she dare wed a man she'd never even kissed?

Francis stepped away. Weltrude waved another candidate forward. The orchestra played the opening chords of a formal minuet.

Laurentia's rebellion abruptly rushed forth. "No," she mouthed to Weltrude.

Weltrude slashed the air with her hand, and the music ceased so abruptly that all chatter died, too.

Using her gracious princess smile, Laurentia indicated that the festivities should continue. Conversation rose again as if that awkward pause had never occurred, and she made her way toward the one chamber where she could be alone.

The water closet. Inside, she leaned against the door and closed her eyes. Why had her father insisted on this farce? It had been difficult to resign herself to wanting only what she could have. Now, whether she wished to or not, she searched among the endless countenances for one special face that could make her love again.

Her palms slid along the painted wood. Love. As if her wretched heart could continue to beat after another infection of love.

Running away from the party seemed a good idea. Running away from herself seemed even better. If she were alone to think, she felt certain she could drive these inconsistent doubts from her mind.

Opening the door, she glanced up and down the hallway. Empty. Her first instinct was to tiptoe away. Her good sense forced her to walk easily, as if slipping away from her own party was appropriate behavior. She strode through the study, the handle to the French doors opened smoothly, and she stepped onto the empty terrace where squares of light alternated with night's shadows.

Placing her palms against the wide, low, cool marble railing, she took gulps of fresh air. Gradually the scents of perfume and warm, nervous bodies faded from her consciousness, to be replaced by the fragrance of lilac from the garden, the salt-tang of the Mediterranean harbor below, the earthy odor of the vineyards clustered around the palace, and from somewhere, the faint scent of tobacco. Her brief rebellion against fate faded, too, as she concentrated on the palace that enveloped her, the mountains behind, the city spread out like a cloth spangled with lights.

She loved this palace of hers. Her crusading ancestors had planted the original sandstone castle into the rocky soil. Succeeding generations had grafted on wings of pale, copper-streaked marble and towers of granite and tile. Now the whole edifice grew like a gnarled and protective tree above the ancient city of Omnia. Garden terraces descended in floral steps down the cliff, each blushing with pleasure in daylight, each steeped in fragrance at night. The lights of Omnia glowed, and faintly Laurentia could hear the sounds of celebration as the inhabitants took a day from the rigors of fishing and trading to rejoice on her birthday. God bless them; she knew many of the merchants and shopkeepers personally. She knew the farmers and vintners of the countryside, too, and the harvesters who lived deep in the Pyrenees, growing that rarest of herbs in their welltended fields. These people were the ones who kept her kingdom alive. The common folk never knew that every day she and her father balanced on the tightrope of statesmanship to allow them their ways of life.

Automatically her gaze traveled to the far end of the bay. The border of Pollardine began at the sea and nestled against Bertinierre all the way into the Pyrenees. The countries had once been allies. Now . . . they were not.

She heard doors opening around the far corner, and the music from the ballroom spilled out. Perhaps it was getting warm inside, or perhaps lovers sought the darkness, there to perform the rituals of courtship. She had no way of knowing what occurred in those brief moments, yet she'd observed the woman's feline smile of satisfaction, the man's concentration on his mate. It would be pleasant, Laurentia thought, if any man ever concentrated on her instead of on her kingdom.

She wished—quite fervently—that such a man would come forward. The door behind her opened. For one moment, she thought her prayer had been answered. She felt a small thrill go through her body. Then her wits rescued her, and she realized she had simply been found, as was inevitable. Found by Weltrude, by one of the suitors, by her worried father. Turning, she faced the lone man silhouetted against the glass doors.

"Your Highness?" A faint, foreign twang accented his voice, and he wore a uniform. No, a livery. The royal livery.

Puzzled, she studied him. She had never met him. "Yes?"

Steadily, he walked toward her, a beefy man whose bulk strained his jacket and smelled of sweat. His beefy hands reached out for her; she tried to sidestep as she sputtered, "What do you think you're doing?"

Without a word, he grabbed her around the waist and hefted her onto his shoulder.

Chapter Two

Laurentia hung there, immobilized by shock. A man, a stranger, a servant had laid hands on her! It wasn't until he put his foot on the balustrade and prepared to leap into the garden that she gave a shriek and grabbed for his hair.

His musty wig came off in her hands. She shrieked again and thumped him on the spine. That knocked him off balance, more than she expected, and he rocked backward, flailing his arms. Emboldened by her success, she thumped again and threw herself sideways.

She flew through the air and hit the marble floor, cracking her elbow, knocking the breath out of her. The thug fell on top of her. Something—someone—landed on top of them both.

The someone knocked the hulking knave off her. Released from the crushing weight, she gasped for breath, strained to hear through the ringing in her ears. In the distance, yet far too close, she heard the crack of bone against flesh. Feet pounded along the terrace; stupidly, all she could think was that she couldn't be caught with her clothes rumpled and her dignity compromised. Sitting up, she swayed as she glanced around.

It was her attacker and her rescuer whose footsteps she heard. The two men raced along the terrace, away from the ballroom, going deeper into the shadows. The one in the lead leaped over the balustrade. The second started to follow, then drew back. The land dropped away there, and only a desperate man would dare the leap.

"Coward," she muttered. That was unfair, but her ribs ached and her elbow hurt and she was the princess and she didn't have to be fair. Not when she had just been attacked by some smelly beast and only one of her loyal subjects or supposedly eager suitors had come to her aid.

Her rescuer limped back toward her—oh, fine, he was injured and required compassion when she had none to spend. He was another broad-shouldered fellow, although not as tall as the villain. As he crossed through the squares of light coming from the windows, then entered the shadows between, he seemed more phantom than man. She strained to behold his face, but could see only dark hair, lightened by a streak of white at each temple, eyes deep-set above a craggy nose, and lips pressed tightly together.

He wore a dark frock coat, a black silk neckcloth, and black trousers over black boots. Obviously, he had no imagination when it came to color, but he wore a gentleman's outfit. Thank God for that.

When he came within speaking distance, the gentleman demanded, in a tone quite unlike any she normally heard, "What the hell was that about?"

Astonished, indignant, and in pain, she stammered, "Who . . . what . . . How dare you?"

"Was he a suitor scorned?"

"I never saw him before!"

"Then next time a stranger grabs you and slams you over his shoulder, you squeal like a stuck pig."

Clutching her elbow, she staggered to her feet. "I yelled!"

"I barely heard you." He stood directly in front of her, taller than he had at first appeared, beetle-browed, his eyes dark hollows, his face marked with a deep-shadowed scar that ran from chin to temple. "And I was just behind those pots."

Tall and luxuriant, the potted plants clustered against the wall, and she looked at them, then looked back at him. He spoke with a Sereminian accent. He walked with a limp. He was a stranger. Suspicion stirred in her. "What were you doing there?"

"Smoking."

She smelled it on him, that faint scent of tobacco so like that which clung to her father. Although she knew it foolish, the odor lessened her misgivings. "I'll call the guard and send them after that scoundrel."

"Scoundrel." The stranger laughed softly. "You *are* a lady. But don't bother sending anyone after him. He's long gone."

She knew it was true. The scoundrel—and what was wrong with that word, anyway?—had leaped into the wildest part of the garden, just where the cultured plants gave way to natural scrub. The guard would do her no good.

So rather than doing what she knew very well she should, she let the stranger place his hand on the small of her back and turn her toward the light.

But he only examined her features impersonally, and in a kinder tone asked, "Are you hurt?"

"Just bruised."

He clasped her wrist and slowly stretched out her injured arm. "It's not broken."

"I don't suppose so."

He grinned, a slash of white teeth against a half-glimpsed face. "You'd recognize if it was. A broken elbow lets you know it's there." Efficiently, he unfastened the buttons on her elbow-length glove and stripped it away, then ran his bare fingers firmly over the bones in her lower arm, then lightly over the pit of her elbow.

Goose bumps rose on her skin at the touch. He didn't wear gloves, she noted absently. His naked skin touched hers. "What kind of injury are you looking for?"

"Not an injury. I just thought I would enjoy caressing that baby-soft skin."

She jerked her wrist away.

He laughed, obviously amused by her indignation and probably lying about wanting to caress her.

Damn him.

She snatched her glove back and pulled it on, and found she had trouble thrusting her fingers into each proper cavity. They trembled, as did her voice. "I don't know why anyone would . . . that is, what he was . . ."

"Aren't you the princess?"

Her heart gave an irregular thump. Wariness returned in a rush, and she took one edgy step away. "Yes."

"Then I'd have to say it was a kidnapping attempt."

She stared at the stranger blankly, straining to see through the darkness at the possessor of that inscrutable voice. "That's absurd!"

"Hardly. You're the only heir to a quite wealthy little kingdom. I imagine your father would pay a fortune to have you back. I'm only surprised no one's tried before."

He made her feel naïve. "We're at peace here—"

"One bad apple, and all that. But he did get away, and if he's desperate enough, he might try again. Or there might be more than one of them. Consider hiring a bodyguard."

Who did the man think he was? How dare he give her advice? "Who are *you?*"

"Dominic of Baminia—except they changed the name, it's Sereminia now, and everyone calls me 'Dom.' " He strolled to the tall potted plant and dug his cigar out of the soil where he'd tossed it. "I'm one of your suitors."

She was shaken, but she hadn't lost her wits. "You were not presented."

"There's no cozening you, is there?" The cigar still smoldered, and he knocked the dirt off and placed the end in his mouth. Lifting his head, he puffed until the end glowed red, then looked down at her. Smoke eased from between his lips as he said, "I didn't get here in time."

He was rude, he was crude—not to mention late— and he spoke so offhandedly, every hackle rose. So she mentioned it. "If you want to court a princess, it seems worthwhile to cultivate punctuality."

"Punctuality." He mocked her patrician accent. "Actually, I didn't see the sense of it. You're not going to marry me."

She wasn't, of course, but it annoyed her that he was so sure. "And why not?"

"I am the brother of the king of Sereminia."

Startled, she searched her memory. The brother of the king of Sereminia? Did he have a brother? But why would this man tell such an easily detected lie?

In fact, would this man lie at all? On the contrary, he seemed honest. Suspiciously honest. "Well," she said cautiously, wondering if he knew the truth, not wanting to give anything away, "that's not a bad connection. We share our northwest border with Sereminia—"

"I'm the bastard brother."

"Of course." Of course. That explained so much. It explained why he didn't seem to know the secret Bertinerre and Sereminia shared. And this gentleman, for such she must call him, must be sensitive about his illegitimate status, else he would have come and taken his chances with the rest of the suitors. "There are other bastards here."

"They don't stand a chance, either." Crossing to the wide marble railing, he sat on it. "Do they?"

He wouldn't get such an admission out of her. "As much of a chance as any."

"Ah, then you've made your choice." The lights from the French doors didn't quite reach him as he stretched out his long legs and crossed them at the ankles. "Who's the lucky leg-shackle?"

She didn't have to stay out here with this cynical brute. She should go in and report the incident to her father. But she found herself several steps closer, still trying to get a good look at Dominic of Sereminia, although why she didn't know. She shouldn't care if she ever spoke to him again. "I haven't picked anyone."

He continued as if she hadn't spoken. "I watched you dance with all those jackasses."

Had it been his gaze that created a chill?

"I would say it was that fellow ... Who is he? ... The tall one with the pompous streak wide as the sea."

She caught her breath on a chuckle. He'd hooked Francis precisely!

"Yes, I've got it!" Dom said. "Little Lord Francis de Radcote."

Her amusement died. "Is that the gossip?"

"Part of the gossip, certainly not all of the gossip. Speculation ran rampant with every swain who took you in his arms." He tilted his head back and blew out a cloud of smoke. "Especially among the debutantes. They're not crazy about you, you know."

He jumped from subject to subject, telling her things no one else would dream of mentioning. "Who isn't?"

"All the young ladies who line the long walls and cluster around the ivory-framed mirrors. The sooner you're married, the happier this year's crop of maidens will be." He tapped the cigar on the edge of the railing. "They don't like playing cat's-paw to a woman of your advanced years."

Her head swam oddly, as if she'd been underwater and out of air for too long. "I suppose not."

"Although you're holding up well for a woman of

twenty-five. Quite pretty, actually. Is your hair really that color?"

"You are a boor!" she exclaimed, but again she found herself swallowing a laugh.

"It's not, then. I had wondered."

Recovering her wits, she said, "You have to admit, it is natural-looking." And the chignon felt rather loose after her tumble.

"Not really. Not many women really have hair of ebony and skin white as snow, as the old fairy tale says. Lemon juice on the complexion?"

He was right about that, at least. "I find it helps bleach out the freckles."

He nodded. "It's good to be a man."

"I have always thought that must be true." She poked at the hairpins holding her coiffure in position. A few had been lost in her fall. But Weltrude instructed that not a hair on the princess's head should ever be out of place, so what matter a few hairpins more or less? Her classic style would not fail. It dared not, or it would answer to Weltrude. "Men have all the advantages. They get to scratch where it itches, stride about in clomping boots, and let loose with any body function they see fit."

"Most important, we have these . . . inappropriate reactions to ladies even when we know they dye their hair."

Her hands froze, her eyes widened. Confused, her mind in turmoil, she stared forward, into the hallway lit by candelabras, her eyes aching with the strain of never blinking. Did he mean what she thought he meant? In his careless, unrefined way, was he calling her attractive?

"If I promise not to belch too loudly, may I see you into supper?"

Slowly, she lowered her arms. What was she doing out here in the dark, chatting with a man to whom she'd never been properly introduced? Weltrude would have apoplexy. "That doesn't seem like a good idea."

"Little Lord Francis wouldn't like it." From the corners of her eyes, she saw Dom nod sagely. "Of course. I just thought you might be grateful. I did grapple with that brute and chase him off." He rubbed his hip as if it ached.

Irresistibly, amusement rose in her again. Just when she thought herself mad to allow herself this freedom with a self-proclaimed rogue, he disarmed her with an offer to be seen with her in public. Then he ruthlessly used his injury and her obligation to get his way. "You're good," she said admiringly. "Very good. But why should I take you into dinner with me when there are so many other men who arrive on time, don't skulk behind plants, and are willing to take their chances as my suitor?"

He was silent so long that she turned to look up at him. He was staring at the glowing red end of his cigar, then he smiled. "Let's face it, Princess. This is probably your last chance at courtship. You might as well make the most of it, and why not? You can play the lads against each other, tease and flirt, enjoy yourself as any woman does when she makes a multitude of men desire her. You can do as you like with me at your side, for I'm not a prince or a even a legitimate commoner, just a buffer against honest courtship."

Vaguely offended, she said, "You have a lovely opinion of my character!"

He shrugged. "I can't imagine this princess duty is any fun, so you might as well kick up your heels. Besides"—he looked down at her, and for the first time she recognized the gleam of the predator in his eyes—"you need a bodyguard, and that's what I am. Your own personal mercenary sent to guard you from the wicked world."

Chapter Three

If she were smart, Laurentia knew she would turn and flee back to the ballroom. But this man was right about one thing. Being a princess wasn't all fun, and conversation with Dominic of Sereminia exercised a mind numbed by ceremony and protocol.

Moreover, she needed to know about him. For the safety of her kingdom, of course. "Mr. . . . ."

"Dom," he said. "Just Dom."

"Dom." She tried the name and found she could utter it easily. Odd how exchanging a few quips with a man gave her a sense of familiarity. "You're a mercenary?"

"There aren't many positions for a bastard brother of the king. I have to earn a living somehow."

A mercenary. A man who fought on any side with the lucre to pay him. That explained the swift action toward her attacker, the scar, the limp, the knowledge of broken bones . . . the cynicism. The almost visible aura of danger that surrounded him.

"Are you shocked, little princess?" Laughter curled in his voice once more, and he towered a head above her as they sat.

But she never allowed a man to imagine such

physical domination made him superior to her. At least . . . not for long. "Not at all," she said with what she considered admirable aplomb. "I was just wondering—if you're my bodyguard, who's going to save me from you?"

"You're a clever girl. You'll save yourself."

"I'm not a girl at all." She'd ceased being a girl the day she married her first husband. "I'm a woman."

"A woman at the ripe old age of twenty-five."

She narrowed her eyes at him. Could the man be a bigger wretch? "I'm clever enough to know if a man like you decided to kidnap me, or harm me, you'd get the job done before I could defend myself."

He didn't move or indicate his displeasure in any physical way, yet the air perceptibly cooled. "If I had decided to kidnap or harm you, Your Highness, the job would be done already."

Rubbing her palms over the goose bumps that had formed on her arms, she thought she would like to learn this trick of influencing the atmosphere. He was efficient, she knew. He wouldn't have bungled it; she would be gone, and no one would know it yet. No one had even come looking for her.

Then a large, dark form stepped into the doorway of the study from whence she had come and looked out. Francis.

And despite her uneasy thoughts about Dom, she wished Francis would go away.

He didn't, of course. He stepped out onto the veranda and asked, "Laurentia? What are you doing out here? Everyone's wondering if you ran away from your own party."

"I did," she said.

"Bad form, dear." That this always proper noble-man allowed himself to chide her spoke volumes. That he stared with offended dignity at the man be-side her said even more. "You're out here with a ... gentleman."

On Francis's lips, the word "gentleman" sounded like an insult. An insult which seemed to affect Dom not at all, but raised Laurentia's hackles. Francis took too much on himself. He always had.

Easing her bottom backward on the marble railing, she made herself at home beside Dom, and swung her feet in a parody of relaxation. "Yes, this is Dom-inic of Sereminia. He's the brother of King Danior of Sereminia and one of my suitors."

As soon as she'd said the words, she wished she could call them back. The brother of King Danior of Sereminia, indeed.

Francis moved closer, out of the light, dismissing Dom and concentrating on her. "The brother of King Danior would be a prince."

"No, Lord de Radcote," Dom said. "Not without the bonds of holy matrimony to bless my parents' union."

Dom didn't sound offended that she'd placed him in the position of declaring his illegitimacy, but she put her hand on his arm anyway. He looked down at her with what she thought might be surprise, and she saw the shadows around his mouth deepen. He was smiling at her, and her heart sang a funny little trill.

"The princess and I have just been discussing my star-crossed debut on the wrong side of the covers and how it will influence my courtship." Dom laid his hand over hers, trapping it against the warmth of his arm. "I shall have to be extra gallant to convince her I am the man she seeks."

She stared at him, unable to tear her gaze from the dim-shadowed face. She knew he said so just to worm his way into her affections, and probably—no, definitely—to annoy Francis. Nevertheless, that combination of danger and charm worked on her like Beethoven's Ninth Symphony. Her pulse pounded in her trapped hand, her breath quickened. She felt if she opened her mouth, her every thought would be expressed in the chorale "Ode to Joy"—and she couldn't carry a tune in a coal scuttle.

"How touching." Francis, not surprisingly, managed to sound both stern and disapproving. "But I'm sure Her Highness would agree it would be best if she came inside and led us into supper."

Supper. Dom had asked to take her into supper. Now he held her hand, and patiently waited for her decision. Damn him. The man read her . . . as well as she read him. He knew that if she didn't accept his invitation, she'd feel guilty for rejecting him and discontented with Francis.

What had been totally acceptable an hour ago—declaring Francis her favored suitor—now seemed the act of a woman who worshipped the dull and predictable. Even the cowardly. She ought, really ought, to give the others a chance. After all, many of them had traveled over mountain and river for a chance to woo her. With Dom at her side, she could tease and flirt in one last grand gala before settling down to the serious business of being a wife, princess, and that which she prayed for, mother.

Never mind that she could do so equally well with a little sensible caution and without Dom dancing attendance.

"Is it time for supper already? Thank you for reminding me, Francis." Sliding off the balustrade, she faced Dom. "Shall we go in?"

He pushed away from the railing and walked away from her, leaving her feeling foolish and abandoned. But he only stubbed out his cigar in the dirt of a potted plant before returning and offering his arm. "Your Highness, you do me great honor."

The guilt she dreaded reared its head before they'd taken a step, and she said, "Come along, Francis. I must introduce Dominic to His Majesty, my father."

"Yes, Francis, come along." Dom couldn't have sounded more patronizing or more unceremonious.

Francis despised a lack of ceremony, and he hurried to catch up as they walked into the darkened study. "Your Highness, you have not been properly introduced to this gentleman, thus you should not be going into dinner with him." Then the light fell on her, and he gasped, "Your Highness!"

Confusion brought Laurentia to a halt. "What?"

"Look at yourself." He pointed to one of the mirrors lining the walls. "You look like a trollop!"

She did. The struggle with her attacker had left her gown askew, her glove smudged from her fall, and her hair was more than just loose, as she had fondly supposed. Tendrils straggled over one shoulder and the whole exquisite creation listed to one side.

She stopped in her tracks and stared at her reflection. "Oh, my."

"Yet, my Lord de Radcote, I would hesitate to use the word 'trollop' in conjunction with Her Highness." Dom sounded amused, but with an edge that effectively chided Francis.

Francis found himself in the unusual position of being in the wrong, and his apology lacked conviction. " 'Trollop' was indeed an unfortunate choice of words on my part."

"I find her disarray charming," Dom said.

"Of course. You would. I'm glad I didn't come out sooner, Your Highness. I would not have wished to interrupt your romp with this fellow."

For a moment, she didn't understand what he meant by a "romp." When she did, she experienced a confusion of indignation, amusement, and, lurking beneath it all, a totally unjustified self-consciousness. Because she hadn't been "romping," yet in the depths of her mind, she rather wished she had been. Certainly it would have been better than being attacked and landing too hard on her ... dignity. "Francis, no! I was—"

"Barely saved from tumbling over the railing. By me." Dom gripped her elbow. "I think perhaps Her Highness has had a little too much to drink."

She rounded on him. "I beg your pardon!"

"Deny it if you like, Your Highness." He dipped his head in respectful salute, but his eyes watched her meaningfully. "But how many glasses of wine have you imbibed?"

For some reason, he didn't want her to reveal her ordeal, but his false accusation meant nothing now.

Not when the light fell full on his countenance and showed her . . . showed her . . .

His forehead was broad, his jaw was a powerful statement of obstinacy, his cheekbones were broad and classically Sereminian. His nose jutted out in a most imperious manner. That scar divided his face into uneven portions, a white streak through rough, tanned skin. For no reason should he have been called handsome.

But he was. He was splendid. Stunning. Magnificent.

Deep in her mind, an alarm sounded.

Black lashes any young lady would envy formed a frame for his eyes. Eyes of pure blue, virginal in their clarity, piercing in their intensity, overwhelming in their sensuality. In his eyes, she could see every slight, every compliment, every battle, every lust, every cruelty. A woman could fall into his eyes and travel the routes to his soul.

Slowly she stepped back.

His mouth . . . his wide mouth hinted of a heated afternoon spent in exchanging long, slow, shudderingly sweet kisses.

A faint dampness trickled across her palms, and she formed fists to dry them on her gloves.

She already knew he was tall and broad-shouldered. But she hadn't realized how his body defined his clothing, making them superfluous decorations on a perfect form.

This man was a stranger to her, but she recognized his breed. He moved, ate, and spoke like a normal man.

But he was a walking, breathing heartache.

Chapter Four

"Laurentia, are you intoxicated?"

Francis's furious question pulled her back from the brink of worship, despair, and resolution, and into the real world.

"What?" She tore her gaze away from Dom and stared at Francis.

"I can't believe it of you," Francis said furiously. "What were you thinking?"

"Thinking?" She'd been thinking she was a woman who learned from her mistakes, that's what she'd been thinking.

"You imbibed unwisely on this, your special night?"

She stared at Francis for one more dazed moment. Then her brain snapped into action—but she didn't dare look at Dom. Fortitude was a fine thing, but she already knew she was susceptible to the idiocy he induced. "I *was* thinking," she answered. "Or rather, I wasn't thinking. I'm better now. The fresh air has done me good, and I'm sure the food from the supper will correct any lack of coordination . . ." She was rambling, confirming her intemperance and deepening Francis's appalled amazement.

Unable to resist any longer, she cast a helpless glance at Dom and lost momentum. He was smiling at her, and she staggered from the almost physical impact. Deep in those tanned and rugged cheeks resided dimples.

Two.

Devastating ones.

If she had known what he'd looked like when she stood outside with him, she would have been speechless. Instead she'd snipped and teased, proving she could be coherent, and that left her looking even more silly right now with candlelight bathing him in a glow and she as blushing and tongue-tied as any green girl.

"Your Highness." Francis broke into her garbled thoughts. "I assume you would prefer Mr.—"

"Dom." The mercenary's broad hand still held her close to his side. "Just Dom. We bastards don't have the luxury of surnames."

Francis flushed; he hated being placed in a position in which he didn't know the proper protocol. "Your Highness. You would prefer *Dom* to take you into supper, I presume."

"It might be better," Dom said. "I'm an old hand with these cases."

Indignation crashed through her. "These cases?" She watched Dom give Francis a manly, fraternal nod, and after a moment of surprised indecision, Francis returned it. Executing a military turn, he strode off, leaving Laurentia and Dom alone.

"These cases?" she repeated, torn between chagrin and mirth. Even when she knew she should be wary, Dom disarmed her.

He watched until Francis had cleared the doorway. Then he pushed her toward the mirror and stood at her left shoulder. With the delicacy of a lady's maid, he plucked the pins from her hair, and she caught her breath as she wondered, for one spectacular, unwary moment, if he intended to seduce her.

Madness. Did it now affect her, too?

"Hold these." He dangled his hairpin-filled hand over her shoulder. "I'll put your hair back up. I have experience in these matters."

Experience. She would wager he did, and she knew how he'd got it. Cynicism made her clearheaded. Cupping her palms, she accepted the pins and demanded, "How could you insinuate those things about me?"

"I didn't want you to tell de Radcote about the abduction attempt." Taking her hair in his palm, he scraped it into a tail at the back of her head and twisted it. "We don't know for sure the nature of the beast, and if I'm going to be your bodyguard, I don't want the palace in an uproar."

Her bodyguard. She looked in the mirror and his virile beauty struck her again. Wary or not, cynical or not, if she made him her bodyguard, she wouldn't be able to act on anything but instinct, like a jellyfish floating on an inexorable current. Maybe even the fundamental performance of a jellyfish would be beyond her, since she seemed to be having trouble breathing. Not that jellyfish breathed— She cut herself off before her thoughts could ramble further. "His Majesty, my father—"

"Should know." Leaning forward, he plucked

three of the pins from her hand. "For one thing, if there is a threat it may extend to him."

That hadn't occurred to her. Panic cleared her mind of any other thought, and she tried to walk away, to go to her father.

Dom stopped her. "Stand still! I don't want to jerk your hair out by the roots!"

She clutched her fingers around the pins, and several sprang into the air and landed with tinny pings on the table and floor. "My father—"

"Is fine. Abductors are cowards, and stupid ones at that, but they'll not attempt anything in a ballroom in front of everyone. They would be caught and executed."

"Yes." She swallowed. "Of course."

"His Majesty is under no more threat than he ever is." Dom used up the hairpins, and pried her fingers open for more. "You *did* realize he—and you—were always in danger."

"Yes," she said, but her voice was small.

He scowled, unimpressed. "Listen. Before the union of Serephinia and Baminia, there were several groups of revolutionaries operating in both countries, and they were almost successful in overthrowing the government."

She knew the story. Every ruler in Europe knew that story, and the tales of all the revolutions spawned by Napoleon's shake-up of the old kingdoms. "But in Serephinia and Baminia, the rulers were corrupt and the economy weak. The people were starving, and starving people will revolt." She grasped his wrist as it dipped down for more pins. When he met her gaze in the mirror, she said, "In

Bertinierre, our people are not starving."

"You're naïve if you think that's all there is to it. There'll always be someone who wants the biggest slice of the cake. You fare well in Bertinierre. Did you think no one would notice?"

On the veranda, he'd soothed her with his patter. Now intensity radiated from him, convincing her she'd been living an illusion of invulnerability.

Ruthlessly she cleared the veil of pernicious desire from her mind. She was the princess, responsible for her country, and Dom seemed the voice of reason. She would listen and decide. Letting go of his wrist, she offered a hairpin. "Who?"

"I don't know." He plucked the pin from between her fingers and used it to anchor another swath of hair. "That idiot tonight, he was an amateur, but an almost successful amateur. If he hadn't underestimated you, and if I hadn't been conveniently in place, you'd be gone."

Very conveniently.

Not that he could have known she would go outside, or that she really thought he had planned a fake abduction just to ingratiate himself as her suitor. But despite his opinion, and her own baffling reaction to a too-handsome face, she was nobody's fool.

Or at least she hadn't been for almost five years.

Holding up a pin, she watched it. Steady, without a tremor. "So you think the attack was a plot?"

He plucked the pin from her fingers. "Not at all. It could have been—probably was—just that smelly mullet-head with a slapdash plan and a lot of nerve."

She handed him another pin. He inserted it, and

her hair took a familiar shape as she watched him pinch and twist. "That would be best."

"By far. But the arseworm . . . excuse me . . . *scoundrel*—"

He paused, waiting for her to laugh. Inviting her to laugh.

She didn't, and after a brief look of surprise, he continued. "The scoundrel could try again. Or this could be the first volley from the discontented."

"Perhaps." Certainly, this explained her father's penchant for extraordinary precautions and plans.

"Or it could even be another country, envious of Bertinerre's wealth."

She started.

It would be too much to expect that he wouldn't notice. Taking her shoulders, he turned her to face him. "That's it, is it?"

"Maybe. No, surely not. That was years ago." Right after Beaumont's death, and she remembered so little of that time, yet vaguely she recalled a conversation between her father and their most trusted servant, Chariton.

Dom waited, but she didn't confide her country's secrets in anyone, especially not men she had the good sense not to trust.

His eyes narrowed, his lashes a sooty fringe. "You're not as innocent as you appear."

"Ignorant," she corrected him gently. "I'm not as *ignorant* as I appear. I'm going to be queen. My father consults me in every matter, tells me his opinion, and asks my advice."

A subtle tension around his mouth relaxed. "That explains much."

"Explains what?"

"Why someone would try to take you. You're privy to the nation's secrets."

He answered easily, but his air of satisfaction, hastily concealed, made her regret confessing her authority. Yet everyone knew; it was common knowledge throughout the kingdom she was His Majesty's most valued emissary. Hiding her capabilities would gain her nothing.

"Stand still for just one moment more. I'm almost done." He turned her back to the mirror and set to work. "I have connections. I'll ask around down by the waterfront tomorrow and see if anyone is talking."

"If they are?"

"Then I'll have earned my still-unnegotiated wage." He grinned at her, all dimples and allure.

Desire rushed back, a giddy aphrodisiac against which she had no defenses, and she almost dropped the last of the pins. But if exposed often enough, a person could get callused against such charisma. "You are no longer a suitor, then, but a servant?" she asked.

He still held a smile, but the character of it changed to tempered steel. "I am never a servant. A servant is someone who waits upon another's pleasure. I am free to come and go, destined to work outside of your tiresome protocol."

She smiled, too, flint to his steel. "Very well. You agree you have decided to take this assignment, and if my father concurs, and we are pleased with your credentials, I agree you should be hired." She allowed him one moment of triumph before putting him firmly in his place. "And I must know the amount you demand as reimbursement."

She watched him, and he watched her, two adversaries locked in undeclared, unarmed combat.

"Re . . . im . . . bursement." Like the yokel she knew he was not, he sounded out the syllables, as if he'd never heard of such a word. "You want me to tell you what I desire in re . . . im . . . bursement."

She waited, wondering how he could appear both menacing and protective, affable and intimidating.

"Your Highness." His hands dropped away from her hair and onto her bare shoulders. They were rough, a workman's hands, and long-fingered . . . a lover's hands.

They moved, his palms stroking the smooth curve of muscle, his fingertips tracing her collarbone, his caress a promise of retribution.

She watched, mesmerized, panicked, amazed as her skin flushed a delicate pink, wordlessly confessing her agitation and desire.

She'd been wrong about a man before, but she didn't think she was wrong this time. This man wouldn't make promises he couldn't keep. Using nothing but his expression, his touch, and his strength of character, he promised her pleasure. The kind of pleasure so intense as to make her weep.

"I will deal you in this round, Your Highness, and show my cards if you care to look. I will protect you and keep you from harm, and when you are satisfied I have kept my word, then I'll present my fee." He leaned down and with his lips by her ear, he whispered, "To you. And you'll pay."

*   *   *

Where was she? King Jerome spoke easily with several likely suitors. No one could tell from his demeanor that he worried because his daughter, trained in the most minute matters of protocol, had disappeared for the past hour.

Yet his knuckles were white from gripping the arms of the throne, and his gaze constantly searched the ballroom, hoping to see her as she stepped out from behind a marble column, expecting her to stroll up to the formally-dressed orchestra and request a waltz, anticipating her reflection in the gilt-trimmed mirrors.

Why had she vanished? Had she gone to treat the headache, or gossip with the women, or . . . dear God, was she bleeding to death in one of the many crannies in the palace, while the orchestra played and he made carefully unworried conversation?

He tried not to panic. Since the incident five years before, he'd been prey to these forebodings. Laurentia didn't know the truth of what had happened. Nor did any but a select few.

He could have asked Chariton, of course, but Chariton was checking the preparations for tomorrow's festival.

Nodding as if he actually comprehended a French count's babbling, King Jerome surveyed the ballroom, thankful for the dais that set him above the crowd.

There. There was Francis, walking in from the corridor with a frown puckering his even features. He'd gone in search of the princess; had he found her?

Stopping, Francis made conversation with a lady of impeccable lineage, and King Jerome relaxed infinitesimally. If Francis thought the princess was in danger, he would have returned at once.

But where was she? So many strangers milled about. So many suitors sought her. What was she doing? Even Weltrude, Laurentia's personal tyrant, scowled.

Then Laurentia entered the ballroom—almost at a run.

King Jerome half-lifted himself to his feet.

Color burned in her cheeks, and her clothing was rumpled. She glanced about wildly and plunged into the crowd.

An unknown gentleman followed close on her heels.

Anger, concern and then, finally, delight buffeted King Jerome as he sank back onto the throne.

He didn't know the fellow who watched his daughter with such hungry eyes, but beneath the surface sophistication King Jerome observed an undercurrent of fiery emotion, and he recognized the gentleman's look of intent as he followed the princess Laurentia.

Without taking his gaze from the young man, King Jerome summoned Weltrude with a crook of the finger. "Why haven't I been introduced to that young man?"

Weltrude's bony hands flexed into fists—the lady hated any insinuation she might have been negligent. But although King Jerome normally took the time to smooth her ruffled feathers, right now he had no patience. Couldn't the woman see the situation required swift action? That fellow moved after Laurentia like a man with a purpose. If Laurentia's father wished to determine his suitability, he would have to interrogate him at once. Genially, of course. With all appearance of hospitality.

"Dominic of Sereminia arrived late, Your Majesty," Weltrude apologized.

"Bring him to me."

As always, when he gave her a direct order, she stiffened. *Then* she moved to do his bidding.

As she sliced through the crowd like a cutter through unruly waters, he once again wondered how he could have been so wrong in his initial judgement of her. Within weeks of his queen's death, a thirty-year-old Weltrude had applied for the position of first lady-in-waiting to the twelve-year-old princess. Her references had been impeccable, but more than that, King Jerome had suspected she belonged to some vanquished royal family. He had hired her in the hopes she and Laurentia would become friends. But although Weltrude's service had never been less than perfect, she had shown neither compassion nor understanding for Laurentia as she dealt with the loss of her mother. As the years had gone on, thirteen of them now, Weltrude's sensibility had hardened into dogmatism. Yet Laurentia insisted Weltrude remain in their service; like him, Laurentia hesitated to release a servant without good cause.

Without appearing to, Weltrude was moving briskly after Dominic. She managed to catch him by the arm just as he reached Laurentia, saw the impatient shake he gave, saw him tense as Weltrude spoke to him, saw him glance toward him.

King Jerome smiled genially, knowing full well Dominic of Sereminia dared not disobey.

But he could, and did, subject Laurentia to the full glare of his displeasure.

She, too, glanced at her father, then lifted her chin at Dominic in open defiance.

My God, what intimacies had occurred between those two that they could quarrel without words? King Jerome couldn't imagine—doubted if he wanted to imagine. But he knew that Dominic wanted Laurentia desperately, with all the ardor and depth of emotion King Jerome wished for her.

If the young man lived up to his promise of passion, King Jerome would help him catch her.

Chapter Five

Did the king suspect? Did he know?

Dom strode across the ballroom toward the beaming monarch and wondered if this assignment would be his last. Yes, King Jerome was smiling, but while in his cradle Dom had learned not to trust royalty. An aristocrat could rend a man to bloody bits on a caprice.

And Dom knew that this time he deserved exactly such treatment. He had told the princess he was a mercenary and a bastard, and that was the truth . . . but not the entire truth.

He had been sent to Bertinierre on a mission.

Somewhere in the Pyrenees
March 1829

"I don't kill for money anymore. I'm retired." Dom *slouched against the wall, hands on the wooden table and carefully relaxed, revealing no sign of strain to the man sitting military-straight in the chair across from him.*

"A mercenary." Marcel de Emmerich smiled slightly as he tapped his fingernail on the damp, worm-eaten table.

"One who conquers for vast sums of money. You have rather failed in that department, I hear."

Of course de Emmerich had heard. He had summoned Dom to this stinking little public house on the edge of nowhere for just that reason. Because he knew Dom was desperate, although he didn't know why. Being the man he was, de Emmerich thought greed had brought Dom here, when in fact he was tangled in the bonds of affection and obligation.

A child depended on him. Not even his child, but the child Dom had come to think of as his last chance for redemption.

"I believe you have a way with the ladies." The sputtering candlelight softened de Emmerich's appearance, effacing the smallpox pits and giving a faintly yellow cast to his pale flesh. His teeth were pocked with black. He wore the uniform he had designed for himself, with subtle touches of gold braid and porcelain buttons. He looked like a catchpenny nobleman, earning his title by gaining influence over Pollardine's frothblower king and conferring it on himself.

He was so much more.

"So you've given up being a mercenary and have become a gigolo instead," he said.

Dom kept his hands still, his expression disinterested. *"A man of my antecedents learns to be versatile."*

De Emmerich studied him, seeking the weakness he sensed existed beneath the composed exterior. Inevitably, he found it. *"That last little tiff in Greece decimated your band."*

Dom's hands didn't twitch. *"I lost some good men."*

"You lost all your men," de Emmerich corrected.

Dom would wager he could kill de Emmerich in a fair fight . . . but he never made the mistake of thinking de Emmerich fair.

"Yes. All of them." Dom allowed a smile to twitch at his mouth as he told the lie. "So I'll be of no use to you, and I'll be on my way." Placing his hands flat on the table, he shoved back his bench—and saw the flash, heard the whistle of a blade past his ear. It stuck in the wall, the thin dagger rattling like a dying man's last gasp.

De Emmerich leaned forward, his eyes glittering with something slimy, vicious. "I don't need your men. I need only you. I will pay you twenty-five thousand crowns Pollardine when you complete the job. Now sit."

Dom sat.

Reaching his long arm across the table, de Emmerich pulled the knife out of the half-rotted wood and slipped it back into his sleeve. Summoning the cowering barmaid, he said to Dom, "I will buy you a drink and tell you what you will do."

For twenty-five thousand crowns Pollardine, Dom would have risked any danger. But it was not danger de Emmerich wanted from him, but shameful treachery.

Now, as Dom stood at the foot of the dais, he wondered if that sword King Jerome kept at his side was entirely ornamental, or if Dom would soon feel the sharp edge against his neck. He deserved it, he knew.

As King Jerome stood and walked toward him, Dom was hard-pressed not to flinch.

But the king stepped off the dais and took his arm.

"Come into my study," he invited. "We'll have a brandy."

"A brandy." Dom limped through the ballroom, his hip aching from the earlier exertion. Every gaze pressed in him, examining him, weighing him, but he cared about only one.

The princess watched with round-eyed dismay as her father led Dom away.

Dom grinned at her. If anyone was more alarmed by this turn of events than he was, it was Princess Laurentia. Surely that was a good thing.

"Don't you like brandy?" King Jerome asked, almost as if he cared about any man's opinion but his own.

"Yes, Your Majesty. I find brandy goes well with cigars." Cigars, stored in a handsome box, kept in the pocket of Dom's well-tailored suit, and all of it, even the man himself, bought by de Emmerich. Dom was aware of the irony, yet he concealed his wariness with an assumption of ease. "I have some of the finest cigars here, if you would like to indulge."

The king slapped his hand on Dom's shoulder. "Excellent! Yes, and we'll have some conversation."

"Conversation?" *Why*? The question hovered unspoken between them.

"I'd like to get to know you, Dominic of Sereminia." King Jerome turned down the long corridor.

Dom turned with him, noting that the uniformed guards stood at attention as their monarch walked past. He breathed easier when they didn't fall in behind—hopefully a continued a sign of health.

Yet he wasn't completely relaxed, for when they halted at a closed door, protected by two more guards, one of them stepped out to turn the knob and Dom went for the knife in his sleeve. He stopped just in time, his fingers on the hilt. Luckily the king didn't appear to notice, and the stupid guard looked puzzled.

What a foolish country, that a man could almost draw blade while standing beside the king!

But as they stepped into the broad, book-lined chamber and the door closed behind them, he found his wrist grasped in King Jerome's fingers.

The king stared into Dom's face, and all trace of friendliness had evaporated. "We aren't eating anything in here, lad," he said. "There's no need for a knife."

So the king was perhaps not a fool. Yet did he know what Dom had come to do? Dom thought not, for if he did, Dom wouldn't be visiting the royal study, lavish with wood trim and maroon brocade, the huge fireplace alight, the desk a behemoth of royalty. No, if King Jerome knew of Dom's intentions, Dom would instead be an inhabitant of the royal dungeon.

So Dom moved to ingratiate himself, and advance de Emmerich's plot. "Forgive me, Your Majesty, but after the attack on Princess Laurentia, I find myself uneasy."

Dom expected to have to give explanations. He did not expect King Jerome's ruddy complexion to visibly pale, or that the older man would clutch his arm so vigorously he cut off Dom's circulation.

"Attack?" King Jerome snapped. "When? Where?"

So the king and the princess were as fond as they appeared to be. Dom stored that information away.

"Tonight, Your Majesty. On the terrace."

King Jerome moved toward the door. "I'll call the guards."

"No!" Dom stopped him with one emphatic word. "No, please, Your Majesty, she's in no danger in the ballroom, and I want you to hear me out."

Halting, King Jerome muttered, "No, of course. We mustn't cause alarm. Not now." Wheeling away toward the sideboard, he commanded, "Tell me." His voice was strong, but his hand shook as he lifted the decanter.

Protocol demanded Dom stay away; good sense brought him to King Jerome's side. "Your Majesty, allow me."

King Jerome surrendered the decanter and sank into the nearest armchair as though his knees would no longer hold him. Yet he stared at Dom imperiously, silently demanding an explanation.

"A man dressed in the royal livery tried to abduct Princess Laurentia as she stood on the terrace."

"A single man?"

"No accomplices."

"You saw this?"

"Yes, Your Majesty." Dom poured two brandies into crystal snifters. "Her Highness screamed and struggled while I seized the villain, and when he dropped her, I gave chase."

King Jerome accepted one of the glasses. "You caught him, of course."

Kings. They expected everything to proceed as they wished. A brief surge of bitterness caught Dom and held him suspended. Then, as he had always done, he controlled it. "No, Your Majesty. I am cursed with a hip wound which makes running difficult.''

"Where did you get such a wound?"

"In battle, Your Majesty, in Greece."

The king leaned back in his chair and studied Dom long enough to make him want to squirm. "Who are you, Dominic of Sereminia?"

Who was he? A knave who plotted to inveigle his way into Laurentia's life. When first Dom had stood in the shadows of the ballroom and watched her dance with her father, he'd been critical. He'd decided Laurentia wasn't beautiful, not really. She was a little short for his tastes, small-boned and delicate, and when he imagined having her beneath him in bed—and he'd allowed himself to imagine it far too intently and with too much detail—he thought he would have to keep his passion under tight control or risk hurting her.

But he was in no hurry. He'd get the job done; he always did.

So he'd gone out onto the terrace for a smoke.

Having Laurentia come out later had been a stroke of luck. Having an attacker appear had been a bigger one. Dom had reacted on instinct, and as always, instinct had served him well. Getting himself hired as her bodyguard was even better than being her pseudo-suitor. It kept him closer to her and the secret she guarded—the secret he must discover.

So after the excitement was over, he had done his best to captivate her, this dainty, privileged princess.

What he hadn't expected was that she would captivate him. She had turned out to be witty and self-deprecating, with a sense of humor he admired and an intelligence that rocked him back on his heels. And when Radcote had stepped out and with meticulous civility tried to freeze him out, she hadn't allowed it. She had defended him.

He would have laughed if he hadn't been so touched.

Yet when they'd stepped inside and she saw his face, she'd reacted with horror. Horror, as if he were deformed, as if he carried the stain of his illegitimacy on his forehead, as if she knew the degeneracy of his past and read the treachery of his soul. The old doubts had leaped up like hell's flames to burn him, and he'd reacted. Just reacted, lashing out, alerting her to the danger she courted in his company.

But now he had the chance to redeem himself. If he could just convince King Jerome that he and he alone could adequately guard the princess . . . "Who am I?" he repeated. "I'm the bastard son of the old king of Baminia, and a mercenary."

King Jerome's eyes narrowed. "Of course. You're one of old Leon's sons. Has anyone ever told you you look like your brother, King Danior?"

Dom worked the carved wood box of cigars out of his pocket. "Yes." Opening it, he presented it to the king.

King Jerome selected one. "A tender subject, is it? No wonder you came here to try your luck with Laurentia."

"I don't expect to wed her." Dom took a cigar, too, then snapped the box closed.

"Competition too much for you?" Closing his eyes, King Jerome sniffed the cigar and smiled.

"I don't imagine—"

King Jerome waved the unlit cigar. "Yes, yes, I know. You think you can read my mind. It's a handy skill to have, young man, but I assure you you do not have it."

"Of course not, Your Majesty. I wouldn't be so presumptuous." Except that Dom knew damned good and well what the king was thinking—that a bastard could not be a prince. Well, Dom didn't want to be a prince. He just wanted to live like one. "I don't need to tell you that the incident tonight was serious. If I hadn't been there, Her Highness would be gone. So I propose that I—"

"You should be her bodyguard."

Slowly Dom let out his breath. He was one step closer.

Chapter Six

To the untutored eye, the hut appeared to be a laborer's home on a country estate, slumbering under the chilly moon. If a man were cursed with criminal intention, the hut might seem an easy mark.

Dom knew better. Before he stepped foot on the rickety bridge over the ravine, he gave his mercenary band's traditional signal—the call of a hunting hawk.

Although it was irrational, Dom shivered in the chill wind that had sprung up off the mountains and with a fine-drawn tension waited for the door to open. Brat was the sole surviving member of his original band. Dom didn't fear a random felon. Brat might be the girl he'd grown up with, but she could easily take care of that type of trouble. But Dom and his mercenaries had made enemies, and now that only he and Brat remained, those enemies would love to seek them out and wipe them off the face of the earth.

More, Dom didn't trust Marcel de Emmerich. He had told de Emmerich the band had been decimated, but de Emmerich had his spies, and if he found out about Brat and the child, he wouldn't hesitate. He

would do anything—kidnapping, torture, murder—
to break Dom to his will.

Dom would break, for Brat was his comrade, his
friend . . . his heart's sister.

In only a moment, the door swung wide.

She was not even a shadow in the darkness of the
house. "Walk on the left." Her voice carried as far
as his ears and no further, for three other huts rested
not far off the road that wound out of the city. The
families had worked on this estate their whole lives,
and they eyed their new neighbors with misgiving.

If they only knew, they would cower in their beds.

Dom ran lightly across the bridge and into the hut.

"What are you doing back here?" Brat shut the
door behind him. "I didn't expect to see you."

"I still can't see you." Standing still, he waited
while she removed the layer of ash from the coals
and blew them to life.

"How's your hip?" she asked.

He rubbed the place where the jagged piece of
shot had torn through his flesh. "Good. I only use
the limp when it gives me an advantage."

The glow of the rising flames gave form to the
single room, and he saw her grin at him. Then as
she laid the kindling he went to the wide bed, rumpled from her rising, and knelt at its side. Carefully
he examined the child who slept there. Gently he
touched the purple bump on her forehead. "She's
hurt."

"She tripped and fell against the bedpost."

He looked at Brat, dressed in a rough brown
homespun gown. Mercenaries never wore bed-
clothes; one never knew when one would have to

rise and flee. "Was she running again?"

"She's always running." Brat's voice resounded with a mother's boundless love. "She acts as if life will escape her unless she catches it *now*."

It was so true, and he sifted the gold of Ruby's hair through his fingers.

"She likes this place. We climb the hills into the forest. And the children in the meadow—they let her play with them."

Dom frowned. "Are they trustworthy?"

"They're fat peasants." Now Brat sounded torn between contempt and jealousy. "They grow their own food, they fish and hunt, and they've not had a war here in generations. They don't know about real life."

"Don't tell them. They'll discover soon enough."

Tucking her chin-length hair behind her ears, Brat settled the logs on the wavering flames. "It doesn't seem right. Maybe I could just mention . . ."

"No!" He came to his feet.

"Sh!" She stood, tall and thin, yet strong in ways most men couldn't imagine, and gestured to the child.

He lowered his voice, but not his intensity. "Are you mad? We need this fee, and we won't get it if we warn the populace. Anyway, we don't know what de Emmerich is going to do after I get him the information."

"Yes, we do. We don't have to be in his confidence to figure that out." Brat sounded just as intense, and she stepped close to stand nose to nose with him. "He's going to try and gull us out of the money."

"He doesn't know about you or the child"—Dom

hoped—"so it's me, and if he's stupid he'll try to kill me."

The fire illuminated her thin face and hollow eyes, testaments to the days of hunger they'd experienced since Greece. "If he succeeds, I can sell the bloody diamond, but—"

"Not just any bloody diamond," Dom said, "the holy Pollardine diamond, attained at great risk to myself."

"I know, I know." She quivered with irritation at his flip attitude. "I can take the money and go to America. But it's *you* I'm worried about."

She was. He knew it. More than she would ever say. They'd grown up together, two children born to depravity and corruption. He'd protected her when he could. She'd nursed him when it was necessary. They had never been lovers. They weren't related by blood, at least he didn't think so, but by the bonds of common experience, and no one could change that.

Yet Ruby's birth had changed *Brat*. The girl who had fought ruthlessly, who had sought pleasure heartlessly, had discovered compassion where formerly there had been none.

Worse, he understood. The child had brought his own hitherto unacknowledged protective instincts to the fore. He and Brat were like wild animals, tamed at the hand of a babe.

"If you're worried about me," he said, "then don't warn the peasants and bring de Emmerich's wrath down on us."

"They're just such"—she lifted her hands—"duffers."

He heard the envy, and he understood. He and Brat had never been so innocent. "Don't warn them."

She turned away. "No, I suppose not. But I've been thinking. We could be happy in a place like this."

He looked around. The dim light showed only rough stone walls, a dirt floor, and primitive wooden furniture. "Like *this*?"

"Yes. You know who we are. Two bastards put to work waiting on the whores when we could barely talk, put to work on a mattress as soon as we—"

"I remember." He had spent his life trying to forget. She never had recounted those early humiliations before; bewildered and hostile, he wondered what had gotten into her now. "What has that to do with anything?"

"You saved me from the bordello. If it hadn't been for you taking me away so quickly, I'd have died screaming mad from the pox."

"Like my mother." He could still taste the bitterness. "And yours."

Brat struggled for composure, and she blinked away tears. That sentimentality had developed since Ruby's birth, also, and he didn't like it. On those occasions when his failure weighed on him, when the death of his warrior friends seemed too grievous, he lashed out, although sometimes his eyes swam with tears and he just wanted to tell them he was sorry. So sorry.

So when he shouted, he wanted someone to fight with, not someone who collapsed. Gritting his teeth, he waited until she controlled herself enough to speak.

"Sometimes we've lived like kings. We've had our fine clothes and our carriages, and we've dined with royalty." Brat dabbed at her nose with her sleeve. "The rest of the time we've lived in forests or mountains, and maybe we've had enough to eat and maybe we haven't. We've fought in wars and been wounded, and we've buried our dead."

He crossed his arms over his chest. "Whatever you're trying to say, just say it."

"Compared to all the rest of our lives, this isn't so bad. We could settle down here, raise Ruby like a normal child, I could grow fruit and sell it in the marketplace, you could—"

He erupted in incredulous rage. "You think we could stay here? Here? I know de Emmerich, and he has spies all over this country. One of those dullards you feel sorry for could be passing reports to him. One of those children you let Ruby play with could be selling us to him."

"No . . ."

"Yes! You know it's true. They *are* duffers, and they'll betray strangers like us for a copper." Running his hands through his hair, he muttered derisively, "Stay *here*."

Brat didn't put up with that kind of mockery. In a lightning-swift strike, she boxed his ear, and while it rang, she ranted into the other one. "As you say. Not *here*. But somewhere where we're not making deals with the devil. Maybe we didn't learn goodness at our mothers' knees. Maybe we could claim ignorance when we fought in Baminia. But we know better now. We don't have to make a deal with de Emmerich.''

"We already did!" Dom flung himself away, pacing across the room and back to face her. "I already did. I promised I would deliver Bertinierre's secret into his hands. I'm a man of my word!"

"A man of your word! You have fought and killed for money, without care for right or wrong or the consequences war would bring to anyone. Most folks consider you the lowest form of life. You're sneaking into the palace on false pretenses and pretending to be a friend of this Princess Laurentia so you can betray her. And you balk at lying? To de Emmerich?"

Brat was right. It didn't make sense. He knew it didn't, but on this one point he dared not yield. If he did, the cornerstone on which he had built his character would be gone. He'd be like the other old mercenaries—shifting sides on the turn of a coin until no one would hire him again and when he looked at himself in a mirror, he'd see a desperate, contemptible man without even the honor granted to thieves.

She waved her arm. "You don't even trust de Emmerich enough to go collect the fee without a guarantee. How did you get Pollardine's diamond?"

"I stole it."

"So you're a thief!"

"No, de Emmerich can have it back—when we've got our money and our lives. All we need is this one job, and we can quit forever." He spread his hands, palms up, appealing to her to dream this one dream with him. "If we score this one, we can buy land, build a mansion, have our ice in the summer instead of the winter."

"We don't need those things."

Carried away, he continued, "Ruby can learn to be a lady, not like you and me; we're just playacting. But a real lady, where the hardest work she does is stitching, and she'll marry a lord." Brat still stood shaking her head. She didn't care what he said. She didn't understand. In desperation, he added, "She won't ever be hungry again."

Brat flinched. "I don't want her to be hungry again, either, but there's a difference between being hungry and sitting on your arse all the time, sewing a fine seam. Can you really imagine my lively girl becoming a lady? It would be like the time I caught a wildcat and tried to tame it."

He didn't listen. He didn't want to listen.

He closed his hands into fists, and Brat sighed. "Where do you propose we buy this land and have this manor?"

This was the tricky part. "I want to go . . . to Baminia."

Nothing could stop Brat's shriek. "What?"

Ruby sat up and wailed.

"Now see what you've done?" Glad of the distraction, Dom bustled to the bed and lifted the child into his arms. "You woke her."

"You must have known I would." Brat stalked toward him. "Have you gone mad? Baminia?"

Ruby snuggled into his arms, murmuring, "Dom," and Dom laid his cheek against the short, soft hair. He'd never had anything to do with children, but from the moment he'd delivered Ruby in a cave in the mountains of Montenegro, he'd been in love. Nothing but the best for this child.

"We haven't been back to Baminia since they chased us out thirteen years ago."

"It's time, then."

"We tried to overthrow your brother."

"He wasn't the king then."

"He is now, and soundly in command. You know what we've heard. The people adore King Danior and Queen Evangeline, the country is united—it's not even Baminia and Serephinia anymore, but Sereminia—the peasants are getting as fat as . . . as the peasants here! Dom, this is madness." She cupped her hands and raised them toward his face. "We lived through hell on earth there. Why would you ever want to go back?"

Ruby lifted her head and stared. Pointing a finger at her mother, she said, "Bad Mommy. We love Dom."

Brat transferred her hands to her head and held it as if it ached.

He felt so sorry for her he would have given an explanation if he could. But how could he tell her when he didn't understand it himself?

Yet Brat knew more than he thought. "It's in your blood. You really are a king's son."

He'd struggled with the truth, unwilling to accept he had inherited anything from the man who had so callously used and discarded his mother. But the longing in his soul wouldn't leave him. He had to do this thing, no matter who get hurt.

"Have you thought about what the old woman

said?" Brat demanded. "You do remember the old woman."

He swallowed. He didn't even need to ask the old woman's name. He knew to whom Brat referred. "I remember."

"And, let me think . . ." Brat placed a finger on her chin in feigned confusion. "Didn't what she said burn your ears when she was throwing us out of the country?"

Ruby's head drooped on his shoulder, and he rubbed his palm up and down her little spine. "The old witch," he muttered.

"I won't argue with you there. She scared me half to death, all bent and misshapen. And those eyes!" Brat shivered. "When she looked at me, she stripped me down to the bone."

A thousand years old, so the legend said. The crone was a thousand years old and a saint to boot. Dom didn't know if the legend was true, he only knew that when she looked at him, he trembled. He, twenty years old, leader of the rebellion, bastard son of the king, afraid of nothing, not even torture, not even death: he had fallen to his knees as if she commanded him.

"King's son," she said, *"listen and listen well. The blood of royalty flows through your veins, but hatred corrupts your heart so that it is a puny thing, twisted and deformed."* Her gnarled finger lifted, and she pointed away from the mountains and toward the great, unknown lands of Europe. *"Take your mercenaries and leave, and don't come back until you've become a* man.*"*

The way she said that phrase, *"until you've become a man,"* called everything he was into doubt. His leader-

ship, his virility, his courage. And he hated her as he had never hated anyone, not even his brother the prince, not even his father the king.

"I'll never come back," he swore.

The old eyes, the color of blue flame, burned him with their power, and she uttered the prophecy that had pursued him throughout the countries and the years. "Yes, you will. The land will call to you, the rivers will sing to you, and you'll return. You'll return—begging on your knees."

She was at least partially right. The land called to him, the rivers sang to him—but he would never go back, begging on his knees. He would go back on his own terms.

"Dom, please, not Baminia," Brat moaned. "Can't we just run away?"

The child Ruby slept now, her body limp against him, and he stroked her head one last time before he placed her in the bed. He tucked her in, then turned to her mother. "Am I not still the leader of this band?"

Brat laid her hand on her chest. "You know I follow you always."

"Then I say—we do this thing."

Her head drooped. "As you wish." She looked up again. "But you're wrong."

He'd never felt more sure. Their luck had changed. They would succeed. Yet he couldn't do it without Brat. "I need your help," he told her.

She tensed, his to command now that they'd settled their strife. "Why are you here? I thought you were going to talk your way into the palace."

"I did. I have. But something happened tonight—lucky for me, but too much of a coincidence."

"And you don't believe in coincidence." She straightened, becoming before his eyes a strategist of war. Motioning him to a chair by the fire, she pulled up a bench. "Tell me."

With a last, lingering glance at the sleeping child, he seated himself and with a minimum of words told her about the kidnapping attempt. Before he had finished she had grasped the importance of the events.

"Do you think de Emmerich is behind this?"

"Why would he give me the money to dress like a suitor, then try and circumvent me with a kidnapping?"

"If one plan doesn't work, perhaps another will?" she suggested. "Or he thinks he'll learn what he wants by torturing her?"

"Or by blackmailing her father." He'd already considered each possibility. "Maybe the country isn't as stable as de Emmerich would have me believe. Maybe the kidnapper was some bold bandit with more nerve than brains. Maybe one of Laurentia's suitors thought to wed her the old-fashioned way. I don't know the answer, and I need you to find out."

"I'll go into the city tomorrow. Visit the market. Talk to the shopkeepers." She frowned. "Could de Emmerich be positioning you to take a fall?"

Leaning down, he touched the hilt of the newly honed knife in his sleeve. "I don't know. I try to think as he does. I never succeed." It was the middle of the night, and he had to be back at the palace, awake and perceptive, by dawn. "I do know we won't get anywhere with this speculation."

She leaned back, her hands on the bench, a sly smile nudging her lips. "But you turned the whole mire to your advantage. Does the princess trust you implicitly? Did you already bed her?"

"I made some mistakes." Had he ever.

"Mistakes?" Brat straightened. "What sort of mistakes could you have made?"

"When she saw me—"

"She fell in love."

"No." *Why not?* He considered his features one of the most valuable weapons in his arsenal. That, and his expertise between the sheets, but the comeliness had provided his entry into many a bedroom. "She couldn't wait to escape."

Clearly, he stretched the bounds of Brat's credulity. "When women see that wounded-angel face, they always fall in love."

"Not this one. She's sharper than the usual good-for-nothing princess." He'd liked her, so much he'd developed a cockstand big enough to use as a hat rack.

Worse, he had one now, just talking about her. If Brat saw, she would never stop laughing, but fortunately the gloom hid his condition. At least, so he hoped. Trouble was, when a man's organ developed a mind of its own, there was no controlling it.

Elaborately casual, he leaned back in the hope of making himself more comfortable and draped one arm across his lap.

"Then she's ugly," Brat suggested. "So ugly you couldn't hide your disgust and she noticed."

"No!" His cock ached, and he pressed his arm

against it in the futile hope it would take the hint and subside.

"Old?"

"No." He didn't want to talk about the princess and how she looked, with her dark hair fallen around her pale shoulders and her dress rumpled. It would have been amusing that Radcote had thought Dom had had his hand up her skirt, only it hadn't been his hand Dom was interested in getting up there. "She's . . . attractive."

Beneath that expensive veneer he'd glimpsed a terrible fear tempered by a hint of steel. She would survive his treachery.

Probably.

"She's clever," he said. "That's why she holds the secret to the kingdom. De Emmerich says there are riches here he can't explain."

"Why doesn't he just march in and conquer Bertinierre?" Brat asked, a practical mercenary to her bones.

Dom knew the answer to that. After accepting the commission, he'd investigated. "De Emmerich isn't as omniscient as he would like us to think. If he can bring enough money into Pollardine, he'll be set for life. If not . . ." Dom shrugged. He didn't care if de Emmerich lost his position. He rather hoped he did. Yet Dom cared only to complete his mission. "Apparently de Emmerich tried an assassination attempt here some years ago; unsuccessful, of course, and he regrets it."

"On the king? I never heard that!" Brat eyed him dubiously. "How do you know?"

Her disbelief didn't bother him a whit. "After he

dictated the terms and told me my mission, I demanded information. To succeed, I said. He's shrewd, telling me just enough to get me in trouble, but—"

"So they send you to seduce Princess Laurentia and get the information out of her . . ." Brat considered that, and shook her head. "That's such a delicate scheme. It doesn't fit."

Dom didn't move. Sometimes Brat had insight where he did not, and something had smelled fishy about this case all along. But when a man stuck his head in a barrel of decaying garbage, it took him a while to locate the most rotten of the sardines. "That's true. He likes to be direct. De Emmerich didn't plan this, then. But who did?"

Chapter Seven

The private dining chamber off the stone terrace glowed with late morning sunlight, and fresh air faintly scented with rosemary and sea air wafted in from the open French doors. With a flourish, the cook presented the plain food King Jerome preferred—eggs and sausage, steaming rolls, golden melons, and whole oranges. Without ever looking up from his paperwork, King Jerome approved each concoction. The royal chocolatier placed the pot of chocolate over a flame. The nervous taster sampled each dish, and after a cursory wait, pronounced the food free from poison. The butler put the dishes on the small round table between Laurentia and her father, and Weltrude ladeled the food on their plates according to their preferences.

Catching Laurentia's napkin by the corner, Weltrude flipped it loose, then placed it in her lap. "Is there anything else, Your Highness?"

"This looks delicious." The stream of chocolate wavered as Laurentia poured it into her father's cup, then her own, but she smiled with as much grace as she could muster. "Everyone may go."

The footman opened the door, and the clink of

silverware and the murmur of many conversations filtered in from the large dining chamber across the corridor. Laurentia always rejoiced in the tradition which allowed her and her father to dine alone in the morning, and never more than now, when every other moment had been slated for parties, hunts, and the annual festival celebrating her birthday.

She wanted to be alone with King Jerome. She wanted to talk to him. Needed to talk to him—before it was too late.

But Weltrude knew her charge too well, and she hung back as the others filed out. Looking at Laurentia, she lifted the thin, painfully curved line of her penciled brows and inspected Laurentia like a general inspecting her troops.

If only Laurentia weren't the lone soldier.

Laurentia's gown of pink cotton cloth was trimmed in braid, with a high collar, a frill right under her chin and braid around the hem to hold it out stiffly. The leg-of-mutton sleeves were large, but not large as Weltrude would have liked—Laurentia drew the line at being unable to place her arms at her sides because of the vast expanse of gathered material. Beneath the gown she wore a corset that emphasized her waist while still allowing her to breathe, another concession to comfort that made Weltrude frown. Laurentia's three petticoats of white linen allowed no glimpse of the outline of her legs under any circumstances. The whole outfit was perfectly respectable. Laurentia had no reason to feel shame. Weltrude could not tell that Laurentia had removed her black leather slippers beneath the table and tucked her legs under her for comfort.

But as Weltrude continued to frown, Laurentia lowered her feet to the floor and groped for her shoes with her toes. In as casual a tone as she could muster, she said, "Go, Weltrude. I'm sure you must have work to do to organize the birthday festival."

Weltrude stiffened her already rigid back. "I have the situation well in hand."

If it hadn't been undignified and common—as defined by Weltrude—Laurentia would have slapped her forehead. She'd handled that badly. Weltrude had been with her for years, instructing her on the proper way a princess should behave, teaching her how to run multiple households, sternly supervising her transition from impetuous adolescent to mature adult. Weltrude had proved herself to be both an immovable object and an irresistible force.

She did not take well to insinuations that she was incapable of handling a house party for a mere one hundred suitors, their important relatives, and their servants.

"Your competence could never be in doubt." Laurentia located her shoes and slipped them on, determined to tie the laces around her ankles as soon as possible. "However, I worry about so many men of different backgrounds. Some are quite volatile, I fear. There *are* those romantic Latins among them."

An emotion close to alarm flared in Weltrude's eyes, and she moved briskly out the door. "Latins," Laurentia heard her mutter.

Laurentia looked around to find her father putting aside his papers and regarding her over the top of his reading glasses. "What was that all about?"

"I wanted to talk to you." Laurentia smiled at him

and spoke so diplomatically and convincingly she impressed even herself. "Papa, I don't think this notion of a bodyguard has merit. Chariton is busy, but there are others he might recommend. And who is this Dom, really? How did he happen to be on the terrace when that person tried to take me?"

With a swift swing of his knife, King Jerome decapitated his soft-boiled egg and laid the cap to one side. "Didn't he explain it to you? He came late to the ball—apparently he thought his illegitimacy removed him from contention as your suitor—and he went out on the terrace for a smoke."

He'd told her father the same story he'd told her. His consistency should have made her feel more at ease. Instead it gave her the unsettled sensation of being outflanked. As, of course, she had been.

Last night, Dom had strode to meet her father. Weltrude had done the honors, and after a short conversation the two men had disappeared into King Jerome's private study.

His private study! None of the other suitors had been taken into the private study, and Laurentia had caught many a sideways glance aimed her way. Indeed, Dulcet, Countess de Sempere, had sidled up and said, "He must have been quite persuasive to keep you from the ball and return you in such a condition. Tell me, Your Highness, what is his name?"

Although only a year older, Dulcie was already twice a widow, thrice a mother, and even as a child she'd been a superior imp. Laurentia knew she should refuse to lower herself to Dulcie's level.

Yet she still winced as she recalled her own reply—"Go wrap your trap around a persimmon, Dulcie."

After a moment of stunned silence, Dulcie threw back her head and burst into laughter. "There's hope for you yet, Laurie."

Laurentia blushed as she recalled how quickly the word had spread that the princess had already tried out one of the suitors and found him to her liking.

"Is there something wrong, dear?" King Jerome sat with his spoon poised about his half-empty egg and watched her with concern and a gleam of curiosity. "You're looking a little flushed."

Anxious to act as normally as possible, Laurentia picked up her fork and gingerly slid it into the mound of steaming scrambled eggs. "I just think I would be safer surrounded by a band of our own guards."

Beneath the mustache, his mouth tugged up in a smile. "The suitors would be discouraged by such an entourage."

Daintily, she lifted the proper-sized bite to her lips—and grimaced. Sawdust eggs. Weltrude had been supervising in the kitchen again. Weltrude did everything well—except cook, and she insisted on trying to learn. "Then I should have one man who we know we can trust."

"I believe we can trust Dom."

Trust him. Her father trusted Dom, when the man was clearly wicked from the crown of his straight dark hair to the no-doubt perfect toes on his no-doubt exquisite feet.

Lowering her voice, she said, "You do remember the duty I must perform tomorrow."

"As if I could ever forget that." He blotted his mustache with his napkin and frowned, and in the quiet voice of diplomacy said, "I don't know, Laurie, I still think it would be better if someone else did it this time."

She ruffled up like an offended hen. "Who? It isn't safe for anyone else to know!"

"Nor is it safe for you to *do* with so many people here."

She couldn't subdue the smile that tweaked the corners of her lips. "Don't you trust me to lose our guests?"

Her father sighed, no doubt remembering the constant and clever escapes she had performed as a child. "I know you'll lose them. It's just that I fear someone will somehow stumble into the middle of the affair and—"

"Believe me, Papa, if someone should so stumble, I will make it seem the most innocent of circumstances. I think well when cornered."

Clearly he wasn't convinced. "Someone tried to take you last night, Laurie, and not even Chariton knows who it could be. I don't need to tell you he's worried."

"I know. I saw him early this morning. But he doesn't have another suggestion, and he did no more than counsel me to be careful." She stretched out her hand, palm up, and he grasped her fingers in a father's grip. "He trusts me, and you must, too."

"I do. You know I do. You've a good head on your shoulders, and I'm proud of you, Laurie."

He'd said it before, but she loved hearing it from him, for the price for her "good head" had been costly and painful. "I'm the logical one to be doing this. You distract our guests with entertainment led by Your Majesty, I disappear for a few hours, and when I return the kingdom is wealthy for another year. There's too much money involved to trust another soul, and I like earning my keep as princess."

"You earn your keep with your care for your duty. You don't have to put yourself in danger, too." But she had reassured him. "If only you weren't so much like your mother. How I was blessed with two such women in my life, I will never understand."

"Think how dull you would be without us." She gave his hand a last squeeze and reached for her fork.

"Dull would be pleasant occasionally," he grumbled. Poking at his melon with a spoon, he said, "You will have to lose Dominic, too."

"Another reason not to have him."

"Don't you think you can fool him?"

"Of course I can, but—" She halted the impetuous flow of words, but too late. She had betrayed herself. "Did he confess to you he had been a mercenary?"

"Yes, of course. He told me when I asked his qualifications as bodyguard."

"Doesn't it bother you to have a man you know has sold his sword protect your daughter?"

With unanswerable logic, he said, "I would be much more uneasy if he were incompetent, my dear."

Incompetent? She flushed as she remembered the caress of his hands across her shoulders. The man reeked with competence. Competence in battle. Competence in bed.

King Jerome smiled, understanding her all too well. "Dom said that when he first suggested it, you didn't seem adverse to having him as a bodyguard."

She should lie, but lying to her father had never been easy, or even possible. He had a regrettable tendency to know she was prevaricating. So she admitted, "Not at first."

"What changed your mind?"

"Just a vague uneasiness." She shoved the plate of eggs aside and reached for a warm, crusty roll. Breaking it apart, she watched the steam rise, then nibbled on an edge.

The bread was excellent. The bakery in Omnia must have baked it. "He's hard to talk to and to have him hanging about at all times would put a damper on my effort to secure a man." There, that should do it.

"Dom also claimed you chatted with him quite freely on the terrace."

The butter, direct from the dairies on the higher slopes of the Pyrenees, had been molded into the shape of a rose. Morosely, Laurentia scraped the yellow petals off. "That would have been the shock of having been almost abducted."

"I think it would be that it was dark out there."

She concentrated on buttering her roll.

"Not all handsome men are like Beaumont."

She snapped her knife down on the table. "Yes . . . they . . . are." She glared at King Jerome and pointed her thumb at her own chest. "Take it from me, Papa, there aren't that many handsome men out there and the ones there are have everything handed to them. Women throw themselves at them, everyone assumes they're nice because surely God wouldn't make a bad person handsome, and they never have to work as hard because everyone wants to spare them the burdens of life."

As mild as she had been emphatic, King Jerome said, "I was handsome once."

"As you still are! But you're . . . different."

He held up one hand. "And Dom doesn't seem to me to be spoiled."

"Rotten. I don't even have to get to know him. He's rotten to the core."

From the open terrace door, Dom said, "Thank you, Your Highness. I shall endeavor to scrub any stench away while protecting your person from harm."

Chapter Eight

Dom stood in the doorway, a dark, rugged silhouette surrounded by a nimbus of light. Where had he come from? How had he moved so silently?

And why was Laurentia embarrassed? She was the princess. She should be able to speak her mind in the privacy of the dining chamber with her own father. *Dom* should be disconcerted at having his sneaky nature caught out.

Yet color flooded her cheeks, and she wished she had spoken less harshly. He might be sensitive, this bastard without a last name.

King Jerome took no notice of her annoyance and chagrin. Instead he waved Dom inside. "Ah, good morning, my man. Her Highness and I were just discussing how lucky it was you came along when you did."

"Yes," Dom said. "I heard."

He limped slightly as he stepped inside, a silhouette no longer, but a living, breathing man.

Laurentia refused to turn her eyes away. If she did, he might get the impression her churlish judgment shamed her. Worse, she might give herself the impression she feared to gaze on a handsome man because she was still susceptible to his kind of charm.

She wasn't. In fact, she wanted to laugh at him. Did he really believe a short, tight-fitting jacket without creases or gathers would encourage her gaze to slide downward, over his broad chest and tight stomach and narrow hips to that place in his trousers where he had stuffed a sock?

She blinked.

He must have incredibly large feet.

When she looked up at his face, she found him watching her sardonically. He challenged her with those eyes, blue as the Virgin's cape, with those dimples, deep and beguiling, with the grin on his delectable lips, with his fists placed firmly on his outthrust hips. He'd seen her scrutinize his body. He would repay the favor . . . later.

For now, in front of her father, he was a gentleman. He shut the doors behind him, then bowed to the king. "Your Majesty. Your Highness." He bowed to her, a masculine ballet of power and grace.

And she realized she had been right. This selfish man cared for nothing but himself. He had planned his entrance to impact her senses. That was what handsome men did. They used their virility like a weapon, bludgeoning mawkish women into service to them using nothing more than a smile, a touch, an attention that seemed totally focused but was in fact nothing but a façade to cover the inherent narcissism of their beings.

Not that she was bitter. Just prepared.

Dom earnestly addressed the king. "May I speak

frankly, Your Majesty, about something that has appalled me just this morning?"

"Of course," King Jerome said. "That's what I'm paying you for."

How much? Laurentia wanted to ask. *How much are you paying him?* And irrationally, she thought Dom ought to protect her for free.

"I must counsel caution, and by that I mean you should be aware of lurkers and be suspicious of anyone, even your most loyal servants, who might be in the position to listen to your conversations."

Laurentia bristled. "We are careful."

He spoke to her, but he concentrated on King Jerome. "Talking about the abduction with the doors to the terrace open? I heard you, and God only knows who else heard you before I came along. You have to be vigilant, Your Majesty, always."

"We were foolish. There's a chair." King Jerome pointed. "Pull it up to the table. Have some breakfast and tell us more."

Couldn't her father see this man was ruthless as any pirate who sailed the high seas? What good was King Jerome's claim to being an excellent judge of character, when he fell for the same balderdash that felled so many ladies?

"I'm sure he ate with the rest of the suitors," she said.

With one hand, Dom lifted the heavy chair and placed it at the table, midway between Laurentia and her father. As he seated himself, he condescended to answer her. "Actually, no, I haven't eaten since last night. I just returned from setting my inquiries in motion. I bathed and changed and came at once to make my report."

He did look heavy-eyed, she noted. Any compassionate woman would feel sorry for him. "Here." She passed the scrambled eggs. "They're delicious."

She watched him spoon them onto his plate, and waited while he took the first bite. He chewed, swallowed, and without a change of expression, lifted his cup. "Would you pour for me, Your Highness?"

He liked them?

"Try the sausage, too," King Jerome said.

"Thank you, I will."

Dom liked the eggs? He helped himself to the sausage, mercifully untouched by Weltrude, as Laurentia steadied his saucer by its edge, lifted the heavy pot, and poured.

"Is that chocolate?" Dom sighed. "I should have expected it. It's a lady's drink."

"Actually, His Majesty prefers it," she said in a frosty manner.

"I find the sugar sweetens Her Highness's disposition," King Jerome said.

Bristling instantly, Laurentia glared at her father as the two men chuckled together. "You're the king," she said. "If you wished for another beverage, you had only to ask."

He patted her hand. "I was teasing, dear."

His very tone reduced her to a sulky child, insulted by a jest. If Dom hadn't been there, would she have laughed and whacked her father on the arm, and answered in kind?

Oh, heavens, she would have.

This was Dom's fault. He'd caused her to lose her sense of humor.

"Do you know who might be behind this attempt on the princess's person?" Dom asked.

"No," King Jerome answered.

"Who are your traditional enemies? Is there a reason they should be stirring?"

Dom still focused on her father as if she didn't exist, and she would have been irritated if she were not so interested in the answer. Her father kept her abreast of developments within the kingdom, yes, but if he thought she might feel threatened or worry unduly, he downplayed them. His caution originated at the time of her husband's death, and she acknowledged she had been overset by his death. Yet despite her assurances to King Jerome, he continued to coddle her in matters of national security.

"The world is changing. Traditions are changing. Countries that for a thousand years have been our enemies are no longer. Countries who have been our allies are—" King Jerome hesitated. "Well, perhaps it is to our advantage to examine our friendships. I confess this attempt on the princess took me by surprise. I fear we have grown complacent."

Laurentia watched her father, straining to read his thoughts by his expression, yet nothing showed but distress and a royal embarrassment. He had sent Chariton out, she knew he had, but he said nothing of that. He only demanded of Dom, "Young man, how long will it take you to get information?"

"This isn't going to be easy." Dom took a bite of egg and followed it with a swallow of chocolate. "Unfortunately, this hubbub about Her Highness's birthday has attracted more than just suitors. There are gypsies and tradesmen and farmers and thieves all milling around in Omnia, strangers all. My man will not be noticed among the crowd, but I fear neither will our abductor."

"So you don't foresee success," Laurentia said.

"I have formidable gifts, Your Highness, but I don't count fortune-telling among them. The only thing I can foresee with any accuracy is trouble." His long arm reached for the basket of rolls. "I'm always right."

"Yes, trouble has a tendency to make itself at home when one least expects it," King Jerome agreed.

The more Dom insisted there was trouble, the more she wanted to insist none existed. But she couldn't, not after that pesky kidnapping attempt. "Trouble comes to those who are unprepared," she snapped.

"You're saying you're prepared?" Dom chose a roll and broke it apart, exposing the white center.

She thought of the addition she'd made to her handbag. "I am."

"I agree." Like a swordsman toying with an inferior opponent, he sank his teeth into the roll, chewed, and swallowed while she waited. At last he added, "You *are* prepared for trouble. You have hired me."

She'd lost her appetite, but to give herself something to do she took an orange from the bowl and intently watched her own fingernails as she dug them into the thin, dimpled skin. Damn that fake footman for showing up when he had! If he'd been earlier or later, she wouldn't have to be dealing with this exasperating Dom . . .

No, some small shred of remaining reason whispered, *I'd be dealing with that horrible smelly man who wanted to hurt me, maybe kill me, in who-knew-what kind of conditions.* She was being unreasonable and illogical. She knew it, but this Dom person drove her past sanity.

Her finger sank into the fruit and a squirt of juice struck her on the brow.

Dom's broad hand appeared beneath her nose, and she jerked her head up. With his thumb, he brushed her lower lip. "Stop sulking, Your Highness."

To her dismay, her lip trembled. Just from his touch, it actually trembled.

Her horrified gaze flew to his. He hadn't noticed, had he?

Yet he watched her mouth, all brooding and attentive, as if the thought of kissing her absorbed him beyond all other interests.

And how could she even connect kissing and Dom in the same thought? What was wrong with her? A man touched her, and lightning struck her blind, deaf, and insensate to anything but him. He was a mercenary, not some student of her soul.

He drew his hand away so slowly she might have thought him reluctant to part from her, and she stared at the long fingers and broad, callused palm. A good hand. Not soft like the other suitors', but strong and capable. A soldier's hand.

Glancing at her father, Dom cleared his throat, the sound harsh and obtrusive in the waiting silence.

She looked, too, to find King Jerome watching the byplay with unabashed fascination, and she blushed, just as if he'd discovered them in some guilty pleasure.

Dom said, "Princess Laurentia, when I guard you, I'll be so quiet, you'll never know I'm around."

She couldn't help it. She laughed at such an absurdity. Not notice? *Him?* He had to be jesting!

He was. He smiled back at her, his lips stretching across perfect white teeth, fine lines crinkling around his teasing blue eyes. He plucked the orange from her hand. In a few quick movements, he peeled the fruit clean. He shook out his napkin and laid it on the table, then placed the orange in the middle and separated it into sections. With a bow of his head, he presented the delicacy to her while she stared at it, and him.

Handsome. He was so handsome. And competent, qualified, knowledgeable, an earthy man capable of providing for her in any circumstances, no matter how primitive. And no matter how smitten he appeared, she had to remember her experience had proved she was no irresistible Venus. She *had* to be sensible.

When she didn't take the orange, he laid it at her elbow with a smile that told her how much her reluctance amused him. "What's the schedule for today?"

"The traditional observance of the princess's birth." King Jerome leaned back in his chair, his gaze fixed fondly in his mind's eye on that long-ago event. "Twenty-five years ago, when she was born, I called for a holiday to last no less than three days, and it has continued as our own, unique celebration."

"How . . . touching." Dom wore that bit of a smile again, the one that said she was spoiled and he wasn't. "What do we do to celebrate the blessed event?"

"There's a high meadow outside of Omnia where the nobles and the people meet and mingle," King Jerome said. "We have a marketplace, with goods from our country and abroad. We have wandering minstrels and jugglers, we have games for prizes."

Dom finished his eggs and sausage. "What sort of games?"

"Archery, shooting, wrestling, races—"

The orange smelled rich and ripe, the kind of fruit that would dribble down her chin if she weren't careful. "Where the noblemen can make fools of themselves trying to best our huntsmen and our laborers," Laurentia said.

"Your Highness doesn't appreciate a good competition?" Dom asked.

Giving in to temptation, she took a section of the orange. "If a nobleman can aim an arrow better than a commoner who stalks game for a living, he has too much time to practice. And a nobleman who enters his thoroughbred horse in a race with men who have nothing better than a mountain pony is taking unjust advantage."

"They try to win her favor that way," King Jerome explained.

"Obviously, it hasn't worked yet," Dom said.

"But they keep trying." She bit into the orange and savored the tart sweetness. It didn't matter that he'd peeled it for her; it wasn't as if he were feeding her.

"I won't enter the shooting contest, then."

Although she didn't look up, she knew he watched her much too closely. "*You* can. You're a soldier of fortune. I imagine if you didn't shoot well, you'd not be here with us today."

"I wouldn't have made it through my first battle. Nevertheless, I can't watch over you if I'm showing off for the ladies. What about tomorrow?"

Laurentia took spiteful pleasure in informing him. "A hunt. Do you think you can keep up?"

"I think if I can't, you'd best slow down for me." He looked straight at her, a man with a message to convey.

And he conveyed it very well. The fine hairs stood up on the back of her neck as she endured the sensation of threat and retribution.

After what seemed to be a very long moment, King Jerome said, "My daughter is a marvelous huntress, the best rider I've ever seen, excepting her mother, but she's also as smart as a whip. She would not put her safety at risk by riding ahead of her bodyguard."

She didn't know about that. Right now it seemed like a superb idea. She looked up to see two faces turned toward her, one admonishing, one sardonically amused and reading her like a book when he'd barely met her and had no business knowing what she thought or how much she resented being backed into a corner—although heaven knew why she should care now. She spent most of her life in that corner. "No," Laurentia said reluctantly. "Of course I will not."

Her father gave her a quick, approving smile.

"And I will endeavor to keep up with Your Highness," Dom promised.

The spy stepped back from the panel concealed in the wall of the private dining room.

A kidnapping. Someone had attempted to take the princess, and unlike Dom, the spy knew who it was.

De Emmerich had become enraged again and tried to hurry things along.

Damn him. He should listen and trust, but de Emmerich thought the princess was a bit of frippery to be captured and racked. A quick way to reveal the information, he thought. He didn't believe she would never break under torture. She would never willingly reveal the source of Bertinerre's wealth.

No, fear and pain would never work on Princess Laurentia.

Only trust and love would achieve their objectives.

And in hiring Dom, de Emmerich had done one thing right, at least.

Dom would seduce her. Princess Laurentia would trust him.

And de Emmerich and his spy would have the kingdom and all its riches for themselves.

Chapter Nine

Dom walked from the private dining chamber onto the terrace just around the corner from the place where he'd rescued Laurentia the night before. The sun shone with blinding impartiality on the white marble floor and rail and on the stairs that descended into the garden. It was a glorious morning—and he just wanted to spit. He'd eaten worse food in his time—hell's fire, he'd eaten snakes in his time—but those eggs came close to being putrid. Only the princess's eager anticipation had kept him from spewing the wretched fare across the table.

That, and King Jerome's kindness. Dom rubbed his hand across his lips in a futile attempt to clean the bad taste from his mouth. Damn, the old man was a gudgeon. Didn't he know better than to trust a stranger with no letters of references and a vague story of being a king's bastard brother? When Dom finished this job, he would tell King Jerome—

"Excuse me." Francis's crisp, superior voice stopped Dom in his tracks. "Were you eating breakfast with His Majesty and Her Highness?"

Dom turned to face him, and found the princess's pride and joy leaning against the door frame, watching him with narrowed eyes. This stinkard was suspicious.

Dom smiled, the amiable, edgy smile of a man facing off with his rival. "Are you the royal monitor?"

"I am the home minister," Francis corrected him, without an ounce of humor, "and a personal friend of His Majesty and Her Highness."

Dom had ruffled feathers last night with his interview with King Jerome. He was ruffling feathers again this morning. Good. "I'm a personal friend of the king and the crown princess, too." Dom moved toward Francis. They were of a height, and Dom looked him straight in the eye. "King Jerome likes a man who's bold and grabs what he wants, not one with his knickers tied so tight he can sing soprano."

It was true. Dom had diagnosed the king's weakness at once.

"I'm not interested in what King Jerome likes," Francis said. "Only what his daughter likes."

Damn. It would have been easier for Dom if Francis was a fool. Not nearly as much of a challenge, of course, but in recent years Dom had discovered that he no longer liked to do everything the hard way.

"Nevertheless," Dom said, "I'll drop by to converse with His Majesty and Her Highness whenever they want."

Vague surprise rippled over Francis's prissy, handsome face. "Of course. If they request your presence, you will do as you are told. That is only proper. However, I cannot imagine such a trend will continue. While His Majesty does indeed prefer the swashbuckling type, Her Highness is quite sensible."

"She likes them bold too," Dom said glibly. "She just doesn't know it yet." Dom had discovered the night before that she secretly lusted after adventure. That made him irresistible.

It wouldn't be a hardship to seduce her; her sweet little mouth begged to be kissed.

Yet perhaps Francis could explain why, when Dom had had that little silver fish of a princess dangling on his hook, she suddenly had slipped away. What fear shadowed her eyes?

He would goad Francis—surely not a difficult endeavor—into revealing her secrets. Then he'd hold her in the palm of his hand, and the thought of that held remarkable appeal. "Perhaps you don't know the princess as well as you think you do."

Francis blinked as if the thought hurt his brain. "Nonsense. I have known her since her childhood."

"And she was always sensible?"

"She has grown sensible," Francis corrected. "As do all women as they mature."

"You don't have a lot of experience with women, do you?" Dom recalled Laurentia's intrigue with him, his occupation . . . his touch. He could have touched a lot more out there on the veranda, but he had wanted to survey the terrain first, give her no reason to retreat.

She'd retreated anyway. Worse, this morning she'd gone from retreat to attack. Hell, he might as well have advanced on her last night. All his light, winning talk had done him no good once she'd seen his face; she couldn't have reacted more strongly if he'd pulled her against him and kissed her silly. After talking to this jackass, Dom could tell she needed to be kissed silly.

And Dom was the man to do it. With an assurance he felt clear to the bone, he said, "I say her wild side is only lying dormant, waiting for the right man to set it free."

"You jest, of course." Francis couldn't have been more stodgily unmoved. "Her Highness matured"—something in the garden captured his gaze—"earlier than others I could name."

Dom turned to look, and saw a lush and rounded lady, walking among the hedges with one of the suitors, a handsome boy who looked dazed at being singled out for flirtation. "Some never mature at all."

"Of course they do. They must." Francis circled around so he could turn his back on the garden. "They're women."

He had an irritating way of making grave pronouncements of such absurdity Dom didn't know whether to smash his face in or laugh in it. "Her Highness isn't so sensible. She's fascinated by my occupation."

"You're a tradesman."

God, Francis was a snot. "I'm a mercenary."

Francis's nostrils pinched as if he smelled something putrid. "Does His Majesty know this?"

Dom almost laughed—this was too much fun. "Yes, of course."

"And he let you take Laurentia into dinner last night and ate breakfast with you this morning?"

"He says my money's as good as anyone's."

Francis made a small sound of disbelief. "No one can buy the princess's hand in marriage."

"It's not her hand I'm interested in." Dom grinned at Francis's horror. "Come on, man, confess. Among the suitors, you're leading the pack. You can't tell me you haven't given a thought to the wedding night!"

"This is a crude conversation and one I have no intention of continuing." Francis marched past Dom, then swung on his heel to face him. "No one should think of the princess in that manner. It isn't decent."

"You mean she's never been out in the garden with you? Like ... er ... what's-her-name out there?" Dom gestured toward the woman, who now drew the young suitor's head down toward hers.

"That woman is Dulcet, Lady de Sempere, a woman of light morals who is interested in nothing but the pleasure she finds in physical contact." Francis stared at Lady de Sempere with scorn. "She frequents the garden far too often, and Her Highness can in no way be compared to Dulcie."

"Dulcie?" Dom carefully noted Francis's topple from the heights of propriety. "Dulcie?"

Francis blushed a blotchy color of red. "I have heard her called such."

"I'll wager you have." The way Francis blushed, Dom would wager he had an interest in Dulcie protocol and ambition couldn't surmount. He would also wager that Dulcie, smart girl, returned his interest and made a career of taunting him.

Good. Francis was not even a bump in the path anymore. "Her Highness was married. Surely she gained an appetite for those physical pleasures."

Francis's color faded as rapidly as it had come. "This conversation is beyond belief!"

"Maybe her husband needed a splint on his lizard. Maybe he didn't treat her well."

"I cannot believe you are so vulgar as to speculate about Her Highness's married life!"

"I'm pretty vulgar." Dom shrugged off the slur with the insouciance it deserved. "You say you're a good friend of the princess's. Surely she's said something about her marriage to you."

"I don't know what kind of gossip you've heard—"

"Not a thing, unfortunately."

"—but Her Highness does not confide her personal life to anyone, and I assure you that, contrary to any rumors that circulated, her marriage was civilized and mannerly, as is proper in a royal union."

"Civilized and mannerly." Dom could scarcely believe it. Laurentia had had a civilized, mannerly marriage? No wonder she had no children. They'd probably met once a month on the scheduled night in the royal humping chamber.

And she'd be happy with another one? That might be what Francis believed, but Dom knew better, and it would sure never be that way with *him*.

"This has been an enlightening conversation," Dom said. "But now we should join the other suitors." And tell them the princess Laurentia liked to see a man show off like a strutting peacock, then watch them make asses of themselves.

While Dom, of course, proved himself to be the true hero—even if he had to set up the circumstances himself.

"Look." Dom stood at Laurentia's left shoulder and directed her attention toward her English suitor.

"Mr. Moneybags Sharparrow has joined in the log-splitting contest."

The surrounding pine forest blocked any view of the Mediterranean, but a cooling breeze off the bay flipped back her wide-brimmed hat. Tugging it forward to protect her eyes against the afternoon sun, she looked across the meadow. The sight that met her gaze made her want to groan.

Conceited Mr. Sharparrow gave her what might have been a competent nod in any other man. But dressed as he was, she couldn't take him seriously. Mr. Sharparrow wore some tailor's idea of an outdoorsman's garb—rough wool breeches, woolen socks, and an artistically draped smock—and he looked like the consummate fool.

He hefted an ax high above his head to take a practice swing, and she shut her eyes as he brought the glittering blade down with great vigor and no control. When no scream rent the air, she cautiously opened one eye, then the other.

Mr. Sharparrow stood looking down at the ax impaled in the still-intact log with a most perplexed expression on his face.

"I wonder if he understands the idea is to *split* the log," Dom said.

Laurentia clenched her teeth to keep from swinging around and commanding him to stop carrying on such a rude, nasty, perfectly pointed commentary of the day's events.

And how did he always know what she was thinking, anyway?

The wretched Dom had taken his place beside her as soon as she left the palace. Her mounted guard surrounded them, but *his* horse paced beside her as she rode down to the docks through a flurry of cheering and calls of "Happy birthday." He held her pocketbook when she christened a new fishing boat, named the *Laurentia*, leaving her side only briefly to speak to a tall beggar-woman half-hidden by the crowd and to press some coins into her hand. Laurentia could not complain about being left for such a charitable undertaking, and unfortunately he had kept Laurentia well within his sight. Again her guard rode with her up the winding road into the mountains that rose like a spine behind the palace. But *his* horse remained at her right hand.

On the wide flats King Jerome had designated Laurentia Meadow, a party atmosphere reigned. Booths selling ale, roast fowl, and crusty rolls lined the meadow. Pushcart peddlers added their shouts to the rumble of the crowd. The scent of pine and crushed grass mixed with the sharper smell of sweaty bodies. A physician stood in front of his booth and tended the inevitable wounds and illnesses that resulted from rough-and-tumble play and too much food.

Ruthlessly, Weltrude had organized the contests, selecting a place and a time for each. Now she moved from place to place, making sure each event proceeded on schedule, taking care of any crisis as it arose and crushing it without mercy. Laurentia suspected that Weltrude didn't approve of such unrestrained frivolity, yet at the same time loved the chance to display her formidable organizational skills.

A cheer erupted at Laurentia's arrival, making

Dom smile, for apparently her popularity impressed him. And the fact that she noticed his smile and cared whether he was impressed irritated her almost into speaking.

But she valiantly held her tongue. As he helped her dismount, she refrained from digging her elbow into his ribs. He stood beside her while she gave her brief speech of welcome and listened as officials and noblemen wished her a long life and good health. Then, all the rest of the wretched morning and into the afternoon, the despicable man walked when she walked, stood guard when she sat, saw to her comfort with such dispatch she could scarcely form a wish before he granted it, and when they were alone, he spoke engagingly about each event as if he were an expert on every subject.

Which, she grudgingly admitted, he seemed to be.

Laurentia's stony silence and evasive gaze seemed to bother Dom not at all, and although she took care to act like a woman placed unwillingly in the company of a rogue, it didn't matter, for he acted like a gentleman who had her father's permission to keep her company.

"Ah, I picked the winner of the archery contest." Dom nodded, pleased with himself. He had proved himself quite skilled at choosing the winners. "Needless to say, it was not your Russian suitor, Lord Mischa."

No, Lord Mischa had proven to be a loss, too.

"You must go down and present the prize, Your Highness."

Dom's reminder nudged at her, and she wanted to snap, *Of course I have to go down and present the prize, you dolt! I always present the prize on my birthday.*

But she would not harangue Dominic of Baminia. No matter how much she wanted to, no matter how against her naturally loquacious nature this might be, she was not speaking to him.

Not that he seemed to care. If anything, her silence gave him encouragement.

"Right this way, Your Highness." He bowed as she walked past him over the crushed grass toward the area designated for archery. Her shawl lay over his arm. He'd taken it when she began to get warm, and held it as if he delighted in being her servant.

Only he wasn't her servant, and no one could ever make the mistake of thinking so. According to her father the king, who took good care to stay on the other side of the meadow, Dom was her hired body-guard. Her bodyguard, not her suitor. She badly wanted to shout that fact to the milling, cheering, lighthearted crowd of nobles and commoners. The only thing that stopped her from giving vent to such an undignified explosion was the fact that no one would believe her.

"I'm honored, Your Highness." The bowman ducked his head and shuffled his feet as she placed the medal around his neck. A blush stained his ears bright red, but he grinned like every one of her male subjects grinned when he'd won first place, as if it had nothing to do with skill and everything to do with his virility. She had noted that men did this regardless of class or wealth.

"Thank *you*, good huntsman," she answered him. "Without your skill, Bertinierre would be hungry and defenseless. We are all grateful."

All atwitter, he said, "We just want to say—all of us huntsmen—congratulations on your birthday."

"Thank you." She touched him lightly on his shoulder and began to turn away.

Someone hissed from off to the side, and he added rapidly, "Uh, Your Highness? On behalf of the huntsmen, we just want to add we're glad you're getting married at last." He looked right at Dom.

She couldn't stand it. She couldn't bear this. "There is no betrothal."

Dom, blast him, grinned at the huntsmen. He didn't speak a word, but Laurentia and every man there could hear his thoughts. *Yet.*

With a gesture of dismissal, Laurentia let the archer go, to be teased and congratulated by his friends.

She couldn't bear to speak to Dom as she walked away from the shooting range. She didn't know where she was going. She didn't care, if she could just go there *alone*.

That, of course, proved impossible. Dom kept pace easily, his arm so close it almost brushed hers, his presence emitting a magnetic field that brought the fine hairs on her body upright.

The huntsman's comment proved what she already knew. If the world rotated on her command, her opinion of a gentleman should have been the most important factor in the selection of her husband; in fact, only her father's opinion mattered. He was the king, he was her father, and he could give her hand where and to whom he pleased. Those who didn't know Dom and his chicanery thought he had somehow won King Jerome's favor, and that drove the gallants into fits of jealousy. Certainly that could be the only explanation for the extraordinary efforts her suitors were making to secure her attention.

Dom's hand on her elbow brought her to a halt, and he gestured toward the stretch of river that wound its way across the meadow on its way to the sea. "Prince Germain of Bavaria is entering the rowing contest. That can't be good for a man of his age."

"Or his girth," Laurentia muttered. For a moment, she entertained herself with the vision of Prince Germain's corset strings bursting and striking around to slap some sense into him.

"Did you want to go and watch?"

Dom sounded only remotely interested in her response and something inside her snapped. Drat this stupid man. Drat her father, drat the huntsmen, drat the whole dratted gender, and most especially . . . "What's wrong with these fools?" she burst out.

"What do you mean?"

He didn't sound delighted that she had at last spoken to him. He sounded idly interested. She shouldn't carry on a conversation, but the words she'd held back all morning bubbled within her and demanded to be spoken. "Who do they think they are, to compete against men who labor in the fields and on the seas? These silly coxcombs don't stand a chance!"

"That silly coxcomb over by the trees seems to be removing his coat so he can join the knife-throwing contest." Dom scanned the rough-hewn men milling around the target. "Unfortunately for him, the fellow in the crimson knickers will finish in first place."

He had unerringly picked out last year's winner,

irritating Laurentia once again. "How did you *know* that?" she demanded.

"Your countrymen are very able, and their skill seems to challenge your suitors." He paused delicately. "They aren't doing too badly for gentlemen who, in the course of their normal lives, exercise only in the saddle. Perhaps they'll fare better tomorrow during the hunt."

For the first time since breakfast, she looked directly at him. "I would feel better if, until that time, they would avoid handling sharp objects."

He smiled at her.

He looked as sculpted and flawless as Michelangelo's David, then his smile added the glow of a thousand candles. He looked as delectable as a bowl of cream vanilla ice, then his smile added the sweetness of strawberries. He looked as exciting as a mighty merchant ship, then his smile added the wind to fill the sails.

Carefully, she stepped a little away, trying to tear her gaze away from his, trying to put space between them so she didn't make a fool of herself in front of her father and half the kingdom. She had been right to refuse to look at Dom, and now in the dazed recesses of her mind, she jotted a notation. *Don't say or do anything to make him smile.*

But it was too late.

"Laurentia." Dom's husky voice sounded deeper than normal, too appealing, too seductive. His eyes gazed into hers as if he sought the Holy Grail of her soul, and she could almost feel herself compelled to step forward, into his arms and into his heart.

Then a woman's dramatic scream rose above the babble of the crowd.

The sensual haze around Laurentia disintegrated, and she glanced toward the commotion not twenty-five feet away.

Someone shouted, "There's a cart overturned!"

Still half-dazed, she looked back at Dom. His brows were lowered, his nostrils flared. He looked, she thought irrelevantly, like a thoroughbred primed for a race, then held at the gate.

The woman screamed again. The spectators moved toward the accident.

Dom scowled at Laurentia, and in a voice of goaded annoyance said, "Not *now*."

Chapter Ten

"Not now," Dom repeated. *He had Laurentia where he* wanted her. He recognized her soft, yearning expression, the way her breasts lifted beneath her deep breaths, her open, upwardly cupped hands. If he had one more minute, he could change that thinly veiled hostility into rampant passion.

Impatient and insistent, Brat screamed again. He was forced to take the stage.

Grabbing Laurentia's hand, he hauled her behind him across the rugged ground.

After a brief, startled gasp, Laurentia hurried with him into the gathering crowd.

Positioning her so she had a good view of the proceedings, he leaned over the merchant, trapped beneath the ring of the wheel.

"Uncomfortable?" he asked.

The merchant examined his face. "About time . . . you got here."

"I came as fast as I could." Sotto voce, Dom instructed, "Groan loudly and writhe around like you're in pain."

"I can't move." Sweat beaded the merchant's forehead. "I think . . . I broke a rib when I brought the cart down on me."

"Damn." More bad luck. The bad luck that had dogged him since ... A crowd was gathering, and on the outskirts Dom located Brat holding Ruby's hand.

Over two years ago, it had been her rape that had signaled the onset of their bad luck. Yet he knew when he'd pulled off this assignment, all would be well. He'd be in control of his destiny. Brat would never be in peril again. And Ruby would never face the life they'd led.

Straightening, he removed his coat and rolled up his sleeves. Boxes—empty, but who knew that?— had been tied on the bed, and the wheel had been carefully placed over a rabbit hole so that when the merchant pulled at the cart it tipped over easily. A good operation, and one guaranteed to make Dom look as if he had the strength of ten men and the heart of a hero when he lifted the cart away.

He glanced at Laurentia. She was watching. Grasping the corner of the cart, he strained to lift it. The sturdy cart weighed more than he expected. His hip burned like fire. He hoped Laurentia noted how he struggled as he set the cart upright and shoved it out of the way.

But when he turned to receive her praise, she wasn't standing where he'd left her. She knelt beside the merchant, speaking to him in a soft voice. Worse, Brat knelt there, too, Ruby standing off to the side, while the two women gently removed the bloke's smock.

"Your Highness, what are you doing?" Dom asked. As if he didn't know.

She ignored him as royally as she had done all

day, and he wanted to grab her by the shoulders and say, *No. Don't look at that smelly old man. Look at me! I'm your sweetest dream come true.*

But she seemed truly compassionate to those less favored, Dom grudgingly admitted, and not at all high in her instep.

Not that that mattered. She was spoiled and royal, and if cozening her achieved his objective sooner, then the deception was well worth it.

To the wounded man, Laurentia asked, "What's your name?"

"Monty, Your Highness." He sounded breathless from pain or awe.

Frustrated, Dom said, "I'll go find some rags."

"Clean ones. From the physician," Laurentia instructed as she untied her wide straw hat and laid it in the grass beside her.

More than just ignoring him, she seemed to have dismissed him from her mind, her whole attention centered on the bruised chest now exposed to the sunlight. Brat looked up at him apologetically, but her concentration, too, focused on the wounded man.

Walking quickly to vent his frustration, Dom found the physician putting stitches in a long, oozing cut in Mr. Sharparrow's arm. He listened to Dom's description of the accident and said, "Her Highness can handle it. Here." He found a ball of clean cloth bandages, and handed it to Dom. "Take that to her. She'll know what to do."

Dom came back to find the crowd bigger than ever, drawn by the spectacle of their princess caring for one of them with her own hands. Impatient, he shouted, "Let me through." A path opened before him, and as he walked he heard someone say, "Her Highness picked a likely-looking one, heh?"

That made him feel marginally better, until he got back to the cart.

The women were talking. If there was one person he didn't want Laurentia talking to, it was Brat, but what could he say? *Don't talk to Brat, she's gotten soft, she might slip and warn you.*

"We can wrap his ribs tightly," Laurentia was saying, "but he won't be able to pull his cart for some time."

"No," Brat answered. "The bone's badly cracked. He won't be able to do much for several weeks, and he'll be in pain for months."

Dom dropped the bandages by Brat and grimly sacrificed some of de Emmerich's cash to salve Brat's guilt. "I'll make sure he's cared for."

"Why? You had nothing to do with his injury." Laurentia picked up the ball of bandages and began unwrapping them. "You saved him. He'll stay at the palace, perhaps perform light labor as he's able, until he can work again."

That's why, Dom wanted to say. *I don't need you charming the man who knows what an imposter I am.*

Even Monty saw the drawback to her plan. "I'm grateful, Your Highness, but that's not necessary."

"The palace contains many chambers, Monty. You'll be no trouble, and eventually you can be a help." Laurentia smiled on him, and the big stupid dolt went soft as a mushroom.

"Let me lift him while you wrap his ribs, Your Highness," Brat said.

"He's heavy." Laurentia frowned as if having tall, strong Brat lift a man worried her.

"Then Dom can lift him and I'll wrap his ribs." Brat glared meaningfully at him, as if having the small, delicate princess close to such dubious company worried *her*.

Well, it worried him, too. Yet before he could agree, a man pushed forward out of the crowd. "Let me." He smiled, an amiable fellow with brown hair, a light complexion, and a proper accent that told Dom he must be one of the suitors.

"An excellent notion," Dom said, intent on whisking Laurentia away.

But his bad luck had not yet run its course. Ruby took her finger out of her mouth and pointed at him. "Dom."

Laurentia broke into a grin. "She's so bright! Is she yours, Gloria?"

Gloria? Laurentia knew Brat's real name? Why, he could remember when Brat had pounded grown men to a pulp for calling her Gloria.

"Yes, that's Ruby." Brat confiscated the bandages, nudged Laurentia aside and as the stranger carefully lifted Monty, began the process of tightly swaddling his ribs.

Now Laurentia turned a gentle smile on the child and held out a hand. "Greetings, Ruby. Are you having fun today?"

Assailed by an eighteen-month-old's shyness, Ruby put her finger back into her mouth and nodded.

Laurentia coaxed Ruby to answer, and Dom's anxiety mingled with pride as the child toddled to Laurentia. But pride for who? For the child who leaned against the kneeling princess and babbled in her thankfully incomprehensible language? Or for Princess Laurentia, who seemed to enjoy the babble, keeping one arm around Ruby, and holding her as if she were precious?

Nudged from behind, Dom turned to an old couple demanding his attention. The man's hands were callused, his nails thick, yellowed, and split. The woman wore a colorful bandana to keep her braids out of her face, and the sun had etched premature lines into her skin. Dom, whose life had so frequently depended on his ability to sum a man up, found himself thinking, *Farmers.* Then he looked into their shrewd eyes and thought, *More than farmers.*

That they brought themselves to his attention surprised him. Normally, respectable people sensed the wildness he exuded, and even in a crowd he found himself alone.

No such wariness tinged their smiling regard. "Her Highness is good with the babes, isn't she?" the wife asked.

"Very good," Dom said.

"She's always been that way around children. Loves children, does our princess." The husband tucked his thumbs into his suspenders. "Isn't that right, Minnie?"

The wife nodded at him. "That's true, Roy. Young man, you'll not have to worry she is like those other noblewomen who allow governesses to raise their children."

Dom began to see the direction of the conversation, and found himself torn between embarrassment and a deep-seated, almost belligerent pleasure.

Like the archer, Minnie and Roy thought he was the princess's choice as husband, and they had leaped ahead to that part of her marriage which mattered to them, the production of heirs.

But before the princess could hug a child of her own, she would have to lie beneath a man. And these people thought she would lie beneath *him*.

He glanced at Laurentia again. She knelt on the grass, all uncaring of the stains on her skirt, and smiled at Ruby in an unselfconscious manner.

What a smile! With absolute abandon, she lavished delight and joy on a child because she knew Ruby would demand nothing in return. Laurentia couldn't smile like that to her subjects or her father. They wished her to wed, and wed for their own selfish purposes. She couldn't smile like that at her suitors, or they'd get above themselves. She couldn't smile like that at her servants or her soldiers or her bodyguard . . . but he wanted her to. That smile made him want to turn her face to his and kiss it off her lips. Then charm her enough to bring it slipping back again.

Minnie interrupted his reverie. "To a man like you, family has to be important."

Dom took a step back. Laurentia didn't seem to be listening, but he didn't want her overhearing this conversation. "A man like me?"

Minnie got flustered. "We were told you were a . . . a mercenary and a bastard."

When he turned to grin at her, all aggression and teeth, she took a step backward, close to her husband.

"Woman, I told you not to listen to rumors." Roy

rebuked her, yet at the same time he wrapped his arm around her shoulders and glared up at Dom.

A hundred times along the roads of war, Dom had met men like this. For his wife, Roy would challenge even a warrior in the prime of his youth. He would fight and he would die for her, because they were one, welded together by time, experience and the one condition Dom thanked God he had never experienced—that emotion the romantics called *love.*

Dom knew himself stupid to be offended when someone mentioned a condition he himself had proclaimed. He'd learned on the streets of Plaisance to fight anyone who called him "king's bastard." Fighting eased the pain of his father's abandonment, the anguish of seeing his mother die, the helplessness of a boy taken by women intent on using his youth to briefly regain their own.

He was no longer that boy, and it was time to stop frightening old peasant couples with his narrow-eyed intensity.

Slowly, so as not to further alarm them with a sudden change in mien, he eased the smile from his lips and proclaimed his condition with appropriate solemnity. "No, your wife is right. I am a bastard."

Minnie recovered first. "I would think it important that your children be part of a good family."

"Very important," Dom agreed. Now Laurentia held the child in her lap, her head bent to Ruby's, the soft nape of her neck exposed by the upward twist of her hair. Brat watched Princess Laurentia with a sentimental glint in her eye. That worried Dom yet again. She'd already questioned his orders once. He didn't dare have Brat fretting about the decency of their mission, not when she'd already proved she'd lost that vengeful edge that had driven her for so long.

Dom laid his hand on Minnie's arm. "Doesn't it bother you your princess might marry a bastard?" Immediately he regretted his question. But he really wanted to know what had made these peasants think they had the right to speak so freely to the man they thought to be their future prince.

"Pish-posh." Minnie spoke stoutly. "Princess Laurentia has a good head on her shoulders, and with you at her side, watching her like a donkey who scents his mate—"

Dom threw back his head and laughed out loud. When he looked down at her, she projected the air of an offended matriarch, and he found himself apologizing. "I'm sorry, I've never been called a donkey before."

"I'm surprised," she snapped. Without drawing breath, she continued, "When you're beside her, Her Highness has that glow about her."

"Woman, you're talking too much," Roy said.

"No, I'm fascinated." Dom never meant anything so much in his life.

Minnie ignored them both. "When we saw Her Highness today, I told my man, I said, 'Princess Laurentia is old enough to choose who she wishes.'" She nodded with the authority of a seasoned matchmaker. "At least you have the look of sanity about you." The husband jostled her elbow, and she said, "Well, he does!"

But although Dom could see she found it difficult, she obeyed the unspoken command to cease.

More than farmers, Dom thought again. "You seem to know her well."

"We've served the royal family for years. Even our son—"

"Woman, you're talking too much," the husband interjected.

"Your son?" Dom urged.

"Our son's in the royal service also," Roy said simply.

Tucking her lips in tight, Minnie glared at Dom as if she knew how he wanted to grab her and question her.

Instead he took her hand and kissed the swollen knuckles. "Thank you," he said. "It's been a pleasure speaking with you."

As he knew she would, the old woman smiled at him, for few could resist when he was charming. But then she did the most extraordinary thing.

She curtsied.

To him.

Royal servants were dragging Monty away on a sling. The crowd around Dom was dispersing. Ruby stood with her mother, holding her hand while Laurentia spoke earnestly. Dom stared at the place where the old farmwife had stood, the image of her bobbing figure emblazoned on his mind long after she had left.

Taking a breath, he eased the constriction in his chest.

The old woman had curtsied. To him. As if she'd meant it when she said it didn't matter if he were a bastard and a mercenary.

He looked up at the princess. She had taken

Ruby's other hand and was swinging it, and Ruby squealed with delight. Brat surreptitiously wiped her nose on her sleeve. The fellow who had helped with Monty stood off to the side, watching the tableau with interest. Too much interest.

It was time for Dom to whisk Laurentia away.

Chapter Eleven

Brat adjusted Ruby in her arms as he escorted Laurentia off, and she easily read the warning glance Dom cast back at her. *Don't bungle this*, he warned mutely.

She wouldn't, but she didn't like the whole mad scheme.

"Mama." Ruby laid her hand on Brat's face and turned it toward her.

Brat looked at her daughter absently, her mind on the man who had been her commander for so many years. "What, Ruby?"

Ruby smiled, a bright toothy grin. "Nice mama."

Brat focused on her child, the sweetest, brightest, most adorable child ever created. "You are a darling."

Ruby. A gem found in the wilderness of her life. She would do anything for Ruby: steal, cheat, murder.

Yet as the baby grew into a child and that child observed and imitated every act her mother performed, Brat realized the truth known by all mothers everywhere.

It was up to her to show Ruby right from wrong.

She settled the child more firmly on her hip. "Do you want a biscuit?"

"Sweets!" Ruby shouted.

"Biscuit," Brat said firmly, and started toward the baker's pushcart.

She, Brat, a nameless, homeless bastard from a whorehouse, had to become a woman her daughter would be proud of. But how?

"You've been so good to help one of my subjects," Princess Laurentia had said. "As a thanks, come to the palace and let me find you new clothing." She'd waved off Brat's horrified objections. "I have so much, and yet you have more than me. I envy you your lovely daughter." She had caressed Ruby's silken hair, smiled at Brat's child as if she really loved her, and confided, "I hope when I marry I have a child half as fair. So you'll let me do this."

Brat's numb nod of agreement had met with beaming satisfaction from the princess. The princess knew how to be good. She'd been taught from the cradle.

No one had ever taught Brat anything except survival. She'd spent her life despising folks who went to their churches every Sunday to pray to some mythical God for help. They were dupes, she said, supporting some fast-talking priest so he didn't have to work. She didn't need that kind of narcotic to keep her happy with her life.

She drank too much, laughed too loud, fought too hard, and never ever found peace.

Then she'd been raped.

Even now sometimes when she shut her eyes she could see the pockmarked face, feel the pressure of rough hands, smell his sour stench . . .

The scent of fresh bread drew her the last few steps to the pushcart.

The baker watched suspiciously as Brat dug the copper out of her pocket and handed it over. Then Ruby smiled at him, and he melted like butter on one of his hot cross buns. "You've got a beautiful girl there," he said, handing over the largest turnover in his case. When Brat would have pointed out she'd paid for a biscuit, he added, "Children grow fast. Can't ever give them too much to eat."

Brat smiled at him, too, adding her pleasure to Ruby's.

Then, juggling the turnover and her daughter, she looked around for a place to sit. All along the perimeter of the meadow, families sat in the shade of the trees. They ate or lounged, watching their children play, talking . . . being normal. One oak in particular caught Brat's eye, for under the tree sat the women who held sleeping babies, the women dressed in a widow's black, the women alone.

The old Brat would have disdained such a seat. Now she found herself trudging toward that tree, gripped by a shyness almost too painful to bear.

Stupid thing, really, that rape. A moment of inattention, a moment of pain, disgust, and wretched humiliation. Not worth brooding about.

Except she hadn't been able to stop crying, or blaming herself for saying the wrong thing, dressing the wrong way, somehow enticing that brute of a sailor . . . Dom and his mercenaries had been furious, roaring about as if anger could cure her hurt. She thought probably they'd hunted down her rapist and killed him, and that seemed just. If ever a man needing killing, it was him. But then, with typical male ineptitude, her mercenaries had tried talking her out of her grief. It wasn't as if she was a virgin, they'd said. Sure, she'd always chosen her mates before, but this wasn't that different. And besides, she'd got her first experience in the brothel.

Where she'd been forced.

Rape made the difference between pleasure and pain, between joy and humiliation.

That knowledge changed her relationship with the troop. Before they'd all been tough together, comrades in battle. Now she forced them to view their actions as others viewed them.

And when she'd discovered she was pregnant! Ah, they almost ran into that battle in Greece.

Conversation died as Brat approached the ladytree. Even Ruby clutched her harder, warned by her mother's rigidity that she should be alarmed. Brat smiled at no one in particular and asked, "Is it permitted for me to sit here?"

With her Sereminian accent, she didn't sound like these people of Bertinierre, and she felt like a target standing there.

Then one of the old women leaning against a trunk moved aside. "Sure," she said in the overly loud manner of the deaf. "Sit down and feed the baby."

Conversation started again as Brat settled her back against the tree. Adjusting Ruby in her lap, she fed her bits of baked apples and raisins baked in the bread-like dough. All the while she relentlessly remembered.

Only Dom had come back for her, a warrior who

worked his way out from under a pile of bodies and staggered off the battlefield. They'd fled into the mountains, burdened by her increasing bulk, stunned by the magnitude of the disaster, missing their friends. She and Dom were nothing but walking corpses—until she'd given birth to Ruby.

Then they'd discovered a new purpose. A purpose that drove them to succeed.

Yet Brat no longer wanted the old successes. The ones they knew how to achieve. She wanted to do what was right.

If she only knew how.

Ruby was drooping now, and Brat adjusted her in her arms. As the toddler slipped off to sleep, Brat finished the turnover. Her own eyelids were drooping, but old habits died hard. She looked around the meadow first, noting the courting couples strolling arm in arm, the two men who had stripped down to their breeches and wrestled in front of a growing crowd—and that Dom and Princess Laurentia were nowhere in sight. Brat sighed, worried but unable to do anything but listen to the laughter of the children and the conversations nearer at hand.

Dom would do what Dom knew how to do, seek a fortune the way he knew how, even if his actions destroyed this bucolic scene and the princess who fascinated him. He tried to pretend he would seduce her only for the job. For his *honor*. She knew better; he stalked Laurentia with a sexual intensity that scorched the air around them.

Brat's eyelids slipped lower. She drifted on a current of light slumber, safe yet aware.

Then she came wide awake, her heart pounding,

sweat beading her flesh in clammy heat. She gathered the sleeping Ruby firmly in her arms, preparing to flee, as her gaze darted around, seeking the peril. She saw again the couples and the crowds. Children still laughed, women still chatted, but somewhere danger threatened and the hair on the back of her head lifted in response.

At last she saw him. A man, standing in the clearing not far away. The sun beat on his brown hair and light skin, and while he stood no taller than she did she had the impression of solid strength.

She recognized him. He was the man who had held Monty as she wrapped his ribs, the one who'd observed Dom and Princess Laurentia so intently. The one who had made her stir restlessly beneath his regard.

Now, again, he watched her, his brown eyes steady and perceptive.

She'd been unconscious, defenseless, and the way he held her gaze rattled her, made her want to check her buttons and cover her face like a harem girl.

Then he smiled and started toward her.

A threat? He didn't look like a threat, but neither had that sailor . . .

The old lady beside her poked her in the ribs, and loud enough for the man to hear, declared, ''He likes you.''

Brat blushed.

Blushed. For the first time in years, maybe in her life, she blushed.

The man knelt in front of Brat, still smiling, one hand knuckled into the ground for balance, one hand open, palm up, on the knee of his trousers. He looked harmless, friendly, open, and Brat relaxed under the unusual attention of an admiring man.

Relaxed, until he said, "I've been watching you."

Chapter Twelve

"I have needs that must be attended to," Laurentia said haughtily. She and Dom stood at the edge of the high meadow, away from the main body of the festivities where the flat land gave way to the beginnings of the Pyrenees. One of the ladies' conveniences had been set up just inside the shadow of the forest in an abandoned hut, part of a hamlet forsaken long ago, and she started up the rugged, winding path toward it.

"Wait." Dom laid his hand on her arm, a warm and callused reminder of his presence. "I'll scout out the area first."

He waited to hear her objections, but she had lost that battle too many times. Without a word, she gestured for him to go. She didn't even flinch when he touched his thumb to her lips and said, "Wise girl."

Everything about him—his grin, his challenging stance, his tone of voice—was deliberate provocation. What was it about her that made him want to poke at her like a boy with a stick?

She laughed softly. A *big* stick.

She watched while he climbed the rugged path. To her, even his black trousers were a provocation, clinging to his thighs and buttocks in a manner that demanded attention. Her fingers itched to explore the firm muscles showcased there, and she found her mind wandering along pathways of exploration and discovery.

Fortunately for the last remnants of her good sense, he disappeared around a tumbled wall, and she caught nary a glimpse of him. Beneath the forest's canopy, she knew, the village was old and wretched, the huts widely scattered, and whatever ghosts haunted it were undoubtedly annoyed by the nosy bodyguard poking about the tumbled stones and fallen roof beams.

When she saw him returning, she wondered what made him smile so wickedly. It couldn't be that he knew his smile destroyed her resolve and turned her into a weak and pitiable creature. Most men weren't so observant, and Dom was very much a man.

Yet the smile mocked her and her dignity. "Don't be long," he said.

"There's no problem," she assured him. "Weltrude scheduled all my duties for the morning, for His Majesty insists I be allowed time to do as I wish at my own festival."

"Nevertheless, don't be long."

She didn't like his tone, his assumption of authority, or the fact he was right, so she brushed past him without acknowledging him or his efforts. Unreasonable, she knew, even deplorable, but how much more deplorable was a woman who couldn't look at a handsome man without desiring inappropriate behavior? Better he should think she was haughty than easy.

She walked cautiously, not wanting to trip and make a fool of herself, yet each sway of her hips seemed like a wanton invitation. And while it really wasn't, she could feel his gaze on her as she walked over the pine needles littering the path. Rounding the corner and moving out of sight proved such a relief she placed one hand on the rough bark of a tree. Her heart raced as if she'd run up the hill, and she wanted to sit and catch her breath. But she didn't dare; she wouldn't put it past Dom to decide she was taking too long, leave his post at the bottom of the hill, and come to find her.

So she hurried to finish, and as she reached the last hut at the far end of the village, she heard a moan. She stopped, her mind flashing to the injured man she'd just treated. Had someone else been hurt? She thought the cry had come from behind those two walls, once part of a hut and still almost intact.

Another moan, followed by a woman's scream. Someone . . . Oh, heavens above, was someone being attacked? Last night's assault sprang into her mind, and panic made her gasp for breath. Someone needed help and she . . . No, she wasn't afraid. She was the princess.

Blind pride and pure determination pushed her into a run, and as she ran she fumbled with her handbag. No one was going to be abducted. Not on *her* birthday.

She barreled around the corner of the standing wall—and came to a complete and humiliating halt.

Dulcie writhed half-naked in the arms of some man who was obviously *not* attacking her.

No wonder Dom had been smiling.

In their lovers' frenzy, they hadn't seen her. Sweat beaded Laurentia's forehead as she eased backward and out of sight. When she came to a large fallen boulder hidden in a grove well away from the action, she sank down and put her head in her hands.

Here paths wound up into the mountains through pine forests that stretched toward the highest peaks. Ivy climbed the rough trunks. As the forest thickened, badgers moved boldly from their dens to waddle about in search of prey, and Laurentia knew wolves and bears roamed the woods. Yet it wasn't insentient nature that she feared, or the animals that lived by instinct alone. It was her, Laurentia, who hurt herself.

Stupid! She was so stupid! Rushing to rescue someone fortunate enough to be involved in passionate embrace.

Not fortunate enough, she corrected herself, wanton enough.

But she couldn't even convince herself. Dulcie chose her partners with an eye to quality, and Laurentia envied her that. Envied her everything, if the truth be told. Dulcie had blossomed early, becoming tall and lushly rounded while Laurentia had been short and straight. And while maturity had eventually blessed Laurentia with a curvaceous figure, she hadn't grown much taller, leaving her looking up while Dulcie flirted her way in and out of trouble. And in again—Dulcie had had to marry at sixteen.

"At least," she'd boasted to Laurentia, rubbing her swollen belly, "I made sure I got caught with a duke."

The duke died, the second husband died, and now

Dulcie was a rich widow with three children she loved dearly and a wandering eye.

From the direction of the pathway, Laurentia heard passionate murmurs, then the tromp of boots as Dulcie's lover strode away, apparently invigorated by their embrace. Laurentia scrunched herself into a little ball and kept watch in the direction of the path.

Which is why she didn't see Dulcie until she spoke from behind her. "Your Highness! Spying on me?"

Laurentia jumped so hard she bumped her head against an overhanging branch, and Dulcie laughed.

Swinging around, Laurentia found her nemesis—and friend—standing downhill at the corner of a single, standing wall.

She was plumper than she had been at adolescence, her gown a little more daring, her hair a red so bright Laurentia could have read by its brilliance, but essentially she was the same Dulcie, studying Laurentia as if she were some silly little girl in need of guidance.

"Dulcie, how did you—"

"I was pretty sure you'd be too stunned to go far, so I searched." Dulcie grinned. "You got an eyeful that time, didn't you?"

It was too late to pretend she didn't know what Dulcie was talking about, so Laurentia said, "I didn't mean to!"

"What did you think was happening? Did you think he was killing me?" At the expression on Laurentia's face, Dulcie laughed harder. "You did. You were going to rescue me!"

"I didn't know it was you or I wouldn't have bothered," Laurentia muttered.

At that, Dulcie laughed hard enough for tears to smear the henna on her lids.

Laurentia watched morosely. One thing about Dulcie, she might laugh now, but she wouldn't tell anyone else. Laurentia knew that for sure; she had a tendency to make a fool of herself around Dulcie.

When Dulcie finally got control of herself, she said, "You should see your face. You look like my maiden aunt when she found out I'd delivered Sammie six months after the wedding."

For some reason, talking about Sammie made Laurentia feel better. She was his godmother, and he was a charming boy of ten who adored her and the gifts she brought him. "I'm sure he came early."

"Of course. Early babies always weigh ten pounds." Dulcie scampered up the hill. "Your Highness, if you would permit me, I'd like to converse with you."

Laurentia didn't want to converse. She didn't want to hear what Dulcie had to say. But on the occasions when she had not consented to let Dulcie speak, she'd gone into situations unprepared. As Dulcie had said on one such occasion, *someone* in Bertinierre had to tell the crown princess the realities of life, and no one else had the nerve.

Dulcie had a plethora of nerve and a lot of heart, so Laurentia might just as well let Dulcie get whatever it was off her extremely ample chest. Gloomily, she gave permission. "You may sit down."

Perching herself on the stone next to Laurentia, Dulcie pulled a handkerchief from her sleeve, dabbed at her face, then turned to Laurentia. "Am I smeared?"

One eye had a smudge of black in the corner and Dulcie's spontaneous tears of laughter had washed one cheek clean of rouge. "Here." Prudently placing her pocketbook on the stone right beside her, Laurentia took the handkerchief. "Let me."

Respect for the royal family ran deep in Bertinierre, and Dulcie hesitated. "Are you sure, Your Highness?"

"If I didn't want to do it, I wouldn't have offered," Laurentia said irritably.

As Laurentia rubbed at one cheek, then another, Dulcie said, "You're taking this too seriously."

"What too seriously?" Laurentia frowned at Dulcie's cheeks, still unevenly colored, then scrubbed all the rouge away.

"This picking of a husband. You've been marching around here like some martinet on parade. If I didn't know better, I'd think you were Weltrude."

Laurentia pinched at Dulcie's cheeks. "Unfair."

"Ow." Dulcie jerked her head away. "You don't need to enjoy that quite so much!"

"It brought your tender blush back."

"Tender is right." Dulcie touched her skin with her fingertips. "I wanted pink, not black and blue."

Laurentia grinned at her, Dulcie grinned back, and Laurentia went to work trying to fix the smudges under Dulcie's eye.

"You've got all these men, and all you do is official duties." Dulcie looked right into her eyes. "You should be having fun."

Laurentia had heard this before. "I can't. I'm fixing the mess you made of your face."

"Dom." A little smile played around Dulcie's cherry lips. "Dominic of Baminia, or so he says. That's exactly who I'm talking about. He's your suitor, and he's following you about like a stud on the trail of a mare."

Laurentia sucked in a breath to blast Dulcie for her crudeness.

Until Dulcie baldly said, "Bed him."

Laurentia's heart skipped a beat, then started thumping so loudly she feared she would cause the earth to shake. Bed him. Bed Dom?

"You can't tell me you don't want to," Dulcie said. "I saw your disarray when you came into the ballroom last night. I saw the way you two stared at each other today, and when you say his name you look like my little girl drooling over a sweetmeat."

Laurentia did not appreciate the description, especially since she feared it was true. "Having fun is not the same as bedding a man."

"That's a lie." Dulcie settled back, leaning on her hands, and looked as satisfied as a pasha who had been serviced by a harem. "And unless I miss my guess—and I'm seldom wrong—your Dom definitely knows what he's doing."

"He's not *my* Dom."

"Don't you want to bed him?" Dulcie asked encouragingly.

"Yes." Laurentia hoped confession would ease her distress, but if anything it made her feel sillier. "But I'm like that with all handsome men. I just . . . want them."

"*All* handsome men?" Dulcie's mouth quirked. "Did you want Jaime?"

"Who?"

"That rather vigorous fellow you caught me with."

Laurentia shrugged. "He's not a man, he's just a boy."

"He's twenty-two, old lady, and if you took a vote, every woman here would agree he's the handsomest bow in the quiver."

Laurentia tried to remember how Jaime had appeared when he had been presented to her last night, when his pants had been around his waist and his charisma had been directed at her. Tall and dark, with melting brown eyes and a tortured beauty . . . "He's too young."

"What about that Persian, Kalil? Or Mr. Shanahan?"

Laurentia recalled the swarthy Easterner and the auburn-haired Irishman. "Very comely, but not like Dom."

Dulcie grabbed Laurentia by the arm. "Yes . . . they . . . are. Better than Dom, even, because they haven't got that scar across their faces."

Indignant, Laurentia said, "The scar gives him character."

"We're not talking about character. We're talking about sheer good looks." Dulcie took a breath that raised her quivering breasts to new heights. "Now if we're talking about a dangerous air, that's a different tale entirely. Your Dom is positively mesmerizing."

"He doesn't want me." Laurentia twisted the

handkerchief in her fingers. "He's just like Beaumont, all powder and no shot."

"You mean he doesn't love you, he only wants you for your ... position."

Laurentia floundered before Dulcie's obvious scorn. "Well ... yes."

"I can't imagine being so blessed, Laurie, or being so bloody stubborn. A breathtakingly handsome man who knows how to give a woman a good time is after your money *and* your body—believe me, he's not faking *that*—and you won't even try him out."

"I tried out one breathtakingly handsome man, and look what it got me."

Dulcie smiled crookedly. "I know what it got you, Laurie. I tried to ride that horse myself. Your husband was a gelding, and unless I miss my mark"— she lowered her voice dramatically—"you're still a virgin."

"Sh!" Laurentia looked frantically around. She half-expected Dom to step out of the trees in high dudgeon because she hadn't returned immediately. "For pity's sake, be quiet!"

Dulcie *was* quiet, so quiet Laurentia realized she'd been tricked. "You didn't know," Laurentia said.

Dulcie wore a pensive expression. "Not for sure. How could I? I feel so bad for you."

She truly did, Laurentia could see that and that, in general, made Laurentia want to hide herself under the nearest rock. Except she was sitting on the nearest rock, and it was too heavy. "That makes it worse. Suffice it to say, he did not choose to make me his wife in the fullest sense of the word. And Dulcie, I can't tell you more."

"Of course it shall be as you wish, Your Highness."

"Thank you."

"But I can speculate!" said the irrepressible Dulcie. "That wedding night must have been a hell of a disappointment."

"I was only sixteen, I didn't know everything"—Laurentia glared at Dulcie—"but *someone* had given me the details about being deflowered."

"Who else was going to tell you?" Dulcie spread her hands in mock innocence. "I was just trying to help."

"You scared me to death."

"The first time's a little painful, and you were such a whiny little girl."

"I was not!"

"Were too." Laurentia started to argue, but Dulcie lifted one finger. "We can't sit here and squabble like infants."

"Why not?" Laurentia asked. "We've had enough practice."

Dulcie poked the finger at Laurentia. "Because we're trying to get you on your back with an experienced man above you so you can have a little fun before you settle down to marriage."

"That's what you're trying to do." Actually, the idea appealed more and more.

"You're twenty-five and a virgin, Laurentia. This is a state emergency." Dulcie looked as serious as Laurentia had ever seen her. "Listen to me. This makes what I'm telling you even more logical. At your age, any other woman has had a few little romps. A husband or two, maybe a dozen lovers.

You've had nothing, and you owe it to yourself to find out what you've missed."

Laurentia rolled her eyes.

"All right. You owe it to your future husband. He's *expecting* to marry a woman of the world, not a little celibate."

Dulcie could produce a good argument, so good she was beginning to make sense. "He's *expecting* that our first child will be his."

"It doesn't matter if the first child is his, only if it's yours. You bear the royal bloodline, not him. Don't you dare let any husband of yours tell you different."

With unshakable confidence, Laurentia said, "I know who I am, Dulcie."

"You don't have to take this Dom forever," Dulcie continued persuasively. "Just test him out. It's like buying a horse. You ride him, see if he has a good gait and staying power. If he doesn't, you move on to another stud."

"That's an awful way to look at it!" Something rustled, and the hair on Laurentia's neck lifted. "Be quiet!"

"Why?" Dulcie continued, blithely impervious. "That *is* what you're looking for, a stud with good teeth and strong legs to give you children, and if he gives you a romp in bed, well then, all the better."

Laurentia looked around at every bush, but she caught sight of nothing suspicious. No Dom, thank heavens. And much as she wished to, she couldn't ignore Dulcie's enthusiastic plans. "Yes, but how do I . . ."

"Smile at him, Laurentia. Bat your eyes like this."

Dulcie fluttered her lashes like a bedouin in a dust storm. "Rest your hand on his arm. Lean against him. Lower your voice so you purr like a well-cared-for cat. Did I say smile?"

"I can't—"

"Yes, you can. It works." Dulcie sighed in exasperation and with the patience of an instructing parent said, "This is your last chance, Laurie. You're the princess. You can't go fooling around after you've picked a husband, but no one will notice if you take a lover now. My God, do you think I'm the only one slipping away for a quick spike?"

Laurentia wanted to cover her ears.

"If he turns out, keep him. If he doesn't, there are others here willing to audition." Dulcie pried the mangled handkerchief from between Laurentia's fingers, then stood up and stepped away. "And don't forget, you could always take dear ol' boring Francis."

Even the thought of Francis failed to bring Laurentia back into a sensible frame of mind. "Francis wouldn't have me if I've been wanton," she said feebly.

"Francis might huff a bit if you draw it to his attention, but if you don't tell him about it, he will politely turn his head and pretend he didn't notice a thing. The man is riddled with ambition. I've never had him, but let's face it—he would be a bore in bed." An odd note sounded in Dulcie's voice, and she ruthlessly straightened her skirt and brushed at her hair. "Do I look presentable?"

"You look fine," Laurentia said. "You always look fine."

Dulcie tapped Laurentia's cheek. "Don't be bitter, dear. You're quite attractive yourself, with a betraying freshness about you. Men find naïveté fascinating, and you should learn to use it to your advantage. In the meantime, think about what I said."

Digging her gloves out of her cleavage, she pulled them on and buttoned them up, then climbed to the path and strolled away, elegance and femininity personified.

Dulcie was fearless, a wicked widow with an insatiable taste for men. Laurentia wasn't like that, but she couldn't stop thinking about Dulcie's advice.

Sleep with Dom just for the experience? Keep him if she wished, toss him aside and try another if she didn't. It sounded good, but Laurentia couldn't see Dom accepting her rejection and moving on. No, if she took Dom as a lover, he'd expect things. Marriage. A title.

Yet . . . he would be a magnificent lover, just the man to introduce her to the complexities and pleasures of mating. So why shouldn't she have a fling? Just a little one. And with a man who reeked of experience. Oozed sexuality. Radiated the kind of appeal she could warm her hands by. And more than her hands if she were lucky. There had to be a way—

A twig snapped. She snatched up her pocketbook and twirled.

Not fast enough. A black cloth descended over her head. Strong arms wrapped her up like a package for transport. And in a nightmare repeat of last evening's abduction, someone lifted her. Flung her over a broad shoulder. And carried her away.

Chapter Thirteen

Dom climbed the mountain at a steady pace, taking care not to limp, seeking a private place in the forest in which to wreak his vengeance. Inside the black cloth, Laurentia wriggled.

He supposed she was uncomfortable, draped across his shoulder. Hell's fire, he *hoped* she was uncomfortable. Never had any woman made him as furious as Princess Laurentia of Bertinierre. The damned woman had the gall, the *gall*, to sit down for a gab when she knew she should return immediately. And she'd been talking about him, listening as one of her lecherous friends described him— him!—as the original easy ride.

He couldn't believe it. He hadn't heard much—he couldn't get close enough—but he'd heard enough, and good women didn't talk that way. Dulcie had a lot to answer for.

Blasted Laurentia, giving him a scare, making him search the hillside. He'd even gone into the ladies' convenience and that high-voiced, incensed old bat had insinuated he was some kind of satyr. Explaining he sought the princess certainly hadn't appeased her. If anything, it had made her more indignant, and he'd left with her fulmination burning his ears. She would report him to Princess Laurentia's body-guards, she said.

But that was him, and for the first time since he'd been hired, he'd lost the princess.

He winced. In less than twenty-four hours, he'd lost the princess.

She had to have been hiding from him. She had to have been. That pig who had tried to snatch her before couldn't have slipped past him. He'd in-spected the surroundings before he'd let her walk alone. There had been only Dulcie and her para-mour.

In the end, Dulcie's voice led him to Laurentia. Laurentia, sitting demurely as she pleased, chatting about taking a lover.

Dom didn't like to admit to panic. Didn't like it, but had to.

The little she-devil's disappearing act had brought him to a fever pitch of worry. He wanted to catch her in his arms and hold her, kiss her, and make her cling to him.

He wanted to teach her a lesson she'd never for-get.

And he couldn't hold her and kiss her. Not while he was in a passion. It had to be done coldly, delib-erately . . .

Damn her!

So he'd gone and bought a long sack full of clean rags and, much to the peddler's puzzlement, dumped out the contents. Returning, he'd waited while Dulcie gave her parting advice and left. Then he'd sneaked up behind Laurentia, threw the bag over her head and down her arms, and kidnapped her, intent on giving her the scare of her life.

She was quiet now, not moving, and he hoped she hadn't fainted. That would diminish the authority of his lesson, and besides, that would make him sorry. He didn't want to be sorry, he wanted to be angry. Anger made it easier to deal with a woman like Laurentia.

He moved off the path and into the deep forest. Here the trees muffled the sound of the crowd in the meadows far below. Sunlight sifted through the tangled branches. Pine boughs littered the rich brown dirt, and a stream babbled nearby. In this lonely place, no one could hear Laurentia scream.

This was a good spot.

Gingerly he stood her on her feet, supporting her until he realized she could stand. Beneath the cloth that dangled almost to her knees, he saw her hand move. Good; she was awake, aware, frightened, ready.

Quickly, he jerked the bag off.

And saw the small, neat, shiny pistol pointed at his chest.

He dove sideways as she squeezed the trigger. He ate dirt as he slid, and pine needles rained on him.

"Dominic?" She shrieked his name in disbelief and horror.

"Damnation!" Sitting up, he touched the abrasion on his cheek, and his fingers came back bloody.

Her eyes were round and horrified, and she took a step toward him. "Are you all right?"

"You shot at me!"

She waved the pistol, empty of its single bullet. "I

tried to miss when I realized it was . . . you." Then she looked at the bag, rumpled on the ground, and looked at him. "You!"

Rubbing his hip—it hurt now—he staggered to his feet.

"*You* kidnapped me. *You* scared me to death?" The weapon dangled from her fingers; her pocketbook dangled from her wrist.

"What the hell are you doing with a pistol?" He marched over to her, so furious he made a conscious effort to tower over her. It wasn't difficult—she was tiny.

And fierce. Doubling up her empty fist, she punched him in the sternum hard enough to knock the breath out of him. "You kidnapped me. You dimwit, you scared me. What do you think you were doing?"

He rubbed his chest and exulted when she shook her aching fingers, wincing as if she'd cracked every knuckle. "I was teaching you a lesson."

"A lesson? What kind of idiot would throw a bag over my head and carry me up a mountain to teach me a lesson?"

"The kind of idiot who is your bodyguard and who lost the princess he was supposed to be guarding." Grabbing the hand with the pistol, he wrestled it from her grasp.

"You didn't lose me." She jerked her pocketbook off her wrist and threw it to the ground. "I was right there on the hill."

"Hidden from sight. Having a nice little conversation with that trollop!"

"Don't you call her that!"

"Why not? That's what she is."

"Well . . . don't you call her that." Her hair had tumbled from its chignon and hung loose around her face, and she shoved impatiently at the importunate locks. "I thought someone was kidnapping *her*."

"That's ludicrous. Why would anyone kidnap her?"

"I heard her scream."

"That's because—"

"I know why it was. I went to rescue her!"

"Wait." He took a breath to calm himself. It didn't work. "You heard a woman scream, you thought she was being kidnapped, and you went to *help?*"

She glared up at him, not at all intimidated, fearless and implacable. "Of course. Someone might have been assaulting her. Or raping her. Or—"

His temper snapped. He dropped the pistol. He grabbed Laurentia's shoulders. "Or murdering her? Someone might have been killing one of your friends—"

"I didn't know it was Dulcie," she said hotly. Then she must have seen something in his face that gave her pause, for with a good deal less vehemence she said, "And sometimes we have an acrimonious friendship."

"Why didn't you come to me for help?" He spaced the words deliberately, giving her a chance to consider her answer before she replied.

She didn't consider. She didn't give the right answer. "You were clear down the hill. She was screaming *then*."

"You are small and delicate, you're pampered and spoiled, you're the princess—and you're my responsibility." Her shoulders were so slight of muscle and bone he could cup them in his palms, and the knowledge of her vulnerability, and her valiance, made his voice rise again. "If you ever come upon trouble again, you'd better run like a scared rabbit. Let someone who knows what he's doing handle it."

She snorted.

Snorted. A vulgar, unladylike snort. As if his dictates meant nothing to her. As if she was big enough and tough enough to take on every villain between here and Transylvania. The top of her head reached only to his chin, and she made him want to hold her and take her and make her so vibrantly aware of her vulnerability she would never again chance her own life.

She needed that lesson. She needed it now, because of him, and what he had been hired to do.

Deliberately, he allowed a slow smile to curl his lips, the kind of smile he used on those few warriors who had ever dared to challenge his authority. "Princess Laurentia of Bertinierre." He used her whole title, savoring each syllable. "Once upon a time I would have given anything to hold a princess of royal blood between my two hands." He slid his palms down her back.

He felt her stiffen beneath his touch, and that gave him satisfaction. His first taste of satisfaction.

"And for no benevolent reason . . . Your Highness." Although her feet dragged, he pulled her closer, giving her no choice although she tried to wedge her elbows between them. Her petticoats whispered as he crushed them between their bodies. "I'm a mercenary, and I understand why a man would want to abduct you. For money, of course, but with you there would be something wicked added. You're easy on the eyes, not big enough to hurt me if you struggle. Some men take pleasure in taming fiery women, and you are certainly that." He saw the moment alarm turned to dread.

He was glad; that had been his plan, to replace her rash self-confidence with some common sense.

But he didn't like seeing her proud chin tremble or the apprehension that filled her wide eyes. For one moment, she looked like a woman who had learned humiliation at a master's knee.

Why? Why did she look like she knew about fear?

Despite Dom's royal blood, he wasn't an aristocrat. He didn't believe some people were inherently better than others, or that some should be protected from the realities of life while others suffered in their stead. Yet he loved Laurentia's fearlessness, her sense of invincibility, and that odd air of innocence no woman of her age and experience should possess. Amazingly, he wanted to protect Laurentia.

Hastily he counted the lesson of prudence well taught. She was frightened. She knew herself defenseless. She would be aware.

No, he would not frighten her further, but still, she'd frightened *him*. He'd been terrified on her behalf, and while he didn't understand it—it wasn't the same, after all, as having his professional abilities cast in doubt—he felt the need to make her pay.

Smoothly, he switched tactics. Leaning back, he examined her face with every appearance of sobriety. "So. From what I overheard, your friend thinks I would be a likely lover for you."

Laurentia jerked in his grip, and guilt brought swift color to her face. "You heard? How much did you hear?"

"Enough." He let her know he baited her by his tone of voice. "A stud, I think she called me."

"Is that *all* you heard?"

"Isn't that enough?"

She studied him hard, then had the nerve to look relieved.

He tried again. "A stud with good teeth and strong legs."

Anger sparked in her eyes as she pushed away her uneasiness. "*She* said so, not me."

He liked this better, this indignation and embarrassment. It meant . . . "You thought it."

She had, for she broke into a frenzy of motion, trying to escape him, looking everywhere but at him, shoving at his chest. He had caught her out.

Pleased and for some reason relieved, he laughed and caught her wrists. He held them out, up and over his shoulders, forcing her full against him.

She felt . . . good. When he made love, he usually managed a fair amount of coherence. He'd learned a few essential phrases to be repeated in the heat of the moment, and the women loved it, God bless them.

But right now, in this stilted, tantalizing embrace, all he could think was that she felt . . . good. And he could not think of one thing to say.

She, however, was not so encumbered. "You . . . you scurvy knave," she hissed, giving her best imitation of an outraged princess who had never been soiled by a man's touch. "You let me go."

"Scurvy knave?" He pretended astonishment, pleased he had showed her the danger without crushing her spirit, half his mind and all his senses intent on the impression of warmth and life she exuded. "Is that the best you can do? I will teach you how to swear."

"You'll teach me nothing!"

His merriment died. He didn't plan it, hadn't thought beyond giving her a taste of him. But her arrogance touched something inside him. He would show her what manner of man she disdained.

Chapter Fourteen

Dom looked down at the princess until she realized his change of mood. Her breath began to hitch as she stared up at him, her dark lashes a tangle, her mouth full and rich and trembling.

Languidly, as if they had all the time in the world, he brought her hands down, slid them behind her waist, and leaned to her. "Laurentia," he whispered. Her scent wafted up from the tumble of her hair, a rich combination of cinnamon, roses, and *her*. "Little princess."

He held her tenderly, as if he could break her with the least of his strength. Her flesh glowed with the subtle shade of peach he'd seen only once before in the fragile twirl of a Venetian glass goblet. Her lips parted, showing the gleam of pearly teeth and making him want . . . want.

If she had said, "No," or even wrinkled her nose at the suggestion such an unworthy should kiss her, he would have drawn back. He would have laughed at the thought that he wished to share passion with a princess, and repeated his warning that she take care.

She did no such thing, and that compliance sealed her fate. He pressed his lips against hers, savoring the freshness of her. Obviously, she hadn't been with a man since her husband's death, and she didn't pretend a deftness she hadn't retained. Nor did she mask her curiosity; her eyelashes parted, then closed, then parted again as if his proximity confused her.

"Open your lips," he said.

Her eyelids fluttered again. Then she nodded and opened her mouth with the resolute determination of a woman facing her first tooth extraction.

He couldn't help it; he smiled at her again. "You are adorable."

She shut her mouth with a snap. "Just don't tell me I'm precious. Short women are always precious. I'm going to be a hundred years old and still be precious."

He tilted his head and studied her. She was right. She was precious, and age would not dim that. But perhaps the term had been overused in her praise. "You're charming. Defiant. Brave. Stupid. Achingly beautiful. And you need to learn how to kiss."

"I'm trying to learn." For the first time since he'd taken her into his arms, *she* smiled at *him*, a siren intent on seduction. "But you won't shut up."

He chuckled.

Yet . . . yet when she looked at him like that, she knocked the breath out of him. Yes, she was beautiful, but more, she challenged him with every weapon in her arsenal, and he was too much the mercenary not to take the challenge.

The taste of her fanned his desire to a roaring blaze. When he probed her mouth, he was inside her. This wasn't an imitation of intercourse. It *was* intercourse. Wet, intimate, so good it brought tears seeping into the corners of his eyes. And when she touched her tongue to his . . .

He let her wrists go. He wanted to raise her skirt, lower his trousers, and release the tyrant that had given him such trouble since the first moment he'd laid eyes on Laurentia. Laurentia, who had leaned against the marble rail and smiled over the moonlit countryside as if it were her only lover.

If he held her, he would take her, and if he took her in this kind of a passion, he would never let her go.

But if he let her go and she turned away . . .

For one long second, he released her from the kiss. She took a gasp of breath and glanced aside. Then she gripped the sleeves over his upper arms, and lifted her face to him again.

He backed her up against a tree, crowding her, holding her with the urgency of his body against hers. He reached around her, one hand on either side of her waist, and clenched the bark as if the long, rough ridges could keep him sane. The ends of her unbound hair brushed the backs of his fingers, teasing him with each touch.

He kissed her again. She was eager, gauche, learning how even as he grappled for fortitude. She should know what this kind of loving did to a man. How her kind of enthusiastic seeking lashed him with passion. He was nothing more than a predator, a wolf who prowled among the lambs and took what he would. As all men were. She *had* to know that. Every woman knew a man's true nature, to take and go, then return and take again. What madness made a soft and tender woman think she could ever tame the wolf, he didn't understand.

"Dominic."

She murmured his name against his lips, giving identity, blessing, to the lonely bastard he was.

"Dom, please." She rose up on tiptoe, crowding back at him, trying to get closer when only their clothes separated them. Her fingers slid up his shoulders into his hair, stroking the strands against the back of his neck, finding the tingle of nerves as if they'd been lovers for decades.

A shudder rose up his spine. He feasted on her mouth, loving the textures, the scents, the pure unbridled pleasure of possessing her with his tongue. His hand lifted away from the tree and hovered next to her breast just beneath her upswung arm. A sensitive area, one that could lift this kiss from curiosity on her part to blind, binding abandon.

If he dared.

He grasped the tree bark again.

Only a stupid man would dare. Already this craving was too much, too deep, too powerful. He held on to control by a thread and to be carried away by such madness . . . well, it was not to be borne.

Gradually, he lightened the kiss, forcing himself by mere willpower to pull back, to lessen his domination, to give her a chance to reclaim the discipline of a princess.

Peasants and nobles roamed the meadow below and in the woods around. A tittering drunk or another pair of lovers could catch him and Laurentia. Their embrace would become a lesser thing, soiled by the amusement of gossips and the avid interest of Laurentia's own people. People who thought they had the right to observe their princess and her courtship.

More important, the kidnapper could be lurking nearby, waiting to catch Dom unprepared.

Dom kissed her gently now, retreating as lightly as a thief.

Nothing left a man as vulnerable as fornication. He had used that knowledge to his advantage on many occasions, all the while swearing he would never be caught so unaware. Yet this time he dared not put his resolve to the test. The violence of his response to a mere kiss forewarned him that lying with this woman would rob him of sight, of good sense, of the very wariness that had kept him alive.

One part of him resented that—a woman who could rip his defenses away with only a kiss.

Another part of him wanted that—passion beyond price.

All parts knew he could not live with himself if he allowed Laurentia to be hurt. As she would be hurt when de Emmerich had his way.

Dom's eyes sprang open as the knowledge slammed through him. She would suffer when he had succeeded in his mission. She would be alone, seduced and humiliated.

But he couldn't contemplate that now. He would think about it later. Later, when her fingers weren't still in his hair, rubbing through the strands as if the touch gave her pleasure. When her mouth was not still on his, accepting the softness of his retreat as if it were only a prelude to more.

"Your Highness," he whispered, hoping formality

would succeed where discretion had failed. When her title didn't touch the haze of voluptuousness enshrouding her, he reached behind his head, grasped her wrists, and lifted them away.

Her eyes opened, and she gazed at him with sleepy dismay. Her hair had hooked itself on the rough bark behind her head, creating a dark and rumpled halo. Her mouth looked well kissed and passion's flush stung her cheeks.

She would look just this way after he'd loved her to sleep, and woke her to love again.

At the thought, he dropped her wrists and stepped back so quickly he stumbled over a protruding tree root.

"Dom?" Her hands dangled, then lifted to cradle her shoulders as if she were cold. Bewilderment as transparent as hers could not be faked, although he almost wished it could.

Her wide mournful eyes and trembling mouth made him want to pull her back into his arms and assure her he wanted as much as she wanted. *More* than she wanted.

"Princess Laurentia." He bowed jerkily. "Your Highness, I think we should return to the festival before Weltrude misses you."

She stroked her lips with her fingertips. "I don't want to go back."

"It's your birthday." He smiled at her, showing her he could be reasonable even while suffering from trousers that fit with uncomfortable snugness. "We can't just disappear. People will gossip."

Her forehead crinkled. She glanced down the path, her gaze lingering as if remembering their ascent. Was she considering vengeance? He would have been. But when she looked back at him, he found himself the object of a very thorough visual examination. "You could give me a gift. Right now."

He took pride in understanding women, but not this one. An hour ago, he would have sworn she didn't know one feminine wile, and now she actively taunted him! "A princess should be above vulgar speculation."

She smiled a close-mouthed smile, almost as if she were laughing at herself. "There has never been vulgar speculation about me."

She was being reasonable. He hoped his relief would transmit itself to a more rambunctious part of his body—soon.

She added, "It's about time, I would say."

Relaxation evaporated.

She pursed her mouth with a display of regal impatience. "But you're right. Now is not our moment." She shook out her skirts, lifting them as if trying to rehabilitate the crushed starch of her petticoats. Darting a glance at him, she lifted her arms and created a frame for her face. Brushing the clinging locks from her forehead, she said, "My hair needs to be put up again, but the pins are gone." She turned her back to him.

Because she had contempt for him? Because she trusted him?

"Would you like to braid it this time?" she asked.

Reaching almost to her waist, the black strands glistened in the dappled sunlight, and as she gathered them in her hands and pulled them over her shoulder, she looked back at him, smiling so mysteriously it would have made Mona Lisa proud. "Don't you want to braid it?"

That answered his question. Laurentia turned her back on him to tempt him. And doing a damned fine job, too. Her pink skirt flared across slender hips. Her hem, shortened for the outdoor activities, allowed him a glimpse of white-clad ankles and black ribbons from her slippers laced up to . . . where?

Brusquely he said, "You do it." Leaning over, he picked up the empty sack and wondered why he had ever thought he should try to teach her a lesson. "I'll gather our things."

"As you wish." The little witch sounded submissive, and kept her back turned as she divided her hair into three parts and began the process of weaving it into a braid. The more her hair came under control, the more her figure was revealed, and the harder he searched for their belongings. He found her pocketbook, trampled and dirty, and dropped it into the sack. The pistol, when he lifted it, seemed no heavier than a toy, but he knew a bullet from its barrel would have punched a hole right through his chest. The fact that she carried it at all stunned him. He thought he knew everything about women like her. So how did she continue to surprise him?

He weighed it in his hand. "Do you always carry a gun?"

"Not at all." She faced him, holding the end of her braid with one hand. "Do you have something I can tie this off with?"

He unraveled a thread from the loose weave of the sack.

"I like that in a man." She smiled at him *again*.

"No matter the situation, you know how to provide."

"Yes." If life had taught him one thing, it was to provide for those he loved. *Brat and Ruby.* He owed them. He would not forget about them and the deal he'd made for their sake.

Laurentia plucked the thread from his hand, wrapped it around the braid, and tied it firmly. "His Majesty gave me that pistol some years ago, soon after my husband died."

She continued to smile, but he detected a waver in her voice, a hesitation she had not ever shown before, and he again sensed a mystery.

"Of course I know how to shoot it," she went on. "His Majesty taught me well. I've just never had occasion to carry it until now."

"Until now?"

"Someone *did* try to kidnap me last night. While I believe you are a capable bodyguard, nothing is certain, and I refuse to be helpless in a fight." She touched his shoulder lightly and smiled that smile. The intimate one that suggested they had shared— or would share—something more than a kiss. "You *do* realize I'm not stupid."

His eyes narrowed on her. "I am starting to suspect it."

"Good." She tossed her braid over her shoulder and reached for the pistol.

Against his better judgment, he let her take it, but he questioned her anyway. "What are you going to do with it?"

"When I get back to my saddlebags," she said, "reload it."

"I'd like to see you shoot."

"More than into the air, you mean?" Her voice lowered to a whisper. "I'd like that, too."

Now she made gunplay sound suggestive! He didn't know what she was thinking, but whatever it was could only be hazardous.

She put her hand on his arm and rested it there. "Shall we go?"

He looked down at her hand, intimately warm. "You walk ahead. I'll finish picking things up and be right behind you."

"But you said I should stay within sight."

"You will be."

She released him with a show of reluctance. She smiled at him again. She batted her eyelashes. And as she walked away, she swayed her hips like a gypsy on the prowl.

He didn't need this now. Not when his mind already struggled against his body's urgings. "Have you got a kink in your back?"

Turning, she put a hand on her hip. "What?"

"It looks as if it hurts when you walk."

Straightening to her full height, which was not much, she glared, then flounced away as he grinned after her.

Then his smile faded.

Where did women learn these maneuvers? And why was she using them on him?

He bundled their belongings into the sack, and glared at her as she made her way down the path, walking carefully down the steep parts, sometimes slipping on the fine dust and pine needles, once stopping and emptying a stone from her shoe.

Yet for all their suspected phoniness, he liked her smiles, and the small touches on his arm and shoulder. If he thought their kiss had healed the rift between them or even swept her into that other universe of rampant desire, he would be hardpressed not to gloat. But she kissed like a girl, all awkward curiosity and eager interest. *He'd* been the one swept away, carried upward on a burst of passion so strong he'd had to struggle to escape.

His palms stung. He looked down at them.

His skin was raw from clutching the bark, and along the string of calluses just beneath his fingers ran a line of splinters dug deep into the skin.

Yes, he had suffered the sting of painfully explicit passion. She had barely noticed his agony and she had certainly not experienced overwhelming desire. He knew what that meant; a simpleton could make this deduction. Little Miss Princess had suffered a frigid marriage. Now she wanted to explore the heavens and, just as de Emmerich had so accurately predicted, she'd chosen him. Chosen him for his looks, for his air of danger and his suspected expertise. Chosen him for exactly the same reasons all the other women had chosen him.

So be it. He'd make it so good for her she'd beg to tell him her nation's secrets. When they were done, he'd walk away heart-whole, a wealthy man, his honor intact and another piece of vengeance wreaked on the royals of the age.

He flexed his wounded hands.

Never mind that for a brief breathless moment, he had wondered if Brat and the farm couple were right, and he could be a better man—and the husband to a princess.

Chapter Fifteen

That had gone well, Laurentia told herself bracingly. Coquetry wasn't so difficult. She'd got him to kiss her, she'd teased him, she'd proved to herself he wanted her.

He wanted her. A grin broke across her face. A man she wanted, wanted her. During the time Beaumont had courted her, she hadn't known what to look for, but she'd learned by observation in the intervening years.

Dulcie wanted her to take advantage of that desire.

Laurentia's smile sagged.

She didn't think she had the audacity to bed a man just because he was handsome. Especially a man she had just met, a man who had taken advantage of circumstances to finagle a place in her life, a man she didn't trust. She had always thought she could never bed a man she didn't trust.

Stopping, she shook a stone out of her shoe and glanced back. Yes, Dom still followed her, keeping her within viewable range.

Of all the virtues, trust carried the most weight for her. As princess, she had learned only too well how many people liked her only as long as they could use her. In her life, she truly trusted only four people. Her father. Francis. Dulcie. And Chariton, God bless his ubiquitous self. Her reliance on them had come only after years of their discretion and support.

She didn't trust Dom. For all his openness, she sensed a mystery about him, depths he deliberately buried. Perhaps his secrets were no more than any other mercenary's—surely those were bad enough—but prudence and well-developed instincts warned her to utilize caution around a man of his background. Her secrets, after all, carried an impact his never could.

Yet he had saved Monty from the crushing weight of the cart. She loved the evidence of his fiery emotions. And . . . although she trusted Francis, she didn't care to bed him, and for a few moments up there on the hill, she had definitely—

She heard Dom shout right before someone tackled her and knocked her sideways.

She hit the ground hard. She slid through the pine needles, weighed down by a heavy human form. Massive, sour with the stench of bad teeth and piss.

The kidnapper.

She tried to catch her breath. She swallowed a lungful of dust and coughed.

He shoved her off the path into the woods, out of sight.

Dom. Where was Dom?

He had said to scream. She screamed. She tried to strike out at the kidnapper.

He struck back, a thump on the head hard enough to knock the sense out of her. As her head bobbled, he hefted her over his shoulder and started running through the woods, uphill, away from the celebration.

Dom. Where was Dom? He should have caught them by now.

Her face stung. The running jarred her belly where it met the kidnapper's shoulder. Her head throbbed from the blow. She wanted to vomit.

Instead she lifted her head and looked around.

Behind her she could see the primitive track they followed. She could see broken branches from their passing.

She should be able see Dom, tracking them relentlessly.

She could not.

Her suspicions were correct. Dom had planned her abduction all along. What other reason could there be for his charm and his kisses? He knew she couldn't marry a bastard, and no man in his sane mind would court her unless lured by the promise of riches. She had been a fool. Again.

Dom wasn't coming. She had no one to depend on except herself. So she would free herself, or die trying.

She didn't have bullets in her gun, thanks to Dom and his fake kidnap attempt. Was that why he had done it? To scout out her defenses?

Tears trickled from her eyes, sliding over her forehead, and she dashed them away. She would not think about Dom. She had to free herself.

This kidnapper was big and brutal, but also lumbering and awkward.

As a child, her ability to run, escape, and hide had

gotten her out of many a lesson and many a function. If she could do that now . . .

In a thicket, he set her down on the ground so hard her spine vibrated. She got a glimpse of wide, frantic eyes in the kidnapper's broad face. A huge horse, seventeen hands high, stood almost right on top of her, its hooves restive and menacing.

She didn't even think of flight, only of avoiding those hooves, but when she tried to roll away her kidnapper grabbed her arm in a crushing grip.

"Keep still," he muttered.

She couldn't place his accent. Right now, she didn't care. She just wanted to live through this. "You won't get paid if that horse kills me." For a woman quaking in fear, she produced a fair imitation of fury.

"They won't care if ye're hurt a little. They're just goina hurt ye more."

"They?" He wasn't on his own. He had been hired—and that, she knew, meant a conspiracy. Dom had warned her . . . She cut off the thought. "Who are *they*?"

"Ye'll find out soon enough." The brute shook her arm, bruising her more. "Don't move or I'll hurt ye m'self." Letting her go, he stepped back slowly.

She bent her head to her chest, gathered her skirt in her hands.

He kept watch on her as he untethered the horse and led it out of the embracing thicket to the well-worn trail. It wasn't the gelding she had first assumed, but a stallion with all the inherent flightiness of the male of the species. Each slap of a branch brought a snort and a defiant prance.

With her hand, she surreptitiously scrabbled in the dirt until she found the right rock: heavy, jagged. Weighing it in her hands, she waited. When the stallion stood sideways and only a few branches blocked her shot, she tucked her feet under her.

"Don't move, bitch," the kidnapper warned again. "Don't—"

Standing, she threw at the horse's flank, threw as hard as she could. The stone bounced, the stallion reared, and she ran. She heard a crashing behind her, a howl of pain or fury, but she didn't stop. As she dashed along, taking the easiest route, underbrush tore at her skirts and at her skin. A branch snagged her; she jerked free. She slowed only when she heard nothing but her own breath. She looked behind her—no one. Then she crept along, concealing her tracks as best she could. She feared to head toward the meadow or even the palace, sure Dom, or someone, would be watching for her. Instead, she looked for a hiding place.

She found one, a tall cluster of stones and bushes. Hitching up her skirts, she climbed the rocks. She snatched up a few broken branches and carried them into the deepest concealment. Crouching down, she made herself as small as possible and arranged the branches over her. She held one stick, pointed side out, toward the breach where she had entered. And she waited.

She twitched at every birdcall, at every creak of the trees, but she saw no one and she wondered—what had happened to her kidnapper? Had the horse trampled him? Had he gone in the wrong direction? She didn't understand this silence. She didn't trust her easy escape.

She didn't trust Dom.

Nor did she understand him. Why would he arrange the kidnapping? As he once said, if he had decided to take her, she would have been already gone. But he hadn't rescued her, either. He had had her in sight. What could have kept him from saving her?

Unless someone had attacked him, too. Maybe the shout she heard had been Dom, falling under an attacker. She closed her eyes and fought back a stab of pain. Could he be dead on the path, a casualty to some villain's greed?

But in that case, where was the accomplice? Everyone should have been after her.

Her head ached from her newly acquired lump. Her cheek was skinned and stiff with blood. She desperately wanted to stand, to stretch her stiffening knees, to creep downhill to the safety of the festivities. Instead she stayed where she was, smearing dirt on her cotton skirt to conceal the vibrant pink color and listening ... listening.

Had they missed her down in the meadow where the revelry continued, or had her disappearance gone unnoticed? If her father had allowed Weltrude to schedule more duties for her, Weltrude would have launched a search by now. But Laurentia knew from previous years that the increasing crowds gave her anonymity—an anonymity she usually enjoyed. She had probably been gone only two hours, and even her father would presume she had done nothing more foolhardy than sit in the shade of a tree to gnaw on a roasted goose drumstick.

And if he did notice her disappearance and Dom's, would he construe the worst from their joint truancy? She winced at the thought, and winced again at the realization that she didn't care about the gossip, if only she could get back to the palace in one piece.

Finally she heard the noise a horse would make.

When Dom parted the bushes, she rammed the pointed stick into his belly.

He grunted and bent at the waist, but when she raised the stick again, he caught it in his hand. "No." He wheezed. "I captured him."

What kind of fool did he think she was? She snatched up another branch and raised it over his head.

This time he just ducked aside. "Go look! He's tied on the horse."

She hesitated. She didn't trust Dom, but she knew well enough she had not done him a permanent injury. If he had wished, he could have knocked her unconscious.

Still, she couldn't allow herself to hope.

Skirting around him, she jumped off the rocks. The enormous stallion stood there, wild-eyed at carrying an unconscious man tied to his back. Going to the man, she smelled his acrid odor even before she touched him. With a moue of disgust, she looked carefully into his face.

Those nasty eyes were closed, one by a swelling that purpled his nose and most of the right side of his face.

"Your Highness, may I come out now?" Dom called.

"You may." She wasn't feeling relief at being rescued. Or anger at the man who had menaced her. All she felt was a bone-deep gratification that Dom had not betrayed her.

From the rocks above her, he said, "I'm sorry it took so damned long for me to find you, but you're good at this. I backtracked three times before I found you."

She looked up to see him cautiously peering down, and she just stared at him. At that marvelous face enriched by the old, long scar—and by a newer, shorter wound, fresh from a blade.

"You ran a long way."

"I did what you told me!"

"Yes. You did." He rubbed his stomach. "I didn't tell you to ram me with a stick, though."

She narrowed her eyes on him in absolute indignation.

"But I approve," he added hastily, "considering you didn't know who it was. I especially approve of your intention to knock me in the back of the head. Never hurt a man just enough to make him angry, Your Highness. You want to disable him completely, and then run."

"I know that," she said. "And I knew who it was. I just didn't know who commanded your loyalty."

He grinned at her as he slid off the stones. A bruise of magnificent proportions colored his cheek. Just below that the knife wound, thin and shallow, curled back the skin. Still grinning, he sucked at his scabbed knuckles.

Why was he so happy? She'd just told him she suspected him.

"Do you forgive me for not liberating you immediately?" He didn't wait for her reply. "I wanted to see where the nasty oaf was taking you and if he had a partner, but once he got to the horse I knew I had to get you at once." His eyes gleamed. "Brilliant thinking, throwing that stone at the stallion."

"It was my only choice."

"Most people, when they're terrified, *can't* think. That stone gave me the chance to take the fool's legs out from under him." He touched his face. "Too bad *he* had a knife, too."

She brushed his hand away and examined the gash. "When we get back to the festivities, the physician will tend to that." Looking earnestly into his eyes, she asked, "Aren't you insulted I suspected you?"

"Of course not. In your position, you should trust no one." He said emphatically, "Trust no one, Your Highness."

"No one," she echoed. But it was too late for that.

On the horse, the kidnapper stirred and groaned. "We'll take him to the palace, put him in the dungeon," Dom said. "Let ol' Smelly here find out what real odors are. Give him a chance to worry all night. In the morning, we'll question him, find out who hired him and what they wanted you for."

Dom was chattering, she realized.

He dabbed his fingers lightly along the lacerations on her cheek. "I'm sorry you had to suffer these, and during your celebration, too. They aren't pretty, but they're not serious. But you realize this attempt has been a godsend. The kidnapping, I mean. Not your face. But with him in custody"—he jerked his head toward the struggling kidnapper—"we'll soon discover who is behind this."

Enlightenment burst on her. Dom was exhibiting masculine triumph. That kind of triumph the bowman had shown when he'd won the archery contest. Dom had fought, he had beaten his opponent, and now he swaggered as if he'd never fought and won a battle.

This odd, ritualistic celebration had never impressed her before. Did he think it would now?

She blessed him with a trembling smile.

It did. Merciful heavens, it did.

"Dom." She walked toward him, and his arms opened. "Dom." She leaned against him, loving his strength, reveling in his virility . . . trusting him.

Brat walked quickly home, Ruby heavy in her arms, and listened for footsteps behind her.

Night had fallen too quickly for her taste, enveloping the countryside in shadow and leaving her an easy target for the man who said he'd been watching her.

Oh, he'd smiled, charmed the old ladies, and introduced himself as Chariton, one of His Majesty's loyal servants, but she trusted her perceptions. In that one phrase, she'd heard a threat.

"I've been watching you."

For how long? she'd wanted to demand. *For what reason?*

Not to court her, as the old ladies believed. He watched her because he suspected her of something.

And she knew she was guilty. She'd come to this kingdom on a mission of destruction, and even though she had objected to Dom's plans, she had complied with them. She was helping bring chaos and anarchy to Bertinierre.

Slowing, she listened again.

Nothing. She heard nothing, but the hair on the back of her head lifted. Chariton lurked out there, skulking along the road, hiding in an olive orchard, sitting among the rocks draped in ground fog. *Watching her*.

He had followed her for the rest of the day, being *charming*. Charming to her. Charming to Ruby. All the time Brat's wariness had grown.

She could fight better than most women. It was just that, since the rape, the sight of a sinister man froze her into immobility for a few crucial seconds, and in that amount of time a battle could be lost.

Moreover, she held Ruby. She adjusted the baby in her arms. She'd fight for Ruby, but what a hindrance she would be.

Not that she thought this Chariton would harm a child. He didn't look the type. He had none of the cold-blooded killer about him. The truth was almost worse. His eyes, when he gazed at her, were warm and . . . interested. Like . . . if he wasn't stalking her to discover her secrets, he would be courting her.

That frightened her all the more.

He did look the type who would fight for his homeland, and skillfully, too. She'd barely managed to shake him before starting home.

Damn, what was she going to do?

Her hut came into sight, low, small, and oh so

safe. If she could just get inside, nothing could harm her. She'd made sure of that.

She crossed the bridge over the ravine, placing each foot prudently. None of her traps had been disturbed, and the road behind her remained quiet and still.

Standing at the door, she swept a glance around.

Nothing. He wasn't there. Had the whole incident been nothing but a figment of her imagination? She didn't think so, but perhaps, if she were wily, she could avoid this Chariton from now on.

Leaning her shoulder against the door, she pushed it open and stepped inside.

And as it swung shut behind her, she heard him say, "I've been waiting for you."

A guard woke Dom in the predawn hours with a message.

While sentries stood at the dungeon door, the kidnapper had been poisoned.

He was dead.

Chapter Sixteen

"Laurie."

The hand on her shoulder was gentle, the voice was her father's, yet Laurentia came out of a sound sleep with her fist swinging. King Jerome ducked out of the way before she made contact with his jaw, and she cried out an apology as soon as she saw his face lit by the flicker of the night candle at her bed, but her gesture displayed her disquiet as nothing else could have.

"Dear girl." He took her clenched hand in his. "I worried about this. You're afraid even in your sleep."

"I'm *prepared* even in my sleep." She took a few breaths, trying to calm her racing heart. "And you would have frightened anyone, Papa! What are you doing sneaking into my bedchamber at—" she squinted at the bed clock "—four-thirty in the morning?"

"I wanted to talk to you in private."

He already wore his gray riding costume. His hair was combed, his cravat knotted loosely, yet with style. He'd wakened his valet even earlier than normal to prepare himself for the day's hunt, and she knew why. She knew what he wanted to talk about. Dom had reported her abduction to the king, and if she were to do her duty, she had to think quickly, to somehow thwart her father's protective instinct. "Papa, did you come to tell me you're pleased with me?" she asked quickly.

He frowned, covering his bafflement with gruff courtesy. "Always, my dear. But for what reason am I to be pleased with you now?"

His confusion gave her hope of outwitting him. "I escaped that kidnapper all by myself. I told you I think well when cornered."

"Yes." He knew what she was doing now, but still he couldn't hide his pride. "I'm very pleased with your quick thinking. But Laurie, you are a sensible girl, and you know today can't go as planned."

So first he would try to put her in her place, use his influence as his elder. But she knew how to answer that. "I'm not a girl, I'm a woman. A woman of quite advanced years, you know." She pulled a droll face. "I'm so old, Papa. Twenty-five is a great age."

"Don't be foolish, my dear. *Sixty* is a great age, and six decades bring a vast amount of wisdom, which I must apply in this case. I would have to be a fool to let you go to the cottage today after two kidnapping attempts."

"I've had other birthdays, Papa, with gifts that will help me survive. Don't you remember the year Beaumont died? You gave me a pistol, and I keep it well-oiled, loaded, and I practice with it."

"Neither a pistol nor quick thinking is a match for an armed force whose orders are to carry you away."

"Do you know of such a force in Bertinierre?" she asked, wondering if he had more than warnings to impart.

"No, but I—"

She relaxed. "I've heard you say it yourself. An armed force could not hide in Bertinierre for long. We're too small and too well-populated. This adversary who tried to take me deals in stealth and deception, and Dom and I disarmed them."

He pulled at one corner of his mustache as he always did when uneasy. "I hope so, but I suspect I know our villain, and he is not easily deterred. Our relations with King Humphrey of Pollardine have not been cordial for many years."

"Humphrey?" She searched her mind for what she had been told of neighboring Pollardine's king, and found none of it flattering. "I thought he was an idiot."

"He is. If not for his wife's skills at ruling Pollardine would surely have succumbed to a revolution, for Humphrey is a man without intelligence or skill. A man easily guided by others." Gingerly, he seated himself on her bed. He had an expression on his face she saw seldom and wished never to see at all; the look of a man who had to admit to a mistake. "Unfortunately, it is the man who guides him who is my enemy."

She replied stupidly; she knew it, yet she couldn't fathom this kind of animosity. Not toward her beloved father. "You don't have enemies."

He tapped her cheek. "A king has enemies. But this hatred is personal. Marcel de Emmerich was once a friend."

"Marcel de Emmerich." She'd overheard his name one time in a conversation between King Jerome and Chariton. "Isn't he a noble of some kind?"

"Humphrey conferred a title on him, yes. Some would say he even deserves it, for he is the son of one of my own barons, the son of an ancient line, albeit an impoverished one. His father put his son in service to me while I was in the cradle. Marcel and I grew up together, friends I thought. Until we were seventeen. Then I found him selling his services, trying to influence me for a price—" King Jerome's voice rose. "—That wasn't friendship. He was a leech, and since I was young and tactless—"

"And hurt."

"Yes, that too. So I told him so."

"I sense this might be one of those circumstances in which honesty was not wise."

King Jerome's voice quieted again. "He has hated me since that day. He left, I didn't know where and didn't care. Then seven years ago I saw him at that diplomatic meeting between me and Humphrey, and he was standing at Humphrey's shoulder and smiling. I knew then . . . I tried to warn Humphrey, but that was another mistake, a bigger mistake, for Humphrey *is* a fool. Maybe all kings are fools when it comes to reading character."

She smiled at her father, trying to comfort and admonish him at the same time. "I don't think kings are bad readers of character so much as I think that for kings, one bad reading carries disastrous consequences."

"A royal curse." He touched her cheek.

She nodded, well aware of the repercussions her

own mistakes had caused. Yet still she was determined, and she said gently, "Papa, I'll be all right."

"Dear, I would rather lose my entire kingdom than allow you to be harmed."

"Isn't such sentimentality against the rules of kingship?"

"I didn't say I would give Bertinierre away, Laurie. I will fight for it, too, you know that. You know all about the precautions I have taken."

"Yes." Yes, she knew all about his plans. Should war or insurrection ever occur in this land of theirs, King Jerome had his plans in place—plans in which she had a function. She had a function today, too, one she would not easily give up. "In the last five years, Papa, I have come to understand duty and honor in a way I never understood it before. Before my marriage, I thought my only important task would be to produce an heir for Bertinierre. As it was slowly borne in on me how impossible that was, I realized I had to serve some function in my kingdom, and when you trusted me to go into the mountains and meet the messenger from Sereminia, I felt . . . blessed."

His voice rose in royal protest. "But—"

Her voice rose above his. "No *buts*. This task means more to Bertinierre than any other duty I perform. It gives me substance. It makes me whole. If I never launch another ship or give another speech, even if I never produce an heir or become queen, I know I have brought wealth into Bertinierre that helped us to remain independent."

King Jerome rubbed his forehead fretfully. "I'll pull Chariton back from his sleuthing."

"Yesterday he said he had a lead about the kidnapping, and he disappeared. Do you even know where he is?"

"Then someone else can go meet the messenger and perform the exchange."

"No one suspects me."

"Someone else for this year only."

"You've impressed upon me the importance of letting no one know, and Papa, the messenger brings so much gold. There is no one else you can possibly trust."

"Then the messenger from Sereminia can wait." He held up his hand when she would have protested again. "*Everyone* in Sereminia knows you *always* go on a retreat on the day after your birthday. The suitors probably don't expect it, but the kidnappers will be watching. They'll be waiting."

So the time had come. The time had come to make her decision, and only a coward would vacillate now. Taking a careful breath to steady her voice, she said, "Much as I hate to admit it, you were right about Dom. He's a good bodyguard. He saved me yesterday." The lace on her sleeve drooped over her shaking fingers as she pushed loose tendrils of hair out of her face. "If I took him with me, would that ease your mind?"

King Jerome studied her as if he sensed a hidden motive. "You trust him that much?"

She thought about the first night out on the terrace, how she'd liked Dom, yet sensed depths which she dared not name. Something about his man called to the wildness in her, and she had to respond or spend the rest of her life wondering . . . "Yes, Papa. I trust him that much."

Hastily, the spy stepped away from the door and hurried down the corridor. At last, a break in the mystery of Bertinierre's fortunes. The princess's annual retreat on her birthday was not simply the little darling's escape from the so-called pressures of her life. Laurentia went to her mountain home to exchange goods for money. What kind of goods remained to be seen—but with the place and the time known, that information would be easy to discover.

The spy smiled, a rare, genuine smile that appeared to startle Dominic of Sereminia as he hurried toward the dungeons.

Let him go to investigate the death of that lump of a kidnapper. The spy had another death to arrange.

The messenger would not be returning to Sereminia.

"Good morning, Your Highness." Weltrude threw back the curtains to allow the early light to trickle into Laurentia's bedchamber. "It's five-thirty. You must rise if you're going to take part in the hunt."

Laurentia smothered a grin in her ruffle-edged pillow. As if her father or the guests would leave without her. But Weltrude had drummed an irrefutable principle into her; a princess never took advantage of her royal privileges. Laurentia agreed, although for different reasons than Weltrude. Laurentia thought the people forced to defer to her should never have to endure anything less than kindness, punctuality and good manners from their princess.

Weltrude thought anything less than perfection tarnished the royal family's patina of glory.

Two different philosophies. Same results.

As Laurentia stirred, pretending to be just wakened, Weltrude gave her instructions to the lesser maids. "Today, Her Highness will wear the dark blue brocade riding outfit with her veiled blue hat and her black leather gloves."

Laurentia normally allowed herself to be guided by Weltrude, for her chief lady-in-waiting's taste could not be faulted. But Laurentia had plans, and they didn't include Weltrude's rigid code of conduct or a conservative blue riding outfit. "Today," Laurentia announced as she sat up in bed, "I will wear the brown velvet riding costume."

At the challenge to Weltrude's authority, one of lesser maids gasped. The other two giggled with delight and hustled toward the capacious closet in Laurentia's bedchamber.

Impassive as always, Weltrude in no way indicated astonishment or displeasure, but moved closer to the bed. In a low voice, she said, "Your Highness, perhaps you don't recall. The brown velvet riding costume did not turn out as the tailor promised. It is less than modest."

Laurentia plucked at her lower lip thoughtfully. "I seem to remember it covers all my flesh, and I definitely remember how very much I adore the material. I'll try it on, at least."

Weltrude smiled one of her reproving smiles. "You don't have time to model everything in your closet."

Usually, Laurentia remembered that Weltrude had guided her through adolescence, and she allowed Weltrude her liberties. Today, she remembered that she was twenty-five, a widow, and more pathetically, a virgin. She had to change that. She had no time to waste. And although she seldom wielded her authority like a sledgehammer, that did not mean she didn't know how. As she slid out of bed, she said, "Then I shall wear the brown velvet riding costume."

She meant to ignore Weltrude's civilized outrage, but something, some movement on Weltrude's part, perhaps, made her look.

There was nothing civilized about Weltrude's outrage. For only one moment, the mask created by wig, rouge and gentility fell, and Laurentia saw only too clearly a vast hidden reservoir of fury.

Then Weltrude's emotion shimmered, softened, became an intense distaste apparently directed at herself. "Of course, Your Highness. Forgive my impertinence. Sometimes I forget that you are not only my former pupil, as it were, but also the princess of Bertinierre."

Feeling oddly disorientated, Laurentia nodded her forgiveness. She knew how very seriously Weltrude took the privileges of royalty, and how seriously she would take her own lapse of respect. Yet . . . yet . . .

Weltrude took the brown velvet riding costume from the two maids. "Here it is, Your Highness. Try it on and see what you think. The hunt will, of course, wait for you."

"Yes." Laurentia hesitated just a little. Just enough. "Yes, I'm sure they will, but . . ."

"Is there a problem, Your Highness?"

"I would be embarrassed to leave them waiting." Shamelessly, Laurentia used Weltrude's sense of duty to get rid of her. "Would you perhaps direct that they be given a cup of warmed spiced wine before we ride? It would give me extra time, should I need it, to prepare."

Weltrude straightened to military readiness. "I will go and supervise the preparation myself."

"That would be excellent," Laurentia said. "You would cover for me, as you have done so many times in the past, and the guests would be pleasured by your wine."

"Yes." Given direction, Weltrude marched to the door. But before she exited, she doubtfully looked back at the maids.

"You have trained them well," Laurentia assured her. "My toilette is in good hands."

Weltrude nodded decisively.

Laurentia waited for a full minute past the time when the latch had clicked before she swung into motion.

Chapter Seventeen

When Laurentia stepped into the stable yard, teeming with suitors and guests dressed for the hunt, the talking stopped for one very telling moment. She saw a flash as Mr. Sharparrow lifted his ringed hands to his chest. She saw Weltrude turn her head away as if mortified. She saw King Jerome lifted his eyebrows in astonishment. Then the din began again with rising excitement. She smiled, hoping no one could see how tightly she clenched her teeth as exultation and nervousness fought for supremacy. If only she could see Dom, gauge his response, be sure she had initiated a sound strategy.

Instead she saw Dulcie, and Dulcie's kohl-lined eyes widened.

As they should. The riding habit wrapped Laurentia from shoulders to ankles, gloves covered her hands, a saucy squared hat rested atop her head, heeled brown leather boots rose almost to her knees. No flesh could be seen, yet just as Weltrude had feared, the rich velvet which covered her so well also traced her bosom, her waist, her hips. The material shivered with each movement, catching the sunlight and reflecting it in slivers of sensuality.

Most important was what she wore beneath—or rather, what she did not wear beneath. Her chemise was of the finest, thinnest cotton, soft against her skin, protecting her from the seams of the riding jacket. Her skirt was tight enough to restrict freedom and the use of undergarments, and yet the material was thick enough no one could ever notice she wore no petticoat and no drawers. And the shirtwaist that provided modest coverage beneath the jacket all the way up to her neck . . . was draped over a chair in her dressing chamber.

Second thoughts? She had nothing but second thoughts, until Dulcie gave a wildly inappropriate, far too obvious gesture of approval. Francis saw it, saw her, and his round and scandalized gaze would have done a priest proud. When he started toward her, his mouth pinched and condemnation radiating from him, Dulcie put her hand in the middle of his back and shoved him right into a horse trough.

The splash brought a roar of laughter from the suitors who still considered Francis serious competition. Dulcie grinned smugly and backed away from the wet and glowering man who rose from the trough. He didn't even glance at Laurentia, but stalked toward Dulcie.

King Jerome spoke close to Laurentia's ear. "I hadn't realized it before, but those two . . ."

Laurentia turned to him and saw him smiling as he watched Francis and Dulcie. "Those two . . . what?" When he didn't answer, she looked back to see Francis place his wet hands on Dulcie's shoulders and shake her. That wasn't the stiff, formal Francis Laurentia knew, and the way Dulcie thrust her chin at him and grinned defiantly might mean—

Dom stepped onto the palace's terrace, and Laurentia forgot Francis, forgot Dulcie, and stared.

She didn't care that Dulcie thought the other suitors were more attractive. Only Dom was mouthwateringly handsome. He stood above them, one hand on the railing, one hand on his hip. One foot rested on the step, the other on the terrace floor. His black hair was bare, the wings of premature white catching the light. Sun and shadow sculpted his harsh face and too clearly showed the knife wound he'd acquired in her defense. His black riding gear hugged his form as sweetly as a maiden. Shoulders like his resulted only from hard labor, and in her world of aristocrats and fops, those shoulders happened only too seldom. Behind him the white palace glowed like a nimbus around his slash of dark sexuality.

His narrowed gaze swept the crowd. It lingered, observing, weighing, seeing more than normal men, she thought, and when his gaze found her, she stopped breathing for one long moment. Could this beautiful man know what she had planned? When he looked at her, did he see a wanton begging for attention? Could he read her secrets, delve her soul . . . or was he truly like Beaumont, concerned only with himself?

He didn't smile as he stared, but gradually warmth began to curl in her belly and heat to flare in her cheeks.

He wanted her. Life had taught her how easily she could misread another, but about this she was sure. He wanted her.

"Papa," she whispered, "it's time to ride."

"Yes, I suppose it is." King Jerome pulled on his riding gloves and spoke in a low tone. "You promise you will keep Dominic at your side?"

"Yes, Papa."

"You'll be wary? If there's any sign of danger, you'll retreat at once?"

"I promise, Papa."

He smoothed his mustache. "I shouldn't allow you to do this, you know."

"You trust me, and rightly." Dom was descending the stairs, his gaze still fixed on her, and she didn't want to speak to him yet. Not with everyone in the stable yard looking on. "Now, Your Majesty, go and lead the hunt, and keep the riders challenged so that they don't watch me!"

"I'll keep them challenged." Like Laurentia, King Jerome was a natural horseman, and he knew how to compel his courtiers' attention. No one would mutter, at the end of the day, that they could have gone farther and faster with a younger man in the lead. Before he strode toward the mounting block, he added, "And by the way, my dear—you look smashing."

Dom was watching her, Laurentia knew. All around them the hunt thundered through the woods. Dogs barked, closing on the scent of a deer. Suitors, ladies, and courtiers spread across the land for miles, riding hard after the hounds. Meadows gave way to brush, brush gave way to timber. Far ahead, her father King Jerome led the hunt, galloping with grace and determination.

Dom's gaze singed her as it had all morning. He observed as she swerved right, toward the center of the pack, then he followed with more caution and less speed. She imagined the man was trying to decipher her mood, trying to decide what had caused her transformation from a resentful lady to a woman demonstrating . . . interest.

She wanted to tell him, *Dulcie persuaded me.*

But that would be an abdication of responsibility, and Weltrude would not approve.

More likely, she, Laurentia, had been ready to change. Suffering from ennui, ready for something besides duty, influenced by her father's hopes, impatient with Francis's stodginess, jolted by her first sight of Dom, infuriated by the lesson he'd decided to teach her with the false kidnapping . . .

Yes, that was it. Dom had auditioned well, and with his kisses she had experienced a jolt of exhilaration such as she hadn't felt since the day she'd married Beaumont. Since the moment she'd discovered that the spoiled little princess couldn't have everything her own way, and that passion, like honor, carried a price.

As the pack of riders neared the cutoff, the trail narrowed. A cliff rose on her right side, ground dropped away on the left. The shouts of the riders quieted at they concentrated on guiding their horses through the narrow flats. Dulcie and Francis jostled for position, each trying to outride the other, locked in eternal competition.

Riding with seeming random carelessness, Laurentia urged Sterling toward the edge of the pack.

Actually, she positioned Mr. Sharparrow between her and Dom, effectively blocking Dom's view, and when she had the Englishman's attention, she smiled at him.

He checked in surprise, and she surged ahead, cutting around one of her huntsmen and off to the right as soon as the cliff dropped away. At once she slowed Sterling, turning him to face the galloping pack of hunters and bring him to a halt behind a tree.

Mr. Sharparrow rode past, looking frantically around, but her brown velvet riding costume matched her brown velvet gelding and helped her blend into the granite cliff. The other riders continued on their way, hallooing and laughing. She caught a glimpse of Dom, too, as he rode past, his gaze intent and narrowed.

He'd be back. He was an intelligent man. When he realized she had vanished, he would reconstruct her actions and remember the cliff. He'd curse her and come for her, and once more he'd be angry that she had not kept him informed of her intentions.

She smiled. The fingertips inside her riding gloves tingled, and excitement curled in her loins.

Yes, he'd be angry and she had no doubt she was a fool for inciting him. Yet she wanted to prove her competence in at least one arena, and a princess learned early to evade her entourage. It was the only way she ever had privacy, and in recent years it had proved to be a practical skill.

More than that, some stubbornness inside her refused to let him have his way about everything. With a man like Dom, if she didn't establish her independence immediately, he would run roughshod over her for the rest of her life.

For the rest of her life. The phrase echoed uneasily in her mind, and as the sounds of the hunt faded in the distance, she avoided the thought with action, turning Sterling toward a cleft in the rocks and urging him forward.

Only three paths led to her cottage. She alternated routes to avoid obvious signs of use, yet without hesitation she guided Sterling between the two boulders behind her. The path took an abrupt upward swing, but Sterling had been chosen for more than speed. He had also, time and again, confirmed his deft footwork and patient nature as he carried her to the rendezvous that had dominated her life these last five years.

She concentrated as the trail narrowed and steepened still more, but when it smoothed out she could think again, and irresistibly her mind returned to Dom. To Dom, to the course she was pursuing, and to her own expectations.

For the rest of her life. What was it she expected from this unlikely mercenary? Mating, marriage, a family? A helpmate, a lover? A life as normal as was possible for a princess and the heir to the throne? Was that what she wanted?

"Yes." She whispered the word to the wind. "Yes, Dominic is what I want."

Why him?

The real reason? Dom himself. He was handsome, alarmingly handsome, so handsome she still fought the urge to flee. She'd learned her lesson well. Handsome men were cold.

Yet his air of danger, while alternately frightening and attracting her, also reassured her. This man cared passionately about . . . about what? She didn't know, she wanted to find out, but the way he moved, the slice of his gaze, the grace of his gestures proved he hated, he loved, he *felt*. The coldness that afflicted Beaumont would never afflict Dom, and that was what she wanted. A man who experienced life, its joys and sorrows, its hatreds and its . . . loves.

Dom desired her. She'd seen the proof in his body, braved the thrill of his kisses. And she wanted to feel, too, as passionately and as intensely as he did. He could teach her. She had no doubt about that.

Most important, after yesterday's rescue, she trusted him.

Far away, the huntsmen sounded their horns, signifying the end of the chase.

Yes, Dom would be along soon, furious that she had evaded him, and heaven only knew what he would do to her as vengeance. As she remembered yesterday's kiss, her skin flushed from the inside out.

Dom . . . She fingered the soft, white silk fichu she wore draped around her neck and tucked into the low cut of her button-front jacket.

The path climbed again, winding around pitted boulders the size and shape of haystacks. Pine peppered each breath of air, so fresh and sharp it almost hurt her lungs. Sterling kicked up small puffs of dust, and she heard the trickle of water from the brook near her cottage. Stopping, she allowed

Sterling to drink, and when he had finished he raised his head and pricked up his ears.

From behind her she heard the faint and steady clop of a horse's hooves.

Dom had found her.

It was time to put all Dulcie's immoral advice into action.

Laurentia's heart pounded, and her knees shook so hard Dom might have been chasing her on foot through the wilderness, rather than this civilized pursuit through the woods only two hours from the palace. Her imagination tossed forth pictures of her running, of him after her, catching her, pulling her to the ground . . .

The trouble was, he filled the role of ruthless hunter only too well.

She touched the silk fichu at her neck again, and swallowed. Maybe this provocation from a virgin widow had not been so wise.

She was sure Dom made the sounds she heard; in the short time she'd known him, he'd honed her instincts about him. Yet she well remembered the abduction attempt. Stripping off her riding gloves, she stuck them in one of her overladen saddlebags, then fumbled for her pistol and pulled it free.

By urging Sterling to quicken his gait, she arrived at the cottage before Dom. She barely glanced at the building, knowing she would see the small, neat white box of a house, the steps going up to the front door, the shutters over the windows. The messenger hadn't arrived yet, and that was good. Just as she'd planned.

Dismounting with some difficulty—the tight-fitting skirt hindered her—she slid out of the side-saddle to a jarring meeting with the ground. She tied Sterling to a branch and, pistol in hand, stepped behind the edge of the tall blackberry brambles that rose near the stables. She watched through the overhanging branches as Dom rode into sight.

His gaze noted the gelding, the cottage, the sheltering trees, and as he looked around, she looked at him.

He sat his horse easily even though they had been matched only the day before on her father's instruction; the black stallion he rode was the finest in the royal stables.

He was a man who could control a horse without reins—indeed, although Oscuro exuded an air of tempestuous savagery, Dom allowed the reins to hang negligently from his fingers.

He was a man who could control a woman, and Laurentia found herself caught between fear and excitement. She wanted this, she'd planned this, yet no woman in her right mind could face the possibility of an angry Dom without wondering about her own sanity.

At this moment, she couldn't remember why she'd deliberately lost him.

As uncertainty whirled through her mind, he spoke. "You can come out now, Your Highness." He looked straight at the blackberry bushes.

Chapter Eighteen

Laurentia didn't allow—wouldn't *allow*—her uncertainty to show as she stepped into sight. Keeping Dulcie's instructions in mind, she smiled enticingly at Dom. "I knew you would find me."

"Always." He grinned back at her, but she would never call that stretching of lips over teeth mirthful. "Never think I won't."

He *was* angry. She had known he would be. She had thought she was ready to face him, but her mouth dried and her smile wavered as he swung out of the saddle.

Rather than move toward her, he walked to his mount's head, his slight limp in evidence, and she hated the relief that swept through her. Calming the tremble in her lips, she acted as if he were an invited guest and she a proper hostess. "There are no servants here. We have to care for our own horses."

"Of course." His gaze rested on the pistol still clasped in her hand. "Still not stupid, I see."

"Never." She hoped.

Grasping the leading rein, he looked again at the cottage. "Where is *here*?"

"*Here* is my personal refuge." She walked right

past Dom, acting as if she were confident he would not grab her. He didn't, but he watched her, his gaze oppressive with heat and laden with the promise of retribution. "Papa had it built for my mother. After my . . . after Beaumont died, he thought I might need a place to go where I could have privacy." Replacing the pistol in the saddlebag, she untied Sterling and led him toward the stable.

Dom followed. "Why would a princess want privacy?"

She hesitated, but it was too soon to tell him all the truth. She had learned discretion at a hard school. Lightly she said, "Here I can scratch wherever it itches."

"Ah, yes." Unwilling amusement shaded his voice. "That evening on the terrace, I seem to remember a fair amount of envy that men could scratch as they pleased."

"Oh." Did he have to remind her of how inane she had been two days ago? "I did say that."

"You said quite a lot for such a reticent princess as you have proved to be."

His voice sounded close, and she turned to find him moving past her, toward the closed stable. He lifted the bar from its brackets and laid it aside, then swung the doors wide. Musty air rushed out, but immediately Laurentia moved to guide Sterling inside; the shadows in the dim stable would protect her from Dom's incisive gaze.

As she passed him, he caught her fingers in his, and her gaze flew to his. "Is it only in the darkness you speak your heart?"

"Yes." Her throat seemed suddenly too small,

constricted by alarm, and she cleared it, all the while thinking, *He's holding my hand*. And then, as his thumb stoked the remarkably sensitive center of her palm, *He's caressing me.* "Yes, it must be the dark."

Bending from the waist, he placed his lips on the backs of her fingers. Just placed his lips there for one long moment. It wasn't a kiss; she'd had her hand kissed many times. This was more of a savoring, an appetizer before the first course.

Then his lips moved, opened, tasted her middle finger in gourmet delight. His eyes fanned shut, his lashes shadowed the faint circles beneath. A lock of hair fell over his forehead, and this tableau, played out in a stable doorway on the top of a mountain, should have seemed ridiculous.

Instead the romance of it brought tears to her eyes.

His lips, his tongue, slowly slid toward her fingertip. His mouth wrapped around it. He turned her hand and slowly stood, sipping her flesh as if it were intoxicating brandy.

"Dom," she said faintly. "I don't think . . ."

And he nipped. One small, stinging bite.

She snatched her hand away. She cradled it in the other, staring at him and wondering if he were a maniac to bite her . . . and if she were mad to feel a quiver of excitement.

He smiled at her, all promise and enticement, and, as if nothing untoward had happened, said, "It's dark in the stable."

She had no idea what he was talking about. Right now, she could scarcely remember her name.

He returned to Oscuro with a loose-limbed gait

that held her gaze. "You can talk to me in there. You can tell me what you like."

As he led Oscuro around her, the significance of his words broke through her trance. Impetuously she followed him inside. "No." She wailed just a little, and she hated that.

She hated it more when Dom said, "You forgot your horse."

Sterling was a sensible beast, and when she turned to get him she found him right on her heels. "I didn't." She grasped his reins.

"So I see." Dom hummed a little as he opened the door to one of the two stalls and led Oscuro inside. "Is there straw?"

"In the loft." She untied the bow at her chin, pulled her hat off, and hung it on a nail.

"Do you want to go up and pitch it down, or shall I?"

"You do it. My skirt is too tight." She pushed Sterling into the remaining stall and pulled off all four saddlebags. Grimacing with the effort, she tossed them, one by one, out into the aisle.

"Who usually does it?"

"I do." She unbuckled the flank cinch on the saddle.

Dom leaned his arms over the wooden wall between the stalls and in a tone of disbelief said, "You really come here by yourself."

"Yes."

"And His Majesty doesn't object?"

She grasped the heavy saddle in both her hands and, with a grunt, lifted it down. "I would never do anything to cause His Majesty undue worry."

Dom mulled that over. "So he objects, but not enough to coerce you."

There was more to this retreat than her own selfish desire for solitude, so she said nothing as she dragged the heavy saddle over to the low wooden stand. She hefted the saddle up. The stand teetered on uneven legs; boards and nails were an enigma to her, but she'd built it herself, for herself, and she was proud of her work.

He said nothing. He only watched, his face and form in shadow. What he thought of Bertinierre's princess grooming her own horse, she couldn't imagine. She didn't even know if he believed her, and thought perhaps he scrutinized her to gauge her expertise. But she did know she would rather he question her about the cottage and her activities here than about *what she liked.*

When the silence had become oppressive, he said, "His Majesty lets you have your head. But with a kidnapper on the loose?"

She clipped off the words. "He trusts me to take care of myself."

"That little popgun's not going to do you a lot of good against a gang of kidnappers."

"I have you."

She could have bitten out her tongue when he said, "So you do."

Seeing him still draped over the wall, she asked tartly, "Do you want me to unsaddle *your* horse, too?"

He laughed appreciatively. "Little witch." He disappeared back into the stall, and a moment later his riding jacket was tossed over a post.

That meant he was in his shirtsleeves. That meant only fine white cotton covered the shoulders she so admired. Unwillingly she waited motionless, waiting to see if other pieces of clothing were removed and hung over the post. The shirt, or perhaps his trousers.

She closed her eyes. She had to gain authority over her watercolor fantasies. They had dominated her thoughts far too much, and a woman could live on daydreams only so long. Someday the outlines had to be filled in with bold brushstrokes of reality.

Controlling her nomadic thoughts proved impossible when Dom was climbing the upright ladder to the hayloft. Her eyes had adjusted to the dimness only too well, and she observed him with a salivating gratification.

Did he know how his slight state of undress affected her? Of course not. Not even Dom could imagine that the princess of Bertinierre would paint flights of fancy around his muscled thighs and broad shoulders. She wondered about the exact color of the skin on those shoulders, longed to see the muscles of his thighs flex, and whether—she took a hard breath—whether Dulcie had been lying when she'd described the mighty expansion that occurred in the male organ.

Laurentia's own wickedness amazed her, for as Weltrude had told her many times, good women did not speculate about proper gentlemen in any physical sense. By that, Weltrude unquestionably meant that Laurentia should not imagine Dom in a total state of undress. But Dom was not proper, not a gentleman, and Laurentia, sadly, did not fit Weltrude's definition of good.

A shower of straw interrupted her reverie, and with gritty determination, she walked to the window on the opposite wall and struggled with the catch on the shutters. When at last she opened them, she stood in the breeze and waited for it to cool her.

Only she couldn't wait that long. Dom would be down when he finished, and after all she had said she wouldn't have him think the pampered princess expected him to do all the work. She did do the labor here, no one else, and she would not have him doubt that.

Turning away from the window, she shoveled grain out of a feed bin into the trough. Gathering the grooming brushes and pick, she went to Sterling and spoke to him, removed his bridle, and picked his hooves. Dragging her stool over, she stepped up and with firm strokes of the currycomb began the job of grooming the massive horse.

She heard Dom descending the ladder. He tossed bedding in Sterling's stall, then in Oscuro's, and left a mound in the back corner. "For later," he said.

She glanced at him occasionally, observing his expertise with a pitchfork, wondering if there was anything he didn't do well, then blushed at her own audacious speculation.

Reality had begun for her. She herself had set it in motion. This intimacy was what she wanted, and nothing could stop her now—not even her own maidenly indecision.

When he finished with the hay, he moved back into Oscuro's stall and out of her sight, but she listened as he removed the saddle, gathered the spare brushes, and began to groom his horse with the same care he would use—

No. She wouldn't think of that now.

The circular curry motion, the repetitious brushing, and the companionable silence relaxed her as surely as it did Sterling. She finished Sterling's head and neck, and moved the stool to work on his back. At last she stepped down on the packed ground and groomed his flanks. In the other stall, Dom performed the same labors. She suspected he would finish first. He had, after all, the advantage of both height and experience.

Apparently the labor gave Dom pleasure, too, for he started to hum, first tunelessly, then a new waltz she had never heard before.

"Who wrote that?" she asked, not realizing what the contentment in her voice revealed.

"Johann Strauss. It was all the rage when we were in Vienna."

Curiosity and an absurd kind of jealousy sank their twin fangs into her mind. "We?"

"My pack. My mercenaries."

That surprised her. Dom had mentioned his pack before, but he had such an air of an outcast about him, she had forgotten. "What happened to them?" she asked.

"They're dead."

"Oh." She didn't think Dom truly felt nothing, only that he refused to reveal himself to her.

She understood. People who had been betrayed too often were cautious. In the end, it would be easier to bare her body to him than to bare her mind.

Yet if all they were to each other was two bodies, she might as well have chosen Francis.

In a cheerful tone that had even Sterling pricking up his ears, she plunged into speech. "I'd love to hear about your mercenary adventures, but first I think you'd like to hear about me, and I don't object." *Much.* "What is it you want to know?"

She waited, half-cringing, for him to ask her what she liked.

Instead he asked, "Are you done?"

After a last few strokes down Sterling's legs, she tossed her brushes onto the shelf. "I am." Sterling was dry, clean and contented, and she experienced the gratification she felt when she performed a labor to her own satisfaction.

"Aren't you warm?"

She paused, half-standing, totally astonished. "What?"

He'd draped his arms over the wall again. They were bare, his shirtsleeves rolled up to his elbows, and she noted the dark hair that covered his muscled forearms and the scars that broke the tanned skin with their irregular patterns of white.

He fixed his gaze on her. "This is hard work, and you're all trussed up like a mercenary's pilfered chicken. You have to be warm."

Gradually she straightened to her full height, which in this instance wasn't nearly high enough.

While she'd been busy, she hadn't been aware of the heat, but now that he was looking at her, she was more than warm. She was hot.

She was also the princess, unused to personal comments and unsure how to deal with them. And she was almost sure this comment went beyond personal, and into familiar.

Which was what she sought, she assured herself. Familiarity, and in more than words.

She looked at him, right into his eyes. "I *am* warm."

He smiled at her, a practiced smile. "Come here and let me help you."

She didn't like that smile, with its smug dimples and suave appeal. He must have used it in hundreds of seductions. But she didn't think she should complain. Didn't know how to tell him she wanted him to be sincere, even if he had to pretend. So she walked out of Sterling's stall and met Dom in the aisle.

The sun stood directly overhead, the whole mountain stilled to receive its blessing. The horses were comfortable, chewing their grain. The shadowed stable was a world of its own; its silence hung heavily in the air as the princess and the mercenary stared at each other.

Laurentia discovered something right away. When they stood this close, it didn't matter that Dom smiled like a magician performing a card trick; her heart still thumped and her breasts rose and fell in quick little breaths.

"This scarf is very pretty." He touched the fichu with one large finger. "But you can do without it. Let's take it off, shall we?"

She nodded, giving permission.

This was all right. He was half-undressed, too, with his shirttails pulled from his trousers and his collar gone. He'd loosened the tie at the neck, and in the vee below she could see a thatch of chest hair, dark and dense, but no matter how hard she stared, she couldn't tell if it descended down his stomach.

And she shouldn't be staring quite so openly. She jerked her gaze to his face to find him smiling with genuine amusement, but loaded for seduction.

His hands, square, strong, capable, reached for the silk. She kept her gaze on his face as he slowly pulled one end from the neckline of the jacket. His eyes narrowed as the bare skin of her upper breast appeared.

His practiced smile didn't survive the shock. His cheeks went slack. She saw him swallow. He paused and then, in a flurry, unwrapped the length of silk from around her neck. The jacket was cut almost to her nipples, and the tight cut pushed her bosom up and out. Her chest and her shoulders were bared to his gaze, with only the barest frill of lace showing above her jacket.

Dom didn't move; his hands stilled. He stared without finesse, without a sign of the skilled debaucher. The breath he took was rough and deep. The fichu fluttered to the floor. "Woman, what do you have under that riding habit?"

She'd rattled him, and she couldn't keep the triumph out of her voice when she said, "As little as possible."

Lifting one hand to cup her chin, he looked into her eyes, and said slowly, "You don't even realize what you've done."

Abruptly his fingers tightened, his free arm snaked around her waist, and he pulled her against him, up onto her toes. He held her face still for his kiss, a kiss without subtlety, without restraint. Yes, the seducer was gone. The man who held her was the mercenary, ferocious and untamed.

He was the man she wanted.

He opened her mouth with his, ravished her with his tongue, moved his hips against her.

She let him, urged him, soaked in the impressions of heat, of passion, of a man beyond control. Dimly she thought Dulcie was right; the organ he pressed against her was much larger than it had been. She'd looked too many times to be deluded. He wanted to put it in her, too. He made that clear when he pressed his hand against her bottom, probing between her legs, restrained by the tightness of her skirt.

Tearing his mouth from her, he said, "Damn it!" with such feeling she felt his frustration through to her bones. Still holding her, he backed her toward some unspecified goal. When her soles slipped, he tipped her over his arm.

She sank into the pile of straw, and he sank on top of her. He was heavier than she expected, *more* than she expected, surrounding her with his scent, his weight, his size. Her hands scrabbled on his chest, slid up to his shoulders . . . his shoulders. They flexed beneath her fingers, as broad and strong as she'd imagined, the muscles clearly delineated beneath the fragile material of his shirt.

He adjusted her beneath him, wrapping his legs around hers. He leaned down to her mouth, kissed her again with swift impatience. "You shouldn't have done this," he said, and with one arm he lifted her just enough for her head to fall back. Her neck and chest were exposed, and he growled like a wolf presented with a feast of soft flesh.

Yet his lips, when he laid them against her throat, were soft, open, his tongue a precursor of delight. He sucked hard on the skin, then smoothed the sting, and laughed softly, so softly. "I've marked you, Your Highness."

She didn't understand what he meant, she only knew his mouth resumed its downward trek and with each kiss and taste, she wanted more. Her nipples tightened, anticipating what he would do, how he would suckle. A low groan broke from her throat, a startling sound, a sound she'd never made before, and she half-lifted her head.

He, too, had lifted his head, and his eyes glinted. He watched her with a smile, a real smile this time. "Sing for me again, sweet princess." His free hand roamed over her rib cage, approached the soft lower reaches of her breast, caressed it with sure strokes she felt through the velvet and cotton and right through to her flesh. Nerves leaped, her head fell back again, and she groaned once more.

"Beautiful." He bent to her, but this time his mouth missed her bare skin and rested right where she wished. His breath warmed her nipple through her clothing . . . and then not through her clothing.

She dug her fingers into his shoulders and shouted, "Dom!" But his name came out in a whisper.

He'd unbuttoned her, pushed away the soft lace and thin cotton of her chemise, and now he tormented her. The barbarous kisses he had crushed to her mouth he now smoothed to her breast. He didn't care that no man had ever touched her there. He offered her no quarter. He sucked at her nipple, bringing it to a peak. His teeth skimmed her skin, a threat and a promise.

Agony. This was agony,

She was tense, she was ready, she was surging beneath his body, frantically gripping his hair between her fingers, trying to get away, trying to get closer . . .

He moved off her onto his side. His hand slid down to smooth the mound between her legs. The pressure he put there felt right, added another brushstroke to the reality of lovemaking, made her writhe, and she moaned in soft, short, continuous bursts. Now he tried to separate her legs, but the tight skirt she'd been daring enough to wear thwarted him again. He swore savagely. She almost wept with frustration.

He slid his fingers into her hair, plucking pins free and tossing them away. He held her head still, looking at her so intently she was forced to open her eyes and look back at him.

"Wear all your clothes from now on," he commanded. "Don't leave anything off."

"Is that what you really want?"

"No." He examined her bare chest, one breast exposed, the brown velvet crushed every place his hand had touched. "No, I want you naked, but not in a stable, not for the first time, not you." He took a breath and for one moment, the insincere smile she hated returned. "And for damn sure, not me."

Scruples. Scruples from Francis. Scruples from a

bastard mercenary. "Why do I always get a man with scruples?"

The smile disappeared. "Has this happened a lot then"—he brushed her nipple with his knuckles— "Your Highness?"

"No." In frustration, she slapped his hand away, rolled away from him and sat up. "Just with you, yesterday. Francis, I could never even get this far."

His mouth tightened in further bad temper. "Maybe no one's ever told you, Your Highness, but it's bad form to discuss your previous lovers with your new lover."

The ecstasy was fading, leaving her cranky and disgruntled, and the straw made her itch. "He was never my lover." She pulled up her chemise and set to buttoning her jacket.

"Good." Dom stroked his hand down her back, then down again, removing the straw. "If the world were just, I would be your first lover, and your last."

She froze.

He thought she'd had other lovers. Of course he did; she'd been married. Even if she hadn't been, that would have been a fair assumption. After all, she was older, and because of her position, she was poised and debonair.

The touch of his hand on her back made her shiver so, she could scarcely finish buttoning the jacket.

But she wasn't experienced, and Dulcie said there was a world of difference between a virgin's initiation and a sophisticated woman's lark. Dulcie said a woman should tell her first lover so he could ease her first time. So Laurentia ought to tell him the truth.

Purposely she wriggled around until she faced him—and found his gaze fixed on her loose hair as he combed it with his fingers. "Dom, you *will* be my first lover."

Lifting a handful of her hair, he buried his face in it. "Yes."

As he bent, he presented the shell of his ear, and she couldn't resist stroking it with her fingertips. "I want it that way."

"I want it that way, too." Somehow his mouth wandered to her cheek, and he kissed it softly. "I want it to be however you want it."

"All right, then." She liked his gentle caress after so much intensity. She liked what he said.

But somehow, somehow, she felt as if he hadn't really heard a word.

He wrapped an arm around her waist. "Since that's why you brought me here, I say we should go up to the house."

"Yes."

"And finish what we started."

"No."

He drew back, startled, but he had promised it would be however she wanted it. And—

"First, I want to talk."

Chapter Nineteen

Talk. *Just like a woman. She wanted to talk.*

While Laurentia bustled around the one-room cottage, sweeping and dusting and generally giving off housewifely sparks of satisfaction, Dom stood in the doorway, so aroused he could scarcely walk. How could he, when he couldn't take his eyes off her?

Just as she'd planned. She might as well have lit the fires of hell between his toes as stroll around, pretty as you please, with her hair dangling down her back, her eyelashes fluttering, a flirtatious little smile touching her lips—and that damned fichu gone. The slope of her chest was lovely, creamy pale skin without a freckle, but he'd seen that before just the other night. Women showed these things in a ball gown, and the princess's ball gown had been cut low enough to pleasure his gaze.

But when a woman didn't wear the correct garments beneath her clothing, a man leaped to the logical conclusion that all garments could be removed, in fact *should* be removed, and as soon as possible. Never, since the dawn of time, had a man realized a woman wore insufficient clothing and thought, *We should have a conversation.*

Talk. As she wished, he'd talk. And as soon as they were done talking, he'd take her hand, lead her to that bare rope bed built into the corner, and love her until *she* couldn't walk. He braced his hand against the door frame. Sometimes in this world justice reigned. He couldn't walk before, she couldn't walk after.

She paused in the act of transferring food from her saddlebags to the cupboard against the wall. "You look so ill at ease. Why don't you sit down?"

"I'll stand." This was all his fault. He should have just swived her in the stable, but he'd fornicated in enough places to know his lousy pile of straw wasn't thick and well stacked enough to protect her royal behind during the crucial moments. And women got funny about things like straw sticking them in the back. Of course, he could have put her on top, but he got funny about straw sticking him in the back, too.

More important—the first time with Laurentia, by God, he would be on top. Usually it didn't matter, but this time it did. Oh, yes, this time it did.

So in the stable he'd been a gentleman and called a halt, and this was his reward. She wanted to *talk.*

She stepped in front of him, smiling whimsically. "You can come in. You don't have to hang around the door like some dog I'm going to kick."

She took his hand between both her own, holding it, raising it to her mouth, kissing it, a soft, affectionate peck on the back of his knuckles. A gesture that looked so natural coming from her, he might have been the prince and she the bastard.

"I came to the cottage just for you," she said.

For him? "Why?"

"Mostly just for you."

In his opinion, she corrected herself most unnecessarily.

"I wanted you to see what I love. To see if you love it, too."

His gaze swept around the cramped room. She'd opened the shutters all the way around, the sunlight streamed in, and he didn't see anything to love. The fireplace dominated one wall, a huge behemoth that must consume logs at a great rate. The rough, rounded rocks that rose in twin pillars beside the iron grate looked as if they had come from a riverbed. The hearth could only be called primitive, with a hook for a cooking pot and old mortar turning to gravel between the stones.

"Who chops the logs?" Dom asked, seeing hard labor ahead for him.

"Papa won't let me do that. Not when I'm up here by myself. He worries about me with an ax, and I have to admit I'm not good with sharp blades."

Appalled, Dom reversed their grip, holding her hand between both of his while trying to make her clarify herself. "You mean you tried chopping wood?"

"No."

"Good."

"I couldn't heft the ax."

It did him no good to realize she was here, safe, and relatively sound. His mind conjured up a picture of her raising an ax above her head and—

She gave a gurgle of laughter. "You look just like Papa did when I told him!"

Yes, Dom understood her father's anxiety. The

thought of Ruby dancing on her little feet toward danger horrified him, and he always wanted to keep her wrapped in cotton wool to keep her safe. Laurentia's father would feel the same way about her . . . and King Jerome would feel like the lowest of criminals when he realized he'd brought the greatest peril to her when he'd hired Dom as a bodyguard.

Yet Dom was the best man to thwart the kidnappers, whoever they were. Protection for the princess was truly appalling, and so Dom would tell King Jerome after he'd . . . betrayed them.

He looked down at Laurentia. He had never played a lover false before. Not even a royal lover.

Yet he'd never betrayed an employer before, either. His honor was at risk. Brat needed security and safety. Ruby's future was at stake. Laurentia didn't matter when compared to those three great loyalties.

And she was using him for his body, for his expertise. He had to keep that in mind.

"The chores I can't handle are taken care of by a couple loyal to my family for generations," Laurentia explained. "Minnie and Roy stock the hayloft and the woodshed—you were speaking to them yesterday, remember?"

He remembered, and now he understood why the old couple had been so free with their opinions.

"Papa closed the house when Mama died, so except for that family no one else knows I come here."

"Even if someone stumbled on the place, they wouldn't think it was a royal abode," Dom said dryly.

The bed stood in one corner, a rough wooden frame hooked to the wall and ropes looping back and forth to support a mattress. The mattress was nothing more than a large, flat, empty sack which Laurentia had dragged toward the front door. She was going to fill it with fresh straw, she had said. He had thought she was hinting that he do it; maybe she was, but he was coming to realize the princess could do it for herself. Had done it for herself many a time.

They still held hands like lovers, and Laurentia tugged him into the room. "My father made the cupboard for my mother, and she decorated it. Isn't it lovely?"

The food cupboard graced one corner, a precarious piece of furniture. Dom thought it looked as if rodents with large teeth had done its decorative carvings, but he wouldn't dream of dissolving Laurentia's delight. "It's lovely. Did His Majesty make the table, too?"

"And the chairs."

That explained a lot, like why one chair tilted on uneven legs and why, if a man put his bare elbows on the table, he would come away with splinters.

But compared to the two primitive chairs and legless seat in the middle of the floor, the table looked good. "What are those for?" He pointed.

She got a foolish grin on her face and moved to the other door, the one at the back of the house. Opening it with a flourish, she gestured him outside.

Transfixed by her smile, by the way her eyes sparkled, he walked across the wooden floor, his boots echoing. Again she gestured him out, and he obeyed, stepping onto the porch—the porch that hung over the mountainside like an aerie over an eagle's kingdom.

Twelve feet wide, as long as the cottage, shaded by an extension of the roof, the porch dug its supports into a slope that dropped rapidly away from the cottage. His breath caught in his throat as he looked into the treetops, alive with birds nesting close enough to touch. Red squirrels dashed from branch to branch. Pines creaked as they swayed stiffly in the gentle breeze.

Amazed at the wealth of beauty, he walked to the whitewashed railing and leaned out. Off to the side, the brook tumbled down a rocky bed, adding its music to birds' song, and far below, the hillside leveled out again and the stream joined another stream on its way down the mountainside. He let his gaze wander to other mountains, blue in the distance. Beyond even that, in the cleft between two mountains, to another blue, deeper and misty with eternity—the Mediterranean.

Dom took a slow, sweet breath of mountain air, almost intoxicated from a beauty that struck at the last remaining remnants of his miserable, cursed soul. He'd viewed a lot of scenes in his travels, but none of them had filled him with awe like this. No place had touched him since the day he'd been thrown out of Sereminia, but this cottage almost hummed with tranquility, with peace, with the sense that sometime, somewhere, someone had been happy here, and someone would be again.

"Do you like it?" Laurentia didn't sound tentative, but quietly proud and delighted to be showing him her domain.

"Yes." He nodded, captivated by the splendor. "I understand why you come here."

"I knew you would." Coming to him, Laurentia put her arm around his waist and laid her head on his arm, against his biceps. "It's my own personal treehouse."

His focus shifted from the distant to the immediate. She was touching him, but not in any salacious way. She leaned against him as he'd seen hundreds of women lean against their husbands, for comfort and support, to share a moment or to rest their head. The familiarity of the gesture caught him off-guard, and the man who knew just how to respond to an advance found himself unable to do anything but stand immobile.

Which apparently was just what she wanted. For a long moment, she remained tucked against him with every appearance of contentment. A contentment he could have shared, if only she were not royal, and not the object of his assignment.

Then she rubbed her head against him like a domestic cat and stepped away. "The chairs are for out here." She tucked her hands behind her and looked out into the distance. "If you like, we can sleep out here, too. It's cold in the mountains, but we have lots of blankets, and the cold keeps the midges away and the stars are beautiful . . ."

She was nervous, he realized. Nervous about suggesting such an intimacy? As if he would reject her!

But maybe someone had. Turning, he seated himself on the rail and looked at her. In the stable, she'd said he would be her first lover. He hadn't been paying a lot of attention to anything but that one breast, pretty and pink, but he remembered that.

He supposed she'd been trying to tell him she'd never found satisfaction, and his function in her existence was to provide it. He acknowledged that easily enough, but it made him wonder about her again. She really did brim with passion and exuberance, so what kind of man could have failed to hit the bull's-eye with her? "You're going to have to tell me about that husband of yours."

The excited flush faded from her cheeks. "I don't want to."

"You said you wanted to talk."

"About this." She gestured past him at the view. "And about you. I scarcely know you at all."

His enjoyment of his surroundings died a rapid death. What was it with women wanting to pry into his background? Did Laurentia think it would make her choice of him more ethical if she could pretend they were friends? "I'm not worth talking about."

Chapter Twenty

Laurentia watched him walk inside, stiff-legged like a stalking wildcat. She'd offended him. He didn't want to talk about himself. She could understand that; he was a mercenary, and contented men didn't travel that route. Only the desperate left home to fight for strangers and die in a foreign land. Still, she wanted to know. A hunger gnawed at her, a need to delve into his mysteries, to heal the wounds and soothe the anger.

Dulcet could have bedded him without knowing his name. Laurentia wanted to be part of his life.

Shaking her head at her own folly, Laurentia went back into the cottage. The mattress was gone, the back door open, and she couldn't help but be happy he'd taken that job in hand. It seemed a sign of domesticity, as if she'd taken the wildcat and had begun the process of taming him.

Drawing on her feminine instincts—she came, after all, from a long line of women—she went to work to pacify the beastly man.

She pushed the chairs outside, placing them side by side in the center of the porch. She dragged out the swing and hung it on chains that dangled from the ceiling of the porch. She gave the swing a push, imagining Dom seated there, reclaiming a bit of his childhood.

The house had been built close to the stream, and in the last place before it rumbled down the mountainside, King Jerome had commanded that a small pool be created. Pail in hand, Laurentia went outside to fill it with water, then carried it inside and scrubbed the dust off the table. She laid out dinner. Cook had packed cold chicken roasted in rosemary and garlic, crusty bread and olive oil, fresh strawberries and clover honey, and a bottle of ruby red wine. Cook had sent cheese, too, but Laurentia would save that for tonight, and hardtack for tomorrow. Laurentia could imagine how word had flown through the palace when she'd asked for these supplies. The speculation would be both vulgar and hopeful—and this time, it would be true.

Dom still hadn't returned, and Laurentia tried to think of what else she could do to prepare for him, wondering if she dared take the time to wash herself. Yet how did she dare not?

If she moved quickly . . . She dragged a linen towel and washcloth from the cupboard, groped in her saddlebags and found her hairbrush, and headed out the back door. She heard cursing from the stable; not pain-cursing, but the monotonous mumble of cursing in which men indulged for no discernable reason. Probably he swore at the slippery straw or the awkward mattress. No matter, as long as he was occupied.

Fist-sized stones lined the edge of the pool, fine rounded gravel formed the basin; King Jerome had wanted only the best for his wife. Laurentia knelt on one wide, flat stone, placed to keep her up out of the dirt, and swished the washcloth in the cool water. Efficiently she went to work, and when she finished every bit of her body not covered by her chemise and boots had been cleansed and dried.

Dom still hadn't appeared, so she sat down and shook out her hair. Wisps of straw had woven themselves into the tangles, and using both fingers and brush she went to work. But she was the princess; a maid usually brushed her hair, and never when she came here had she been rolling around in the stable in a state of abandon. As she worked she leaned over the water, utilized its quivering surface as a mirror. Yesterday's scrapes on her face were fading, but she winced and complained under her breath as she brushed.

Sometimes she really enjoyed being wealthy and pampered. She hated learning new skills; except for diplomacy and statehood, she never mastered any subject easily, and she dreaded appearing stupid.

And she had come here to learn from Dom. She felt like the child Laurentia again, faced with a swimming teacher and a deeper pool than this. She remembered only too well how loudly she had squalled. She hadn't wanted to learn, but her father had insisted, even going so far as to ask if she were a coward.

Laurentia had squalled louder at that, but she had advanced on the water. She had put in a toe, pulled it out with a squeal, and complained about the cold. She'd sat on the side and splashed both her feet, then pulled back. At last, after an hour of working up her nerve, she'd jumped in all the way—and had had to depend on her teacher to keep her from drowning and the water to remain buoyant.

The trouble was, in this case, Dom was both teacher and water.

But she was going to grit her teeth and learn how to make love, no matter how much her virgin body quaked.

"Your Highness?" Dom shouted from the back door, and he didn't sound happy.

"Here, Dom," she called.

He followed the sound of her voice, appearing at once around the side of the house, a shining knife in hand. When he saw her, he sheathed the knife in his boot, and glared at her.

Apparently stuffing the mattress hadn't relieved his ill humor.

So she smiled at him and gestured with the brush. "You can pin hair, and you can unpin hair. Can you untangle it?"

He stalked toward her. "I need to know where you are at all times."

"You caught the kidnapper yesterday," she pointed out.

"I caught one of them." Dom placed his palms on her shoulders. "And he was dead this morning."

"What?" She swung around, dislodging his hands. "He can't be dead."

"Nevertheless, Your Highness, he is. Someone poisoned him."

"How did someone enter into the royal palace and—" She stopped. She knew the answer. "Someone in the palace is a traitor."

He removed the brush from her white-knuckled grip. "Who?"

Who indeed? "So many people work at the palace." She pressed her fingertips to her forehead. "So many people have access to the food. The cooks, the butler, the turnspit, the footmen. In the dungeon, the guards."

"Is there no one you suspect of being a traitor?"

"If I suspected someone, he would already be occupying a cell in the dungeon himself."

"His Majesty said much the same thing when I told him."

So Dom had informed her father. "Did His Majesty tell you what happened"—she took a breath—"five years ago?"

Dom focussed exclusively on her. "No. What?"

She sighed. "I don't know."

"What do you mean, you don't know? You just said—"

"Things happened, but my husband died at the same time, and I . . . I didn't . . ." The guilt of that time rose up to choke her, as it always did. Dom waited while she swallowed and fought for control. "It was only later that I realized how much had changed. My father gave his trust more sparingly and he made extraordinary plans for every circumstance that could affect our kingdom. I was drawn into his confidence in ways I had never been before. I thought at first he did it to distract me from my . . . unhappiness. Later I realized some of his closest people were missing and I heard a rumor they had been exiled. He built up his personal guard and the army. And he needed me to take my place at his side."

Dom slowly slid the brush through the strands around her face, and looked at her with—was it admiration? "You are a very wise and beautiful princess."

She couldn't help it. She beamed.

He turned her, then smoothed the bristles through her hair. "So . . . we are dealing with more than just a kidnapper now. We are dealing with a murderer," he said. "Give me your word you won't disappear on me again."

"No," she promised. "I will always let you know where I am."

Funny, but having her maid brush her hair felt different than having Dom do it. For one thing, her maid didn't swear when she found a tangle. For another she didn't smooth it with her hand after every stroke. The birds twittered, the brook burbled, the air smelled like earth and pine, and Laurentia closed her eyes and enjoyed each curse and each caress.

At last he stopped, wrapped his hand around her jaw, and tilted her head back. "Are you going to sleep on me?"

Without opening her eyes, she murmured, "Not at all."

Leaning down, he kissed her lips, the contact short and sweet. "I'm going inside to eat."

Her eyes sprang open, and he chuckled at her. Then slowly his amusement died. "When I look at you, I see an untouched land to be conquered and held. Why do you suppose that is, Your Highness?"

His fingers rested on her jugular, and her blood surged and pounded in response to his words. "Typical mercenary thinking," she retorted weakly.

"Yes." He rubbed gently down her throat, then pressed the flat of his hand on her chest where her heart beat. "That must be it."

When Dom bent over her, fixing her with his concerted attention, she could sing an aria, twirl in a pirouette, or just laugh for no reason. Dom made her happy. She lavished a smile on him and extended her hand. "Let's go feed you."

And he smiled at her. Really smiled at her. It was, she realized with a shock, the first time she'd seen genuine pleasure from him.

"Come then, O princess." Taking her hand, he helped her up, led her to the cottage, and all the while he kept their fingers entwined and that smile on his face.

Just for this moment, she had been born.

She fed him dinner, teasing him, flirting with him as Dulcie instructed, only now her smiles and touches came naturally. He seemed captivated. More than once, he seemed on the verge of one of those genuine smiles—and she wanted another.

When they were done eating, she sent him back out onto the porch and cleaned up quickly, then hustled out. He leaned against a column at the railing, staring out as if he still couldn't believe the view. She understood that; she couldn't believe it, and she'd been here many times before. Joining him, she slipped her hand into the crook of his arm.

"Isn't it glorious?" she inquired.

"Glorious." He tightened his arm over her hand. "And it's yours."

"Mine."

He glanced down at her, one of those genuine

smiles on his face. "If you knew the possessiveness evident in your voice!"

"Why not?" Her pride for Bertinierre sang in her soul. "From here, I can see my kingdom, all of my kingdom, all the way to the sea, spread before me in the most breathtaking spectacle on earth."

"You love it."

"Of course I do. Who wouldn't?" She laughed. "Don't you?"

He looked out again. He didn't answer right away, and when he did the admission seemed torn from him. "Yes. Yes, I love the view. From up here, it almost reminds me . . ."

She held her breath. He was on the verge of disclosing some tidbit of his life, volunteering the information willingly, and she wanted it. She wanted any piece of him she could have.

"If it weren't for the sea in the distance, I would think I was in Baminia."

She let out her breath. There. He'd done it. "We *do* share a border with . . . with Sereminia, as they call it now. These mountains are a branch of the Pyrenees. And while the roads aren't that well traveled, if you ride northwest from here, you can reach Sereminia in less than a day." A geography lesson! She could do better than this. "Do you miss Sereminia?"

He shrugged. "I haven't been there in twelve years. I was used to being away."

"That's not the same as not missing it." Again he didn't reply, and was silent for such a long time she started to wonder if she'd crossed that invisible privacy line he drew, and if she would be forced to retreat.

But as she searched in her mind for banal subjects to introduce, he answered at last. "I didn't miss it for the longest time. I had my friends, my mercenaries, and they were all Baminian. I had the battles. I had the money. But when war took my friends and the buffer between me and the world disappeared ... I just wanted to go home." His voice changed from yearning to disgust. "Crawl home like a wounded dog."

"Of course you did." To her that was so obvious. "Where else do you go when you're hurt, but home?"

He turned on her so quickly she stepped back. "You don't understand. You—yes, you would want to go home. For you, home is father and food and warmth and love. For me, Baminia held nothing but pain. Do you *know* who I am?"

"The king's son."

"Not the only king's son. That old Judas professed love to dozens of women, and got children on four of them. Only Danior was legitimate, but the other two were taken care of."

"Why weren't you?"

"I was conceived just before the revolution of '96." He smiled, but it wasn't his genuine smile. It was more a curl of the lips. "The queen, his true wife, was killed before Mama could go to her for succor."

Laurentia suspected she didn't want to hear the rest. She suspected this tale would haunt her in its horror. But she had to go on, had to find out what made Dom the competent, cruel, hard man she had seen just yesterday. "What happened to your mother?"

"When her father found out she was with child, he threw her out of her home. The revolution had begun. She found her way to the city, I don't know how. When I think . . ." His hands clenched into fists, his knuckles white with the need to change a past that had happened before he was born. "Even after she'd lived in the brothel for all those years, Mama was pretty. Delicate, like you, with a smile that I adored."

A brothel. Laurentia swallowed the lump in her throat. The best refuge his mother had been able to find was in the stews. Laurentia couldn't even imagine the horror of that. Of having to sell her body over and over again to strangers. And Dom had seen it.

"That's why she got to keep me with her," he said. "Because the men liked her smile, liked her shape, and the old whore who ran the place didn't want her to leave."

"Would you have been better off in an orphanage?" Laurentia asked timidly.

"The revolution left the country starving, and orphans are disposable." He rotated his shoulders as if tension held his muscles in thrall. "Especially the son of a king whom everyone blamed for their troubles."

"How did they know you were the king's son?"

"Mama proclaimed it proudly. She still loved him, damn her"—love and agony etched his face—"so she told everyone and everyone knew I was the only bastard rejected."

Laurentia didn't have any words to comfort him. What could be said that would make an old child's pain go away? She knew of nothing, and she groped for his hand. His fingers closed around hers, and he gripped too hard, but she knew he didn't realize it, didn't know anything but his own anguish.

"I never met my father. He and the queen were killed together, but every time I look in the mirror I see him. I look like him. I look like my brothers. I look like the Leons."

Being one of a royal family . . . ah, this she understood. "Everyone mocked you, blamed you for their troubles, and envied you your bloodlines."

He looked at her. "Clairvoyant, Your Highness?"

He had transferred his hostility to her, she realized. The gulf between the legitimate and illegitimate stretched so wide not even empathy could bridge it. But she answered anyway, paying for his confession with a piece of her own heart. "Sometimes people who don't know me think I'm not too bright, and they ridicule me in sly ways—as if I'm not going to comprehend their beastliness—or they hate me because they think I'm better than they are." She flushed as she recalled the unsubtle mockery. "*They* think."

Tilting his head, he studied her with a little less animosity and a little more interest. "I would have never guessed we had that in common. Did you beat up everyone who mocked you, too?"

"No, but I wanted to." Hastily she added, "I'm not dismissing your adversities."

"I didn't think you were."

She'd interrupted the flow of his confidences, she realized, and she hadn't meant to do that. Neither did she want to force him to remember the agony of his youth.

She needn't have worried.

He withdrew from the wreckage of his life, withdrew from her, and finished his story without a hint of emotion. "My mother got sick. I was put to work pleasuring women. My mother died. I left." That crooked smile bit into his face, and he confessed the last of it. The worst of it. "I led the next revolution to dispose of my brother. I failed." He crossed his arms across his chest, waiting for her reaction.

Shock? Horror? Yes, but not because he'd led a revolution against the Sereminian royal family. Laurentia ached for his pain, for the boy he had been, growing up loving his mother, hating her life, knowing what she had given up for him. A thousand memories haunted him, worse than she could have ever imagined. "What did you do then?"

"I took my band and we sold ourselves as mercenaries."

"How did they die?"

"I picked the wrong side in a stupid little war, and they all—" He stopped. Obviously, this wound was too recent. He couldn't separate himself from this grief, from this guilt.

"All were killed?"

"There is Brat. Just one of the original band."

"Where is Brat now?"

"Poking through the inns and along the docks, trying to find out more about the kidnapping." Turning away, Dom looked out over the trees again, but Laurentia didn't think he saw Bertinierre in all its glory. He saw only, she suspected, corpses on the battlefield. "I miss them. The camaraderie, the jokes. We had done everything together, and been together so long, we knew each other's thoughts without speaking. It was my fault they died, you comprehend, and I have to . . . salvage something for them. Raise one good thing in their memory."

He vibrated with pain and resolve, and Laurentia respected his determination. "Whatever you do, I know it will be the right thing."

He turned on her like a snarling wildcat. "You're really *not* too bright. I don't do the right thing. I'm Dominic of Baminia. I leave death and carnage behind everywhere I go."

"You used to do that," she corrected. "You're like your mother. She did what she had to do. You did what you had to do."

"Such an understanding princess," he mocked.

She could see his temper rising, although she could not fathom why. "No, you're wrong. I could never understand, because I have never had any experience to match yours."

Her tenderness put him into a fury. She saw it in his blue eyes, lit by a flame, and in the way he gathered her into his arms, like a man taking possession. "Are you happy now, Your Highness? You got me to *talk*."

" 'Happy' isn't exactly—"

"Now I'll do that other thing you require of me." He bent close to her face, so his breath brushed her lips. "I'll kiss."

"If you don't want to—"

He took her lips like the mercenary he was, boldly, without compassion. He opened her to his tongue, probed her, stroked her until she ran out of breath and good sense at the same time. When she sank her claws into his shoulders, he pulled back and stared at her, tucked into his arm. Holding her immobile, he slashed at her with his words. "You chose a good candidate to bed you, Your Highness. I learned a lot in the whorehouse. I can bring to you pleasure with my hands, with my mouth." Taking her hand, he placed it on his crotch. "With this."

A good woman would have been shocked. Laurentia was curious. She explored the length of him, trying to get an idea of what, really, he kept within his trousers.

But before she could truly glean the knowledge she sought, he snatched her fingers away. "Damn you, Laurentia, if you continue there'll be nothing left to fulfill your desire."

Now that she *didn't* understand.

"Your Highness." He still held her wrist, and he kissed her fingers with mocking respect. "You aren't the first princess I've kissed, you know. There have been others. One who was curious about how a mercenary made love. One who thought I would be rough and hurried, and she liked that way until I taught her better. I taught them passion, they taught me refinement. They made me the man who could walk into your ball and convince those other upstarts I was your suitor."

But if he thought he could make her hate him with a few phrases of disdain, he was a fool. She had a mind of her own. "If you give me their names," she said, "I'll pen them a note of thanks."

He studied her. "Who?"

"Those other princesses who taught you to kiss." She had startled him, she could tell. Then he laughed, a long, low belly laugh, and he whispered, "I can't even remember their names."

"Will you remember mine?"

Her temper eased his aggression as her compassion could not. His grip loosened; now he cradled her. "Yes," he said, "for I fear it is written on my heart."

She didn't believe him. The only thing written on his heart right now was the old drive to survive, and the new drive to do right by his fallen comrades. But if she could keep him at her side long enough, maybe together they would raise a monument to his friends, and maybe then he would treasure her name and person.

Tilting his head back to hers, he began to kiss her again.

And at the door, someone coughed.

Chapter Twenty-one

Dom responded with the instincts of a cold-blooded warrior. He thrust Laurentia against the post and threw the chair out of his way. He got a swift glimpse of alarmed mahogany brown eyes in a feminine face before he had the interloper pinned to the wall, his knife to her throat.

"Identify yourself," he commanded, his voice a low growl.

"Dom, no!" He heard Laurentia hurrying toward him, her heeled boots echoing on the wooden boards. "It's my messenger."

He didn't release the girl, didn't take his gaze away from her apprehensive regard as he spoke to the princess. "You didn't tell me anyone would be arriving."

"I'm telling you now." She tugged at the arm with which he held the messenger's throat. "Let her go. For heaven's sake, Dom, she's a woman."

"I've seen women who would just as soon eviscerate a man as sew him a shirt." But Laurentia wasn't lying, he was sure. He didn't know why she would and, more important, the peasant girl he held was plain, young, and white-faced with apprehension. Slowly he loosened his grip. "Who is she?"

"Her name is Rosabel, and she doesn't deserve this." Laurentia shoved at his shoulder. "Let her go!"

He heard the snap of command in her voice. Laurentia could act the role of princess when she chose. He freed the girl, but demanded his due. "What do you need a messenger for?"

Laurentia royally ignored him. She placed her arm around this Rosabel's shoulders and led her inside. "We'll get you some water," she said soothingly. "He must have given you a fright."

"Who *is* he?" Rosabel asked.

He stalked after them, and it irked him that Laurentia answered her question before she answered his.

"He's my bodyguard," Laurentia explained.

"He's not your usual bodyguard," Rosabel said.

While Laurentia placed the messenger in a chair, he leaned against the rickety table and glared.

The girl, dressed in a peasant's plain, dark costume, glared back. She had an attitude about her that Dom remembered, but couldn't identify at first. But he knew for sure she didn't like that he had pinned her to the wall or that she'd been frightened.

Laurentia brought Rosabel a ladle full of water, and while the girl drank, Laurentia went to the food cupboard and rummaged through it. "How was the journey here?"

"Good." Rosabel cast a contemptuous glance at Dom. "Until I got here."

Then it struck him; Rosabel acted with the flair and defiance of the younger Brat, performing any task, accepting any dare, doing anything to escape the ordinary run of life.

"I'm sorry." Laurentia placed a hearty meal on the table. "He's really harmless."

Dom didn't immediately grasp that she was referring to him, but when he did he finally had had enough of the chatter. As the girl pulled up her chair and dug into the food with all the enthusiasm of a half-starved waif, Dom caught Laurentia's arm as she bustled past, and for the last time asked, "Who is she?"

"Who are *you?*" Rosabel demanded. "You look just like King Danior."

Dom recoiled as recognition struck. He didn't know *her*, but those eyes . . . "You're Serephinian."

"Sereminian," Rosabel corrected. "No one calls themselves Serephinian, or Baminian, either, except for the people too old to adjust." The girl, who must be all of eighteen, ran an insulting gaze over him. "So who are *you?*"

Dom leaned toward her, coiled and ready to strike terror back into her heart. "I'm Dominic of Baminia."

Rosabel stared at him for a moment. Then she threw back her head and laughed. "He's dead."

Dom jerked back. Dead? Dominic of Baminia wasn't dead. He was the scourge of the Two Kingdoms.

"With that face, you have to be some kind of relative of the Leons," Rosabel said, "but don't try and palm off that Dominic-twaddle. I've heard it before, and that dark, dangerous line hasn't seduced me yet."

Dom heard Laurentia giggle, then choke back her

mirth. He didn't dare look at her. He'd just been slapped in the face with his own mortality.

"Did you bring the packet, Rosabel?" Laurentia asked when she had control of herself.

Rosabel looked at him mistrustfully before she jerked her head toward the back door. "It's in the usual place."

Laurentia went to the food cupboard again, and from the bottom shelf she pulled out an overlarge black rucksack, woven of wool and with straps to fit over the shoulders like a child's sling. She dragged her apparently heavy burden to the table and placed it beside Rosabel.

An earthy, minty odor wafted to his nose, and he tried to place it.

"I have everything for your return journey right here."

"She's going to carry *that* back?" Dom studied the bony girl. "She has a pony, right?"

Rosabel grinned at him, not at all offended. "A pony would attract attention. I have an ancient donkey." She hefted the sack in both hands.

Dom watched the muscles ripple in her arms. If he were still in the mercenary business, he would have recruited her.

"A good harvest," she said to Laurentia.

"Very good." Laurentia glanced at him, waiting for the questions.

He wasn't going to reveal his ignorance in front of the little urchin Rosabel.

"Come back in a fortnight," Laurentia continued. "There will be more. Much more."

They were talking in code, one Dom didn't understand but deeply resented.

"As you command, Your Highness." The girl showed some manners when she stood and curtsied deeply to Laurentia.

Laurentia rushed to assist her in lifting the rucksack onto her shoulders, and while Dom didn't want to help Rosabel, he had to assist the princess. So he gently pushed Laurentia aside and settled the weight on the girl. The scent of mint and earth strengthened, bringing up memories of standing in a forest in Baminia, of stepping on an herb—

But he forgot about that when Rosabel looked him over and snorted. "Dominic of Baminia."

With a sense of relief, he watched her trudge out the door. "If that's how they're raising girls in Sereminia"—he made sure he used the correct designation so he wouldn't sound like an old gaffer—"then the country's gone to hell while I've been gone."

"How old are you, Dominic?" Laurentia asked in a merry tone.

Why did she want to know? "Thirty-three."

"You sound as if you're eighty." She began to clean up the clutter of dishes left by Rosabel, but Dom stopped her with a question.

The most important question, he suspected, he would ever ask. "Why was that woman here? What was that all about?"

Laurentia hesitated, searching his features as if she could read his character in his face. Then she nodded firmly, took him by the hand, and led him back onto the porch. She pointed to the chair where he'd been sitting before.

He righted it and seated himself, sinking slowly onto the hard seat, watching her watch him.

She perched on the wide railing. "Do you know what *mentha nobilis* is?"

"No, I—" He stopped. That scent from the bag.

The scene from the forest.

Dom stepped on an herb, and one of his revolutionaries grabbed his arm and jerked him aside.

"That's a bad omen, Captain," he said.

"What?" Dom asked.

"Stepping on"—the revolutionary shifted his gaze away from Dom's—"on the royal maywort."

Royal maywort. Another one of the superstitions surrounding the imperial family in Baminia, and in Serephinia, too. Lifting his foot, Dom ground his heel into the soft, mossy-looking plant and looked challengingly at his man.

Who paled, backed away, and muttered, "Bad luck. Bad, Captain."

Mentha nobilis. Royal maywort. Dom hadn't believed in omens or luck, but apparently he didn't have to believe to be defeated.

"*Mentha nobilis*," he said, "is an herb that grows in high elevations, in secluded places, in Sereminia. It's reputed to be a remedy for flesh and plants."

She smiled at him like a teacher pleased with her pupil. "That's right. Dried, it's very light, but very potent. Sereminia has a tradition of spreading it on its crops, especially the barley. It's supremely effective at warding off blight—and Bertinierre just happens to be the best place to grow *mentha nobilis*."

Slowly, the truth began to dawn on him, but he didn't dare believe it yet. "In Sereminia, it grows wild."

"Sereminia has not been able to cultivate it. We have. *Mentha nobilis* is a fickle plant, but apparently there's something in our mountains it loves. So we have a most satisfactory arrangement with King Danior and Queen Evangeline. We grow this herb, they pay us for it, and their crop yields have increased twofold."

His mind grasped the significance at once. "They don't buy the herb from anyone else?"

"Right after King Danior and Queen Evangeline took the throne the country was in desperate straits." She considered him with a clear gaze. "*You* know."

He satisfied himself with a tight nod.

"So Papa *gave* them whatever *mentha nobilis* we grew, which wasn't a lot since we had little use for it. Our crops had no blight. A few eccentrics drank it brewed like tea."

"It tastes like dirt."

"You have tried it?"

"My mother made me drink it when I was sick."

Laurentia smiled at him for too long. "She loved you very much."

"Yes." Yes, he knew that, but his mother's love hadn't saved them from scorn, from poverty, from humiliation. He had had to save himself—and he'd been too late to save her. He had never forgiven himself for that. If he could have just grown up a little faster . . . "Tell me about the herb."

"After five years, Papa received a proposal from the royal family of Sereminia. They would pay us well for any royal maywort we produced if we would sell to them and them alone, and they would buy from us and us alone. With the help of the herb, they had surplus grain to sell and the treasury was full." Her shoulders were back, her chin tilted up; she was very picture of pride. "And our treasury is full, also."

"Why doesn't everybody know?"

"It's such a small thing. The farmers harvest and dry the herb. The king's agents collect it, and none but a few understand its importance."

"Why the secrecy?" As if Dom didn't know.

"Our relationships with some other neighboring countries are not as cordial as our relationship with Sereminia, so we find the secrecy prevents any misunderstandings." She leaned forward. "You do realize the magnitude of this, don't you? There are only three people in all of Bertinierre who know this. Three people, and now you."

He understood the magnitude. Yes, he did. *Mentha nobilis*, a damned plant that tasted like dirt, was the source of wealth he'd come to discover. A stupid little plant was powerful enough to change the fortunes of two countries. No wonder de Emmerich couldn't figure it out. The simplicity was the secret of its success. That, and the stealth that kept the business so secret most people realized nothing about the transaction. Dom wanted to laugh out loud.

Yet . . . at the same time, shock held him immobile. Laurentia had freely given him the secret he had come to discover. He hadn't had to seduce her, she'd just told him, and just because he'd beat up a kidnapper without the wit to stay alive in the king's own prison.

Brat, bless her, had pointed out the obvious. De Emmerich had set the kidnappers on the princess. De Emmerich had hired him. De Emmerich trusted no one to do as he commanded. So de Emmerich had to have convinced one of the servants or the courtiers in the palace in Plaisance to turn traitor. The poisoning of the prisoner confirmed that, and knowing someone was a traitor, Dom had watched with a cold and analytical eye.

Ambition rode Francis, Comte de Radcote, with an unrelenting spur. Weltrude . . . some people might say a woman would never act with such perfidy, but Dom knew better. The female of the race could often be the most vicious, and Weltrude, never beautiful, no longer young, and in a position that lost importance every day, had reasons to resent Laurentia. Dulcet, Countess de Sempere . . . the princess allowed Dulcie to be her confidant, so she was the most dangerous of all.

"Who's the third person who knows about this secret?" Dom asked, hoping to pry the truth from her unwary grasp.

Waving an airy hand, she dismissed his question. "That's not important. What is important is what I realized yesterday, when you rescued me. Then, and only then, did I recognize you were truly a man of honor, a man who had given his word to protect me and risked his life to do so. You are more noble than those with bloodlines they can trace for a thousand years. You are a better man than any of those pompous windbags who don't even know the meaning of loyalty. And I wanted you to know"—her eyes filled with tears, and her voice wobbled—"how much that means to a princess."

She'd forced him to talk, had drawn out the story of his childhood, listened when he went on and on about his mother and how she'd earned a living. About him and what a sensitive little bastard he had been. About the humiliations and the hatreds that had nurtured his hatreds.

Laurentia hadn't mocked him, or laughed at him. Indeed, she had brought him up here to show him the deepest secret of Bertinierre, and nothing in his confessions had changed her mind.

Stupid damned woman. What was she trying to do, make him love her?

He jumped back, slamming the back of his head against his chair.

Hell, no. He didn't love her.

And what would it matter if he did? He had no options. He had to pass the secret to de Emmerich.

Dom looked at Laurentia, petite and earnest, framed by boughs and generous to her bones.

He didn't love her, but here in full sight of Bertinierre, he made his vow. He would come back.

He would do his best to negate the harm that must inevitably come to Laurentia. And before he left, he would lay his claim on her.

Laurentia didn't know what to think. She didn't know what she'd expected when she told Dom the truth, but certainly not this tight-lipped concentration. Quietly, she slipped into the chair next to his, and together they sat in silence, waiting, waiting . . . for what?

Laurentia didn't know. She wanted to ask Dom what he thought, again impress on him the importance of silence, but he sat in his chair, his head tilted against the headrest, so motionless she couldn't see the rise and fall of his chest. He might have been asleep, except his eyes were open, staring out into the treetops as if he could read the future in the wind that stirred them. His manner reminded her of her father on those days when he had to sit in judgment in the royal courts.

Yes, Dom was acting like a man with decisions to make.

No, like a man who had made decisions.

Eventually he stirred, and without looking at her asked, "Do you have any other secrets you want to tell me?"

"No," she said faintly. "No, that's the only secret I know."

"Then," he said, "take off your clothes."

Chapter Twenty-two

The thin mountain air must be affecting her brain, Laurentia thought . . . "What did you say?"

In a leisurely manner—no, a lordly manner—Dom turned his head and looked at her, his pure blue eyes hot as embers after a forest fire. "Take off your clothes."

Her breathing developed a serious hitch.

He went on, "I haven't been able to think of anything except you, bare beneath that jacket, since you told me you'd left off your shirt. That was what you intended, wasn't it?"

" 'Intended' is too strong a word," she said, her voice thin.

One of his hands stroked down the smooth wood on the chair arm. Slowly, sensuously. "What word would you use, Your Highness?"

" 'Hoped'?" She just hadn't imagined he would respond with such unmistakable carnality.

Funny thing, though. She wasn't afraid. Waves of savagery rolled off of him like billows of lava down a volcano's slope, and she wanted to dance on the brim just out of danger—and maybe, when she'd danced long enough, she would allow herself to be consumed in a blast of fire.

Lifting her hands to the top button, she carefully slipped it from the buttonhole. And stopped. "I'll take off my clothes if you take off yours."

"Don't tease me," he said, so low she could scarcely hear him and so intense she dared not. "I'm barely holding off as it is. When I'm out of my trousers, princess, your time has run out."

His words struck right to the heart of her.

No, not the heart; lower than that. Deep in her womb she experienced a softening, a yearning, and she wanted him *now*—and she feared him now. Stupid to be afraid, but in this matter he held all the power, and she was nothing but a weak woman. A woman in love.

She stared at him in a stricken daze. In love. She loved Dominic of Baminia, or Sereminia, or wherever he was from. That was the reason she'd brought him here to tell him the very secret that was the core of her kingdom. That was why she trusted with only a foiled kidnapping as evidence that he was reliable. That was why she had chosen him to make love to her. She loved him. All the other suitors paled in comparison to the rough, perilous, genuine man called Dom. She loved him.

"Don't look at me like that, all perplexed and scared." He released his grip on the chair arm and touched her cheek with his thumb. "Nothing ever frightens *you*, O princess of Bertinierre. You're about as brave a woman as I've ever met."

"No, I'm not." She couldn't bear to have him think her courageous when most of her life she had been barely existing. And she didn't dare tell him that she had discovered she loved him. "I just don't let anyone know when I'm frightened."

He chuckled, soft and deep. "That's what courage is, Your Highness. But you don't need courage with me. I'm not going to hurt you, I swear. I don't even have to do this now, but I owe you. Only . . . I want you too much to do it your way. We're going to do it mine." His callused thumb scraped along her chin. "So take off your clothes."

The buttons of her jacket slipped through their holes easily. They should, because she used both hands and watched her own motions vigilantly. When the jacket hung open, she halted to take a breath—and heard his own intake of air. He was looking into the shadows of her jacket, staring as if, with his gaze, he could strip away the meager bit of cloth and see her flesh beneath.

Odd, to be so shy when he'd already bared her breast, but *he* had done that, and in a flurry of passion. This . . . this was passion, too, but a different kind, slower, more deliberate, almost painful in its intensity.

"Take it off."

The arms of the jacket were tight, especially at the wrists, and usually her maid helped her. He wasn't going to help her; one glance at him proved that. She had to stand up, put her arms behind her, grasp one sleeve with the opposite hand . . .

"Face me," he commanded. When she hesitated, his voice became a whiplash. "Face me!"

She swiveled on her heel and glared down at him. Damn the man! Who did he think he was?

He answered the question without her ever speaking it aloud. "I'm your lover."

Will-o'-the-wisps danced on her heartstrings.

"And I want you to face me."

She already was facing him. Him, her lover. He'd said so, so it was true. She was wise enough to know that wasn't the same as a declaration of love, but she was the princess of a wealthy kingdom. She could bribe him into staying with her, give him passion enough to hold him at her side, and maybe someday all those great, dangerous emotions she sensed in him would coalesce around her.

Her old experiences whispered coldly, *Maybe not.*

But she didn't listen. When she was with Dom, she felt strong, invincible, and convinced that anything was possible.

"Take off your jacket."

He thought she was brave; she would be a fool to disillusion him. Reaching behind her again, she grasped one sleeve with the opposite hand and tugged. The jacket gaped open, revealing the light lacy trim of her chemise.

Dom observed her relentlessly, his fingers stroking the chair arm.

She worked the sleeve off and hesitated. The other sleeve still clung to her arm and shoulder. She would have to tug it off, too. Were there rules to be followed while undressing for a man?

She watched the movement of his long, tapered fingers. She wanted those fingers on her. In a burst of courage, she stripped away the jacket and dropped it to the floor.

His gaze followed its course. His fingers stopped

their action. He sat motionless, like a god surprised by the impertinence of one of his maidens.

Languidly, his gaze traveled back up her legs, her hips, to her breasts, and there lingered. In a voice as rich and warm as sable, he said, "I can see your rosy nipples through the white chemise. They're already puckered, and look, you're shivering as if my hand touched them, or my mouth suckled them. Think how you'll moan when we're touching, our whole bodies rubbing, here on the porch."

"On the porch?" She looked about her with dazed eyes, realizing for the first time how exposed they were. When she had thought of making love, she'd always imagined a dark, enclosed place, safe as a womb. But Dom had commanded her, and she had begun to strip without a thought to the eyes that could be watching them.

Again he read her with uncanny accuracy. "The birds fly, the squirrels chatter, but no *person* can see you here. Look, Laurentia." He waved an arm, and like a woman mesmerized, she stared out at the view. "The ground drops away, and the only thing between us and eternity is air and sky. This is almost a treehouse, and here we have the freedom to do as we like. We can laugh, and we can love, and I can make you mine in every way I know how." His lids drooped, and he looked like a man sated rather than hungry. "And I know a lot of ways."

"Dulcie only told me about one."

One side of his mouth curled as if he were trying to restrain his amusement. "Dulcie's been holding out on you. Right now, I would like to see you nude. Take off your clothes."

The skirt buttoned on the side, and Laurentia opened the buttons. She didn't consider that all she wore was the thin knee-length chemise and silk hose tied with thigh-high garters. It never even occurred to her that without the skirt, he could see . . . everything. She might have undressed for a man every day, it was so easy.

Until her boots caught on the waistband when she kicked the skirt away.

She frowned at the boots, fitted and impossible to get off by herself. She hadn't considered them this morning when she'd dressed and contrived at the same time. Now the thought of bending down, clad only in her chemise, and wrestling boots off her feet seemed undignified and not at all appropriate.

But she hadn't taken Dom into consideration. "Here, let me." In a graceful motion, he slipped out of his chair, the chief cavalier in the court of temptation, and did as she had wanted.

He put his hands on her—on the leather of her boots, where she couldn't even feel them.

That wasn't good enough. That wouldn't do at all. She glared down at him, but he knelt before her with head bent.

And if he had looked up, what would she say? *No, I want you to touch me?*

She lacked the nerve.

Nimbly he unbuttoned one boot. "I approve of the high heels." Gently he hefted at her foot.

She wavered. "Why, because it makes me taller?"

"No, I like you just as you are. But these pointed heels work well when some blackguard attacks from behind. If you plant your heel hard enough on his instep, you can pierce his foot."

"Dom!" The idea of such violence horrified her.

"Just remember."

No longer able to keep her balance, she caught at his shoulder, putting *her* hands on *him*. As he slipped off the boot, his muscles flexed, rippling beneath her palm, giving her the barest sample of how it would be when he had removed his clothes and the two of them lay together.

She frowned, looking around the porch. Dulcie said people had to lie down to make love, and while the bed was made, it was far away, clear into the corner. If she could scarcely stand while Dom removed her boots—the other disappeared under his ministrations—she couldn't expect to make it to the bed.

He hadn't planned this very well.

Then his hand wrapped around one silk-clad ankle and slipped up her calf, and she forgot her concerns. He passed her knee, and her vision blurred. He untied the silk ribbon garter at her thigh, his knuckles brushing her bare skin, and her fingers lost their tactility.

So what if most of her senses had developed unexplainable defects? It was worth it to have his hands on her skin as he rolled down her hose. To have them tarry at the back of her knee to stroke the pale and sensitive flesh, then continue down, down to her foot. His fingers lingered on the fine bones of her ankle and stroked the slight arch of her foot. She smiled and tugged against his hold, but the sensation wasn't so much a tickle as a titillation.

She knew what he would do next. He would slide his hand up her other leg and remove her other hose.

Only . . . he didn't. "Now," he said, "you take off the other one."

"Oh." She tried to think how she should do it.

"Here." He patted her chair. "Put your foot up here."

If she did that, she'd have to pull up her chemise to untie the garter and although she had always understood that a lack of drawers left her exposed, the position would leave her . . . more exposed.

"Laurentia, I want your leg here."

She didn't move, bound up with wanting to say no, to assert her authority, to force him to admit he couldn't make her do anything. And above her procrastination was the insight that she balked only because of shyness.

He knew. The man knew females, knew *her*, too well for any woman's peace of mind. "Laurentia." He placed his hand, warm, callused, deft, on her bare calf. "I'm what you want. Out of all the men in Bertinierre, you picked me, and that was right." His hand glided up to her knee—not far enough—and back down.

"I can give you pleasure like you've never had before. Before I'm done with you, you'll have screamed a hundred times." His hand slid up to mid-thigh—still not far enough—and back down.

"But I want you very badly. You look at me, and you think, *He's sitting at my feet, and he can see*"—he smiled wickedly—"*everything*. And it's true. I can see through that material. Did you know that?"

Dumb with anticipation, she shook her head.

"The light shines though it. I can see every curve. I can see your breasts, so perfect, and the indent for your navel, and this . . ."

His hand spiraled up, up, up, until it reached the hair between her legs. He barely brushed the ends, but she couldn't suppress a whimper. Breath held, she waited . . . and hoped . . .

His hand slithered slowly, so slowly, back down to her ankle. "I want you to put your foot up here"— he placed his other hand on the chair seat—"and I want you to take off your stocking. That's all. Just this one time, I want to do this my way. Won't you indulge me?"

"I am probably setting a bad precedent by allowing you your own way about everything." Very carefully, she placed her foot on the chair. Not because she wanted to maintain an illusion of dignity. Oh, no. Because she wanted to remain standing, and that required all of her concentration.

"You are. Give a mercenary an egg, and he'll want the whole damned chicken."

Lifting the hem of her chemise, she placed it just above her garter and smoothed it down. Beside her, she heard Dom take a deep, harsh breath. She untied the garter and dropped it, then began the process of removing her stocking. Easy to do, except that her fingers seemed suddenly swollen and clumsy, the silk attained a life of its own, and her leg stretched on forever. She had never had a man kneeling beside her, holding her ankle, looking at her legs and more, for all she knew. As she leaned over to roll the stocking down her calf, she gingerly glanced down at him—and froze.

He wasn't looking at her legs. He was looking between them.

He *could* see everything, not through the chemise, but beneath it. From his expression of taut enjoyment, she deduced he liked seeing everything, had planned to see everything.

That revelation thrilled her, and the thrill appalled her. What kind of woman was she to enjoy a man's gaze on the place that should be cloistered?

"Dom?"

He didn't look up, or speak a word of comfort. He'd been caught out, as he knew he would be. Without changing expression, he placed his hands on her hips and turned her toward him. She tried to lower her leg, but with lightning reflexes he caught her knee and held it in place, so that she faced him, one foot on the floor, one foot on the chair, exposed and so vulnerable she ached with shock, with fear, with the anticipation he'd carefully cultivated.

He eased the chemise up to her waist, and looked again. He might have been a statue, he was so still. Only the rise and fall of his chest betrayed him.

Tilting his head, he met her gaze. He hid nothing from her now. He let her see him as he really was: mercenary, warrior, a bastard in every way. He wasn't a good man, or a kind man, but he was her man.

It almost hurt to smile at him, and she knew her lips trembled betrayingly, but he read the message she sent him. She had thought his expression would lighten, but if anything the magnificent broodiness of him deepened. Swiftly he turned his dark head to kiss first the upright leg, right on the pulse that beat inside her thigh. Then . . . then he kissed her raised leg, again on the thigh, a little closer to the place no man had ever been.

Oh, he didn't know that. She knew he hadn't comprehended when she said he would be her first lover. Maybe, with his upbringing, he didn't even understand what "virgin" meant. But it mattered to her, that he take a little extra time to allow her to get used to these sensations.

Yet she couldn't complain that he was rushing her. This seduction was nothing like the kisses they'd exchanged in the stable. This was unhurried, tender, teasing. Only it was so much more thorough than she ever allowed herself to dream.

He kissed her again, right on the cord of muscle on her inner thigh, and on this kiss he opened his mouth. He braced his elbow against her knee and his fingers again brushed the thatch of hair between her legs.

"Laurentia," he murmured against her skin, "do you know what I'm going to do?"

"No." Then it hit her. "Yes!" She tried to step back.

He was ready for her. Sliding one arm between her legs, he wrapped his hand around her bottom, holding her in place.

"Dom!" She caught his hair in her hands, but that only made him burrow into her, rubbing his head on her like a great cat. "You can't—"

"No, *you* can't"—he laughed harshly—"stop me."

His fingers opened her, exposing her more when she thought there could be no more. He pressed his kiss on her inner flesh, the naked part, the tender part. He found the most sensitive nubbin and he licked it with the flat of his tongue, just like the cat she thought him. Whimpering, she hung onto his hair, not to pull him away but for support.

Had he no inhibitions? Did he think she had none?

He sucked on her, drawing her into his mouth while his hand traced the entrance to her body. Over and over, his finger circled, threatening, promising, while his lips and breath and tongue drove her to the edge of madness. Her face tingled, her breasts tightened, her toes curled. He subjected her to pleasure until she tried to shove him away. Then he distracted her—with the thrust of his finger deep inside her.

Her back arched, she threw her head back. Her inner muscles twisted, trying to take him deeper— and his mouth fell away. "My God!" His finger eased from her. He stood in one effortless motion, and she got a terrifying glimpse of a countenance drawn tight with driving desire. Then he imprisoned her in his arms and twirled her toward the bed.

She tried to walk.

Apparently she wasn't quick enough for him, for he lifted her from behind and carried her, his hands gripping her to his chest as if she were fighting him.

She wasn't. She was too stunned to fight, to protest. When he laid her in the middle of the blankets, he placed her there so firmly that the straw-stuffed mattress crackled in her ears, and with his hand on her stomach, he said, "Don't move."

She didn't think she could.

Standing, he stripped his shirt off over his head, baring muscles and scars, the thatch of hair, the rippled abdomen. His hands went to the buttons on his trousers. He opened them swiftly, a man absorbed in his need.

A man . . . His erection sprang forth, and while her lips moved, she no longer had breath. "Oh, no." Driven by a maiden's sudden terror, she scrambled to her knees and made for the opposite edge of the mattress.

He grabbed her ankle. "No, sweet, not a chance." He dragged her back to him, his hand catching the hem of her chemise.

She clutched at the covers, tangling them in her fists. No wonder she'd felt him through his clothes. He was too big. "We can't do this. I forbid it." For a woman close to hysteria, she thought she sounded remarkably firm.

For all the attention he paid her, she might not have spoken. He flipped her back over to rest in the middle of the bed. He pulled her so that his knees were between hers. The front of her chemise bunched up to her waist. When she tried to kick him with her free foot, he caught that and held her wide.

He advanced as inexorably as an army, and when he lowered himself to her, she found her courage had vanished. Her hands moved restlessly on his arms, not shoving him away, but not hugging him either. Tears welled in her eyes, and one trickled down her cheek. "Dom, please."

He rested on her, his weight heavier than she expected. He kissed her cheek, her ear, licked the track of the tear from her temple. "I'm not going to hurt you, Laurentia." His voice rumbled through his chest, pressed so firmly against hers, and his deep tone brought her comfort when she knew it should not. "I promised to give you pleasure, and I will. Now."

One of his hands tangled in her hair. The other . . . where was the other? Between them, opening her, finding her again, entering her and drawing out the moisture that hadn't dissipated. Her body hadn't got the message that she'd changed her mind. She squirmed when his thumb brushed the nubbin he had licked, and squirmed more when he did it again. She said, "Dom, stop." But to her dismay, her voice had lost its authority. She sounded languid and almost . . . lustful.

His finger eased out of her. He replaced it with his shaft, shocking, large, too intimate.

He must have heard her swift intake of breath, or perhaps he'd felt it as she felt his speech, through the closeness so cogent she didn't know where she ended and he began.

His hand in her hair moved, a slow massage in her scalp. "How can you think I would hurt you? I'm going to make you happy."

Below, the remorseless invasion began, eased by her body's readiness. His words should have eased her mind, too, but he watched her with a gaze that pinned her to the mattress. He watched every expression, observed every newborn emotion as it clawed its way to the surface. He wanted to know everything she felt, he wanted to observe her passion, and he violently, completely wanted to spend himself in her.

Why did she read him so well?

Why did he fathom the depths of her mind when she barely understood them herself?

He was too big. This was too personal. She felt too much, she wanted to hide until she could comprehend the untried emotions and raw instincts that twisted within her. Yet when she turned away, he caught her chin and turned her back. His pure blue eyes watched her even as his body listened to her body.

After the first assault, he held himself at ready. "Relax. I know it's been a long time, but if you'll just relax those muscles, it'll be easier for you."

"I can't." But her body was his body's ally, and inevitably, as the initial pain abated, her muscles softened and yielded.

Taking her hands, he placed them around his neck, forcing her to embrace him even as he moved forward again, relentless, a mercenary on the march.

The sensation of fullness grew. Her fingers moved restively in his hair, catching the ends and tugging. She found herself flexing her legs around his hips, seeking relief or satisfaction or . . . something. Snaring her knee, he brought it up to his waist, propelling himself further toward his goal.

Inside her, something tore, a swift pain that severed her innocence.

Dom stilled. All sounds around them vanished. The world fell away. Only Dom and Laurentia remained, their gazes locked, their bodies intertwined.

The word fell softly from his lips, comprehension and awe mixed. "Virgin," he said.

At last he understood. At last.

Painstakingly, she tilted her hips toward him,

bringing him all the way inside her, so far inside he touched the entrance of her womb. Her inner muscles clenched and relaxed, holding him still for her proposal.

Taking his face in her two hands, she held him as he held her, and with the voice of a princess and the desires of a woman, she said, "Dominic, I love you. Marry me."

Chapter Twenty-three

Dom stared down at Laurentia. At this princess of Bertinierre's royal house, crushed beneath him, subjected to his dominance.

This was what he liked. The crowning moment of any royal seduction, when the princess became a woman like any other, subject to him and his skill. And this princess . . . she'd fought him. Tried to hide herself from him. Tried to avoid a wanton response, until he'd dragged her beneath him and forced her to respond. Any man would revel in that kind of power, but the king's bastard gloried in it. Dominic taught the untutored princess passion.

In that service, he had justified himself and his breach of faith.

Now he stared into those shining green eyes, damp with tears. Against his breastbone, he felt the beat of her heart. Within her, the dampness of her passion mixed with her virgin blood, her muscles quivered under the shock of his penetration, and in the deepest part of her, her womb awaited his seed.

Although he hadn't understood, she had, and she had freely given him her virginity. Her virginity, her love, and, if he consented, her troth.

Revenge? Dominance? He couldn't remember why he had ever wanted them.

Passion. Possession. They mastered him as if the others had never been.

In a voice he scarcely recognized as his, he said, "You had better mean that, Your Highness, because you are never escaping me now."

He pressed into her, in so far there was no more.

Her eyes widened. "You'll do it?"

Gradually he withdrew. "Marry you? With the greatest of pleasure, Your Highness. While giving the greatest of pleasure"—leaning down to her, he kissed her quivering mouth—"Your Highness."

He thrust again, still slow, and she braced herself against his assault. "No," he whispered. "Relax."

She *had* to relax. The way was slick and tight. Shock no longer held him suspended. Desire grabbed him by the balls and held him in thrall, and for the first time since *his* first time, he knew he would lose control.

He didn't want to hurt her. Please, God, he didn't want to hurt her, so she had to relax.

He withdrew and thrust again.

Her eyes widened, then fluttered shut.

Again.

Her leg moved against him, a restless unguarded motion.

Again.

She bit her lip, and he kissed it softly.

Again.

She lifted her hips in the instinctive rhythm of love.

His discipline crashed around him. He reached

under her and brought her hips up, tilting them up to the right angle. Not to make it easier for her, but because he had to be inside her. Now. Now.

She moaned. Was she struggling? She clawed at him. Was she fighting? He didn't know. He didn't care. She was his. He would make her his. And when he was done—he would make her his again.

Then, deep within her, the changes started. Her muscles clamped down, trying to hold him.

Her legs wrapped around his waist, her arms reached over her head. She clutched the blanket, tearing at it while she cried out, and he recognized that sweet expression of absolute abandon.

He'd done it. He'd done it!

And on a wave of triumph, he penetrated to his full length, and convulsed in the primal sowing of his seed.

She thought he would move off her now that the deed was done. And he did lift himself, but only enough to ease the bone-deep ache caused by his weight and by . . . she didn't know by what. The frenzied activity, she supposed. Certainly he didn't seem to be worried about what had happened inside her. He remained firmly in possession, although without his former proportions, and through her closed eyelids she could almost see the intense concentration he bent on her.

"Did you mean it?" he asked.

A fair question, she supposed. How many other women proposed marriage at such a time? "I want you to wed me."

"No, the other."

Cautiously she opened her eyes. He looked just as she had known he would, brooding, fierce, demanding, and at once she lost the thread of the conversation. "What?" she asked weakly.

"What you said first. Before the proposal."

"Oh." He couldn't even speak the word, she noted. "That I love you? Yes, I do."

Some of the fierceness faded, and he put his forehead against hers. "Thank God. I thought the swelling had spread to my brain."

She couldn't help it. Although he hadn't returned her declaration, although she doubted he knew the meaning of love, he amused her, and she giggled.

He watched her, a half-smile tugging at his lips. Carefully he withdrew from her and moved to one side, closing her legs and tugging down her chemise. He moved to the edge of the mattress, and she heard the thump of his boots as he discarded them at last. He stood. She hoped he would pull up his trousers. He removed them. He walked away from her out of the cottage, his slight limp in evidence, and she found her gaze riveted on the motion of his nether cheeks.

Before, she'd been infatuated with his shoulders. Now, it appeared her obsession had moved lower. She hoped it would stop there, and wondered what his feet were like.

Almost at once he returned, carrying the bucket and an armful of towels. He held the towels to his chest. She kept her gaze fixed on his face.

He stood over the top of her and blessed her with one of those genuine Dominic-smiles. "It's a little late for that," he said. "You might as well look at the whole packet."

She glanced. She didn't mean to, but her gaze just dropped by itself. Everything below his waist looked a lot different now. Not nearly as frightening, until one pondered the magical ability of his body parts to change sizes. The fact that each muscle on his frame was well defined and powerful could alarm a less adventurous woman than she had proved to be. And a scar, momento of his mercenary days, reached long and jagged across his hip.

He put the bucket on the floor and dropped the towels on the bed. Placing one knee on the mattress, he wet the washcloth and wrung it out over the bucket. "You did tell me," he said.

She observed him with alarm, and her over-burdened brain at last deciphered what he meant. "About the virginity, you mean."

Leaning over her, he wrested the hem of the chemise from her grip. "I didn't understand."

What was he *doing*? He couldn't do *that*. "I know you didn't."

"Part your legs, you little innocent. This will make you feel better."

She looked at that washcloth spread over his hand. "No."

"It *would* be better if I picked you up and carried you outside to the pool . . ." he mused.

She dragged a pillow over her face, and contemplated not coming out until her blush had faded. That was to say, never.

"Laurentia?"

She inched her legs apart.

He pressed the washcloth between them. "I feared I was hurting you."

She spoke into the pillow. "Yes." He was right. Of course. The coolness did ease the sting. "But what you did before . . . it was so much that . . . well, you promised me pleasure and . . ." She peeked out.

His eyes half-closed as he listened to her stammered explanation, and that half-smile lifted his lips again. "You don't need to be afraid I'll hurt you again." He dropped the cloth in the bucket and eased the chemise out from underneath her.

"Dom," she groaned, and pressed the pillow over her eyes again.

He paid no heed to her distress, but moved the pillow and pulled the chemise over her head. She brought the pillow back immediately and held it to her face, hoping to cool her blush against the muslin.

Silence followed, the kind of silence that had her poking her head out in a sort of dreadful curiosity.

He was looking at her. His gaze touched her shoulders, her nipples, the narrow waist and womanly hips.

She could scarcely breathe, wanting him to like what he saw.

"Perfect," he said. And, "Mine."

He reached for her. His fingers trickled like cool water over her collarbone, along the outer curve of her breasts, and down to her hips. "We won't even try to dance the mattress jig until tomorrow morning—"

The phrases he used!

"And only then if you're not in pain."

He sounded matter-of-fact, but she noted a small

tremble in his fingers, and he touched her nipples once more, circling them with one finger until they tightened the cord that reached low in her belly.

Then again he lifted her, pulled the covers down, and placed her on the sheets. "In the meantime . . ." He wrung out the cloth, and this time when he brought it back, he opened her and washed everything. Everything!

She squeaked and tried to object, but as soon as she began to speak, he discarded the cloth and placed his head between her legs.

And this time he brought on that glorious and exhausting sensation with his mouth, just as he had promised he would.

Chapter Twenty-four

When Laurentia woke, evening had fallen. Although the sun had gone down, light lingered, bathing everything with a golden glow that seemed fitting for her mood. Gingerly she sat up, pushing the hair out of her face, listening without interest to the complaints of her muscles. Better that every bone in her body ache than she should have remained unenlightened for even one more day.

What had awakened her, she realized, was the absence of Dom's heartbeat under her ear. She groped in the bed and, finding his pillow still warm, she called, "Dom?"

He came through the doorway at once, carrying a tray, with his saddle bag dangling off his arm.

If he wanted to wash her again, she would have to object. Or maybe not.

He was still nude, and this time she wasn't quite so shy. She noted that his muscles defined his body shape, sleek, strong, and graceful. Scars of various shapes and origins occurred everywhere, but especially on his arms and chest. That ugly scar sliced across his hip. Hair liberally sprinkled his chest, hugged the line of his stomach down to his groin, and surrounded his privates, which shifted and moved as she stared.

Her observation, she realized, aroused him. In that they were alike.

"There's no use looking at me in that manner. I am determined that my virgin princess should rest tonight. Besides"—he set the tray and the saddlebag on the floor beside the mattress—"I want to *talk.*"

From his amused expression, she got the impression he was paying her back for something, although what she couldn't imagine. "We can talk," she agreed cautiously. "But aren't you cold?" With the sun down, the mountain air quickly cooled, and already she was grateful for the layers of blankets on the bed.

"I'm naturally warm." He lifted the covers, slipped in beside her, and put his cold feet on her legs.

She squealed and pushed at him.

He laughed and hugged her.

It was all so natural, as if they'd been lovers for years, yet underneath the normalcy lurked a sense of the exotic. They had known each other for three days only; they knew each other better than any two people in the world. They had discovered everything about each other that mattered; they had everything to discover about each other.

Lifting the tray, he placed it between them on the mattress. "This cheese you brought stinks like a soldier's socks."

The cold air crept down under the covers, and she hugged her arms around her waist and shivered.

"Don't tell me you're one of those men who only eats prissy cheese."

He dug through his saddlebag and pulled out a shirt. "I've eaten enough disgusting things in my life without subjecting myself to rotten cheese."

"Like awful eggs?" she asked slyly, remembering their breakfast together.

He whipped his head around. "You did know!"

She laughed and contented herself with a noncommittal "Huh."

"It's too late for that." He wrapped his shirt around her shoulders. "I've caught you now."

"I let you catch me," she corrected, gratefully sticking her arms in the sleeves.

"And you'll stay caught."

He sounded pleasant enough, but she heard the undercurrent in his voice, and she experienced a surge of protectiveness. The poor man couldn't believe she had committed herself to him. She groped under the covers, found his hand and squeezed it. "Nothing could happen that would change my mind."

"I wouldn't allow it," he said coolly. "There's your stinky cheese. I cut some bread, and I dug out these brown things."

"Brown things?" She didn't remember bringing brown things, and twilight was falling quickly. She couldn't quite see what they were.

"Dried apples."

"Don't you like dried apples?"

"I *eat* anything. I *like* meat." He popped an apple in his mouth and chewed. "I'll go hunting tomorrow."

"Tomorrow?" She was startled. "I thought we'd start for Omnia tomorrow."

"No. We'll stay here for a day. As a honeymoon. I need you to know whose woman you are."

His wish to remain seemed a sign of insecurity, but he sounded so decisive, she had to say, "Before we go back to all my suitors, you mean."

"Your suitors." He shook his head. "You never wanted any of them."

"No, but—"

"Eat." He broke off a piece of cheese and brought it to her lips, waiting until she accepted it. "You'll need your strength." He fed her, alternating bites of apple, bread, and cheese, and when she began to flag, he said, "I would like to know. Why were you a virgin?"

She pulled back from the bite he offered.

Still he proffered the bread.

Her appetite gone, she pushed his hand away. She would tell him, but only the barest outline. Anything else would constitute whining, and princesses did not whine. Not when, raised by the turmoil of passion and surrender, their emotions already drifted close to the surface. "Madness afflicted my husband's family. His Majesty believes Beaumont married me for security and eschewed my bed to avoid producing more . . . tormented souls."

"Was Beaumont tormented?"

The night grew darker by the minute. She was glad, for she didn't want Dom to read her face. "He suffered from bouts of dementia."

Dom dusted his fingers over the tray, then lifted it and set it on the floor, removing the barrier between them. "Why did His Majesty let you marry him?"

"Papa didn't know. He sent someone to England check up on Beaumont's antecedents, and our courier came back confirming that Beaumont was indeed titled, of ancient family and the last of his line. Everything Beaumont told us was true. It was what he didn't tell us."

"His Majesty would not marry his beloved daughter to a stranger on that flimsy evidence."

Laurentia couldn't hold back a smile, albeit loving and exasperated. "I love His Majesty, and I would never speak ill of him, but in one matter he is deluded. He thinks, because he is king, he can on meeting a man judge that man's character."

In a hard voice, Dom said, "In that, he is most definitely deluded."

Laurentia bristled. "It seems to be a common problem among the male gender."

"And among royals."

She had no answer. She didn't even understand why Dom would be so offensive.

"Beaumont was handsome," Dom stated.

He sounded so positive that a picture of Beaumont rose in her mind—blond, noble of brow, suave and elegant. "How did you know? Have you been asking about my marriage?"

"I ask only you, Your Highness." Dom sounded not at all offended, although her query had been abrupt and rude. "But the first time you laid eyes on me, you didn't like my face."

"And women always like your face," she deduced. "Have I been so transparent?"

Lifting her hand, he kissed her knuckles. "You are a boundless and infinite mystery to me."

She jerked her hand back. "Are you jesting?"

"No." Reaching out to her, he took her hand again and held it forcibly. "I do not know what would make a princess of your intelligence and background choose me."

She took a breath to tell him.

But he asked, "Did he hit you?"

She knew he felt the quiver in her fingers, so she threw back her shoulders and in her princess voice said, "You wanted to know why I was a virgin. I told you. I can see no advantage to continuing this conversation."

"I told *you* about my mother."

She stiffened more, staring out into the darkened forest and hoping, praying he wouldn't continue.

"I told you who I was, who I am. Do you think I don't want to know the same about you?"

She brought her knees up to her chest.

Dom released her hand and slid under the covers. "Did you propose to him, too?" He rested on the pillow, his hands cupping his head, his elbows akimbo.

She ought to lie down, too, huddle beneath the blankets for warmth, but she liked looking down at him. Being taller, in this instance, seemed almost an advantage. "No. He asked Papa's permission, and when my father had bestowed his blessing, Beaumont proposed to me, on his knees, in a bower in the garden."

"I feel hurt. I didn't get such a romantic setting."

His spurious humor allowed her to relax—a little.

And reflect—a little. Dom might joke, he might allow her head to be above his, but he would relentlessly pursue his information. "I gave you the setting I thought you would most desire."

Taking her hand once more, he laid it on his chest. "Your Highness is most astute."

His chest hair crinkled beneath her hand, his heart beat, his warmth made her want to rest her head on him and beg him to make the memories disappear.

But that they could not do for each other. "Beaumont never hit me, he just . . ." She took a moment to breathe, to try and relieve the tightness in her chest. "I was sixteen when we married. He was twenty-four. I thought I was in love. We went to one of my country homes, and the first night he just didn't . . . present himself. I waited and waited, and finally I . . . sought him out." Even the remembrance brought a rush of blood to her cheeks. "He was asleep. The next morning I . . . He was affable. But I was sixteen, I was in love, and I pursued the issue. I think at first he really didn't want to hurt me, but I was the princess and demanded my rights as a wife. And he said . . . he said . . ."

"That it was your fault." Dom sounded so calm, and he pressed his hand over the top of hers and demonstrated how he wished her to caress him.

"Yes!" She stroked, running her fingers down the arrow of hair. "How did you—"

"If he had told you the truth, you and your father would have sought an annulment. You are the royal heir. You must produce a child, and the Church would not deny you that."

Dom was so logical. His very serenity soothed her

agitation and made Beaumont appear, if not mad, then cold-blooded. Yes, she knew rationally what Beaumont had done, but to hear Dom deduce that he had played upon her youthful insecurities like a master steadied her.

"So instead he told you . . . what?" Dom asked.

"At first, that I was too young. Then . . ." She hated this. This reliving of the days when her world had been thrown into turmoil and she had been annihilated by a few well-chosen phrases. "I do admit, I was spoiled, and given to tantrums even at that advanced age."

"Did he not know that?"

"Before we were married, he said he thought my temper fascinating."

Dom grunted.

"But when I told him he should do his duty, he said he didn't want to. He said no one wanted me. He said the only reason any young man had paid court to me was that I was the princess, and rich, and he had done so for the same reason. He said that was the only reason he'd married me, and he wasn't going to force himself to bed a woman as unattractive and spoiled as I was."

"Lord Maggot said quite a lot."

And she remembered every word, every nuance. No matter how hard she had tried to forget, she still remembered. "He got quite agitated as he spoke. He frightened me, and I wanted to go home to my father, but Beaumont laughed. He said Papa wouldn't believe me because I was a new bride, and a woman, and men knew all women were hysterical. He said

I was a stupid girl." She found herself clenching a handful of chest hair.

Dom caught her hand and carefully loosened her fingers.

"Beaumont said he and Papa were friends. As they were. That was one of the reasons Papa approved the marriage, because they got drunk together and hunted and were comrades."

"No matter what you do, your father will not turn away from you."

"I know." She did know now, although she also had learned enough about love not to test its limits. "But Beaumont used just enough truth mixed in with his lies. I knew I was spoiled. Weltrude had told me. I knew I had a temper. I'd broken the crockery." She gritted her teeth before confessing, "And I must warn you, sometimes I still do."

"You can throw the vases at me anytime." Dom sounded warmly amused. "I'm a good catch. In more ways than one."

"Modest, too." She appreciated his humor but found her face too stiff to smile. "I didn't think I was stupid, but Beaumont said that reading Latin in the original and calculating yields per acre didn't make me wise, only overeducated."

"I'll wager he didn't read Latin."

"Not well, but I didn't think of that then."

"So you didn't tell your father."

"I didn't tell anybody. My own husband, the man who'd slept with countless women all over Europe, wouldn't touch me." She shivered, the chill of the night reaching through his shirt and raising goose bumps. "I kept hoping he would relent. I thought if it were dark enough perhaps, or if I wore the right clothes or knew the right thing to say ... but nothing worked."

"Your Highness, I don't want you to think I revel in your unhappiness"—reaching up, Dom cupped her head and brought it down to rest on his chest—"but for me, for now, I'm glad."

She pressed her nose into Dom's chest and smelled his scent. He was real, and here, and she loved him for knowing she wished to be in his arms. "Beaumont could be a very pleasant companion when I wasn't ... bothering him."

Dom slipped an arm around her shoulders and brought her closer to share his warmth all along his length. "If you want to grope my crotch, I swear I will never call it bothering."

She chuckled as his heat and humor began to relax her. "We put on a good façade, but eventually the servants gossiped that we never shared a bedroom. And I was not with child. My father began to question me."

Dom ran his fingers through her hair. "You denied everything."

"I couldn't talk to him about *that*."

"No. Of course not." Dom actually sounded like he fathomed her bashfulness.

"Beaumont's outbursts became more noticeable, so unbeknownst to me, Papa placed a spy in my home." Dom stroked his hand across her back in slow circles, and she stretched like a cat. "It was Chariton."

Dom's hand stopped. "Who is Chariton?"

"Chariton is our friend, our servant. You remember—he was the man who helped Gloria wrap Monty's ribs."

"You didn't introduce me."

"Chariton prefers to remain unrecognized. He says his tasks are easier that way."

"His tasks?" Dom asked sharply.

Laurentia didn't mind explaining. She should have foreseen that Dom would want to know. "He's an investigator when we need one and usually my bodyguard."

"Why isn't he your bodyguard now?"

Beneath her ear she heard his heartbeat increase. "Because you came along and Papa liked you, and he realized *I* liked you although I didn't want to admit it. I think—no, I know—Papa was playing Cupid."

"Where's Chariton now?" Dom persisted.

"Papa sent him off to discover what he could about the kidnapping attempt. Chariton will ask around Omnia, see if anyone was talking about it. Chariton has contacts all over the docks and at the inns."

"I wonder if he ran into Brat," Dom said.

"That's right. You did say your Brat was searching for clues." She laid her hand on Dom's chest next to her cheek. "Do you suppose they know each other now?"

"I suppose they do." The beat of his heart slowly resumed its normal speed, a calm, strong thrumming beneath her ear. "So Chariton found out you were a virgin."

"He suspected. So Papa suspected. I think Weltrude suspected. And the entire kingdom speculated."

"It's rough when you know every time you walk out the door, people are whispering behind your back," he said with the air of someone who knew. "Finish telling me about the little pissant you married."

She rather liked the way Dom talked about Beaumont, as if he were a boogeyman to be sent back to hell with the proper incantation. In truth, she could now see him becoming nothing more than a footnote in the text of her life. "Papa also sent to England for more information, and found out the whole family was mad. Beaumont's only surviving aunt lived in Bedlam, and no noble family in England would give their daughter into Beaumont's keeping, for Beaumont's father killed his mother in an insane rage."

Dom sucked air into his lungs.

"Beaumont fled England and came to the continent, looking for a wife who was ignorant of his family history. Of course, when Papa knew the truth, he demanded Beaumont attend him at all times, and Beaumont died while in his service."

"How?"

She hesitated. "I was never quite told."

"You were never quite told?" Dom sounded incredulous.

"Papa insinuated he died of a hunting accident, but once Chariton said he'd died on the terrace. I should have demanded the truth—"

"But by now you'd been told so many truths that were hateful lies you were afraid to ask."

Dom had a rare way of understanding human torment, perhaps because he'd personally visited those hells himself. "Yes, and I felt . . ."

"Guilty. Because you'd married a crazy incompetent and you couldn't cure him with your love. You didn't even love him."

She started to lift her head, but he pushed it back down and tightly wrapped his arms around her.

"All right, Your Highness, I've listened to everything you've said, and here's the truth. Your jackass of a husband used you, and when you confronted him about it, he destroyed you. He was a ruthless bumhole, and I don't ever want to hear you give excuses for him."

"He was just trying to find himself a haven where he could—"

"Go crazy in peace?" Dom snorted. "Men don't do that. They don't take a girl and hurt her in the basest way possible for their own purposes. He was insane. He was weak. He didn't deserve you."

She could tell that was that, as far as Dom was concerned. He had made his pronouncement; she should listen. But inquisitiveness led her ask, "What would you have done, if you were him and saw the darkness coming to envelop you?"

"I would have rowed out to sea and when the winds and rain came for me, I would have fought until I knew I had lost to nothing less than God Himself."

It was true, she realized. Dom would never have permitted madness to take him. He would have taken matters in his own hands, and died as he wished.

"I never want to hear you apologize for being

spoiled, high-handed, or hot-tempered." Making his point, he poked at her back with his finger. "You're the crown princess of Bertinierre. The responsibility you carry would break a lesser woman, and—although if you ever repeat this, I'll deny it—most men are weaklings and would crumble beneath the burden."

"I know. That's why I can christen ships and visit orphanages and come here to deliver our goods. I'm *good* at being the princess."

"Believe me, darling, you're good at being a woman, too."

The way he said it, so warm and amused, made her press her knees tightly together in a combination of anticipation and excitement.

She'd made him happy.

He'd made her ecstatic.

Maybe, if she were clever, she could convince him that morning was too long to wait.

"Your father also has a temper, I saw it this morning when I told him of the kidnapper's death. No one reproached him for breaking a vase. Nor would they you if you were a man."

"And men get to scratch whenever they want," she mumbled.

"Sure, women have a pitiful lot." He rolled, putting her beneath him, and leaned over her in the manner she already recognized. "What do you think?"

The aches in her body had diminished while she slept. The night air nipped at her nose, the brilliant stars shone from a midnight blue sky, the blankets created a cocoon of warmth, and within that cocoon was a man, her man. He wanted her. "I think I see the break of dawn."

Sliding her hand down his body, she found his erection.

He jerked and gasped as she wrapped her fingers around him. "Seems kind of early."

Again the size gave her pause, but curiosity drew her to explore the silky skin, the cap, the ridges and veins. "Can't you hear the birds chirping 'Good morning'?"

"My hearing's not too good right now."

She thrilled at the power she held in her hand. "You'll have to trust me, then."

"I do, Laurentia." He kissed her with the sweet ardor that had stolen her heart. "Do you trust me?"

"Being with you is the first thing I've done in years"—she caught her breath at the swirl of his breath on her nipple—"that is willful and not . . . no . . ."

He lifted his mouth. "Not what?"

"Not well thought out." When he wasn't touching her, she could actually speak. "You're my one moment of passion."

"One? Only one?"

She circled his ear with her fingertip. "So far."

"But do you trust me?" He covered her mouth with his hand. "Say 'I do.' " He released her.

"I do."

"Then"—he moved between her legs—"we're as good as married."

But when morning really broke and she woke up to a new day, his pillow was cold and he was gone.

Chapter Twenty-five

Dom read the signs. An army had obviously passed this way within the last week. The forest road had been widened by the tramp of many feet, a tobacco pipe had been smashed against a rock, squirrels had been shot out of the pines for sport. Pollardine's invasion force had moved into the mountains above Omnia, and now awaited their chance to swoop down and conquer Bertinierre. All they needed was information. The information he brought them.

Marcel de Emmerich had a talent for snooping, indeed for every kind of underhanded dealing, and he had paid Dom to learn the facts.

No, Dom had to be honest—he had accepted payment to learn the facts. He had agreed to do so less than a month ago, and the man he had been then had seen his action as dishonorable, but necessary. And after all, his treachery will affect only a princess, one of the hated nobles, a woman of the same class as his wretch of a father.

Then he had met Laurentia. Fire and intelligence, beauty and loyalty. She was more than he'd ever dared to dream of having. . . . and she'd given herself to him. He hadn't had to seduce the secret out

of her; she'd given it to him. She'd given him everything, offered him a life at her side.

He wanted that life, and not because of the power
and the prestige and the wealth. He wanted it because somehow Laurentia had bound him to her. If
he were a dishonest man, he would have said she'd
shackled him with the bindings of the flesh. But he'd
swived many women, and he'd never experienced
this tug of . . . what? . . . responsibility, he supposed.
So this attachment he felt had been caused by her.
By Princess Laurentia and her candor and vulnerability and charm. She was so obviously his.

His to throw away because of the deal he'd made
with the devil.

Oscuro shied as they rounded the bend, and Dom
flinched. Three male bodies in tattered clothing dangled from a sturdy limb, hung by the neck and left
for the buzzards. Were they hunters who had stumbled into the midst of the army and found themselves the first victims of this invasion? Or had they
been part of the invasion, men who had found a
hanging to be their reward for insolence? No matter
which, de Emmerich showed his true colors with this
cold-blooded display, and Oscuro did not need
Dom's urging to hurry past.

Some might say—Dom might say—that he himself was no better than de Emmerich, for he cher-
ished his principles above the safety and security of
his woman.

Yet what kind of man gave his word, took his payment, did the job, then deliberately failed to deliver?
He was Dominic of Sereminia. He was a mercenary
whose services had been sought because he could be

depended upon to never change alliances, never betray his employer, never falter before overwhelming odds. He had been a warrior his whole life, doing what others would not, but always he had taken pride in his unfaltering sense of honor. That honor had been the bedrock of his character, and that honor had brought him here, to the outskirts of the Pollardine war camp where he would deliver the secret, Bertinierre—and the princess—into the clutch of the most dreadful monster of all.

If he did not, he would lose the money that was Ruby's. . . . and his very soul.

He'd left his princess after too brief a time. He hadn't wanted to. He'd planned to keep her in the cottage with him, encouraging her passion so that when she learned the truth about his ruse, she'd be so in love with him he'd be a part of her, grafted onto her soul.

Instead she'd told him of her servant Chariton, who was investigating the kidnapping attempt. If Chariton was as competent as Laurentia said—and if he were not the traitor—Chariton would see Brat, study her, and Dom would be revealed as a scoundrel.

Dom could not allow that to happen. Better that he finish this dreadful task with some scrap of control than to allow destiny to sweep him along. If only he saw a way out of this tangled web of conflicting loyalties. If only . . .

Abruptly, Dom turned Oscuro onto a side trail. He tethered him out of sight of the road and dismounted. He pulled his black cloak with its custom made pockets from the saddlebag and donned it.

Then he cleared his throat. Looking up at the towering pines and feeling as foolish as ever he had, he called, "God?"

His voice echoed oddly in this silent place, and he flushed. Probably such informality wasn't the way to approach an unknown deity, but in all the years since his mother died Dom had never made the attempt, for he'd always known all the answers. Now he didn't, so he cleared his throat and repeated, "God? I need a sign. One woman and one war aren't much when stacked against my loyalty to Ruby and my duty as I . . . as I understand it, but I can't convince myself I'm doing the right thing. So if you would show me what I should do, I would be grateful." That seemed rather abrupt, so he added, "Amen."

He didn't know what he was supposed to do now. Wait, but for how long? He supposed God was busy, but Dom could smell the smoky scent of campfires that signified Pollardine's camp was close at hand, and he couldn't dodge their sentries for long. If he didn't get the sign soon, he would be forced to go to the king's tent and finish the job for which he'd been hired—and for that, he would probably die.

Hell, with the odds stacked against him, he would probably die, anyway. In fact, he might as well stop stalling and get it over with, for God wouldn't bother with a man like him.

So he made his way through the brush toward the road, and just before he stepped into the open he heard the jingle of a harness—and Weltrude rode away from the camp.

She was smiling, the kind of smile a murderess and a traitor would wear, and he realized—of course. Weltrude had the motive to betray her mistress. She had control of everything in the palace. She could have arranged to poison the prisoner and no one would be the wiser. And somehow she'd come into the same information he had. Dom couldn't betray the princess. He was too late. Weltrude had already betrayed her.

He'd asked for a sign. He had one. He looked up at the treetops and said, "Thank you."

But there was still the money, which he'd earned, and another matter. The matter of Laurentia's safety.

Briskly, he started toward the camp.

The order hadn't yet come to move, for in the open meadow where de Emmerich had set up camp, the soldiers, conscripts, and camp followers still lounged around. A sentry challenged Dom as he crossed the perimeter, but when he announced he had business with de Emmerich, he was at once waved on.

As he passed the mercenaries around the campfire, he heard his name called.

"Dom!" Toti the mercenary grinned with openly false pleasure at seeing his old rival. "What did they hire you for? Do they want a defeat on their hands?"

The mercenaries around the campfire laughed and shoved at each other.

Dom didn't join in. He just kept his gaze level, and Toti's grin faded. Toti always broke under Dom's examination.

When Toti was squirming, Dom indicated the camp. "It looks like someone is planning a war."

"Are you jealous?" Toti stirred the fire with the charred end of a stick.

"No." Not when de Emmerich was hiring the

cheapest, least dependable mercenaries he could find. "I've got one last job, then I'm moving on."

Toti's straggling mustache drooped over his mouth. "You got enough money to do that?"

"Not yet."

Toti looked over Dom's outfit, stained with sweat from the eight-hour ride, but still elegant and obviously expensive, and his jowled, coarse face fell even further. But he bragged, "When we get into Bertinierre, the spoils are going to be rich."

Again Dom allowed his gaze to roam, resting with particular interest on the amateurs—Pollardine's army. "And you get to work with such good companions."

The men around the campfire made a variety of noises, none complimentary.

Toti spat on the ground. "A bunch of cowed peasants."

"They always are. Poor devils. It'll be a cold grave in a foreign land for them." Dom stared at Toti. "And for you. I have a premonition about this job. Don't you?"

Toti made the sign to protect himself from the evil eye. "Don't say that, Dom. Bad luck."

"Truth," Dom countered. "How long have you been here?"

"A week."

"A week? Of sitting around doing nothing but poking the fire with a stick? Why aren't you training?"

"We don't need to train," Toti muttered.

"A cold grave," Dom repeated. "How much longer until you march?"

Toti broke the stick and tossed it in the flames. "You know how it is. When we're told."

"That stinks."

Toti shrugged again, and his eyes rolled toward the tall blue tent, crowned with flags, that was set in the middle of the camp.

Dom knew why none of the men dared voice a complaint. They smelled of fear. The whole camp smelled of fear, of farmers forced to leave their families, of mercenaries uneasy about the upcoming fight, of camp followers desperate to get out while they could. None of them dared complain, for de Emmerich would discipline them.

Those hanged bodies had been deserters. They hadn't died happy deaths.

"Is that de Emmerich's tent?" Dom asked.

Glum nods all around.

"The king's tent," Toti clarified.

"That's where I'm going." Dom walked off, leaving a horrified silence behind him.

He felt the men's gazes on him, and he took special care not to limp although more than anything, riding hurt his hip. But he wouldn't show weakness. Not to those walking corpses.

By the time Dom reached the tent, de Emmerich had obviously received word he was in camp, for the guard lifted the flap and stood silently aside.

Dom didn't even have to duck as he stepped within. The sun through the silk walls bathed the room, tinting everything—the king's massive camp bed, the trunks, the curlicues on the armor—a peculiar blue. One man sat behind the polished wood table, one man stood at his shoulder. King Humphrey and de Emmerich, both blue-complexioned, both dangerous in their own way. But Dom hadn't received a knife blade as greeting, so de Emmerich wanted confirmation.

Ostentatiously, Dom loosened his own knife in its scabbard. "De Emmerich, you tried to swindle me."

De Emmerich smirked. "Whatever do you mean, young Dom?"

"You tried to kidnap my princess."

De Emmerich's gaze sharpened on Dom. "Your princess."

"*My* princess. Trying to kidnap my princess was a serious mistake." He strolled across the tent and in a lightning-swift move sank his blade in the top of the table.

Pollardine's king didn't even start, the stupid fool. He just sat watching, his big eyes round and vacuous.

"What did you think you were doing?" Dom demanded.

"I didn't know if you would succeed in seducing her." De Emmerich grinned. "Apparently you did."

With morbid fascination, Dom stared at de Emmerich's now-perfect teeth. Surgeons sometimes replaced a rotting tooth with one taken from a corpse; Dom would have sworn de Emmerich sported a new mouthful.

"So you were going to take her and torture her?" Dom allowed his voice to rise. A royal guard stuck his head through the cloth opening, and Dom snapped, "Get him out and tell him to stay away."

De Emmerich's smile faded. He didn't like being ordered around by a mere mercenary, but he couldn't stick his knife in Dom's gut—which was the plan, Dom knew very well—until Dom had revealed Bertinierre's secret source of wealth, confirming what Welltrude had told him not a half-hour before.

"Marcel . . ." the king whined.

De Emmerich patted his head absently. "It's all right, Humphrey. He won't hurt me." He snapped his fingers at the guard. "Out. And stay away from the door."

Dom didn't believe the guard would do it. Not for a minute. The goal of every man in camp was to survive, and he would listen at the thin walls. Dom didn't care. The more people who heard of de Emmerich's defeat at the hands of his hired mercenary, the more people would doubt and desert. "Here's the problem, de Emmerich. You're going to take the information I give you—did I say give you? I meant *sell* you—and you're going to march into Bertinierre. You're going to get astride the country, and you're going to squeeze it dry."

"You're telling me no?"

"I'm telling you, I know you're planning to hurt my princess. Right now, I don't really care if I fulfill the deal I made with you. I would just as soon slit your throat."

At last de Emmerich showed what he was made of. The knife flashed out of his sleeve and whizzed so close past Dom's ear he heard the whistle of its passing. "You'd have to get to it first."

One blade down. "I don't relish the kind of betrayal you tried to set up. You send me to do a job, you step back and let me do it."

De Emmerich didn't like Dom's equanimity, and

he answered spitefully, "You haven't been successful in much lately."

"Just because you have to beat a woman into sub-
mission before she'll bed you, doesn't mean that I
have to," Dom retorted.

King Humphrey giggled. "He's right, you do. I
don't. They like me."

Dom allowed his gaze to rest on the royal place-
holder. "So tell me where the money is, Your Majesty."

"It's—" He started to point at the open trunk
where silks and jewels frothed over the edge.

De Emmerich slapped his hand.

King Humphrey slapped back, hard enough to
knock de Emmerich backward.

In the moment of tense silence that followed, Dom
got a good idea of the balance of power between the
two men. Lazily, as if such displays were common-
place viewing, he said, "I'll take the money, I'll tell
you what the secret is, and we'll all be happy."

De Emmerich didn't think he could lose. A smile
of grotesque proportions spread across his face. "I
never truly doubted you, dear Dominic. Go take
your fee."

Dom didn't hesitate. The skin between his shoulder blades itched, but de Emmerich wasn't done toying with him yet. Turning his back, Dom strolled to
the trunk. He dug through the contents of the trunk,
found a leather money bag stashed in the corner, and
lifted it. "Doesn't feel like twenty-five thousand
crowns Pollardine."

"Did I say twenty-five thousand?" De Emmerich

tapped his lip in fake thoughtfulness. "I thought I said ten thousand."

"No." Dom peered at the contents. Coins. A great many coins. Perhaps ten thousand crowns. Certainly it weighed enough. He opened the wide left pocket hidden in the lining of his cloak and carefully spread the contents within, taking care that the seams should not tear. Then he reached into the trunk again and brought up another bag. "And another ten thousand bonus."

King Humphrey whimpered, but de Emmerich quieted him with a hand to his shoulder and a word in his ear.

Dom opened the right pocket and did the same. "And another . . . damn, this seems to be the last one." He held up the last bag. "How are you ever going to pay your mercenaries?"

"Out of Bertinierre's treasury," de Emmerich said. "So what's the secret?"

Dom came to the table and jerked his knife free of the wood, and without hesitation betrayed his princess and her kingdom.

Then, his honor as a mercenary satisfied and his duty to Ruby done, he said, "I wouldn't pull that knife, de Emmerich."

De Emmerich already held a long, shiny blade ready to throw. "Why not? I already knew the secret. You're telling me nothing new."

Dom continued, "Because if you kill me, your king will never get the Pollardine diamond back."

The blade shivered in de Emmerich's fingers.

"The Pollardine diamond?" King Humphrey squealed, and grabbed for his chest.

"What do you know about the Pollardine diamond?" de Emmerich asked.

"I know where it is." Dom kept his voice level, his gaze level, and his hand on the butt of the pistol hidden in the lining of his cloak.

King Humphrey squealed again and ripped open his shirt.

Dom watched with interest, knowing what the king sought, and knowing he would not find it.

King Humphrey pulled the leather thong with its leather bag from beneath his corset. "It's here." His fingers groped the sack. "I can feel it." But he opened it, dumped the contents onto the table, and a small jagged crystal fell out.

The camp outside rang with men's voices.

The tent pulsated with the battle of wills between the two men.

De Emmerich slammed his knife into its scabbard.

Dom released his pistol into its holster.

De Emmerich snatched up the crystal. "Quartz." He tossed it down and in a white-hot rage headed around the table. "Damn you, you scabby bastard, what did you do with the diamond?" He advanced on Dom, those white teeth bared in a snarl.

Dom stood his ground.

De Emmerich came to a sudden halt two feet away. He was no match for Dom, and they both knew it.

Dom watched as de Emmerich faced that fact and fumbled for his knife. Dom swung the bag of gold and smacked the groping hand hard enough to break bones, then grabbed his wrist and twisted. When de Emmerich dropped to his knees, Dom put his lips right next to de Emmerich's ear. "I took the liberty of getting a guarantee for my safety. Now I'm telling you, that diamond is a guarantee for my princess's safety, too. The holy diamond of Pollardine will be returned safety after the overthrow, when the princess is released into my care." He twisted the arm until de Emmerich whimpered. "With no injuries. No rape, no torture, not even a bruise. Do you understand?"

De Emmerich nodded.

Dom upped the pain level. "Do you understand?"

"Yes!"

Letting him go, Dom straightened. He bowed with a flourish and said, "Sleep soundly, Your Majesty. By the way, you're very handsome in your night-shirt."

He left without, this time, turning his back.

He moved quickly through the camp back to the place where he'd tied his steed, not even stopping when the mercenaries hailed him. "I wouldn't stay if I were you," Dom told Toti as he strode past. "It's a doomed expedition."

Laurentia waited twenty-four hours for Dom to return. One miserable day. One cold, wakeful night.

At last she gave up her hopes and dreams, and faced the desolation that was her life. He wasn't coming back. He had never planned to stay. Not even the promise of an easy existence as consort to the crown princess of Bertinierre could compel the wretch to marry her.

Worse, her misplaced moment of passion and trust had put her kingdom in jeopardy.

Once she came to that realization, she rode back toward Omnia with all speed. She entered the palace to find the halls almost empty. The suitors were gone. The ladies had vanished. Only a few servants remained, subdued and whispering. Laurentia's footsteps echoed on the polished floor as she ran down the long hall, her gaze fixed her father's study. She had almost reached it. She was almost there—when a bony hand grabbed her arm and jerked her to a standstill.

She whipped around to find herself facing Weltrude.

"Walk." Weltrude towered over her as always, and her voice lashed with an unyielding tone. "A true princess doesn't hurry like a hussy. Walk."

Laurentia jerked her arm away and rubbed the five bruises Weltrude's fingers had caused.

Weltrude knew. Somehow, she knew that all her predictions had come to pass, that Laurentia had destroyed everything she loved in a fit of passion.

Laurentia backed away from her grimly triumphant lady-in-waiting, spun on her heel, and walked the rest of the way to the study.

Weltrude didn't matter. Walking didn't matter. All that mattered was getting to her father and doing what she could to cure the wound she had inflicted.

No one answered when she knocked, but quietly she pushed the door open.

Her ashen-faced father sat in his easy chair, holding a note.

Now she ran and knelt at his side. "Papa?"

"Pollardine's armies are in place in the royal maywort fields. If I don't concede defeat, they will destroy Bertinierre. If I don't agree to act as their puppet-king and keep my people calm, they will murder you."

Laurentia took his shaking hands in her own. "Papa, I betrayed you. I betrayed the whole country. This is all my fault."

His sad eyes, so like her own, filled with tears, and he gathered her in his arms. "You flatter yourself. You are not the only one who has made mistakes here. You are not the only one who has misjudged character. I'm the king, and I say this is my fault." Leaning his forehead against hers, he said quietly, "But the rescue of the country will be our responsibility, too, daughter, and we will do it."

Chapter Twenty-six

Dom expected to know the minute he rode over the border into Sereminia. He thought that some part of him, some hidden bit of flesh and bone would say, *Here, king's son, you have set foot on your father's land. The land you were cheated out of by an accident of birth.*

Yet the peaks remained lofty and unattainable, the wind whistled down the canyons, the summits passed without note, and eventually, on the descent down yet another mountain, he recognized one of his old haunts.

He had passed into Sereminia without knowing when.

A path became a trail, and finally a road. In Sereminia, all roads eventually led to the river, and he heard its rushing waters before he saw it. The river gleamed like molten silver in the sunlight, and while it was beautiful, the rivers were just as beautiful in Bertinierre. He dismounted, knelt on the bank, and as he plunged his hands into the water and washed his face, he shivered. The rivers in Bertinierre didn't make a man freeze from their bone-chilling cold, either.

No, he wasn't feeling the exultation he had anticipated on his return to Sereminia. He felt only urgency. He needed to get back to Bertinierre before the war touched Laurentia.

"Ho, there." A man's voice hailed him.

Dom turned in the smooth motion of a mercenary who'd left his back exposed.

No man stood there, but a youth of perhaps sixteen. He leaned on a hoe and examined him inquisitively. "I don't recognize you." He indicated Oscuro, tied to a tree. "You're not from around here."

His pronouncement had a ring of truth that Dom couldn't fail to recognize. He wasn't from around here. He hadn't been for a long time. "No."

"I definitely don't recognize this horse." The lad revealed his true interest. "He's a beauty."

"Yes." Dom rose to his feet. "I'm from Bertinierre."

"Really?" The lad's eyes lit up and he forgot about Oscuro. "Rumors say there's a fight going on in Bertinierre."

"So there is."

The lad sagged against the hoe. "I wish I was there. Not here, where nothing ever happens."

Dom looked past him, into the fields of growing barley. The land was prosperous, each stalk a tribute to Danior's wardship and the advantages of peace. And this stupid youth was complaining.

"What's your name, son?" Dom asked.

"Gregor."

"Well, Gregor, things used to happened here. Haven't you ever heard about the fight King Danior had to gain his throne?"

"Against the evil Dominic," the youth said in a singsong voice. "Yes, I've heard about it. Papa talks about it all the time, and how he played such a big role in saving the prince and princess. But that was years ago, I was just a kid, nothing's happened since, and anyway, I think Dominic is just an ogre made up to frighten little children."

The imaginary ogre stood there and stared at the lad. A tale to frighten children? He'd been gone thirteen years, and returned to find himself a myth? By Santa Leopolda, that girl Rosabel wasn't the only one. "He was real," Dom sputtered.

"You sound like my father." Gregor lifted his smock and wiped off his forehead and smeared dirt on. "You and he ought to get on well. Come on, there's the dinner bell." He invited a stranger to his home without hesitation; another sign of peace. "You and Papa can tell your stories and scare the little ones."

Dom had already gone one full day without eating, and he was too good a mercenary to refuse a meal. "Thank you," he said. "I would like to scare the little ones, but I don't have time to sit down for dinner."

Gregor examined him. "In an awful hurry, then."

"Yes. I have to save my woman."

He wasn't even an ogre, Dom realized. He was a ghost, walking the streets of Plaisance, recognizing landmarks and not being recognized. No one raised a hand in greeting or in blows, no one spoke his name or paid him heed.

Plaisance hadn't really changed. The capital of the

Two Kingdoms still gleamed in the sunshine, an ancient city that had taken root on either side of the river valley and grown into this tangle of streets where merchants, monks, and noblemen lived side by side. If anything, Plaisance looked a little cleaner and definitely more prosperous. The merchants were plumper, the children wore shoes, and a few of the streets now wound out of the flatlands and up onto the slopes of the surrounding mountains to accommodate the city's growth.

The streets thronged with people, but no one looked on his face and ran from him. No one noticed him at all. He had become something they wanted to forget; that mad and mercifully brief moment when they'd wanted to overthrow their ancient royal family and deny an ancient prophesy.

Yet as he walked toward the Palace of the Two Kingdoms, he knew how to get attention. He walked up to the captain of the Royal Guard and demanded an audience with King Danior. The captain was neither dim-witted nor self-satisfied, for he well remembered the revolution. He took one look at Dom's face, his features stamped with the heritage of the royal family, and pointed the way inside. As Dom walked through the doors of the palace, the captain fell in behind him, and Dom could almost feel how the man's hands twitched toward his weapons.

Dom found himself ushered into the prime minister's office, and in only a moment the prime minister himself walked in.

Dom recognized him at once. "Victor! Brother. How good to see you."

"Damn." Victor stood, hands on hips, and glared.

"I hoped the captain was wrong. What are you doing here?"

"Maybe I've come for a job," Dom answered. "Our brother the king seems to be handing out high posts to just about any shirttail relative."

"Worse, His Majesty would probably give you one." Victor turned his back and walked out. "Come on," he called over his shoulder.

Dom hurried to catch up. "Sloppy," he reprimanded. "What if I was carrying a weapon?"

Victor cast him a disgusted glance. "You didn't come to kill us all now. If you wanted to do that, you would have come before, or come sneaking in like a thief. No, you came to fulfill the old lady's prophesy."

The old lady's prophesy?

You'll return begging on your knees.

Victor saw Dom start as he remembered, and he said with relish, "I hope they let me stay and watch."

But he wasn't begging on his knees, Dom wanted to retort. He would never beg on his knees. The old lady wasn't right.

"Did the girl Rosabel return from Bertinierre unharmed?" Dom asked.

Victor stopped in his tracks. He swiveled to face Dom. "You have been busy, haven't you?"

"Did she?"

"Yes. She didn't like the man with Princess Laurentia, so she came home by a secret route. You were that man, weren't you?"

Dom grinned at his half-brother.

"So she was right to be cautious." Victor swiveled

to face front again and marched down the ancient corridors.

He followed as Victor led him up worn stairs. The adornments of the palace he'd once worked to over-throw didn't interest him. Only Danior interested him, for Dom's goal was within reach.

Victor tapped on a solid oak door, then swung it open. "It *is* him," he called, then waved Dom inside.

Dom stepped inside, expecting to see an anteroom, or at the least some kind of office. Instead he stepped into a bedchamber. A vast royal bedchamber, deco-rated in gold and silver, with candles burning to light the dim corners and a curtained bed on a raised dais.

Worse, a woman reclined in the bed, and a man sat at her side. Evangeline—and Danior.

"Don't tell me you're sick," Dom blurted, all his fine plans crumbling with the knowledge that Dan-ior would not leave his beloved wife if she were ill.

But Evangeline only laughed, a hearty peal of amusement. "Not at all. I've never felt better."

"You must have just traveled into town, or you would know the news." Danior's voice sounded the same, only stronger and more sure, if such a thing were possible. "We have just been blessed with an-other daughter."

Danior looked so proud. Obnoxiously proud, but what else was new?

Now Dom saw the cradle beside the fire, and the stooped old nurse who rocked it with her foot. "May I look on my niece?"

Danior gestured his permission and Evangeline smiled at Dom with such delight he wondered if childbirth had driven her mad. Her and Danior both. Dom wouldn't let a man like him close to a helpless infant, not knowing what they knew of him. But they said nothing as he approached the cradle and drew back the covers. "Ah." The sigh was drawn from him. "A princess." The babe slept, her plump mouth moving as she dreamed of milk and comfort. He couldn't see her eyes, but he would wager they were blue, for she carried the same mop of black hair that Victor carried—that Danior carried—that he carried. There could be no doubt that they were all related, and he would have a child who looked like this soon. He knew he would.

If he could get back to Laurentia before it was too late.

Carefully, he slid one hand under the child's head and one under her tiny body, and he lifted the slumbering child to his chest. She weighed so little, yet was so precious.

"She should be swaddled." He knew that from his experience with Ruby.

"That's what I say, too," Danior agreed. "But Evangeline won't hear of it."

"Barbarians," Evangeline muttered.

When Dom had a child of his blood, he would swaddle her. He would guide her and protect her. He looked toward Danior. "I need your help."

Danior watched him in bemusement, as if the sight of his rebel brother and his infant daughter amazed him. "Do you? What kind of help?"

From beside the cradle, a creaking voice asked, "And are you willing to go on your knees to save your princess?"

Dom looked down at the stooped old nurse and recognized the gleam in her eyes. It was the old nun, the old saint who had uttered the prediction before throwing him out of the country.

He had sworn he would not go on his knees, not to Danior, not even for this, but Laurentia's life was at stake. Laurentia's, and their child's, and . . . Laurentia's. He had to make this right. Even if Laurentia never forgave him, even if their children were never conceived, even if he never loved another woman, he had to rescue Laurentia and make her world right.

Somehow he would save her kingdom for her . . . because he loved her.

The babe in his arms squirmed and sighed, a promise for the future, and he answered steadily, "Yes. For Laurentia I will go down on my knees."

And he did.

Chapter Twenty-seven

*The prison chamber was small, but scrubbed and, de-*spite its being below street level, dry. Laurentia had a narrow, straight-backed wooden chair and table and an iron bed with a feather mattress and clean linens. She received only two meals a day, but they were substantial, if plain. The Pollardine guards treated her well, although one had taken her courtesy to mean affection, and she'd had to teach him differently with the heel of her boot on his instep.

Dom had taught her that, but she didn't think about Dom. Instead, she thought about herself.

As each day passed of the slow, torturous week, she paced the cell, back and forth, along the track countless other prisoners had made in the sandstone floor. She examined the scratchings other prisoners had made in the sandstone walls. And she thought about the way she'd changed in the last five years.

Before her marriage, she had been a child, wanting what she wanted without a thought to possible consequences. Her marriage had demolished that girl with her bright, youthful convictions, and Laurentia had had to rebuild herself. From the strengths of the girl and the experiences of the woman, she had created Bertinierre's beloved princess: strong, self-willed, worthy to rule.

She'd had only one weakness: she believed in true love.

Dom had diagnosed her weakness at once, and he'd taken advantage of it. Very well. But she was still the princess of Bertinierre, and neither Dom, his schemes, nor any of his cohorts could destroy her. In the end, she would win all.

A faded cloth covered the small barred window at the top of her cell. Night after night she heard the drunken shouts of the soldiers as they celebrated their victory. She heard occasional gunshots, and feet running on the cobblestones. Yet she couldn't hear the everyday sounds of life on the street. The merchants calling out their wares, the chatter of the women hurrying to the well, they were indistinguishable in the living grave she inhabited.

But on the second day, she discovered that if she balanced the chair on top of the table, carefully climbed up, and stood on her tiptoes, she could push the makeshift curtain aside and her eyes were right at street level. So every morning she watched the shoes of Omnia's merchants as they scurried by and the boots of the mercenaries as they marched past, and pretended she was still an important part of the city. And sometimes . . . a friend would come and talk.

Laurentia was never balancing on the chair when Weltrude arrived.

Laurentia knew Weltrude's schedule, for Weltrude had informed her she would visit every afternoon, and Weltrude never varied her agenda. Every afternoon she left the palace where she now occupied Laurentia's own quarters, and rode in the royal landau to the center of town. The guards bowed her into the prison. The clink of the key in the door leading to the corridor of Laurentia's cell was the signal that Weltrude had arrived, but Laurentia knew Weltrude had first passed through two more doors and walked along two more corridors—corridors filled with Bertinierrian patriots who had resisted the invasion.

Laurentia had a corridor all her own. There were no neighbors in the cells around Laurentia. Apparently Weltrude believed Laurentia could forment a counter-invasion even from prison.

After the sound of the key in the outer door, Laurentia heard the approaching murmur of the guards as they produced fulsome compliments for the traitor who had taken her place. Then the key rattled in the lock of her own cell, and Weltrude had arrived.

Seven days. Seven visits.

Seven letters.

Today, the solid oak door swung wide, and there stood Weltrude smiling with brightly rouged lips.

Laurentia smiled back. She couldn't bear to have Weltrude know the depths of her misery. "Weltrude, come in. Have a seat." She pointed to the chair, now safely resting in the middle of the floor. "I'm sorry I can't offer you better hospitality."

As the door shut behind her, Weltrude said, "Thank you, my dear. You must admit, when you think of the misery of the Bastille, you are quite lucky to be in such comfortable circumstances."

Laurentia still smiled, knowing full well what

would result if she shouted the truth—that she didn't belong here, that Weltrude had raised perfidy to an art form, and very soon her crimes would be punished.

Weltrude seated herself in a rustle of silk, leaving Laurentia standing, as always. "Even my own dear father kept quite a nasty dungeon. Did I tell you he was a king, too?"

"Yes, I believe you did." *Every day, several times.*

"I want to make sure you remember it. I was a king's daughter, too, a true princess in every sense of the word, but the world's diplomats thought my father's kingdom would be better ruled by Russia, so they gave it to the czar and I was left homeless." She unbuttoned her white gloves, took them off, and smoothed them in her lap. "After Father died, I had to make my own way in the world, but I survived because I'm strong. *I'm* running this country now."

"I thought de Emmerich was running the country."

"He thinks so, too, but he's really not good at anything but bullying. He is very good at that." Weltrude contorted her face into an exaggerated expression of conspiratorial amusement.

Horribly enough, Laurentia feared it was true. She knew the strength of Weltrude's will; she had just never comprehended the direction of Weltrude's ambitions. For so many years Weltrude had been Laurentia's anchor; now Laurentia discovered those years had been filled with petty enmity, scheming, and bitterness.

But if Laurentia had her flaw, so did Weltrude, and Laurentia recognized it—her vast, overweening confidence. "What about Pollardine's king?" Laurentia asked.

"Humphrey doesn't care about power! He just spends the money." Weltrude frowned. "And searches for his diamond." Snapping open her painted ivory fan—Laurentia's fan—Weltrude waved it before her face. "This chamber *is* a little stuffy with so little ventilation—"

It's the flames of hell licking at your boots, Weltrude.

"—but it's really altogether quite acceptable for *you*. We could have kept you in the dungeons under the palace, of course, but we feared your father might find a way to communicate with you there."

Laurentia folded her hands before her, put her toes on an imaginary line, and concentrated on not fidgeting.

"Those dungeons are rather dark and dank. That fool of a kidnapper de Emmerich hired died in most unpleasant circumstances."

Laurentia flicked a glance at Weltrude's satisfied expression. "Poison usually is unpleasant."

"But how good of Dominic to bring him back where I had access to the food." Weltrude smiled again, showing a streak of lip rouge on her teeth.

Laurentia took great satisfaction in not telling her.

Weltrude continued, "No wonder he had to take the job from de Emmerich. Your Dominic was not very smart!"

Laurentia found herself wanting to shout in Dom's defense, and the horror of that momentarily shattered her self-possession. For one moment she dropped her mask and the clawing agony was plain to see.

Like a rich, sleek snake, Weltrude had been watching, and she struck. "Yes, *your* Dominic. I knew as soon as I saw him de Emmerich had chosen well. Dominic knew what he was doing all along." She waggled her finger at Laurentia in grotesque roguishness. "He seduced you just for the secret."

In that, Weltrude was wrong. Laurentia had freely given the secret to Dom, and all she'd been foolish enough to do was fall in love.

"No one really wants you for yourself, a spoiled, insolent, impetuous girl like you."

There, you've said it. Give me my letter! "I know that, too."

"Yes. Well." Weltrude rose. "As long as you don't think anyone cares about you anymore. Your people hate you for bringing this on them. Your father still lives in the palace, of course, but he's nothing but a puppet doing as de Emmerich tells him, and de Emmerich does what I tell him."

"I see." The thought of the indignities suffered by her father grieved Laurentia past bearing.

"You should be glad I'm the power behind de Emmerich." Going to the iron door, she banged on it. As the guard noisily turned the key in the lock, she said, "If it weren't for me, de Emmerich would have killed your father days ago. I believe de Emmerich used to be a friend of your father's, and your father discarded him for some reason."

"Because de Emmerich is a treacherous swine?" Laurentia inquired in a polite tone that only emphasized the brutal words.

"It could be that." Weltrude opened her handbag and brought out the daily letter from King Jerome.

She placed it on the table and looked Laurentia directly in the eyes. "But he's no more treacherous than you, my dear Laurie. You destroyed your own father."

In that, Weltrude was right.

Laurentia watched the guard bow the wretched woman out of the cell, saw the door shut, heard the rattle of the key. Only then did she snatch up her precious letter.

The seal had been broken, of course. For security, Weltrude said. So she knew they weren't planning insurrection.

Laurentia smiled.

But the letter said no more than it had in previous days. King Jerome was well. He hoped she was well. She was not to worry. All was going as they had foreseen.

She brushed her hand across her suddenly wet eyes. The letter gave her comfort, yes. It told her everything she wanted to know. But . . . but how she wanted to see her father, talk to him, hug him again and have him tell her he loved her. In those few minutes before the guards had come to take her away, her father had taken the blame for insisting Dom be her bodyguard. She had taken the blame for falling blindly in love. Then they'd abandoned their futile self-reproaches and spoke of the plans they'd made. Plans they would now put into action.

Laurentia resumed her pacing.

Down the hall, she heard the key turn in the lock, and she paused. Weltrude allowed only herself as visitor. Supper had already been served. There were no other prisoners here. So why the change in routine?

Had someone, somehow, found out what she was doing?

She couldn't hear footsteps, but then, she never could. The door was thick and strong. She could only stand and wait, heart thumping, staring at the door.

The key grated in the lock. The door swung back.

And she heard Dominic of Baminia, the biggest bastard in the whole world, say, "Thank you, Toti. There'll be more when you let me out."

The pain of hearing his too-familiar voice almost doubled her up.

This had never occurred to her. That Dom would have the audacity to come to Bertinierre, to her prison, and mock her? No. She hadn't thought that even Dom could be so cruel.

Stepping forward, she blocked the entrance. She didn't glance at Dom, or in any way acknowledge him. "Toti, I give you the word of a princess you'll get your reward if you'll take him away."

Dom crowded her into her cell by his sheer bulk. "Get out, Toti."

Toti grinned, stupid as always, and shut the door. The key rattled in the lock, leaving Laurentia alone—with Dom.

She didn't take the time to brace herself; she didn't dare. If she thought about it, she'd never find the courage. So she looked right at him, absorbed the pain of seeing him without recoiling, and said, "I'd ask why you came, but I'd guess the answer would be to laugh in my face."

His face, that fallen-angel face with a day's smudgy growth of whiskers, changed from watchfulness to a grim impatience. "You don't know me well."

"No, I don't know you at all." He flinched, and she enjoyed that.

"But you *do*," he said. "In the biblical sense."

She should have known he wouldn't let her get away with winning even a verbal battle. He would attack on any front, strip her defenses down with reminders of her own idiocy, and leave her, again, bleeding and helpless.

Only she wouldn't let him. If she woke in the night with tears on her cheeks, he would never know.

"Yes." She nodded judiciously. "That part I quite enjoyed. I think you must be a good lover."

He ceased his satisfied survey of her prison to consider her incredulously. "You think?"

"Perhaps you don't realize it, but since you left I've been unable to investigate any other men or their abilities." She gestured around the bare chamber. "The possibilities here are limited."

"No one's touched you, then."

He wore a different outfit than she'd last seen on him, rather elegant if one liked black leather trousers and a black leather waistcoat. She would swear his black shirt was silk, with close-fitting sleeves and a tight-fitting collar, and if he had a jacket he had failed to bring it into the cell. Only his boots were the same, heavy and black.

She wanted to ask where he was going dressed in

such a bizarre manner. She chose not to care. "No one comes near."

Dom nodded. "I told de Emmerich they weren't to hurt you."

Her breath caught on a jagged bit of emotion. Funny how it affected her to hear Dom admit his culpability. She knew he had used her. She knew she'd been stupid. But to have him admit he'd known, planned for her incarceration, talked to de Emmerich about her and how he made a laughing-stock of the princess of Bertinierre . . . "Good of you," she said.

He considered her, glowering in the plain, short-sleeved dimity gown Weltrude had allowed her. "I didn't come to ridicule. I came to help."

She snorted. Weltrude wouldn't approve, but now everything that Weltrude had ever taught her was suspect. "Help? Help do what? Prepare me for a life-time in prison? Prepare me for death? Strangle me? Break my neck?"

He moved forward, stalking her, tightening the dimensions of the room with his determination. "You're not going to die here!"

She gave way, stepping sideways, keeping herself away from corners. "Not here, but if your de Emmerich gets his way—probably on a gibbet in Omnia's square."

"Listen to me." He caught her shoulder, halting her retreat. "It won't come to that."

His touch hadn't changed. It didn't matter what she knew of him, how he had betrayed her. Her flesh warmed, her heart warbled, each strand of hair and toenail and elbow longed to unite with him.

With a jolt, she realized why he had come. "Is this part of your fee?" she asked hoarsely. "I'm not broken yet, so they send Dominic of Baminia in to finish the job? Or do you get paid extra for torturing women and children?"

His eyes narrowed.

"I recognize that look." She pointed her finger into his face. "That means you're losing your temper. Or not. Maybe it just means you're *acting* like you're losing your temper. Just like you *acted* like you desired me, you *acted* like you could be trusted, you *acted*—"

He folded her finger back into her hand, then jerked her forward by her fist. "I did desire you." He brushed her other hand aside. "I can be trusted." He scooped her up by the waist and brought her full against him. "And I am definitely losing my temper."

The feel and scent of him enraged her. She wanted to flail at him, to flatten him. "Do you think I'm afraid? Of your anger? Under your tutelage, I have done the worst thing a princess can to do her family and her country. I no longer fear lightning, or tidal waves, or raging boars, and I most certainly do not fear you."

With exaggerated and mighty patience, he asked, "You're not going to listen to me, are you?"

That patience, that patronage sent her over the edge into rage. "I was a fool over Beaumont. I was a fool over you. The third time isn't going to happen, Dom."

He held her. Just held her and looked at her, his

eyes like coals from the hottest part of the fire. "You said you loved me."

Victory at all costs. He would leave her no defenses, fling up each individual weakness to her until she crumpled.

Very well. She understood war now in a way she had never understood it before, and she had her weapons, too.

"I said a lot of things. I meant them at that moment. A lifetime has passed since then." Grabbing his hair, she yanked it, then stomped her heel hard on the instep of his foot.

He let her go and grabbed for his foot.

She backed rapidly away. "Love withers, Dom, at the sound of laughter, and you were laughing at me every moment we were together."

Chapter Twenty-eight

Dom thanked God for his heavy leather boots, because they were the only things that saved him from a broken foot.

He looked up at Laurentia who stood, her back against the door, exuding absolute unbridled pleasure, and he thanked God for something else.

"Your Highness, you've forgotten one thing."

She was smart enough to be wary of his cordial tone. "What's that?" she asked cautiously.

Putting his foot on the ground, he stomped it a few times to ascertain its soundness. "We're locked in here."

He saw her breasts rise under her quick breath.

"You just tried to hurt the ruthless mercenary bastard who took your virginity and left you sleeping—"

"And betrayed me." She had every vertebrae on her spine pressed hard against the door now, but she was still defiant.

"And betrayed you," he echoed. "Do you remember that piece of advice I gave you after your second kidnapping attempt, Your Highness?"

She slapped the flat of her hand against the door in a rhythmic motion.

Oh, yes, she remembered. He could tell. "Never hurt a man just enough to make him angry. You want to disable him completely, Your Highness, because an angry man is hard to handle. Do you remember the other thing I told you, Your Highness?"

She balled her hands into fists and began to beat against the door. She didn't turn her back on Dom.

Good. She was smart enough to be worried. She was brave enough to be defiant. She wasn't afraid of him. Good, also.

And she was still furious.

That was fine with him, because he was furious, too. She loved him, she'd said so. He loved her, he'd discovered that. But damn her, she ought to trust him.

He spoke through clenched teeth. "I told you, after you had incapacitated the man, to run like hell. Well, Your Highness, you haven't left yourself anywhere to run. We're in a tiny prison chamber and no one can hear you."

"Toti's got to release you," she said.

"Toti's not going to release me." He knew that as well as he knew his father's name. "I blithely just walked into de Emmerich's trap, and he's not going to let me go until I give him the Pollardine diamond."

She stopped beating on the door and stared at Dom. "The Pollardine diamond? How did you get that?"

"I took it off their sleeping king and held it as a guarantee. A guarantee which I have sacrificed by coming here." Smiling with false affability, he sat in the narrow chair and yanked off his boots. "Your Highness, you're stuck with me."

"Wh-what are you going to do?"

As if she didn't know. "I have just spent the most miserable week of my life," he said. "I had planned to spend two full days and two full nights with you, convincing you in every way I could imagine that you were my woman. Mine, now and forever. But I had to leave early because you told me about Chariton and I knew if I didn't leave, he'd be at the door, telling you the truth about me, and I'd never complete my commission. That's a hell of a way to end a career, Your Highness—in prison."

She laughed bitterly. "I know that."

He glared and stripped off his waistcoat. "So I hurried away, barely giving poor Oscuro a rest, trying to find Pollardine's army, and I get there too late, thank God, and almost get cheated out of my pay and almost get killed."

"I wonder which one concerned you most."

"Then as fast as I could, I headed off to Sereminia."

"Sereminia?" She blinked.

He relished her confusion. "Sereminia, my former home. There I found out that the victor always writes the history books, and my brother the king was the victor. I was a nobody, a worm he had crushed beneath his heel."

"If only that were true."

She didn't think him a worm. He chose to consider that an advance. "But I accomplished my mission there. It took a few days; they needed my advice about the best way to conquer Bertinierre—"

She looked truly aghast. "You brought another army down on us?"

Damn her, damn her! He got his shirt off in record time and started peeling off his trousers. "But when I was done, I leaped on Oscuro and hurried to Omnia."

"You invited Sereminia"—she developed an odd expression—"to invade us?"

"When I got here, I inquired first about you." He pointed at her. "Not about Brat, not about Ruby, but about you, because all the time I was gone all I could think about was you. All I could worry about was you. All I wanted was you. Princess Laurentia, who loved me. Princess Laurentia, who wanted to wed me."

Now she turned her back on him and started beating on the door and yelling. "Toti, open this door. Toti!"

She had finally gotten smart.

He tossed his trousers over his waistcoat and shirt, and stalked toward her wearing nothing but the outfit he'd been born in. "Princess Laurentia, you and I exchanged vows, whether you want to admit it or not, and I'm going to damned bloody well teach you that when you make a vow, you keep it." He could have picked her up from the back; instead he availed himself of the chance to unbutton her gown.

When she realized what he was doing, she tried to face him, but he'd had some experience with struggling women—a lot of noblewomen liked to pretend to be unwilling—and Laurentia's fury interfered with her judgment. If she'd dropped to the floor she might have had a chance, but all she did was struggle, and he took care of that with one arm across her back.

"When I get out," she snapped in royal wrath, "I will have you horsewhipped!"

"I have a better idea." He finished unbuttoning and stepped away and just as he knew she would, she flung herself around and her gown slipped off.

She grabbed for it. It drooped around her arms. The straps of her chemise could not have been simpler: no lace, no ribbons, just pure, plain white cotton so thin as to be transparent, and beneath that—nothing.

Just as he'd hoped. "You never wear a corset, do you? I like that in a woman." Lifting the holster, he extracted his pistol.

"In prison? There's no one to see me here!" She answered him, but her gaze wavered between him, cock-proud and ready, and the gun.

"There's no one to see me, either." He was so aroused he just wanted to pick her up and bury himself in her, but he had something to prove to her. "No one's ever going to know what passes between us this night."

"Night?" She glanced up toward the window where the spring sun still shone from the west.

He checked the pistol. It was loaded. He advanced on her. She shrank against the door. Taking her hand in his, he wrapped her fingers around the gun. "I'm going to take you. There's only one way out."

She stared at his hand on hers, at the gun she held so unwillingly. "What's that?"

"You have to shoot me."

Slowly, she lifted her gaze to his face.

With a gesture that offered himself to her, he said, "Go ahead. The guards can't hear. We're too far away. There's been so much gunfire, no one on the street will even notice. And I won't stop you." He grinned at her in challenge.

Immediately he realized the grin was a mistake, for Laurentia's spine straightened. She dropped her gown. Smiling back at him, she stepped away from the door. It wasn't a pleasant smile.

"Do you have a cigar?" she asked.

"A cigar?" He did. When Danior had discovered he liked them, he had given him a box. "Why?"

"Get it."

He didn't understand, but he knew he wasn't going to like this. He fumbled with his waistcoat and got a cigar out of the inner pocket.

She gestured with the pistol. "Put it in your mouth and step against the wall."

He moved back to the far wall, which wasn't nearly far enough. What had possessed him to try and prove anything to Laurentia? She had a grudge against him, a grudge even he could understand, and he could tell by the sparkle in her eyes and the thrust of her shoulders that his provocation had infuriated her.

"Put the cigar in your mouth and turn sideways," she commanded.

"But if I turn sideways . . ." Sadly enough, he was still aroused.

"You said you wanted a demonstration of my shooting ability." She was still smiling. "I'm going to shoot the cigar out of your mouth."

He would see that smile in his nightmares. "Pistols are notoriously hard to aim, and you've never shot that particular piece."

"You'll just have to trust me, won't you?"

God had answered his prayers last time. Would it be too selfish to beg God for his own safety now? Did he even deserve his prayers to be answered? Thrusting the cigar between his teeth—lucky for him Danior smoked long cigars—he turned sideways. He glanced at Laurentia out of the corners of his eyes. She was lifting the pistol in both hands, an intent expression on her face.

Compulsively, unable to help himself, he found himself praying.

"You'll want to cover your ears," she advised. "It's going to be loud."

It wasn't his ears he covered.

Bracing himself, he closed his eyes.

The explosion blew his prized cigar to smithereens.

But if he were alive to know it, he didn't care. Plaster chips sprayed his face. His ears rang. He opened his eyes and looked at the wall beside him, and the bullet hole smoked from the impact. For the second time in his life, he lifted his eyes upward and said, "Thank you, Lord."

Then he turned to face Laurentia. He tried to speak, but found he had to swallow, first. "Nice shooting, princess."

"Yes." Walking to the table, she placed the pistol on its surface. "You gave me two options—shoot you or bed you. I made a third option. Don't ever try to corner me again."

The pride of the woman! He'd never valued arrogance in a noble before, but Laurentia deserved to be haughty. And she was his. He could scarcely contain himself for happiness. Pretending like he'd never wondered, however briefly, if she would miss, he swaggered forward to confront her again. "So now what? I'm still alive, and we're still alone."

She lifted her chemise. She untied the ribbon that held her simple white drawers and let them fall. He caught a brief, far too brief, glimpse of her belly, the cup of her hips, and the neat black triangle of hair. Then, before he could drag in a single breath to assuage his shock, she let go of the chemise. She stepped out of her gown and followed, a princess in a full-length, peasant-simple chemise. With both hands, she shoved him and he staggered backward. When the chair bumped him in the back of the legs, she grabbed his arms. "You're not going to force me or seduce me. If we're going to do this, we're doing it my way."

He didn't know whether to chuckle or cower. He did neither, but sat down hard when she shoved at his shoulders.

Her breasts were at eye level, and she was breathing hard.

A week ago, for one glorious day and one glorious night he'd observed these breasts, he'd held these breasts, and since that time, he had dreamed about these breasts. The size, the shape, the weight. The tender velvet skin, the sensitive nipples tinted the perfect shade of rose, the way they fit in his mouth and the ripple of her body beneath him when he suckled. Now her breasts rose and fell, so perfect he wanted nothing more than to suckle them again, but when he reached out, she knocked his hands away.

"My way," she snapped.

Lifting her chemise, she daintily placed a foot on either side of him, arranging herself above his thighs. She wasn't tall, the position was awkward, yet ... she was open to him, and his cock strained and shifted, reaching, desperate, wanting. If he weren't inside her soon, he would go mad with desire and her revenge would be complete.

Frustration brought beads of sweat to his brow, and he cautiously reached behind her. Intent on moving closer, she didn't rebuff him or even notice when he caught the hem of her chemise and moved it up out of the way, and held it as he steadied her with his hands on her buttocks.

Her muscles flexed in his palms, and she scorched him with a glance of rage. Or passion. Or ... no matter, she didn't object.

"Your Highness." His voice sounded gravelly, and he had to clear his throat. "With your permission, I would assist when you allow."

Her chin was up, firm, regal, and she lowered it only to give him a single nod.

That was enough.

The warmth, the roundness of her bottom cheeks had haunted him this past week. He hadn't caressed them enough while he had the chance, nor had he had the light to truly examine them, to observe and to imprint the sweet female strength of them in his mind.

Even now, he could only dream of what paradise lay between those buttocks.

But he was a mercenary; he scarcely knew how to

dream. He only knew how to get what he wanted.

She began to lower herself to him, but she was almost a virgin. The way was tight and closed against him. Her pubis touched him randomly, swift little pats that had him grinding his teeth.

"If you would allow me . . ." Sliding his fingers inward, he found her, opened her.

At his first touch, she paused. Her eyes half-closed, her breath froze.

This he had seen during that day and that night. This expression of yearning told him the truth. She wanted him. Even now, even after what he had done, she wanted him, and her rage could not disguise that.

He'd declare a triumph, but first he had to get inside her. He had to possess her again. Then he would know she was his. "Laurentia," he whispered as he opened her.

She looked at him and licked her lower lip, moistening her pouty mouth.

His gut gave a twist. That mouth. He'd observed that mouth every day that he'd been with her, watching her talk, smile, eat, frown, and all he'd wanted was to kiss those lips, soft, pink, generous. He'd imagined the taste of her, thought of the tongue-play they could have, considered how he would take her breath and give her his until they were one and alive with impatience.

He'd done all that, and all he wanted was to do it again.

"Your Highness." He parted his lips, reached for her with his mouth.

She drew back. "My way." Catching his cheeks

between her palms, she tilted his head up. She pressed her lips to his, and this time she opened him, probed him with her tongue, filled his mind with sensations of wetness, of warmth, of bodies and motion and . . . He had to get inside.

Below, he probed her with his finger, and tasted her tiny moan with his lips. She was ready. He was past ready. He removed his finger, guided her down to him. The mere contact of her, open on him, adjusting around him, sent his hips surging up.

He was inside. If he could just push all the way in, have her wrapped around every inch of him, everything would be in order. She would remember whose woman she was and she would say she loved him again.

She had to say she loved him.

She pulled away from the kiss they shared. She placed her hands on his shoulders. She looked into his eyes.

And authoritatively she propelled herself up.

Not all the way, but far enough to make him grab and try to force her back down.

"My way," she said, and before he could grab again, she languidly sank back down. But not all the way.

Her feet rested on the floor. She had control. Maybe she wanted revenge.

As slowly as she was moving, she already had it. But—oh, God—she twisted her hips a little as she lifted herself again, and the friction inside her brought tears of delectation to his eyes.

And why? Could it be that the rage and frustration that drove him goaded her, too? Had the lonely nights been too long, had her fears been too painful?

She leaned against him, stroking him with her whole body as slowly she rose, and deliberately she fell. Each time a little more of him entered her, and each time it wasn't enough.

Her nipples brushed his chest. The fabric between them snagged on his chest hair. He wanted to strip away the chemise, remove any barrier from between them, make this agony a pure indulgence . . . but he didn't dare take his hands away from her buttocks. He kept hoping she would tire, she would let him take over, and he could drive into her again and again . . .

"Take all of me." He was begging. He could force her. Of course he could. But he was a fair man. She had the right to torment him as he had tormented her.

Only this was too much. His balls were pulled tight against his body, he needed his release now, and still . . . *still* she tantalized him. "Please, darling. Your Highness. Please."

"Darling Your Highness," she echoed. "I like that."

She was still talking. She'd reduced him to babbling. But he didn't make the mistake of thinking her unaffected. As she moved on him, he felt the walls within her flexing, a counteraction to the stroke of her breasts along his chest, to her sheath around his cock. With just a little encouragement, she would be twisting in his arms, moaning in that soft voice, tightening on him until he fought his own orgasm to allow her hers.

He knew how to bring a woman to climax with a

single caress. He'd been trained to pleasure a woman until euphoria carried her beyond the physical and into a place of pure sensuality.

Now he knew why. He had found a design in those years of servitude. Fate had prepared him for Laurentia.

So he touched her. He slid his hand down her thigh, cupping it in his palm, and lightly touched that sensorial bit at her front.

She arched back, up, cresting like a wave. That single touch would have been enough, but for her he wanted more. He grazed her, small, rhythmic motions of encouragement. With each stroke, she tightened her grip on pleasure, loosened her grasp on control. The sounds he worshiped broke from her, small, untutored, primitive. Her features became the face of love, classic and timeless. Each undulation brought her higher, straining, reaching for pleasure, contracting on him.

She was wild with purpose, demanding without words that he satisfy her, and he took savage joy in obeying.

When her body had been overwhelmed, and she thought there could be no more, he took her beyond.

Carefully, firmly, conclusively, he pressed his fingers against her.

She dug her nails into his shoulders. She cried out, "Dom!" She shuddered and convulsed, a living flame in his arms.

He could bear no more restraint.

He assumed control. Clasping her hips, he stood, driving her all the way down on his shaft.

She cried out again, wrapping her legs and arms

around him, holding all of him. He took three long steps to the door. He placed her back against the smooth surface and held her there, leaned hard between her legs. As he knew it would, the contrast of the coolness of the wood at her back and the heat between them brought her to consciousness for one long second.

She looked into his eyes.

In his softest, most domineering voice, he said, "*My* way."

Dom was drifting off to sleep at last when he felt Laurentia's shoulders shake. At first he diagnosed a nightmare, but the narrow bed didn't allow for such a mistake.

She was crying. Her head rested on his arm, and tears trickled over his skin and onto the pillow.

Lifting himself above her, he whispered, "My brave girl, what's wrong?"

"I love you," she said.

Such an enormous sense of relief filled him that, for a moment, he thought himself too vulnerable. Love, according to all the sages, was supposed to give him a sense of security, not twist his heart into a knot at the sound of a sob. "I know."

"You don't understand." She took a wavering breath. "I don't want to. I don't want to, and it's almost more than I can bear."

Chapter Twenty-nine

Dom woke slowly, knowing Laurentia had already risen, stretching and feeling the aches she had inflicted. He counted them well received. They were together again. They had spent the night making love: her way, his way, her way. Now he would explain what he had done and why. Now she would be reasonable.

Opening his eyes, he looked for her.

Looked again.

Sat up and stared, then stupidly leaned over and looked under the bed.

He leaped to his feet, not conscious of his nakedness, and slammed into the door. It was locked. He looked up toward the window. Nothing. Nothing had changed; the room was the same.

But Laurentia was gone.

How had she done it? Hell's fire, how had she escaped?

He gathered his clothes as quickly as he could, donning them in a frenzy, then scrambled around the chamber, touching the walls, moving the bed, trying to find a secret exit.

Nothing.

At last he shoved the table up against the outside wall, put the chair on top, and climbed up. He held his breath as he balanced himself and straightened; the furniture which seemed strong enough while on the floor now seemed deceptively fragile. But it supported him until he could shove the curtain aside and grasp the bars at the small slot of a window. He found himself hoping they were sturdy and could support his weight. They were and could. And he realized—Laurentia hadn't escaped this way. She couldn't have piled the furniture while he slept. He wasn't that sound a sleeper. The top of his head brushed the ceiling of the cell, even with his knees bent, but for the diminutive princess to haul herself up and out—no.

Yet this was his best chance. Shiny bolts held the bars in place, but he twisted at them anyway. They didn't move. He jerked at the bars. He succeeded only in almost overbalancing.

The bottom of the window was at street level, and when he peered out he found himself gazing on a side street. It wasn't busy, but merchants and housewives hurried past, some right by his nose, some across the street. An ox-drawn cart rolled along at a tedious rate. By craning his neck, he could see the end of the street; guards loitered there, but by their attitude Dom knew they considered this boring duty.

Damn it, he had an army marching into town soon. He had to get out to meet Danior.

So he started yelling. "Hey! I'm down here, get me out! Hey, come on, I need to get out! Hey!"

No one paid any attention; indeed, most people

increased their speed. The guards grinned, but they stayed at their posts.

"Hey!" Dom shouted.

One brown homespun dress came to a halt by his nose, and he snatched at the hem. "Lady, I need help."

She knelt by the window and peered inside. "I would say you do."

"Brat." Relieved, he rested his forehead against the cool bars and looked into her thin, amused, and welcome face. "Where's Ruby?"

"Safe."

"Can you get me out of here?"

"Maybe."

He lifted his head. Brat was behaving oddly. "What do you mean, maybe?"

"You've made a mess of things, Dom."

"Not that again." He glared at her. "I got the money for Ruby."

"Not for Ruby," she corrected him. "For you. And in the process, you've destroyed a country."

Owning a pair of breasts obviously sapped the mental processes. "It's not destroyed," Dom snapped, "it's just damaged a little, and I'm going to help put it together."

"Do you think when something's broken you can just stick some glue on it and it'll be as good as new?" Brat rested her hands on her knees like someone prepared to stay a while. "Even Ruby knows better than that."

Dom craned his neck and checked the guards. They were passing a bottle and laughing. "You're exaggerating."

"Then where's the princess?"

"She escaped."

"Without you?"

"Don't be such a wiseacre." *Without you*. The phrase echoed through the hollow corridors of his soul. *Without you*. Laurentia had left without him, without even a backward glance.

"She's gone," he repeated. How? His gaze sharpened on Brat's face. "You know her well now."

"Oh, yes. The princess and I speak every day."

He had an uncomfortable moment of wondering what Laurentia had thought when she discovered his one remaining mercenary was the woman she had met and to whom she had been so kind. And did she know about the cart? He'd never had his lies catch up with him, because he'd never before planned to stay.

None of that really mattered, though. All that mattered was—"Then you know how she got out of here."

She smiled.

He straightened and cracked his head on the ceiling. "Damn!" He rubbed his skull, but the blow put his mind to working. "That Chariton person found you."

"Days ago, Dom."

"So *he's* helping Princess Laurentia?" His voice rose in disbelief. Princess Laurentia would rather have someone else help her?

"Better ask what the princess is doing to help herself. She's organized the whole revolt from her cell."

"Revolt." Dom glanced back at the barren room.

Laurentia had organized a revolt, and from here? Why hadn't she told him?

His military mind went to work. "How? When? Give me a report."

Brat responded to his commander's voice as she always had—coldly, efficiently. "Five years ago, the king and the princess concocted a plan in case an invasion occurred, and this last week they've been putting it into action. The princess has been passing and receiving notes through the window, and apparently the letters she received from her father were in code. At this moment, Bertinierre's army is gathering outside the capital. The king has escaped from the palace. The princess has been taken to her command post."

"Will she be safe?"

"Only if they win back their kingdom."

They *would* win back their kingdom. Dom himself had guaranteed it. "Sereminia's army will be here by tonight. Brat, I need to get out."

Brat scrambled just out of arm's reach, and considered him. "Was the princess glad to see you?"

"No. She was angry." If Brat had been talking to Laurentia, she already knew all the answers. "But I made things better."

"Which is why she went off and left you locked in a cell?"

Brat, the old Brat, was truly gone. She questioned his judgment; she called his feints. The wounded, rebellious girl had grown up, and he didn't like the change. "Can you get me out or not?"

"Not until I tell you a few things, Dominic."

He groaned and dropped his head to the bars again. "Not now!"

She grabbed his hair and pulled his head back to look in his eyes. "This is the only way I know to make you listen." She shook him. "Her Highness loves you."

"I know. She told me." He didn't tell Brat what else Laurentia had said.

Brat seemed to know, anyway. "But she hates herself for it."

"She told you that?"

"No, but I know. Do you think I've gone through all these years of battle and passion without learning anything about being a woman? And I've been raped, Dom. I know about bitterness and shame."

"I didn't rape her!"

"No, you made her ashamed of herself. That's worse. Dom, love should make you proud, and I know loving you *could* make a woman proud."

He answered as he always answered any reproach. "I'm a bastard and a mercenary."

Brat slashed at the air as if cleaving his defense. "Don't try and sell me that mare's nest. I know who you are. I didn't follow a bastard and a mercenary all these years. I followed the man I could see inside. A man of honor, a man who protected his own, a leader."

"You're saying that I make excuses for myself." She really knew how to get to him; he hated those spineless worms who shrugged off responsibility.

"I'm saying that whenever you want to hurt someone, you claim to be a bastard and a mercenary."

"I never hurt Laurentia."

"Didn't you?" Brat stood up. "I have to go now. The guards are coming."

She walked away, leaving Dom staring out of the cell onto the street.

Hurt Laurentia? He hadn't hurt Laurentia. She'd been angry, that was all.

But if that was the truth, why had she cried?

The guards strolled past without bothering to speak to him, then strolled past again, while Dom hung on the bars and tried to understand.

"I told her I loved her," he muttered to the missing Brat.

He hadn't, of course. But he'd thought it. Men just didn't say things like that. *I love you.* He'd never heard a man say that. Since the day his mother died, he'd never said it to anyone.

But he'd thought it. He meant it. "Aren't women supposed to be intuitive about stuff like this?" he asked the street plaintively.

Beneath his feet, the chair moved.

He clutched the bars and looked down, and there stood Brat, an urchin grin on her face, the key in her hand. "Are you coming, or are you going to hang there all day?"

Chapter Thirty

The cheerful, charred, worn, exultant, red-eyed, trium-phant, and bloodstained two dozen men and women mingling below the dais in the throne room had become Bertinierre's newest heroes and heroines. They had come to celebrate their victory, to compare wounds, to exchange tales, and most of all to gaze upon their equally grubby and exhausted royal family.

Laurentia knew how they felt. She wanted to look at all of them, too.

All except . . . ah, but Dom had earned his place here. According to reports, he had been like a whirlwind, convincing Pollardine's horsemeat mercenaries it was time to flee, positioning King Danior and Sereminia's army. The two days of fighting had been brief and brutal, but now, as a fresh morning dawned, King Jerome sat firmly on the throne in his palace.

Only . . . none of this would have happened if it hadn't been for Dom.

None of it would have happened if it hadn't been for her, either.

Almost no one knew all the truth. The tale that

circulated spoke of King Jerome's surrender only
when his daughter had been taken prisoner. No one
thought the worst of him for that, especially since
he'd retaken the country in such a timely manner.

But she knew the truth. Dom knew. They were
bound together by the knowledge of his perfidy and
her gullibility at a time when she didn't ever want
to be bound to him at all.

She had proposed marriage to him.

She groped for King Jerome's hand.

And Dom was determined to have her.

King Jerome patted her fingers, and read her mind
with uncanny ability. "You have to stop reproaching
yourself. The mistake was as much mine as yours. I
pushed you into his arms. It's not turned out to be
such a mistake after all, has it?"

"What do you mean?" she asked in horror.

"It's a lucky man who knows his enemies, and
King Humphrey is being escorted back to Pollardine
with his diamond on a string around his neck. It's a
lucky man who knows his allies, too." He nodded
at King Danior, who stood speaking to Dom. "We
can identify our dearest friends." He indicated Dulcie, smudged with gunpowder. Francis, bandaged
and splinted. Chariton with his Gloria—Brat, as
Dom called her—and Ruby, who toddled about the
throne room, not at all impressed by its glory. Minnie and Roy, old and stooped, loyal as always. The
others, noble or not, wealthy or not, who had stood
for their country. "Our people fought for us and
won." Through the open windows, Laurentia could
hear the continuing sounds of celebration.

She blinked away the tears. Again. The anger that

had sustained her through the last week had been burned away in the frenzy of the uprising.

Honesty compelled her to stop, to think, to admit it hadn't been the excitement of the revolt that had cleared away her anger, but the time she'd spent in prison—with Dom. Her emotions had been stripped down to their most basic, and now she had to face the truth. The truth about Dom. The truth about herself. That, she knew, would be the most painful of all.

She found herself observing him. He had fetched Ruby and held her in his arms, but he was staring at Laurentia, an impatient frown tugging at his brow.

If she didn't dry her tears, she feared he would abandon protocol and mount the dais to her side.

"Papa," she whispered. "Let's start the ceremony."

King Jerome squeezed her hand again, then let it go and stood. The talking ceased, the people moved forward to form a single line at the dais, and he said, "Dear friends, my daughter the princess Laurentia and I cannot ever fully express our gratitude for your assistance in the recovery of our kingdom. But we can and do wish to grant you the highest and most ancient honor of Bertinierre, the Cross of St. Simon."

Laurentia gathered the medals and the king's sword and walked to his side.

"First, to our fellow sovereign, King Danior of Sereminia, with our deepest appreciation."

King Danior bowed his head as King Jerome placed the medal around his neck by its ribbon. The two rulers embraced, and spoke quietly for a moment. Both turned to look at Laurentia.

Laurentia stared back.

The resemblance between Danior and Dom was uncanny, but she would never mistake them. Danior was calm, deliberate; the fire that burned in Dom and so attracted her was banked in Danior. Yet he examined her with a proprietary interest, and color rose in Laurentia's cheeks as she wondered what Dom had told his brother.

King Jerome cleared his throat. Hastily she presented him his sword. One by one, as Laurentia called them, the others stepped forward.

Francis knelt before the king. The king tapped first one shoulder, then the other. Laurentia placed the cross around his neck and embraced him stiffly.

Dulcie knelt before the king. The king tapped first one shoulder, then the other. Laurentia placed the cross around her neck, then suffered an enthusiastic embrace and a whispered, "Did you tangle the sheets with him?"

Chariton knelt, was tapped, given the medal and a new title created specially for him while his mother, Minnie, wiped her eyes and sniffled loudly.

His parents came forward in their turn to receive their crosses, and as Laurentia embraced them she thanked them again for the care they took of her cottage.

Dom had given Ruby up to her mother, and Gloria held the child's hand as she accepted her medal. Laurentia gave them both special hugs. How could she not? Gloria had been her strength through this past week; Laurentia would never forget.

All the others received their taps with the sword, each received their medal and an embrace.

At last only Dom was left, waiting patiently, his hands loose at his side. He prowled forward, all loose-limbed grace, while Laurentia thought, *This is not acceptable.*

It wasn't acceptable that he had used her, betrayed her, seduced her, and she still wanted him. Her infatuation proved, as nothing else could, that she was not yet fit for rule. Sovereigns didn't love unwisely, didn't dream of a handsome face, didn't imagine sharing burdens for all the coming years with a crafty devil given to despicable masquerades.

He knelt before her father, and she thought he watched King Jerome with something oddly like wariness. She glanced briefly at her father and thought it peculiar that he smiled at Dom with the same expression he wore when he faced an unusually talented fencing partner.

Danior stood with his arms crossed, grinning. The other men had arrayed themselves around the throne room for a better view, while the women exchanged conspiratorial glances.

Something was going on. Something Laurentia didn't understand.

"Dominic of Sereminia," King Jerome intoned. "I will never forget what you have done to me or my daughter."

The phrasing was curious also, she noted.

"And I now give you your reward." King Jerome tapped him on the shoulder, but as he lifted the sword, it wavered too close to Dom's head. Blood sprang from his ear.

Dom slapped his hand over the wound.

Laurentia gasped and covered her mouth. "Papa!"

"I'm so sorry." King Jerome didn't sound sorry. "It must have slipped. Here, let me finish you up."

Dom tilted his head away from the untapped shoulder and closed his eyes as if expecting a blow.

King Jerome tapped the other shoulder. Again the sword wavered, rasping along Dom's neck. A long line of blood oozed up from the resulting scrape.

"Dreadfully clumsy of me!" King Jerome wiped off his sword with an apparent lack of concern. "I must be growing weary after all my exertion putting down the invasion. You do understand, don't you?"

"I do indeed." Dom got stiffly to his feet, pulled a handkerchief from his pocket, and pressed it to his ear.

Blood on the other side trickled steadily into his collar.

"Laurentia, he's bleeding," King Jerome said. "Have you a bandage?"

"Although I spent part of the night working at the hospital," she said tartly, "I amazingly enough did not think to stuff bandages in my pockets. I didn't know you were going to cut him." Although, from the grins around the throne room, everybody else did.

While she would have liked to reproach her father, Dom was still standing there bleeding.

"Here. I have one." King Jerome handed her a clean white cotton square. "Fix him."

She didn't think that someone else could have done the job. Or that Dom could have held the bandage himself. She just turned—and found him standing directly before her. She still stood on the dais. He stood on the floor. His eyes were level with hers. She didn't think she liked that. But he turned his head and presented his neck, and she folded the suspiciously available bandage and pressed it to the wound.

She glanced up. Everyone was watching them, not even trying to hide their avid interest. Wartime, Laurentia had discovered, stripped away inhibitions.

"I don't know why he did that," she murmured in Dom's ear.

Dom looked at her. "I do."

They stood so closely together his breath touched her face. She could see his pupils dilate as he gazed at her. She could kiss him . . . "Why?"

"A couple of things," Dom said laconically. "Betraying him and his country for one. Debauching his daughter and making her cry for another."

To her horror, tears rose in her eyes again.

Dom's hands rose and hovered around her. Their lowered voices couldn't disguise the drama of this tableau. "Oh, dear one, don't do that. Don't cry. You make me feel like a horse's ass."

"You *are* a horse's ass." She swallowed, and swallowed again, reinforcing her royal discipline. She made a point of examining the bandage. "If I had some linen strips, I could wrap them around your neck—really tightly."

He smiled, oozing charisma as he had the first night she'd met him. "Would that make you feel better?"

He could ooze all he wanted. Charisma wasn't going to work this time. Not on her. Absolutely not. "No."

Now his hovering hands grasped her arms, and he gave her a little shake. "Laurentia, we have to talk."

Her tears dried under a flash of temper. "We've talked too much."

Her voice must have risen, for the people in the throne room chuckled.

She didn't care.

"This is not over." His voice had risen, too. "You said you loved me. You asked me to marry you—"

The listeners gasped.

"—and I swear on this medal that we—"

"The prisoners have arrived," King Jerome announced.

Laurentia and Dom turned to look at the king.

He looked back and indicated the guards who waited at the rear of the throne room. "De Emmerich and Weltrude have arrived for judgment."

Right before Laurentia's eyes, Dom forgot all about her.

Dom turned and stared as de Emmerich and Weltrude paced forward, both grubby and worn also, but upright, unchained, surrounded by guards dressed in stiff, traditional, asinine garb and bristling with spears—and knives.

Hell's fire, King Jerome didn't realize the risk he ran, allowing a vicious boar-pig like de Emmerich into a room with civilians.

With Laurentia.

Brat snatched up Ruby and stepped back. Chariton and Danior went on the alert.

The others just stood there, smugly imagining themselves safe. De Emmerich had lost everything. And if de Emmerich was dangerous when in power, he must be feral in defeat.

Dom started forward, pulling his knife from his sleeve.

And chaos erupted. De Emmerich shoved Weltrude forward, overbalancing the guards in front of him. Hampered by their ruffs and spears, the guards beside him tried to react. He had two of their knives before they knew what had happened. Women screamed and men shouted as de Emmerich slashed around him, clearing a space. He sprinted forward, raised his knife toward the dais—and Dom threw his own knife.

Too late. De Emmerich released his blade.

Dom's sank into de Emmerich's chest.

Dom had been too late. He swung around, terrified of what he would find—and saw Laurentia on the floor, King Jerome on top of her, and de Emmerich's knife quivering deep in the wood of the throne.

Dom felt, actually felt, his heart start beating again.

The moment of terrified silence was broken by Weltrude's shriek. "I didn't do it!"

Ruby joined in with a wail. The guards scuffled over Weltrude, and over de Emmerich's twitching body. A babble of horror and relief rose from the crowd.

Danior clapped his hand on Dom's shoulder. "The king and the princess knocked each other down." He looked around the throne room. "There was a lot of that."

Couples lay stretched on the floor like fallen logs. Chariton's parents were rising painfully. Chariton and Brat were trying to comfort Ruby. Francis and Dulcie . . . were in each other's arms, kissing wildly, like adolescents who had just discovered fornication.

Dom started toward the dais, determined to pluck Laurentia from the floor and straighten a few things out.

King Jerome stepped in his way. When Dom would have evaded him, King Jerome wrapped his fist in Dom's silk shirt.

Dom looked at the king.

The king looked back, and he wasn't smiling. "If you could come this way, Dominic, I have a few things I would like to say."

Behind the desk in King Jerome's study, set into the plaster wall, was an enamel crown, symbol of his royalty. The desk itself was oak, ancient, well polished, with a delicate wood grain. An expert craftsman had carved a prominent scepter and crown into the front. The grain on King Jerome's oak chair matched perfectly, and a crown had been carved into the high back so that it appeared to hover above his head.

King Jerome himself sat behind his desk, signing papers, skillfully ignoring Dom until Dom wanted to squirm and confess his guilt. Dom had never been in this position before, toeing the line before the father of a girl he'd debauched. Funny, how it reduced him from a competent, strong mercenary to a groveling lad again.

Which was just what King Jerome planned. Dom recognized a master tactician when he saw one.

At last King Jerome signed his final paper, dusted it with sand, and placed it off to the side. Folding his hands before him, he surveyed Dom from head to toe, and if his expression was anything to go by, the sight did not impress him.

"Well, boy, what do you have to say for yourself?"

About what? What did prospective suitors say to a girl's father? Especially when the wedding night had already been celebrated?

Dom swallowed, the wounds on his ear and neck throbbed, and he wanted to find Laurentia. Now. "Your Majesty—"

"You know"—King Jerome picked up his quill and twirled it—"when I realized the fiasco of Laurentia's last marriage . . . I assume she told you about her last marriage?"

"Yes, but I need to seek her now and—"

"Good. Did she tell you her husband was assassinated?"

Dom's jaw dropped.

"I see she didn't." He put the quill back down. "In all fairness, I have to admit I never told her. She felt enough unnecessary guilt about Beaumont without her thinking he died so she could be free of him."

Dom wanted his explanation. "Assassinated?"

"I required Beaumont to stay with me. It kept him away from her. The assassin shot the wrong man. A stroke of luck for me."

Dom found himself finishing the thought. *And for Laurentia.*

"Yes, after that I resolved to do everything in my not-inconsiderable power to make her next marriage one of irresistible fire. You can imagine my dismay as the years slipped by and no flame poked up his head." King Jerome chuckled. "Poked up his head. Yes, very good."

Dom chuckled, too. It seemed the diplomatic thing to do, and he needed to hear this.

"So I conceived of this celebration and in you I recognized the passion I imagined for my little girl."

"Thank you, Your Majesty."

King Jerome's tone abruptly turned hostile. "Passion is hot. Revenge is cold. If you betrayed my little girl for revenge"—he stood and slapped his hands down on his desk—"I will ban you from my country and she'll marry Francis."

Rage roared through Dom. He slapped his hands on the other side of the desk. "She'll marry Francis over my dead body."

King Jerome thrust his head forward. "That can be arranged."

Dom wanted to hit the old man. Hit the king! For what he was suggesting. "She's mine! If I have to kidnap her myself and take her far away, she'll always be mine. About this there can be no discussion."

"So you love her?"

"I do!"

"Oh." The wrath died out of King Jerome as if it had never been, and he sank back into his chair. "In that case, you want to ask me something."

Dom's head was reeling. "I . . . you . . ." He'd been played by a maestro. He knew it; he deserved it. "Your Majesty, may I have your daughter's hand in marriage?"

"I am pleased to welcome you to the family." King Jerome picked up his quill and another stack of papers. "If you can convince the princess Laurentia."

Dom could. He had to. "I'd be delighted, Your Majesty. If you could direct me to her?"

King Jerome looked up. "She has gone to her cottage."

Chapter Thirty-one

Chariton rode with Laurentia up to the cottage and un-saddled and groomed Sterling for her before mounting his own steed to ride away.

"Thank you, Chariton." She stood in the door of the stable and smiled at him. "I know I don't say it often enough, but I do appreciate you."

"You don't need to say it." He controlled his anxious horse with a firm grip on the reins. "I know that you appreciate me. You treat my parents and me as kindly as if we were part of the royal family, and we are humbly aware of your generosity. That is the reason, Your Highness, I feel that I can tell you the truth. I don't approve of Dominic of Sereminia."

Oh, she didn't want to hear this! She shook her head and tried to speak, but Chariton continued relentlessly.

"In my opinion, he doesn't deserve you. But His Majesty does approve of him, so I feel I must confess what I know Dominic will not."

She didn't want to hear this, but . . . "What?"

"He's not the one who betrayed you and Bertinierre. Weltrude got to de Emmerich first."

"Weltrude?" Laurentia's heart gave a joyful leap

into her throat. Then her happy flush died. "You mean Weltrude beat Dom to the reward."

"Yes."

"How do you know that?"

"Weltrude told me in a discussion in her prison room. Gloria confirmed it."

Bitterly, Laurentia asked, "Did Gloria also tell you Dom would have betrayed me if he'd had the chance?"

"We don't know that."

"I do." Wearily, she waved him on. "Go back to Gloria, Chariton. I'm glad you care enough for Dom to speak for him at all, but the fact he wasn't the actual villain changes nothing."

Chariton looked as if he wished to argue, but after a telling hesitation he bowed from the saddle. "I don't like leaving you alone, so promise me you'll be careful, Your Highness."

"I will." She watched him ride away and reflected on her foolish compulsion to be at the cottage when Pollardine's army was fleeing the country and mercenary soldiers were seeking for new employment. But Pollardine was east, the cottage was west, and she had to complete her mission. For some reason, completing her mission had taken on an importance exceeding any task she'd ever set herself.

She'd explained that to King Jerome just before she went to change into her second-best riding costume, the one that required a corset, a full set of petticoats, and all her undergarments.

Papa had understood. She hadn't even tried to elucidate why she wanted to be here high in the mountains where the stones sang of simpler times, the pines swayed in time, and dreams wafted along on the breeze. She didn't quite comprehend why herself, but she needed peace, solitude, and a chance to think.

To ensure her peace, she had two loaded pistols in her saddlebags. Two loaded pistols to shoot at any intruder who showed up at her cottage and disturbed her solitude. Intruders like . . . Dom.

She wouldn't miss this time. She didn't want him to come. She wanted a chance to heal, to recover a thimbleful of dignity and try to discover what pattern she would stitch for the future.

At the same time, she wanted him here.

She rubbed her forehead against the stable doorsill. So maybe she was stupid.

She wanted Dom to come after her, to go down on his knees, admit his guilt, beg for her forgiveness . . . so she could reject him and throw him out of the country.

Behind her Sterling snorted, and she had to agree. Her fantasies read like a marionette's melodrama.

Wearily she walked into the dim, hay-scented stable and threw back the shutters on the window. Fresh air rushed in, and she took a healing breath. This, yes, this was what she needed.

The most likely scenario, should Dom show up, was that he would toss her over his shoulder and carry her into the cottage where he'd make love to her until he'd driven all reason from her head. Why shouldn't he? It had worked every other time.

And she was sick of being tossed about like a bit of flotsam on the ocean.

Oh, in the heat of passion he might be able to seduce another marriage proposal out of her, but they couldn't stay naked all the time. Sooner or later they would have to put on some sense with their clothes and she knew she couldn't live like that, always wondering if he . . . loved her.

She rubbed the aching place in the middle of her chest right over her heart. That was it in an acorn. She wanted Dom, but only if he loved her, and even if he said so, would she believe him?

She heard his shout even before she heard the sound of Oscuro's hooves. "Laurentia!"

He'd found her.

No, she knew better. Her father had sent him. For some obscure reason, her father really wanted her to take Dom as her husband, and His Majesty, in his own way, could be just as stubborn as she could.

Well, she didn't want to be just standing pathetically, looking as if she'd been waiting for Dom to deign to make his appearance. She had a task to do, and she didn't care if he had to wait all day while she did it. Hastily she picked up the pitchfork and walked to the pile of straw in the corner.

He yelled again.

"In here," she yelled back. That felt good, expanding her lungs, opening her mouth and *shouting* at Dom. She did it again. "In the stable."

He appeared at the door, a hulking silhouette that blocked the sun. With his shoulders hunched like that and his hands twitching, she thought he looked like the portrait of a penned bull in a rage.

Good. Let *him* suffer the results of ineffectual fury.

He stalked into the stable, Oscuro on a leading

rein behind him. "I thought you promised not to disappear without telling me."

Sinking the pitchfork into the pile of straw, she shoved it aside to reveal the trapdoor. "That was before."

"Before what?" demanded the snorting bull.

"Before *you* disappeared without a word." Dropping the pitchfork, she grasped the iron ring in both hands. "Maybe I should demand that promise from you, too."

Dom relaxed a little. "I give it."

She laughed without amusement. "What are your promises worth?"

Frustration must act as fertilizer, for Laurentia would have sworn he grew taller and broader. "My promises are worth everything. Because I fulfilled my promise to de Emmerich, I threw away my chance to marry, to be a prince, to be respectable. I threw away every dream I ever had."

"Touching." Proud of her cool reply, she lifted up on the ring and dragged the door away from the shallow cavity below the floor.

Then he came at her, his hands outstretched as if he would help her, and he stepped into the light of the window. He still wore the black leather and silk. He hadn't stopped to bathe, and smudges of dirt and gunpowder still covered him in liberal amounts. His hair stood on end in a mad frenzy. He probably smelled like horse and sweaty man. And he was so handsome her body ached for him.

Her aplomb abruptly abandoned her. "No!"

He stopped.

"No. I'll do it. I'm strong." She stood, bosom heaving, daring him to come closer.

And he backed away, his hands still outstretched. "Laurentia . . ."

Oscuro stomped his hooves, upset by the lack of attention and, no doubt, by her shrieking. "Your horse," she managed.

Apparently, Dom hadn't even noticed Oscuro's distress. "What?"

"Your horse is lathered. You must have ridden him hard. You had best curry him."

Dom looked behind him at the horse. "Oh. Yes, I . . ." He caught the leading rein again and led Oscuro to his stall. With rags and straw, he wiped Oscuro down. "Yes." His voice sounded a little more like the Dom she knew—hard and confident. "I did ride hard. There are scoundrels out here."

"Untrustworthy knaves like . . . you." She looked at her hands. Her riding gloves hadn't been built for physical labor, but in her haste she hadn't remembered to change into work gloves. The fine leather was scuffed. Would anything ever go right again? "I comprehend my peril. Do you know what I've been doing for the last two days?"

"Directing the uprising in the city." Gathering the brushes, Dom began to groom Oscuro quickly as if the physical exertion would relieve his tension. "Telling men what to do, where to fight, who to kill—"

Picking up the shovel, she threw it in the hole. "I am aware of every danger that threatens me, Dom."

He heard what she didn't say, and answered that. "I am not a danger to you."

She had thought that the days of revolution, of imprisonment, of thwarted passion and disgraceful love had burned the rage away. She had thought she had learned her lesson, and that she would never again tumble into this turmoil of intemperate emotion. But just seeing Dom, hearing him speak, knowing what he had done to her and her country—that brought fury roiling forth from the hidden places of her soul. "Oh, aren't you?" She paced toward the stall. "Wasn't it you who courted me with such charm, rescued me with such efficiency, told me your story with such pathos, that I decided to do what I hadn't done in almost ten years?"

"I didn't lie about my past."

"Then, then you seduced me! You didn't have to. I had told you the most important secret I knew. You had everything you needed to collect your fee." Although she stood right outside the stall, Dom still worked. He didn't look at her, she wasn't even sure he was listening to her, and somehow that made the acrimonious words flow freely. "You could have ridden off and left me hurt, but heart-whole. But no, you had to take my virginity, make me love you, get me to propose. Propose marriage to *you*, because I was so blindly in love! You were my great moment of passion, my leap of faith—and I leaped right into a huge, empty cavern and found myself all alone, naked and shivering."

Dom tossed the brushes in the corner and stalked toward her, and if she had been incensed, he was furious. She took a step back.

He pointed his finger at her and in a low, unwavering voice said, "Yes, I seduced you. I always knew

I could do that. But I didn't *make* you love me. If I
could make a woman love me, don't you think I
would have done it sooner? Do you think I would
have stumbled around this world, an outcast and a
bastard, if I had the power to *make* a woman love
me?" He took another step toward her. "You *gave*
me your love, and you can't have it back."

She had advanced, he had retreated. Now he advanced, and she retreated. Retreated back to the
knee-deep cavity, and picked up her shovel.

He looked at her, standing in that hole, and without demanding an explanation went back to Oscuro's stall. She dug the shovel into the dirt.

His vehemence had shaken her.

All the things she'd sensed, heard, suspected
about him during that day and that night in the cottage were true. He had been a lost soul, resentful
and hostile, wandering around the world seeking he
knew not what. Now like a child with a new toy,
he clung to her declaration of love, imagining that
if he refused to give it up it could not slip away.
Love wasn't like that, but he didn't know.

Or maybe he did, and that explained the desperation that compelled him to ride in all speed up a
mountain after her.

The sound of the currycomb started again. "I
thought you were angry at me."

She tossed out the first shovelful of dirt. "I am."

"I understand that. I'd be angry, too. But I figure,
if you're just angry, I can cajole you out of it."

She wondered how hard she'd have to hit him
with the shovel before he went down. "*Cajole* me?"

"I've been angry most of my life, but you have to

be honed to maintain that kind of hostility. Have to be a bastard and a king's son and be used in a brothel and lose your mother to the pox before you're thirteen." His litany might have sounded like an appeal for sympathy, except it was delivered in such a mild tone. "You, Laurentia, had some bad experiences. I won't deny that. But you could never make anger an avocation. You just don't have the bitterness."

What was she supposed to say to that? *Thank you?*

"But Brat told me something else about you."

Laurentia squeezed the handle on the shovel. "I never talked to Brat about us."

"Apparently you didn't have to. Ever since she gave birth, she's suffered from bouts of intuition, and I can tell you from experience she's pretty good at it."

Laurentia already knew she didn't want this.

"She says you're hurt."

Laurentia scuffed her feet in the dirt. "I have never felt healthier."

"She says you have many layers, and if I can just peel away that layer of anger I'm going to see the pain I caused you."

Laurentia sank the shovel in the dirt, but she was having trouble seeing. The dirt, the shovel, her feet, they wavered with the onset of those endless tears which she would not, would *not*, allow to fall. "There's nothing wrong with me time won't cure."

"They say time heals all wounds, but I'm a mercenary. I know what that platitude means." He'd moved so quietly she hadn't heard him, but now he was as close to her as he could be without actually being in the pit with her. "Sometimes you have to wait to die to be healed. I want you well now."

He stood on the stable floor. She stood in the hole. He was taller than she was. Of course. But— "You can't have your own way about everything." A tear dropped into the dirt.

"Laurentia, I love you."

She tossed the dirt on his boots.

"Did you hear me?"

"I heard you."

"You're not the first person I've loved, you know."

She froze in the process of dumping another shovelful of dirt on him, and her gaze flew to his.

He watched her relentlessly, observing her agitation, the tears on her face, and, for all she knew, every emotion that skittered through her confused soul.

"I loved my men," he said, "and I lost them. I love Brat like a sister. I always have. And I love Ruby."

She thought about how he had held Ruby this morning, and how Ruby had embraced him. "I know."

"When I lost my men, when Brat and I almost starved and Ruby was born in a cave, I swore I would find some way, any way, to provide for her. No one wanted me as a mercenary." He kicked the dirt off his boots. "I had no men, and worse, I had a reputation for bad luck. So when de Emmerich offered me twenty-five thousand crowns to seduce you, I took the assignment, and gladly. With that kind of money, I could go back to Sereminia with

Brat and Ruby, and we could live like . . . well, like kings."

She sank onto the stable floor as far away from him as she could get and still have her feet in the hole.

"I wanted to go home. I thought going to Sereminia would ease that gnawing in me for something—stability, purpose, I didn't know what I needed, but I felt like I was starving." He squatted on his haunches and crumbled a clump of dirt between his fingers. "Then I met you, and I knew getting the secret out of you was going to be easy."

She puffed with exasperation. "You make me sound like an open book."

"You were. You wanted everything that I was. Adventure, danger, excitement, good . . . coupling."

"Coupling" wasn't his first choice of words, she could tell.

"You know I've never thought much of royalty," he said unnecessarily.

"I don't think much of mercenaries, either," she retorted.

"I didn't expect to think much of you. You seemed open, generous, strong-willed, intelligent. All that meant to me was there'd be a greater contrast when I uncovered your viciousness." He tossed a few dirt clods back in the hole. "Only I never found the bad parts."

"No wonder you left me." She was almost embarrassed. "I bored you."

"Bored me." He laughed shortly. "I did discover enough pigheaded determination and foolhardy bravery to keep you interesting. And I discovered those layers."

"I don't have any layers!"

"Layers," he repeated. "And secrets that had nothing to do with Bertinierre and everything to do with you. Your past. Your marriage."

"No layers," she muttered. He made her sound like an onion.

"So I started thinking about how to complete the job and get the money without putting Bertinierre in peril for more than a few days. I had to go back to Sereminia, which I found did not feel like home, because I only feel at home where you are."

She dabbed her nose on her sleeve. He was right, damn him. She *did* have layers. The layer of anger was easier to manage. With anger, all she had to do was stomp around and shout. But this layer was agony, anguish, dolor, torment . . . that was where the tears were coming from, and she didn't want to face this.

"My sister-in-law, the queen of Sereminia, said I should tell you I begged on my knees for Danior to bring his army to Bertinierre."

Laurentia really needed her handkerchief, but if she dug it out of her pocket and openly cried, it would seem like an admission of . . . something. She just didn't want Dom to know he'd uncovered a *layer*. "Am I supposed to be impressed?" She croaked like a frog.

"I told Evangeline that wouldn't win me clemency." He sat on the floor across the hole from her, a man too handsome for his own good. "So here's my question. If you had a chance to save Bertinierre by sacrificing me, what would you do?"

Too handsome for her own good, too. And reasonable, logical, and possessed of every other vice.

She wasn't fooling him a bit; he already knew she was crying. So she stripped off her gloves, dug her handkerchief out of her pocket, and mopped at her face. Then she looked at him with as much honesty as she could muster. "If I had to, I'd put an apple in your mouth and roast you for dinner."

He smiled at her, a double-dimple affair. "You're not just saying that because you're irate with me?"

She hated being wrong. "My first duty is to my country."

His smile widened—perfection taken to its ultimate. "In the rather extended conversation I shared with your father after he threatened to throw me from the country, we discussed you, and he said you had learned to value duty above passion."

"He discussed me with you?" Such a conversation outraged and alarmed her. The two men who knew her better than any others had compared their thoughts? How unfair! What had ever possessed her father? "What did my father think when you told him that Weltrude had told de Emmerich about our deal with Sereminia?"

Dom scowled. "How the hell did you find that out? Did Brat tell you?"

She found herself obscurely pleased to have flummoxed him. "It doesn't matter. What did His Majesty think?"

"I didn't tell him."

"Why not?"

"Because it doesn't matter. I had made a deal. I

was determined to win a fortune for Ruby. So if Weltrude hadn't told de Emmerich I would have."

Laurentia was astonished to hear herself repeat Chariton's words. "We don't know that."

"Yes, we do," Dom said stubbornly. "Once I agree to a deal, I never renege, regardless of the consequences."

Did he have to be honest about everything?

Dom continued, "I pointed that out to His Majesty, and he suggested that made me unlikely to disregard my wedding vows." He lavished his smile on her again. "He's right. When I give you my pledge, it will be forever, and it will include all of myself— my body, most joyfully, and my soul, for all that it's worth."

"My father wants me to get married at any cost."

"If that was all His Majesty wanted, you would have been married to Francis for four years."

All this sound reasoning was giving her a headache. She closed her eyes for just a moment, and when she opened them, Dom's smile had disappeared.

Leaning forward, he said, "I haven't ever loved a woman—not like my woman. I'll admit it, I don't know what I'm doing. I know how to pleasure you. I know which fork to use and just how low to bow, but I don't know how to be a prince consort. Part of finishing de Emmerich's assignment was wanting to put my past behind me, truly behind me. Finish the last job cleanly, settle Ruby's future, before I came to you. Part of it was pride—you're never going to need me to support you, I know that, but I wanted to demonstrate that I can take care of you. If the

world goes up in flames tomorrow, you'll still eat.
I'll keep you safe."

"I know that." She'd never entertained any other
thought.

"So we'll try this again. We'll get married and I'll
devote my life to making babies with you." He
leaned forward, all the way forward, and lifted her
chin with his fingers. "I'll make you happy, Laurentia. I do love you."

His words had eased the pain of his betrayal, there
could be no doubt about that. But even if she could
forgive, she couldn't forget. It would always be there
between them, this dreadful distrust.

She jerked her chin back. "No." Standing, she
stuck the shovel into the earth and lifted it from the
hole. "Dom, it all comes down to the fact I don't
trust you anymore."

He looked at her, standing in a hole, working with
the shovel. "What are you doing?"

"I'm digging up the money Sereminia paid us for
the royal maywort." She tossed more dirt out onto
the stable floor, and said churlishly, "After that little
war you caused, Bertinierre needs this money to re-
plenish our treasury."

Dom didn't say anything. He just sat there, lips
puckered, elbows on his thighs, hands clasped, and
looked at her.

It took her a moment to understand. A moment to
try and think of some way out of this hole she'd dug
herself into, literally and figuratively. She ran her
hand up and down the shovel handle, watching her
own motion with preternatural fascination. "I suppose you're thinking that if I didn't trust you, I

wouldn't dig up my country's fortune in front of you."

He lifted his eyebrows.

"There could be a different explanation." She observed nervously as he stood. "The money might not really be here. I might be testing you to see if you—"

"Throw you over my shoulder and take you away to ravish to you until you make sense?"

"No!"

He halted.

She was getting good at saying that word. Maybe he could be trained.

He took another step.

Maybe not.

As rapidly as she could, she said, "I am tired of being shoved around. Kidnappers grab me, you grab me, I'm always being carried hither and yon like a sack of onions." Layers again. She continued hastily, "I am an adult woman who has just directed a revolt, who carries a nation's hopes on her shoulders, and I will make my own decision in this affair."

As he warily watched, she leaned on the shovel and climbed out of the hole. Then she tossed the shovel back and strolled to the stable door. Pausing there, she looked over her shoulder, gave him a smile and fluttered her eyelashes. "Last one to the cottage has to be on the bottom."

And as she ran, his boots thundering behind her, she thought, *I wonder how he's going to get my corset off.*

But in the end, he once again proved himself resourceful.

*Have you ever wondered why
opposites attract?*

*Why is it so easy to fall in love when your friends,
your family . . . even your own good sense tells you
to run the other way? Perhaps it's because a long,
slow kiss from a sensuous rake is much more irresistible than a chaste embrace from a gentleman with
a steady income. After all, falling in love means taking a risk . . . and isn't it oh, so much more enjoyable
to take a risk on someone just a little dangerous?*

*Christina Dodd, Cathy Maxwell, Samantha James,
Christina Skye, Constance O'Day-Flannery and Judith
Ivory . . . these are the authors of the Avon Romance
Superleaders, and each has created a man and a
woman who seem completely unsuitable in all ways
but one . . . the love they discover in the other.*

*Christina Dodd certainly knows how to cause a scandal—
in her books, that is! Her dashing heroes, like the one in
her latest Superleader, SOMEDAY MY PRINCE, simply can't
resist putting her heroines in compromising positions of all
sorts . . .*

*Beautiful Princess Laurentia has promised to fulfill her
royal duty and marry, but as she looks over her stuttering,
swaggering, timid sea of potential suitors she thinks to
herself that she's never seen such an unsuitable group in
her life. Then she's swept off her feet by a handsome
prince of dubious reputation. Laurentia had always
dreamed her prince would come, but never one quite like
this . . .*

SOMEDAY MY PRINCE
by Christina Dodd

*Astonished, indignant and in pain, the princess
stammered,* "Who . . . what . . . how dare you?"

"Was he a suitor scorned?"

"I never saw him before!"

"Then next time a stranger grabs you and slams
you over his shoulder, you squeal like a stuck pig."

Clutching her elbow, she staggered to her feet. "I
yelled!"

"I barely heard you." He stood directly in front of
her, taller than he had at first appeared, beetle-
browed, his eyes dark hollows, his face marked with
a deep-shadowed scar that ran from chin to temple.
Yet despite all that, he was handsome. Shunningly
so. "And I was just behind those pots."

Tall and luxuriant, the potted plants clustered against the wall, and she looked at them, then looked back at him. He spoke with an accent. He walked with a limp. He was a stranger. Suspicion stirred in her. "What were you doing there?"

"Smoking."

She smelled it on him, that faint scent of tobacco so like that which clung to her father. Although she knew it foolish, the odor lessened her misgivings. "I'll call the guard and send them after that scoundrel."

"Scoundrel." The stranger laughed softly. "You *are* a lady. But don't bother sending anyone after him. He's long gone."

She knew it was true. The scoundrel—and what was wrong with that word, anyway?—had leaped into the wildest part of the garden, just where the cultured plants gave way to natural scrub. The guard would do her no good.

So rather than doing what she knew very well she should, she let the stranger place his hand on the small of her back and turn her toward the light.

He clasped her wrist and slowly stretched out her injured arm. "It's not broken."

"I don't suppose so."

He grinned, a slash of white teeth against a half-glimpsed face. "You'd recognize if it was. A broken elbow lets you know it's there." Efficiently, he unfastened the buttons on her elbow-length glove and stripped it away, then ran his bare fingers firmly over the bones in her lower arm, then lightly over the pit of her elbow.

Goosebumps rose on her skin at the touch. He

didn't wear gloves, she noted absently. His naked skin touched hers. "What kind of injury are you looking for?"

"Not an injury. I just thought I would enjoy caressing that silk-soft skin."

She jerked her wrist away.

What could be more exciting than making your debut . . . wearing a gorgeous gown, sparkling jewels, and enticing all the ton's most eligible bachelors?

In Cathy Maxwell's *MARRIED IN HASTE*, Tess Hamlin is used to having the handsomest of London's eligible men vie for her attention. But Tess is in no hurry to make her choice—until she meets the virile war hero Brenn Owen, the new Earl of Merton. But Tess must marry a man of wealth, and although the earl has a title and land, he's in need of funds. But she can't resist this compelling nobleman . . .

MARRIED IN HASTE
by Cathy Maxwell

"I envy you. I will never be free. Someday I will have a husband and my freedom will be curtailed even more," Tess said.

"I had the impression that you set the rules."

Tess shot him a sharp glance. "No, I play the game well, but—" She broke off.

"But it's not really me."

"What is you?"

A wary look came into her eyes. "You don't really want to know."

"Yes, I do." Brenn leaned forward. "After all, moments ago you were begging me to make a declaration."

"I never beg!" she declared with mock seriousness and they both laughed. Then she said, "Sometimes

I wonder if there isn't something more to life. Or why am I here."

The statement caught his attention. There wasn't one man who had ever faced battle without asking that question. "Well, the clergy has answers to that."

"I know. I've heard the answers." She paused and then said with sudden fervency, "But it isn't enough to repeat prayers. I want to feel a sense of purpose, of being, here deep inside. Instead I feel ..." She shrugged, her voice trailing off.

"As if you are only going through the motions?" he suggested quietly.

The light came on in her vivid eyes. "Yes! That's it." She dropped her arms to her side. "Do you feel that way too?"

"At one time I have. Especially after a battle when men were dying all around me and yet I had escaped harm. I wanted to have a reason. To know why."

She came closer to him until they stood practically toe to toe. "And have you found out?"

"I think so," he replied honestly. "It has to do with having a sense of purpose, of peace. I believe I have found that purpose at Erwynn Keep. It's the first place I've been where I feel I really belong."

"Yes," she agreed in understanding. "Feeling like you belong. That's what I sense is missing even when I'm surrounded by people who do nothing more than toady up to me and hang on my every word." She smiled. "But you haven't done that. You wouldn't, would you? Even if I asked you to."

"Toadying has never been my strong suit ... although I would do many things for a beautiful woman." He touched her then, drawing a line down the velvet curve of her cheek.

Miss Hamlin caught his hand before it could stray further, her gaze holding his. "Most men don't go beyond the shell of the woman . . . or look past the fortune. Are you a fortune hunter, Lord Merton?"

Her direct question almost bowled him off over the stone rail. He recovered quickly. "If I was, would I admit it?"

"No."

"Then you shall have to form your own opinion."

Her lips curved into a smile. She did not move away.

"I think I'm going to kiss you."

She blushed, the sudden high color charming.

"Don't tell me," he said. "Gentlemen rarely ask before they kiss."

"Oh, they always ask, but I've never let them."

"Then I won't ask." He lowered his lips to hers. Her eyelashes swept down as she closed her eyes. She was so beautiful in the moonlight. So innocently beautiful.

Across the Scottish Highlands strides Cameron MacKay. Cameron is a man of honor, a man who would do anything to protect his clan . . . and he wouldn't hesitate to seek revenge against those who have wronged him.

Meredith is one of the clan Monroe, sworn enemies of Cameron and his men. So Cameron takes this woman as his wife, never dreaming that what began as an act of vengeance becomes instead a quest for love in Samantha James's HIS WICKED WAYS.

HIS WICKED WAYS
by Samantha James

Cameron faced her, his head propped on an elbow. His smile was gone, his expression unreadable. He stared at her as if he would pluck her very thoughts from her mind.

"It occurs to me that you have been sheltered," he said slowly, "that mayhap you know naught of men . . . and life." He seemed to hesitate. "What happens between a man and a woman is not something to be feared, Meredith. It's where children come from—"

"I know how children are made!" Meredith's face burned with shame.

"Then why are you so afraid?" he asked quietly.

It was in her mind to pretend she misunderstood— but it would have been a lie. Clutching the sheet to her chin, she gave a tiny shake of her head. "Please," she said, her voice very low. "I cannot tell you."

Reaching out, he picked up a strand of hair that lay on her breast. Meredith froze. Her heart surely stopped in that instant. Now it comes, she thought despairingly. He claimed he would give her time to accept him, to accept what would happen, but it was naught but a lie! Her heart twisted. Ah, but she should have known!

"Your hair is beautiful—like living flame."

His murmur washed over her, soft as finely spun silk. She searched his features, stunned when she detected no hint of either mockery or derision.

She stared at the wispy strands that lay across his palm, the way he tested the texture between thumb and forefinger, the way he wound the lock of hair around and around his hand.

Meredith froze. But he stopped before the pressure tugged hurtfully on her scalp . . . and trespassed no further. Instead he turned his back.

His eyes closed.

They touched nowhere. Indeed, the width of two hands separated them; those silken red strands were the only link between them. Meredith dared not move. She listened and waited, her heart pounding in her breast . . .

. . . Slumber overtook him. He slept, her lock of hair still clutched tight in his fist.

Only then did she move. Her hand lifted. She touched her lips, there at the very spot he'd possessed so thoroughly. Her pulse quickened as the memory of his kiss flamed all through her . . . She'd thought it was disdain. Distaste.

But she was wrong. In the depths of her being,

Meredith was well aware it was something far different.

Her breath came fast, then slow. Something was happening. Something far beyond her experience . . .

What could be more beautiful than a holiday trip to the English countryside? Snow falling on the gentle hills and thatched roofs . . . villagers singing carols, then dropping by the pub for hot cider with rum.

In Christina Skye's *THE PERFECT GIFT, Maggie Kincaid earns a chance to exhibit her beautiful jewelry designs at sumptuous Draycott Abbey, where she dreams of peacefully spending Christmas. But when she arrives, she learns she is in danger and discovers that her every step will be followed by disturbingly sensuous Jared MacInness. He will protect her from those who would harm her, but who'll protect Maggie from Jared?*

THE PERFECT GIFT
by Christina Skye

Jared had worked his way over the ridge and down through the trees when he found Maggie Kincaid sitting on the edge of the stone bridge.

Just sitting, her legs dangling as she traced invisible patterns over the old stone.

Jared stared in amazement. She looked for all the world like a child waiting for a long lost friend to appear.

Jared shook off his sense of strangeness and plunged down the hillside, cursing her for the ache in his ribs and the exhaustion eating at his muscles.

He scowled as he drew close enough to see her face. Young. Excited. Not beautiful in the classic sense. Her mouth was too wide and her nose too thin. But the eyes lit up her whole face and made a man want to know all her secrets.

Her mouth swept into a quick smile as he approached. Her head tilted as laughter rippled like morning sunlight.

The sound chilled him. It was too quick, too innocent. She ought to be frightened. Defensive. Running.

He stared, feeling the ground turn to foam beneath him.

Moonlight touched the long sleeves of her simple white dress with silver as she rose to her feet.

He spoke first, compelled to break the spell of her presence, furious that she should touch him so. "You know I could have you arrested for this." His jaw clenched.

Her head cocked. Poised at the top of the bridge, she was a study in innocent concentration.

"Don't even bother to think about running. I want to know who you are and why in hell you're here."

A frown marred the pale beauty of her face. She might have been a child—except that the full curves of her body spoke of a richly developed maturity at complete odds with her voice and manner.

"Answer me. You're on private property and in ten seconds I'm going to call the police." Exhaustion made his voice harsh. "Don't try it," Jared hissed, realizing she meant to fall and let him catch her. But it was too late. She stepped off the stone bridge, her body angling down toward him.

He caught her with an oath and a jolt of pain, and then they toppled as one onto the damp earth beyond the moat. Cursing, Jared rolled sideways and pinned her beneath him.

It was no child's face that stared up at him and no child's body that cushioned him. She was strong for a woman, her muscles trim but defined. The softness at hip and breast tightened his throat and left his body all too aware of their intimate contact. He did not move, fighting an urge to open his hands and measure her softness.

What was wrong with him?

Imagine for a moment that you're a modern woman; one minute, you're living a fast-paced, hectic life-style . . . the next minute, you've somehow been transported to another time and you're living a life of a very different sort.

No one does time-travel like Constance O'Day-Flannery. In ONCE AND FOREVER Maggie enters a maze while at an Elizabethan fair, and when she comes out she magically finds she's truly in Elizabethan times! And to make matters more confusing, the sweep-her-off-her-feet hero she's been searching for all her life turns out to be the handsomest man in 1600's England!

ONCE AND FOREVER
by Constance O'Day-Flannery

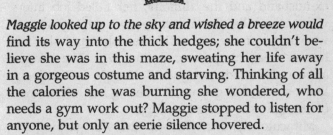

Maggie looked up to the sky and wished a breeze would find its way into the thick hedges; she couldn't believe she was in this maze, sweating her life away in a gorgeous costume and starving. Thinking of all the calories she was burning she wondered, who needs a gym work out? Maggie stopped to listen for anyone, but only an eerie silence hovered.

Suddenly, she felt terribly alone.

Spinning around, she vainly searched for anyone, but saw and heard nothing. "Hello? Hello?" Her calls went unanswered. She stopped abruptly in the path. She felt weak. Her heart was pounding and her head felt light. Grabbing at the starched collar, she released the top few buttons and gasped in confusion. Okay, maybe she could use that shining knight right about now. She didn't care how or where he appeared, as long as he led her out, for the air was heavy and still, and Maggie found it hard to breathe.

"Help me . . . please."

Silence.

Her heart pounded harder, her stomach clenched in fear, her breath shortened, her limbs trembled and the weight of the costume felt like it was pulling her down to the ground.

Spinning around and around, Maggie experienced a sudden lightness, as if she no longer had to struggle against gravity and push herself away from the earth. Whatever was happening was controlling her, and she was so weary of struggling . . . flashes of her ex-husband and the alimony, her failed job interviews, the bills, the aloneness swirled together. It was bigger, more powerful than she, and she felt herself weakening, surrendering to it. The hedges appeared to fade away and Maggie instinctively knew she had to get out. Gathering her last essence of strength, she started running.

Miraculously, she was out. She was gasping for breath, inhaling the dust and dirt from under her mouth when she heard the angry yell that reverberated through the ground and rattled her already scrambled brain.

She dare not move, not even breathe. If this were a nightmare, and surely it couldn't be anything else, she wasn't about to add to the terror. She would wake up any moment, her mind screamed. She *had to!*

Drawing upon more courage than she thought she

had left, Maggie slowly lifted her head. She was staring into the big brown eyes of a horse.

A horse!

She heard moans and looked beyond the animal to see a body. A man, rolled on the side of a dirt path, was clutching his knee as colorful curses flowed back to her.

"Spleeny, lousey-cockered jolt head! Aww ... heavens above deliver me from this vile, impertinent, ill-natured lout!"

Pushing herself to her feet, Maggie brushed dirt, twigs and leaves from her hands and backside, then made her way to the man. "How badly are you hurt?" she called out over her shoulder.

The man didn't answer and she glanced in his direction. He was still staring at her, as though he'd lost his senses.

Shoulder-length streaked blond hair framed a finely chiseled face. Eyes, large and of the lightest blue Maggie had ever seen stared back at her, as though the man had seen a ghost. He was definitely an attractive, more than average, handsome man ... okay, he was downright gorgeous and she'd have to be dead not to acknowledge it.

Wow ... that was her first thought.

Everyone knows that ladies of quality can only marry gentlemen, and that suitable gentlemen are born—not made. Because being a gentleman has nothing to do with money, and everything to do with upbringing.

But in Judith Ivory's THE PROPOSITION Edwina vows that she can turn anyone into a gentleman ... even the infuriating Mr. Mick Tremore. Not only that, she'd be able to pass him off as the heir to a dukedom, and no one in society would be any wiser. And since Edwina is every inch a lady, there isn't a chance that she'd find the exasperating Mick Tremore irresistible. Is there?

THE PROPOSITION
by Judith Ivory

"Speak for yourself," she said. "I couldn't do anything"—she paused, then used his word for it—"unpredictable."

"Yes, you could."

"Well, I could, but I won't."

He laughed. "Well, you might surprise yourself one day."

His sureness of himself irked her. Like the mustache that he twitched slightly. He knew she didn't like it; he used it to tease her.

Fine. What a pointless conversation. She picked up her pen, going back to the task of writing out his progress for the morning. Out of the corner of her eye, though, she could see him.

He'd leaned back on the rear legs of his chair, lifting the front ones off the floor. He rocked there beside her as he bent his head sideways, tilting it, looking under the table. He'd been doing this all week, making her nervous with it. As if there were a mouse—or worse—something under there that she should be aware of.

"What *are* you doing?"

Illogically, he came back with, "I bet you have the longest, prettiest legs."

"*Limbs*," she corrected. "A gentleman refers to that part of a lady as her limbs, her lower limbs, though it is rather poor form to speak of them at all. You shouldn't."

He laughed. "Limbs? Like a bloody tree?" His pencil continued to tap lightly, an annoying tattoo of ticks. "No, you got legs under there. Long ones. And I'd give just about anything to see 'em."

Goodness. He knew that was impertinent. He was tormenting her. He liked to torture her for amusement.

Then she caught the word: *anything?*

To see her legs? Her legs were nothing. Two sticks that bent so she could walk on them. He wanted to see these?

For anything?

She wouldn't let him see them, of course. But she wasn't past provoking him in return. "Well, there is a solution here then, Mr. Tremore. You can see my legs, when you shave your mustache."

She meant it as a kind of joke. A taunt to get back at him.

Joke or not, though, his pencil not only stopped, it dropped. There was a tiny clatter on the floor, a faint sound of rolling, then silence—as, along with the pencil, Mr. Tremore's entire body came to a motionless standstill.

"Pardon?" he said finally. He spoke it perfectly, exactly as she'd asked him to. Only now it unsettled her.

"You heard me," she said. A little thrill shot through her as she pushed her way into the dare that—fascinatingly, genuinely—rattled him.

She spoke now in earnest what seemed suddenly a wonderful exchange: "If you shave off your mustache, I'll hike my skirt and you can watch—how far? To my knees?" The hair on the back of her neck stood up.

"Above your knees," he said immediately. His amazed face scowled in a way that said they weren't even talking unless they got well past her knees in the debate.

"How far?"

"All the way up."

TAKE A HASTY $2.00 REBATE
ON CATHY MAXWELL'S
NEWEST ROMANCE!
MARRIED IN HASTE

Affaire de Coeur says Cathy Maxwell "keeps getting better and better!" Avon Books wants you to enjoy her latest wonderful historical romance, MARRIED IN HASTE, (available in bookstores in August) with the added pleasure of a $2.00 rebate. To take advantage of this great offer, simply purchase MARRIED IN HASTE, send in your proof-of-purchase (cash register receipt) along with the coupon below by December 31, 1999, and we'll rush you a check for $2.00.

Void where prohibited by law.

Mail to:
Avon Books, Dept. BP, P.O. Box 767, Dresden, TN 38225

Name_____

Address_____

City_____

State/Zip_____

CMX 0499

ELIZABETH LOWELL

THE* NEW YORK TIMES *BESTSELLING AUTHOR

"A law unto herself in the world of romance!"

Amanda Quick

LOVER IN THE ROUGH

76760-0/$6.99 US/$8.99 Can

FORGET ME NOT   76759-7/$6.99 US/$8.99 Can

A WOMAN WITHOUT LIES

76764-3/$6.99 US/$8.99 Can

DESERT RAIN   76762-7/$6.50 US/$8.50 Can

WHERE THE HEART IS

76763-5/$6.50 US/$8.50 Can

TO THE ENDS OF THE EARTH

76758-9/$6.99 US/$8.99 Can

AMBER BEACH   77584-0/$6.99 US/$8.99 Can

JADE ISLAND   78987-6/$7.50 US/$9.99 Can